TOO MANY BRIDGES

TOO MANY BRIDGES

A RADIC & MULROY MYSTERY

BILL GORMLEY

LEVEL BEST BOOKS

First published by Level Best Books 2024

Copyright © 2024 by Bill Gormley

All rights reserved. No part of this publication may be reproduced, stored or transmitted in any form or by any means, electronic, mechanical, photocopying, recording, scanning, or otherwise without written permission from the publisher. It is illegal to copy this book, post it to a website, or distribute it by any other means without permission.

This novel is entirely a work of fiction. The names, characters and incidents portrayed in it are the work of the author's imagination. Any resemblance to actual persons, living or dead, events or localities is entirely coincidental.

Bill Gormley asserts the moral right to be identified as the author of this work.

Author Photo Credit: Georgetown University

First edition

ISBN: 978-1-68512-694-0

Cover art by Level Best Designs

This book was professionally typeset on Reedsy. Find out more at reedsy.com

Contents

Praise for Too Many Bridges	vi
Chapter One: A Call For Help	1
Chapter Two: There's No Place Like Home	8
Chapter Three: A Primer on Bridges	18
Chapter Four: A River Cruise	25
Chapter Five: The Bubble Bursts	30
Chapter Six: A Mental Health Day	36
Chapter Seven: Legal Constraints	40
Chapter Eight: Food for Thought	46
Chapter Nine: It's All Greek to Me	51
Chapter Ten: Knocking on Doors	56
Chapter Eleven: Silhouettes in the Moonlight	58
Chapter Twelve: A Grim Business	63
Chapter Thirteen: Meet the Parents	68
Chapter Fourteen: Going Public	74
Chapter Fifteen: Forbidden Thoughts	77
Chapter Sixteen: Hoping for a Break	82
Chapter Seventeen: A Day at the Park	86
Chapter Eighteen: Disposing of Poisons	89
Chapter Nineteen: Bridge Lessons	93
Chapter Twenty: Back at the Park	96
Chapter Twenty-One: The Lord is My Shepherd	100
Chapter Twenty-Two: A Delicate Situation	104
Chapter Twenty-Three: Picking Up the Pieces	109
Chapter Twenty-Four: The Best Thai Dish in Pittsburgh	113
Chapter Twenty-Five: Ancient History	117

Chapter Twenty-Six: Another Special Request	123
Chapter Twenty-Seven: Sheds with Secrets	128
Chapter Twenty-Eight: Spider Man	133
Chapter Twenty-Nine: Brainstorming at the Squirrel Cage	136
Chapter Thirty: A Return to Sewickley	144
Chapter Thirty-One: A Request for Mugs	149
Chapter Thirty-Two: The Sting	153
Chapter Thirty-Three: A Chance Encounter	157
Chapter Thirty-Four: Two Stakeouts	160
Chapter Thirty-Five: An Act of Piracy	163
Chapter Thirty-Six: Picking Up the Mail	168
Chapter Thirty-Seven: Time to Get Ready	173
Chapter Thirty-Eight: A Reluctant Witness	177
Chapter Thirty-Nine: Extra Cheese?	184
Chapter Forty: Second Thoughts	187
Chapter Forty-One: Legal Niceties	193
Chapter Forty-Two: Loose Ends Day	197
Chapter Forty-Three: What's in a Blintz?	200
Chapter Forty-Four: Following the Trail	203
Chapter Forty-Five: Taking the Fifth	209
Chapter Forty-Six: Say Ah!	216
Chapter Forty-Seven: Lost but Not Found	222
Chapter Forty-Eight: Into Thin Air	226
Chapter Forty-Nine: Butterflies	231
Chapter Fifty: Push-Ups	235
Chapter Fifty-One: A Brief Respite	238
Chapter Fifty-Two: A Day at Wrigley Field	241
Chapter Fifty-Three: A Man's Best Friend	245
Chapter Fifty-Four: A Roll of the Dice	249
Chapter Fifty-Five: A Familiar Voice	252
Chapter Fifty-Six: A Disturbing Dream	254
Chapter Fifty-Seven: The Ties that Bind	259
Chapter Fifty-Eight: Free at Last	261

Chapter Fifty-Nine: The Keeper of the Keys	264
Chapter Sixty: Reunited	269
Chapter Sixty-One: A New Game Plan	275
Chapter Sixty-Two: A Whiff of Soap	278
Chapter Sixty-Three: A Difficult Conversation	282
Chapter Sixty-Four: New Evidence	289
Chapter Sixty-Five: Sifting and Winnowing	292
Chapter Sixty-Six: A Bridge to Somewhere	296
Chapter Sixty-Seven: A Daring Escape	304
Chapter Sixty-Eight: The View from the Bridge	308
Chapter Sixty-Nine: A Front-Page Obituary	313
Chapter Seventy: When the Going Gets Tough	318
Acknowledgements	324
About the Author	326
Also by Bill Gormley	327

Praise for Too Many Bridges

"Bill Gormley has produced a tightly written debut police procedural reminiscent of Ed McBain's finest. *Too Many Bridges* takes the reader on an insider's tour of Pittsburgh, from its homeless encampments to its popular attractions. And, of course, of so many bridges under which evil may lurk."—Annette Dashofy, *USA Today* bestselling author of the Zoe Chambers and Detective Honeywell series

"In *Too Many Bridges*, Bill Gormley takes a fresh approach to the police procedural. A sizzling whodunit that's also a wheredunit, focusing on an elusive bridge. May there be many more Radic and Mulroy adventures ahead."—John DeDakis, novelist, writing coach, manuscript editor, and former Senior Copy Editor on *CNN*'s "The Situation Room with Wolf Blitzer"

"I loved this evocative mystery's strong sense of place and compelling characters. It offers plot twists and turns you won't see coming, a smart detective who earns your respect, and a different perspective on the world. Bill Gormley has written a page-turner that will leave you eager for more."—Mally Becker, author of the Agatha Award-nominated Revolutionary War Mystery series

Chapter One: A Call For Help

If there was one thing Detective Branko Radic hated more than a late-night phone call, it was having to answer the telephone while brushing his teeth.

The call from the Pittsburgh Bureau of Police homicide desk reached Radic at his Mexican War District apartment at 10:48 p.m. He had barely scrubbed his upper right molars and a bicuspid when the ringing began. He cursed and managed a half-spit while fumbling for his phone.

Radic recognized the caller's name from last week's orientation session. One of the better new recruits. But he sounded frazzled and wasn't making sense. After a proper spit and a quick rinse, Radic asked him to calm down and start over.

"We just got an anonymous tip. A man said he wanted to report a murder, that he was calling from under a bridge, and that he was homeless. Then he hung up. I'm really sorry to bother you, detective, but I didn't know who else to call."

Radic struggled to process what he had heard.

"You're saying we don't know who called, we don't know where he called from, we don't know who the victim was, and we don't know who committed the murder?"

"That's about the size of it."

"I wish he had called 911. Then, at least, we'd have his location. Did you get a phone number?"

"No, unfortunately, but we do have a recording of the call. Do you want to hear it?"

"You recorded the call?"

"I didn't. HQ did. It's part of the orientation process."

"Well, that's a lucky break. Play it back for me."

Police: Pittsburgh Police, Homicide.

Caller: I'm calling to report a murder.

Police: Where are you calling from, sir?

Caller: I'm under a bridge.

Police: Which bridge?

Caller: Forget about the bridge! What matters is the murder.

Police: We can send someone out, sir, but we need an address.

Caller: Sorry, I'm homeless.

Police: Okay, can we back up? How do you know there's been a murder, sir?

Caller: I know the murderer.

Police: Who is the victim?

Caller: A young woman.

Police: What's her name, sir? And what is *your* name?

Caller: I gotta go. I'll probably be next! (click)

Radic sighed. "Lieutenant Stilton is gonna *love* this one. I suppose we could send some uniforms to a handful of bridges. But which ones? Do you know how many bridges we have in our fair city?"

"A lot?"

"Pittsburgh has more bridges than any other city in the United States. That's 446, to be precise. We can't send uniforms to check out each and every one of them, to find a witness who may or may not be there and a corpse that may or may not be under the bridge."

"What should I do, sir?"

"Find out which of our units is closest to Point State Park. Have them check out a few nearby bridges for suspicious activity. Tell them we have a phantom witness who may have witnessed a murder. Give the unit my phone number and have them call me when they're through. I'll stay up till I hear from them."

"Thank you, sir. I'm sorry about the call."

CHAPTER ONE: A CALL FOR HELP

"Don't worry about it. I'm glad you reached out to me."

Radic hung up, not feeling glad at all. In fact, he felt a knot in the pit of his stomach, a tightening of his shoulders, and a nasty headache boring into his skull. *I'm getting too old for this,* he thought. *And I'm only thirty-six.*

The memory of his thirty-sixth birthday last month did little to cheer Radic up. With impeccable timing, after two years together, Gloria had picked that very day to split up. He remembered every word:

"You're a great guy, Branko. You have beautiful brown eyes and a nice, tight butt. You're smart, considerate, and sexy. But you're not happy. You have a good job, but it's not a happy job. You have a good life, but it's not a happy life. I want someone who can make me happy! And that's not you."

Radic watched the evening news, just in case. No murders yet. He heard back from a squad car just after midnight—five bridges visited, no suspicious activity. He was tempted to dismiss the tipster as a crank, but something about the distress in his raspy voice seemed authentic. He didn't sound crazy; he sounded afraid.

Radic thanked the officer for calling, then went to bed. Alone, thanks to Gloria. But, in all honesty, he didn't disagree with anything she had said.

The following morning, Radic drove the short distance to the Pittsburgh Bureau of Police headquarters on Western Avenue without turning on his car radio or stopping for coffee. It was a gorgeous fall day, which seemed to mock his foul mood.

Radic found a parking spot in the lower lot, barely noticing the panorama before him: a patchwork of skyscrapers nestled between the Allegheny and Monongahela rivers, which created a third, the Ohio, which flows nearly 1,000 miles to the Mississippi River.

It was a breathtaking view and Radic felt fortunate to see it daily. But not today. Unless he was mistaken, this was going to be a pisser of a day. A day for commiseration, not celebration. Perhaps a good day to have lunch with Lucas Renfert.

Radic strode into the weather-beaten brick building, found the stairs, and walked to the second floor. Inside the homicide squad room, he responded to greetings with a brief wave, forgoing the usual banter, and headed straight

3

to his desk.

Moments later, Radic checked in with Lieutenant Charles Stilton. Lean, wiry, with graying temples, Stilton was a good enough boss—reasonable, fair, and calm under pressure. He never blindsided you and expected you never to blindside him. For better and for worse, he was predictable. No blind-siding…but no blinding insights either. Very logical but not creative. Known to many as "the Stilt," Stilton probably would not have objected to the nickname. Had he known that some cops called him "Cheesy," he might have been less forgiving.

"Cheesy" Stilton asked good, predictable questions as Radic briefed him on the strange call. He recommended that Radic contact Missing Persons as soon as possible. He suggested that he determine whether any recently released prisoners had violated their parole. He asked for regular reports. But the bottom line? As expected, Radic was pretty much on his own.

An hour later, Radic knew where things stood. Missing Persons had received a call about a senior citizen wandering away from a Greenfield nursing home Saturday morning. After a four-hour search, the missing senior was found calmly feeding pigeons on a park bench. A young woman from Shadyside had disappeared a few days ago without notifying her roommate. But then she called over the weekend. A new boyfriend had spirited her away to the Bahamas for a romantic getaway. She sounded hungover, the roommate reported, but none the worse for wear. As far as Radic could tell, all 302,000 of Pittsburgh's inhabitants were present and accounted for. At least for now.

Reports from parole officers were equally reassuring…and therefore vexing because it meant no leads. A repeat offender with a penchant for robbing convenience stores had failed to report to his parole officer on schedule. Then, he turned up the following day with good news—he had landed a job at a convenience store. Oddly enough, it was a store he had previously robbed! The convenience store owner must be a saint or a fool, Radic thought. Or maybe a genius. If it takes a thief to catch a thief, who better to spot shifty characters than someone with plenty of first-hand experience?

CHAPTER ONE: A CALL FOR HELP

Over time, Radic had grown accustomed to the slow, often tedious nature of a homicide investigation. One small step led to another small step, then sometimes to a dead end, but also possibly to a giant step forward. Without that last critical step, the process could be very frustrating. With it, the experience was deeply satisfying.

Radic remembered a book he had read in college, *Bird by Bird*, by Anne Lamott. The author's brother, ten years old at the time, had delayed working on a book report until the last minute. The paper on birds in America was due the next day. Paralyzed, the boy didn't know where to start until his father took him aside. "You've got to write this bird by bird," he advised. Which meant one small step at a time.

That was how Radic viewed police work. Don't think too much about all the steps required to solve a murder investigation. It was mind-boggling. Instead, focus on one task and make sure you do it well. Then, focus on a second task and handle that well. Always be willing to revisit your assumptions as new evidence accumulates. If you do, there's a good chance you will solve the case. If you don't, you need a new career. Or a shrink.

In lieu of a shrink, Radic's friend and favorite sounding board, Lucas Renfert, was free for lunch. They agreed to meet at the Squirrel Hill Café (aka the Squirrel Cage), not far from his friend's home.

Lucas Renfert was easy to spot despite a seat in the darkest corner of the restaurant. Black, tall, and muscular, he was still strikingly handsome at age 66. He often chose a dimly lit table near the back in an effort to hide a prominent scar on his right cheek. Years ago, Renfert had explained that he grew up in a tough neighborhood in L.A., Watts. "As a young punk, I thought I had no choice but to join the Crips or the Bloods," he had confided. Then, rubbing his cheek, he said, "Clearly, I chose the wrong gang!"

Renfert was nursing what looked like a glass of iced tea. His tweed jacket, neatly trimmed beard, and thick glasses gave him a distinctly professorial look, and appropriately so. Renfert had taught criminology at Carnegie Mellon University for many years and was only recently retired. He had been Radic's mentor at CMU and had strongly encouraged him to enroll in the police academy 15 years ago.

"How's my favorite student?" Renfert asked with a grin.

"How's my favorite professor?" Radic countered.

"I'm back in the classroom again."

"That's great! I was hoping you would do that."

"Just part-time, of course. What's the use of retiring if you don't have plenty of leisure time?"

"And how are you spending your leisure time?"

"Helping my favorite student solve a crime or two."

"Well, I could definitely use your help. But I'm still not sure that a crime has been committed."

Renfert ordered a triple-decker club sandwich, while Radic ordered an Italian hoagie with capicola, Genoa salami, and provolone.

Confident that the waitress would not be returning soon, Radic reached into his pocket and pulled out his cell phone. No better way to start this conversation than with the eyewitness call.

Renfert listened attentively, sipped his beverage slowly, and puckered his lips. "You either have something to say, or there was too much lemon in your tea," Radic observed.

"That's what makes you such a fine detective," Renfert said. "In fact, I ordered an Arnold Palmer—half tea, half lemonade. With that combination, anyone would pucker his lips. Any dead bodies on your doorstep yet?"

"Not as of noon today."

"Any missing persons?"

"Two, but they've both resurfaced."

"Any thoughts on where the homeless man was calling from?"

This time, Radic puckered *his* lips.

"There are several homeless enclaves in Pittsburgh," Radic began. "Three on the North Side, two on the South Side, and two or three downtown. Maybe more. I thought I'd make the rounds with a uniform today or tomorrow."

"Any homeless communities near a bridge? Like the one he was calling from?"

"One of the South Side communities is within striking distance of a bridge.

But our caller says he was calling from underneath a bridge."

"Any reason to doubt that?"

"No reason to doubt it. No reason to take it as Gospel either."

The waitress arrived with their sandwiches, which provided an excuse to catch up on friends and activities.

After settling the check, Renfert asked to hear the call again. He listened intently, as before, then said nothing. Radic apologized for the background noise.

"Well," Renfert said, "the background noise is a distraction if you want to identify the caller. But the background noise is good stuff if you want to identify the bridge. Somehow, you need to figure out which bridge your caller was calling from."

"I agree," Radic said. "The bridge could lead us to the caller. At the moment, it's our best lead."

Renfert pulled out a pad of paper and jotted down a name and phone number. "You need to talk with a colleague of mine at CMU's Engineering School. He knows a hell of a lot about bridges. He's not a miracle worker, but he might help you narrow your search. When he listens to the background noise, he might be able to say something about the bridge."

"Terrific!" said Radic. "This gives me a new lease on life."

"In your line of work, a new lease on life means you might be able to figure out why someone has died a gruesome death," Renfert noted, with a look of concern in his eyes. "Sometimes I wonder whether this is a healthy line of work for a young man."

"I thought you said this was the perfect line of work for me!" Radic exclaimed.

"That was several murders ago," Renfert reflected. "Too many murders are hard on the soul."

Chapter Two: There's No Place Like Home

Rosemary Dunne was not a worrier. Her roommate, Carol Sloan, had disappeared without warning, prompting her to contact the police. But, thankfully, Carol had gotten back in touch.

Now, a getaway weekend was turning into a getaway week. When Carol let her hair down, she really threw caution to the wind.

Rosemary was not a prude. If Carol wanted to have wild, torrid sex with her mystery lover on the sandy beaches of Nassau, it was not for her to judge.

Still, there was something about the whole escapade that seemed a bit fishy. She and Carol were not super close. But they had a good, cordial relationship. Shouldn't Carol at least have left her a note?

Also, in the two years that she and Carol had roomed together, Carol had occasionally indulged in a glass of wine or two, but she had never been rip-snorting drunk. The Carol who called her over the weekend, in contrast, was clearly three sheets to the wind.

Again, not a big deal. We should all take a walk on the wild side now and then, even an accountant like Carol, whose regular routine was more mild than wild.

Rosemary thought about all of this as she began her nurse's shift at Allegheny General Hospital. Clearly, she should call Carol to see how she was doing. She made a mental note to do just that when she got home.

CHAPTER TWO: THERE'S NO PLACE LIKE HOME

* * *

On returning to work, Radic checked in with Lieutenant Stilton to see who might be available to accompany him to some homeless sites. Luckily, Officer Mulroy was available.

Kathleen Mulroy was relatively new to the Pittsburgh police force but had already acquired a reputation as smart, tough, and reliable. Radic enjoyed working with her because she was a team player *and* an independent thinker. A rare combination.

Mulroy had a background in social work, which made her an asset for this particular assignment. The homeless community was notoriously tight-lipped. If Radic was to make any progress with them, it would help to have someone they could trust at his side.

Radic found Mulroy at her desk. Attractive, blonde, blue-eyed, 30 years old, Mulroy wore her hair in a bun while at work, preferring shoulder-length hair while off duty. Mulroy greeted Radic with a warm smile.

Radic noticed a slight overbite, because of their last conversation. "Do you think I have an overbite?" she had asked after confiding that she had just split up with her boyfriend. "What's an overbite?" Radic had answered. "That's the right answer," Mulroy had responded with a laugh.

Radic sat down with Mulroy in a quiet conference room to bring her up to speed. He played the homicide desk call for her and explained his intent to visit several homeless communities with her at his side. Her connections with Catholic Charities, a well-known social services organization, were likely to help.

Mulroy questioned his reasoning: "I may have some street cred with the homeless community because of the work I used to do for Catholic Charities. But I'm still a cop, and you're a cop. If you really want the homeless folks to open up, you should enlist someone from Catholic Charities like Sister Mary Grace. When you're homeless, there's no one you trust more than someone who's fed you a warm meal or found you a warm bed on a winter's night."

So, Radic and Mulroy drove to Catholic Charities near Liberty Avenue before doing anything else.

Sister Mary Grace O'Malley was petite, reed-thin, and quick to smile. She greeted Officer Mulroy cheerfully at the door, with a kiss on both cheeks. She then escorted the two police officers to a small office and asked how she could help.

Radic decided to play the homicide desk call first, just in case Sister Mary Grace recognized the voice. She didn't.

"I know a fair number of homeless people," she explained, "but our homeless communities are pretty dynamic. People come and go. Also, your man could be a loner. Some homeless people find comfort in being part of an encampment. Others prefer to be alone, for fear of being robbed or molested or harmed in some way. It's a very personal decision. Your caller seems like someone who is very scared. I would think he'd avoid the encampments."

"Is there anything else you could tell us about this man, Sister, after listening to the call?" Mulroy asked.

"Yes," Sister Mary Grace smiled. "I can tell you he's from Pittsburgh."

"Really?" Radic asked. "How do you know that?"

"From the very last thing he said," Sister Mary Grace responded. "I'll prolly be next. Prolly, as in trolley. Not pro-ba-bly. That's classic Pittsburgh-speak. You have yourselves a Pittsburgher!"

Warming to Sister Mary Grace, Radic asked her if she would be willing to accompany them to some homeless sites. But she demurred.

"I want to help. I really do!" she explained. "If someone has harmed a homeless person or threatened a homeless person, then he's a threat to other homeless people as well. I want you to get to the bottom of this. But when it comes to helping law enforcement officials, I have to walk a tightrope. Rightly or wrongly, homeless people see the police as a threat. You might break up their camp, you might arrest someone for a trivial offense, you might ask for proof of citizenship. To put it bluntly, Catholic Charities can't be seen to be siding with the police in a dispute with the homeless community."

"But Sister, you just said yourself that we're trying to *help* the homeless

CHAPTER TWO: THERE'S NO PLACE LIKE HOME

community," Radic argued. "It's not like you're aiding and abetting THE ENEMY!"

"Ah," Sister Mary Grace responded, "but that's exactly how it would be perceived by many homeless folks. And as a representative of Catholic Charities, I just can't take that risk."

Recognizing an impasse, Mulroy intervened. "Sister Mary Grace, I think we understand why you can't be seen with us," she reasoned, "but can you at least point us in the right direction? Can you help us to identify the right people to talk with?"

"That's a horse of a different color," Sister Mary Grace said, brightening. "Some of the homeless encampments have informal leaders, even officers. Not all of them. But some of them. I can give you some names to get you started."

"Thank you, Sister," said Radic. "That would be a big help!"

Chastened by Sister Mary Grace's lecture, Radic and Mulroy parked their police car a couple blocks away from the North Side homeless camp near the Allegheny River that Sister Mary Grace thought might be worth a visit. No need to raise any hackles.

As Radic and Mulroy approached the small settlement, they noticed that several people retreated into makeshift tents or behind concrete berms. Clearly, the police would not receive the same warm welcome here that they enjoyed at Catholic Charities.

By prior agreement, Mulroy spoke first. Approaching a middle-aged man with alert eyes and polished black shoes, she projected friendliness: "Hi! We're sorry to trouble you, but we're trying to help a homeless man who may be in distress. We received a call from him last night. Sister Mary Grace said that if we came here, we should try to speak with Manuel Duarte."

The man sized up the two police officers. "Are you here to shut down our camp?" he asked.

"Definitely not!" Mulroy answered. "That's not our intent. And we don't have the authority to do that. As far as we're concerned, you've done nothing wrong. We're just trying to identify someone who may be in trouble."

The man said nothing for a while. Then he asked, "How do you know

Sister Mary Grace?"

"I used to work at Catholic Charities before I joined the police force," Mulroy explained. "Sister Mary Grace said she would help us, so long as we don't disrupt your community."

The man relaxed a bit and motioned to a man who disappeared behind a concrete berm, then reappeared moments later with another man in tow. He was short, compact, good-looking, possibly Hispanic. He projected an aura of self-confidence as he approached the police.

"I'm Manuel Duarte," the man said. "How can I help you?"

At this point, Radic took over. "Thank you for speaking with us, Mr. Duarte. We received a call last night from a homeless man who says he witnessed a murder and who fears for his own life. We're trying to find that man."

"What is his name?" Duarte asked.

"Unfortunately, his phone call was interrupted before he could say," said Radic. "All we know is that he recently spent an evening under a bridge."

"As you can see, detective, we're not exactly *under* a bridge," Duarte said. "No one here fits that description."

"Can you think of someone who *does* fit that description?" Radic asked.

"There are a lot of bridges in the city of Pittsburgh, detective," Duarte observed. "This man could hang out under any one of them."

Radic sighed, sensing that this was going nowhere. "I grant you that," he conceded and reached into his pocket for a card. "If you hear from this man, or if you hear about him, or if you hear about a murder, we'd greatly appreciate your getting in touch," Radic said. "The killer could be a threat to this man and the entire homeless community."

Mulroy's beeper was ringing when they reached the squad car. A major traffic jam on Stanton Ave. in Lawrenceville. The working assumption was a traffic accident, but no one knew for sure. "Do you want to come along, sir, or shall I ask them to find someone else?" Mulroy asked.

Radic decided to go with the flow. Mulroy and Radic arrived ten minutes later and quickly discovered the cause of the problem: at least a dozen chickens were staging a sit-in right in the middle of a busy street! Whenever

CHAPTER TWO: THERE'S NO PLACE LIKE HOME

a motorist tried to shoo them away, they promptly relocated to another equally inappropriate venue. One even perched on the hood of a car and started pecking at the windshield wipers.

"How are you at catching chickens, sir?" Mulroy asked.

"I don't think I ever tried," Radic answered. "What's your plan?"

"My plan is to go to the grocery store," she replied.

"You gotta be kidding!" Radic exclaimed.

"If it was just one or two chickens, I'd say, let's just try to grab them," Mulroy explained. "But with so many chickens, we need to provide a bit of encouragement."

While Mulroy left in search of treats, Radic directed traffic as best he could. When the traffic thinned a bit, he knocked on a few doors, trying to identify the chickens' owners. Eventually, he located the correct residence, with an open chicken coop in the backyard, though no one was at home to help round up the escapees.

Meanwhile, Mulroy returned with several bags of baby carrots and a few tubs of blueberries.

The treats worked like a charm. One by one, Radic picked up chickens and deposited them in the chicken coop while Mulroy converted the sidewalk into an outdoor café. Traffic began to flow normally again. A few motorists honked their horns in appreciation while others took snapshots. Mulroy wrote out a citation to the owner for creating a public nuisance, placed it in the offender's mailbox, and started up the car.

"What's our next stop?" she asked.

"Let's try the South Side," Radic suggested. "Sister Mary Grace gave us a name there. And it's one of the bigger homeless communities."

To get to the South Side, Radic and Mulroy took the Birmingham Bridge, which connected Pittsburgh's middle-class brain (Oakland, home to three universities) to its working-class heart (the South Side, former home to a leading steel mill). It wasn't Pittsburgh's most beautiful bridge, but it was a vital artery.

Approaching East Carson Street, Radic fondly remembered it as the location of the Cuckoo's Nest, an amazing magic store that had enchanted him as a young boy. He began his magician years with a disappearing nickel trick and graduated to a more sophisticated and more lucrative disappearing dollar trick—always a good bet with aunts and uncles who routinely allowed the dollar to disappear for good. Sadly, the Cuckoo's Nest was one of many old businesses to have closed its doors.

The homeless community in the South Side was close to the Monongahela River, but not particularly close to the Birmingham Bridge. As they approached, Radic tried to imagine someone calling from this site and describing his location as "under a bridge." Definitely a stretch.

Unlike their previous visit to a homeless site, Radic and Mulroy saw less scattering as they got closer, perhaps because the homeless residents seemed older. Several seemed to be snoozing on benches or blankets. No obvious leader appeared to be present.

Again, Mulroy took the lead, approaching an elderly man munching on an apple. "Excuse me, sir, we're not trying to hassle anyone, but we're looking for Vince Gatti. Sister Mary Grace from Catholic Charities thought he might be able to help us out with something."

The man had an odd look about him as he raised his head. Was he squinting? Winking? Angry? Amused? Mulroy couldn't tell for sure. Finally, the man responded: "You won't find Gatti here, coppers!" the man barked. Then he added: "Maybe at work."

"Where does he work?" Mulroy inquired.

"Fatheads!" the man cackled, his eyes bulging.

Taken aback by the insult, Mulroy turned to Radic for guidance.

"I think he means Fat Head's Saloon," Radic said, suppressing a grin. "Is that right, sir?"

"Fatheads," he confirmed. "East Carson Street."

"Thank you, sir, and have a nice day!" Radic said, motioning to Mulroy that it was time to go.

"You up for a drink, Mulroy?" he asked.

"On duty or off?" she asked.

"On duty," he replied.

"If the city of Pittsburgh requires it, I can probably handle a beer," she

CHAPTER TWO: THERE'S NO PLACE LIKE HOME

replied with a smile.

It was late afternoon, and Happy Hour was in full swing. Radic found a booth near the back and ordered an IPA. Mulroy chose a Stella Artois. Radic asked the waiter if Vince Gatti was around. The waiter nodded towards the bartender.

"Is it okay if I get the beers myself?" Radic asked.

"Be my guest," the waiter replied.

Radic explained his business to Gatti, invoking Sister Mary Grace's name. Neither reluctant nor eager, Gatti was willing to talk but would not be on break until 7 o'clock.

Radic and Mulroy quickly agreed to have dinner while waiting for Gatti. Radic ordered the Bay of Pigs sandwich (pork, ham, swiss cheese, and a piquant sauce), while Mulroy ordered a chicken salad with blueberries.

"You seem to have a thing for blueberries!" Radic teased.

"We used to vacation in Maine," Mulroy laughed. "On a good day, we would have blueberry pancakes for breakfast, a bowl of blueberries with lunch, and a blueberry pie after dinner. Sometimes a couple of scoops of blueberry ice cream on top."

"I'm surprised your complexion isn't blue by now!" Radic said.

"Don't knock it until you've tried it!" Mulroy replied. "Blueberries have lots of antioxidants. Food for the brain. They help you to think better."

"OK, Ms. Blueberry, so what are you *thinking* about our homeless guy?" Radic asked. "Or should we wait until you've eaten your blueberries first?"

Mulroy decided not to wait. "One thing I've learn about the homeless is that it's a mistake to generalize about them. Take Gatti, for example. He's homeless, but he also works. That's not the stereotype. Or take Duarte. He's obviously intelligent and has some leadership ability. He doesn't fit the stereotype either."

"Okay, point taken," Radic agreed. "So, what's your take on our caller?"

"Just because he's homeless this week doesn't mean that he's been homeless for a long time," Mulroy said. "He could easily be a hard-working, middle-class guy who just lost his home or his wife or his fortune. He could easily be connected to the victim, or to the murderer. Maybe they were business partners, and something went wrong. Maybe they went to high school together. I'm guessing he's a reasonably good guy because he's reporting a murder. But maybe he's not a saint himself."

"OK, those are good ideas," Radic said. "But how do we find him?"

"Well, we need to make ourselves visible in the homeless community," she said. "He found us once. Maybe he'll find us again." Then, she added, "If he's still alive, of course."

At 7 o'clock sharp, Gatti nodded to Radic and exited the restaurant. After a decent interval, Radic and Mulroy left, too.

The trio repaired to a dark alleyway that afforded maximum privacy. "I can give you ten minutes," Gatti said.

Radic summarized what he had said at the bar: "We're looking for a homeless man who may be in trouble. In fact, we have reason to believe that his life is in danger. All we know about him is that he's spent some time under a bridge. He might even live there. Does anyone you know fit that description?"

"A lot of homeless people I know have probably lived *near* a bridge, detective," Gatti replied. "After all, this is Pittsburgh. But it's hard to get *under* a bridge, even in Pittsburgh, unless, of course, you're out on the water."

Radic nodded. Then he thought of something. A vision of Huck Finn on the Mississippi River flashed through his mind. "Do you know of any homeless people who live in a boat?" he asked.

The question surprised Gatti and Mulroy, too. "Are you truly homeless if you live in a boat?" she asked.

Radic had anticipated the question. "If it's a yacht, of course, then it's the rough equivalent of a home," he answered. "But what if it's just a small fishing boat with paddles?" Turning to Gatti, he asked, "Do you know anyone who has access to that kind of boat?"

A glimmer of recognition flashed across Gatti's face. "Vazzy," he said. "It could be Vazzy."

"Who is Vazzy? First name? Last name? Nickname?" Radic asked.

Gatti shrugged. "Most homeless folks aren't big on sharing last names."

"What can you tell us about him?" Mulroy asked.

"He joined our community a few months ago," Gatti recalled. "But he wasn't a regular. He would drift in and out. He would leave suddenly, like he had an urgent appointment."

"Or like he was afraid of someone?" Mulroy asked.

"Could be," Gatti replied. "He always seemed to have eyes in the back of his head."

"How do you know he had a boat?" Mulroy asked.

"Because he told me once," Gatti replied. "He had a bandage on his hand. He said he hurt himself while docking his boat in the dark."

"Do you know where he kept the boat?" Radic asked.

"No," Gatti recalled. "I asked him once. And he made a joke about it."

"What was the joke?" Radic asked.

"It wasn't a very funny joke," Gatti recalled. "He said: If I told you where the boat is, I'd have to kill you."

Chapter Three: A Primer on Bridges

It was unusual—though not unprecedented—for Lieutenant Stilton to ask to see Radic at 8 a.m. Was he upset with the slow progress on the bridge homicide case? Was a real murder about to displace a hypothetical murder on his agenda?

Radic entered Stilton's office, not knowing what to expect. He certainly didn't expect a big smile.

"Come in, Radic, come in," Stilton said, greeting him warmly. "Have you seen this morning's *Post-Gazette*?"

Radic shook his head.

Stilton pointed to a photo on the front page of the Local News section featuring none other than Radic himself. There he was, cradling a chicken in his arms like a newborn baby, while several other chickens feasted on blueberries and carrots.

The article portrayed Radic and Mulroy as quick-thinking heroes who managed to end a traffic jam and escort 15 chickens to safety with a minimum of fuss and feathers. The headline read, "POLICE FOIL FOWL JAYWALKERS."

"This is terrific!" Stilton gushed. "Absolutely terrific! Police solving real community problems through quick, decisive action. We're always being criticized for this or that. This publicity is worth its weight in gold. You and Mulroy are to be congratulated!"

"Well, I hope you do congratulate Mulroy," Radic replied. "It was her call. I just happened to be there."

"Of course, of course," Stilton said. "Good of you to say that. And I will congratulate her in just a few minutes. But first, I wanted to speak with you about your case."

"We don't have much to report yet, sir," Radic conceded.

"Early days, early days," Stilton assured him. "But do you think that the tip is legit?"

Radic paused before answering. "I've listened to that homicide desk call at least a dozen times," he said. "I don't know what the man saw. I don't know if it was an actual murder. But I'm pretty sure that he saw something very disturbing. And I'm pretty sure that he was scared."

Stilton nodded. "I trust your instincts, Radic," he said. "You're a good cop. I'm going to give you another week to play this out."

"Thank you, sir," Radic replied. "Plus, I have a request."

"What is it?"

"I'd like to keep recording calls to the homicide desk a while longer. Just in case our eyewitness decides to call again."

Stilton was pensive. "You think he deliberately called us directly rather than 911?"

"I do."

"Why?"

"He doesn't want us to know where he's calling from. The 911 team has equipment to locate callers instantly. We don't."

"He's that smart?"

"He's pretty cagey. He's good at dodging questions he doesn't want to answer."

"Okay," Stilton agreed. "We'll keep it going a while longer. The expense isn't that great."

"Thank you, sir."

"Normally, I would pair you with another detective for a murder case," Stilton continued. "But we don't know yet whether it's an actual murder. And I need Scuglia and Turley to handle the suspicious death at the Bellefield Boiler Plant."

"Understood," Radic said.

"But I can give you Mulroy, if you want her," Stilton said. "You two work well together. She wants to become a detective. Has she told you that?"

"Yes, she has, sir," Radic replied.

"Well, she has the right stuff," Stilton said. "But she could use some experience. This case could be the final piece of the puzzle for her. If it leads somewhere, that is."

Mulroy was in a good mood when she connected with Radic mid-morning. She had seen the *Post-Gazette* article and had received compliments from Stilton, plus random chicken squawks from her colleagues.

"It's going to take us a while to live this down," she said to Radic.

"True enough," Radic agreed. "But we've earned enough brownie points to keep us looking under bridges for another week."

"Is that really what you have in mind?" Mulroy asked.

"Not exactly," Radic said. "I'd like you to follow up with Gatti. Try to get a better sense of where our guy hid his boat. Or took his boat. Track Gatti down before he goes back to work. See if he can fill in some of the blanks. Also, check in with the River Rescue Unit. Maybe they've seen a lone boater who fits our guy's description."

"Sure," Mulroy said. "And you?"

"I have an appointment with a Carnegie Mellon professor," Radic said. "It's time for me to learn the A-B-Cs of bridges."

* * *

Carnegie Mellon University, situated in Pittsburgh's Oakland neighborhood near Schenley Park, is one of the world's leading citadels of computer science education. As Radic crossed the leafy campus, he counted at least three robots hustling with a sense of purpose as if they were late for class. Well, he thought, maybe they were. Who knows?

The Department of Civil and Environmental Engineering is located in Porter Hall. A Silver LEED building, Porter Hall boasts many green features and an attractive interior. Radic had taken a course there years ago and remembered getting an A in it.

Professor Shinichi Watanabe greeted Radic warmly when he knocked on his office door. A stocky, middle-aged man with calloused hands, Watanabe gave Radic a firm handshake and offered him coffee or tea. When Radic requested coffee with sugar, Watanabe picked up his cell phone and asked someone to bring tea for him, coffee for his guest.

Do people still have secretaries fetch them coffee? Radic wondered to himself. And at a university?

Five minutes later, as the men swapped stories about Lucas Renfert, a robot arrived with a cup of coffee and a cup of tea.

As Radic's jaw dropped, Watanabe laughed heartily. "I'm just showing off!" he confessed. "We usually get our own beverages at CMU. But when we have a distinguished guest, we sometimes ask our robots to help out." Watanabe thanked "Fred" for the drinks and instructed him to return to base, aka the kitchen.

While drinking a surprisingly good cup of coffee (do robots do the brewing too?), Radic quickly summarized the essentials of the case. Then he played the homicide desk call after explaining what they knew about the caller.

"Can you confirm that the background traffic is on a bridge?" Radic asked.

"It could be," Watanabe said. "There are noticeable irregularities in the sound, and that's consistent with the kind of dynamic pressure and tension you associate with a bridge. Also, it's pretty loud."

"Are bridges always loud?" Radic asked.

"Well, bridges are usually made of concrete, which tends to be noisy," Watanabe said. "And there's not much soil below to absorb the sound. So, yep, they're pretty loud."

"Any way of figuring out which bridge it is?" Radic asked.

"Ah," Watanabe sighed. "That's a much more complicated question, detective. How much do you know about bridges?"

"Not a lot," Radic confessed. "That's why I'm here."

With that as an invitation, Watanabe launched into a mini-lecture on the subject. "There are five main types of bridges," he began. "An arch bridge is one of the oldest types, dating back to the Romans, if not before. The basic principle is a curved design so that the pressure from above does not go straight down but is distributed along the curve and directed to abutments at either end of the bridge. Sometimes, there's one curve. Sometimes more. The Ponte Vecchio in Florence is an arch bridge."

"And in Pittsburgh?" Radic asked.

"We have some fine arch bridges in Pittsburgh!" Watanabe beamed. "You've driven over many of them, I'm sure. The Fort Pitt Bridge. The Fort Duquesne Bridge."

"But those bridges don't look anything like the bridges I remember from when my family traveled to Italy," Radic objected.

"An astute observation, detective!" Watanabe said. "The Romans used stone for their arch bridges. In Pittsburgh, we use concrete and steel. It's a different look."

"And the other types of bridges?" Radic asked.

"The simplest is called a beam bridge," Watanabe explained. "Some of these are quite short, featuring only one beam that extends horizontally from one location to another or from one shore to another. The advantage of a beam bridge is its affordability and the speed with which it can be built. The disadvantage is that it tends to sag over time. The longer the bridge, the greater the sagging."

"And in Pittsburgh?" Radic asked.

"Well, you see them all around you," Watanabe responded. "Especially in parks, with small ponds or lakes. Or overpasses. You're less likely to see them crossing a river these days. Beam bridges are not ideal for trucks or heavy traffic."

"Another traditional bridge design is a truss," Watanabe continued. "A truss bridge includes a lot of parallel and diagonal beams that work together to reduce tension and redistribute the weight. Pittsburgh has a famous truss bridge—the Smithfield Bridge, built in 1881. It was one of the first bridges in the U.S. to use steel in the truss."

"What about the spectacular bridges that cross the Hudson River?" Radic asked, his curiosity growing. "What type of bridge is the George Washington Bridge? And how about the Verrazano Narrows Bridge, the one that seems to go on forever?"

"Ah, ha!" Watanabe exclaimed. "Those bridges are indeed breathtaking. We call them suspension bridges. A suspension bridge uses ropes or cables attached from vertical suspenders to sustain the weight of the bridge and its traffic. It was a breakthrough in engineering design that made it possible to carry thousands of cars a day across a wide river, safely and securely."

"Are there suspension bridges in Pittsburgh?" Radic asked.

"Yes, there are," Watanabe assured him. "For example, the Andy Warhol Bridge, the Roberto Clemente Bridge, and the Rachel Carson Bridge are all suspension bridges, with exactly the same design."

"Last but not least … well, maybe least … is the cantilever bridge," Watanabe concluded. "It's similar to the arch design, but it supports its load through diagonal bracing with horizontal bars."

"Sounds sort of like a truss bridge," Radic observed.

"Again, detective, you have a good grasp of bridges," Watanabe replied. "A cantilever bridge is like a truss bridge, but it's only anchored on one end. And that's often a problem. It's more subject to decay than other truss bridges."

"And in Pittsburgh?" Radic asked.

"The Liberty Bridge," Watanabe replied.

"It seems like it's always being repaired," Radic commented.

"As you might expect of a cantilever bridge," Watanabe replied.

Anticipating more questions, Watanabe suggested another round of beverages. This time, though, he and Radic walked down the hall to the kitchen, giving "Fred" a well-deserved break.

Back in the office, Radic resumed his questioning. "So, Professor Watanabe, you've listened to the eyewitness call. If I play it for you again, is there any way you can tell whether the noise is from an arch bridge, or a truss bridge, or a suspension bridge?"

Watanabe sighed and gazed into space for a while. "I was afraid you were going to ask that question," he said. "Go ahead and try me. But don't get your hopes up."

Once again, Watanabe listened to the homicide desk call, focusing on the background noises, not the message from the caller.

"Well, detective," he said. "I have good news and bad news. The good news is that this is almost certainly a bridge. All bridges have transverse joints to adjust to expansion and contraction as temperatures change. That produces a characteristic sound. Sort of like a moving train. That's pretty noticeable here."

"So, you have yourself a bridge," he continued. "But what type of bridge? I'm afraid I can't tell you whether it's an arch bridge, or a truss bridge, or a suspension bridge. That's just above my pay grade."

Radic couldn't hide his frustration. "So there's nothing you can tell me except that it's a bridge?" he asked.

"Well, your bridge is on the loud side, which probably means it's pretty close to the ground. If your caller is at the base of the bridge, then the height is relevant to the volume you hear. So, I'm willing to go out on a limb and say that this is not the Westinghouse Bridge, because it's one of our higher bridges, 240 feet from the ground."

Watanabe reached for a piece of paper. "You need to speak with a friend of mine, who's a music professor at Pitt."

"A music professor?" Radic asked skeptically.

"Her name is Josephine Donato, and she's an expert on urban soundscapes, including bridges. Listening to a bridge is like listening to a piece of music. Most of us hear simple stuff—a melody line, a tempo. Josephine hears things that you and I would never notice. It's almost like E.S.P. She might be able to help you. Look at it this way: what do you have to lose?"

Chapter Four: A River Cruise

Mulroy's return visit to the South Side homeless camp yielded little new information, but it wasn't a total bust. Gatti had agreed to meet with a sketch artist at Fat Head's Saloon just before work. With any luck, they would have a drawing of their homeless man to help with their inquiries.

With that accomplished, Mulroy turned her attention to the River Rescue Unit. She reached out to a colleague she knew from the Police Academy who was posted there and arranged to meet her early that afternoon.

When she heard what Mulroy was up to, Officer Lexie Davodny suggested that they take a short excursion. "I need to patrol the Allegheny for an hour or so," she explained. "And it might help you to visualize some of the places where we sometimes see odd ducks acting a little squirrelly. Excuse me for mixing my metaphors!"

The River Rescue Unit was located, conveniently, near police headquarters on the North Side, very close to PNC Park, home of the Pittsburgh Pirates. Mulroy decided to walk a few blocks, to clear her head and get a little exercise.

"Just call me Skipper!" Davodny exclaimed as she extended an outstretched hand to bring Mulroy on board. "I was SO pleased when you called. I never see the old gang anymore, now that I'm out on the water. Welcome to one of the finest police boats in the Tri-State area!"

Davodny was as stunning as ever. As a cadet, Mulroy had admired her chic hair styles and her penchant for wrist accessories. These days, she was sporting feathered bangs—a delightfully retro look that accentuated her sparkling green eyes.

Davodny handed Mulroy a life jacket, offered a couple of safety tips, fired up the engine, and gave a war whoop as the boat started moving. "Hold on to the railing if you value your life!" she warned.

The pride and joy of the River Rescue Unit was a sleek Jupiter boat, 43 feet in length, with a Yamaha V-8 engine, 425 horsepower. "Notice the propellers," Davodny gushed. "They're enormous! That's why we can accelerate so quickly…like this."

Suddenly, the boat lurched forward. Mulroy felt a sharp jolt in the small of her back and the bracing spray of ice-cold water on her face. "Would you like goggles?" Davodny asked, with a grin, pleased to have gotten her friend's attention.

"Do…you…always…go…this…fast?" Mulroy sputtered, trying not to sound too alarmed.

"Not really," Davodny laughed, slowing to a more comfortable pace. "I'm just having a little fun. So, how can I can help you and Detective Radic? Who is super hot, by the way. Do you know if he's seeing someone?"

Mulroy didn't know and said so.

"He's a good-looking guy, but I've never known what to make of that earring on his right ear."

Mulroy had noticed the silver hoop earring, too, but had never thought much about it.

"A fashion statement?" she speculated.

"Well, I hope so, on behalf of eligible women everywhere! What's up? I'd like to help."

Mulroy explained the genesis of their case and ran the homeless boater theory up the flagpole. "We're thinking that our guy might have access to a boat, a cheap boat, that he uses from time to time when he wants to be by himself," she said. "Have you seen anyone like that out on the river?"

"Almost all of the boats we see on the three rivers are motorboats like this one, though maybe not as classy," Davodny responded. "And, of course, tugboats with barges heading west for the Mississippi or the other way around."

CHAPTER FOUR: A RIVER CRUISE

"Do you ever see someone all alone in a boat that is barely seaworthy?" Mulroy asked.

"Well, yeah, every now and then," Davodny replied. "If we do, we usually have a word with them, to make sure they're okay and to remind them about the currents."

"Could a boat like that be stored at a regular marina if the guy had enough cash for it?" Mulroy asked.

"Yep, that would be possible," Davodny said, "but who would want to pay a hefty marina fee for a boat that's probably worth a few hundred bucks?"

"I don't know," Mulroy said, "but our guy might have some money, even if he doesn't have a home."

"Well, there's a couple marinas on the waterfront if we turn around," Davodny said. "The Lock Wall Marina. And Washington's Landing. Do you want me to drop you there when we head back?"

Mulroy thought for a moment. "That can wait," she said. "We hope to get a sketch of the man we're looking for this evening. I'd rather have that in hand before visiting."

Davodny performed a few routine duties while chatting with Mulroy. She gave the boat another hair-raising, face-spraying run before docking. Mulroy felt relieved to have survived the excursion with her dignity more or less intact.

* * *

Back in the office, Radic checked Gatti and Duarte for priors, just in case. Duarte was clean, as far as the Pittsburgh police knew. Gatti had a restraining order from an altercation with his wife (now ex-wife), but that was several years ago. Radic was half-tempted to check Sister Mary Grace for priors, just for fun, but decided against it. At worst, she might have participated in a political protest. If so, more power to her!

Radic texted Mulroy and asked her to pick up the sketch at Fat Head's Saloon. Then, he dropped by the Carnegie Library to check out a book or two about bridges.

TOO MANY BRIDGES

* * *

Rosemary Dunne returned to her empty apartment after a tough day. Two patients didn't make it, including an eleven-year-old boy who had been clinging to life for five days. He had a rare blood disease and succumbed mid-afternoon. Rosemary was looking forward to having dinner with a friend to take her mind off the day's death toll.

But first, she decided to call Carol. Rehearsing a speech in her head, Rosemary was a little nervous. Then, her call didn't go through. Service disconnected. Rosemary tried again, with the same result.

Now, she was genuinely worried. Maybe her friend Martha would know what to do when they met for dinner. Rosemary confirmed the rendezvous, took a catnap, grabbed her purse, and headed out the door to Point Bruge Café in Point Breeze.

Martha was already there, gin and tonic in hand. Rosemary was tempted to order a stiff drink herself, but opted for lemonade instead. Though not a teetotaler, she preferred to drink only on weekends. In her line of work, one drink could easily lead to another. She didn't want to travel down that path.

Martha, also a nurse, had lost a patient, too, earlier in the week at Presbyterian Hospital. They shared feelings of defeat and frustration, then segued into a few jibes at their least favorite physicians, quick reviews of Netflix movies, and a debate over hairstyles. By the time their food arrived, they were feeling more normal.

As Martha listened to Rosemary's account of Carol's impromptu romp in the Bahamas, she grew increasingly concerned. She had met Carol only once, but she didn't seem flighty or fanciful. All in all, the whole episode seemed out of character.

"Have you checked her room?" Martha asked.

"No," Rosemary replied. "Carol is a very private person."

"Did she pack a bag?" Martha asked.

A basic question, Rosemary thought. She felt embarrassed that it hadn't occurred to her to look. They asked for the check and split it.

CHAPTER FOUR: A RIVER CRUISE

With Martha in tow, Rosemary returned to her apartment. Together, they entered Carol's room and looked inside the closet. There, plain as day, was a bright blue suitcase with a gaudy tchotchke for easy identification at an airport baggage claim.

"Do you know what her swimsuit looks like?" Martha asked.

"Two-piece, blue and green with small flowers," Rosemary replied.

Martha rifled through Carol's drawers and quickly produced a blue and green swimsuit.

Rosemary gulped, sat on the edge of the bed, and steadied herself. She was feeling a bit light-headed. "I guess I'd better call the police," she said. "Again."

Chapter Five: The Bubble Bursts

Radic was skimming a book about bridges when he got the call. A colleague, Max Volcker, had just heard from a young woman whose roommate was thought to be missing, then thought not to be missing. Now she's thought to be missing again. The records listed Radic as having made inquiries. Did he have an interest in the case?

"I'll be right over," Radic said. Within seconds, he was driving to the young woman's apartment on South Negley Ave. in Shadyside.

The apartment was easy to find, with a squad car sitting out front. Volcker, from the Missing Persons unit, had just arrived. Volcker had a good rep. He had been with the PBP for nearly twenty years and was widely admired for his methodical investigations and his people skills. If he had a vice, it was a small one: he loved to take pictures. Maybe not a bad thing if you were in Missing Persons.

Two young women sat in the living room. One, Rosemary, seemed to be the distraught roommate. Radic noticed that she was a pleasant-looking young woman with curly brown hair and a bracelet on her left wrist. The other, Martha, appeared to be a friend.

Volcker introduced Radic to the two young women, explaining that he had an interest in the case.

"So, Ms. Dunne, the last time we spoke over the phone, you were of the opinion that your roommate was vacationing, not missing," Volcker began.

"That's right," Rosemary said. "She called me up from the Bahamas and said everything was fine."

"When was that?" Volcker asked.

CHAPTER FIVE: THE BUBBLE BURSTS

"Thursday night," Rosemary replied.

"OK," Volcker said. "So what's changed since then?"

"Well, two or three things, really," Rosemary said. "I tried to call her on her cell phone, and it's been disconnected."

"Has that ever happened before?" Volcker asked. "Might she have been late in paying her bill?"

"No, absolutely not," Rosemary replied. "Carol is very fussy about paying her bills on time. She's an accountant."

"OK, what else?" Volcker asked.

"Well," Rosemary said. "I started to think back to Carol's phone call from the Bahamas. It just didn't seem right."

"OK," Volcker said. "In what way didn't it seem right?"

"Carol isn't a risk-taker," Rosemary explained. "Far from it. And she isn't a drinker. Or much of a drinker. When she called me up the other night, I thought she was drunk. But the more I think about it, maybe she was drugged."

"Has she ever taken drugs during the time you've known her?" Volcker asked.

"Not recreational drugs, that's for sure," Rosemary responded. "Maybe an occasional Advil or some allergy medicine."

"Alright," Volcker said. "Anything else?"

At this point, Rosemary started sobbing, and Martha intervened. "We came back after dinner tonight and looked in Carol's closet," Martha explained. "Her suitcase is still there. Then we looked in her dresser drawers. Her bathing suit is still there. Would you leave your bathing suit behind if you were going to the Bahamas?"

"Well," Volcker said, "sometimes people act impulsively."

"That's true," Martha admitted. "But Carol is not the impulsive type. If anything, she's the opposite."

Now it was Radic's turn: "Ms. Dunne, you may have covered this already, but where does Carol work?"

"It's a big accounting firm in downtown Pittsburgh," Rosemary said. "Dobson and Baker. Down on Grant St."

"Do you happen to know her boss's name?" Radic asked.

"It's Cynthia," Rosemary responded. "I don't know the last name."

"Are Carol's parents local?" Radic asked. "Do you know how we can reach them?"

Rosemary confirmed that they were local—from Sewickley—and agreed to find a phone number and an address.

"How about boyfriends?" Radic continued. "Anyone in particular?"

"Not that I know of," Rosemary said. "That's why the whole idea of a getaway weekend seemed so preposterous. She had no romantic interests that I knew about."

"What about other male friends?" Radic asked. "Anyone she might just pal around with from time to time?"

"Well, there's a guy at work she's gone out for drinks with once or twice," Rosemary recalled. "Just to talk about work stuff."

"Do you happen to know his name?" Radic asked.

"The Dude," Rosemary replied. "That's what she calls him."

"The Dude," Radic repeated. "As in *The Big Lebowski?*"

"Yep, that's right," Rosemary said. "For some reason or another, she thinks of this guy as the Dude. Like he's a piece of work, I guess."

"What do you mean, a piece of work?" Radic asked.

"Like, a little crazy?" Rosemary said. "A little eccentric?"

In a murder investigation, Radic never liked to hear the word crazy. Or even the word eccentric. Volcker and Radic thanked Rosemary for reaching out and asked if they could search Carol's room the following day. Rosemary agreed but said she would be working. She gave Volcker a spare key so he could visit while she was at work.

Volcker and Radic parted after agreeing to meet downtown early in the morning to sort things out.

* * *

The following morning, Mulroy tried to track down Radic, but no one had seen him. She texted him. Still no luck. So, she made multiple copies

CHAPTER FIVE: THE BUBBLE BURSTS

of Gatti's sketch of Vazzy. A middle-aged man with intelligent eyes, a prominent nose, and bushy eyebrows. Reportedly about 5'11", with brown hair, brown eyes, and a ruddy complexion.

Giving up on Radic for the moment, Mulroy started making the rounds. No one at the first marina on the North Side had ever seen the man. Nor did they have a low-budget wooden boat on the premises. No one at the second marina recognized him either. And no wooden boats there, though the owner said this did occur from time to time.

On an impulse, Mulroy dropped by Catholic Charities to see if Sister Mary Grace knew the man in the sketch. She did not but agreed to circulate the drawing.

* * *

Radic and Volcker met at the Public Safety Building downtown at 8 a.m. The protocol was not firmly established, but the working assumption was that Volcker would be the lead investigator unless and until it could be established that Carol Sloan was a murder victim. For the time being, she was just a missing person.

Both men agreed that their first priority should be to visit Sloan's place of work. Conceivably, she was on assignment, maybe something hush-hush. Or she had been in touch with her boss. One could only hope. If not, the possibilities got dicier. After seeing her employer, they could turn to the sensitive task of contacting her parents. What do you say to the parents of a young woman who might be salsa dancing in Nassau … or dead as a doornail in a forgotten corner of Pittsburgh? Radic shuddered at the thought of that conversation.

Volcker and Radic flashed their badges at the main desk and asked which floor Carol Sloan worked on. The gatekeeper directed them to the third floor, where they asked for Cynthia. "Cynthia Nolan?" the receptionist asked. "Yes," Volcker said. "If that's who Carol Sloan works for."

Not entirely sure what was going on, the secretary buzzed Ms. Nolan and indicated that the police wished to speak with her.

Cynthia Nolan was a trim, bird-like brunette with glasses thick enough to suggest that she spent many hours sifting through customer accounts. Her office featured a view of some very fine skyscrapers.

Volcker got directly to the point. "Ms. Nolan, we're wondering if you've been in touch with Carol Sloan over the past few days. It's our understanding that she works for you. Is that right?"

Nolan blanched. "Yes, officer, I'm Carol's boss. And no, I don't know where she is. She failed to report to work on Wednesday of last week. I've tried to reach her by phone, but no luck."

"Has this ever happened before?" Volcker asked.

"Far from it," Nolan replied. "Carol is extremely reliable and punctual. She's one of my favorite employees."

"So you're concerned?" Volcker asked.

"Very much so!" Nolan replied. "In fact, I called her parents yesterday to see if she was ill or in a car accident or something like that. They don't know where she is either and are worried sick about her. Her parents gave me her roommate's phone number. I was going to call her today."

"Well, no need for that," Volcker said. "She's in the dark too."

"Ms. Nolan, what kind of work does Carol do here, if I might ask?" Radic asked.

"Well, most of it is tax returns and everything that goes into that, including advice on how to make money and how to save money. Plus some intellectual property work," Nolan said.

"Has she been working on anything sensitive lately?" Radic asked.

"All of our work is sensitive, detective," Nolan replied. "Carol is very discreet and very honest if you're suggesting otherwise."

"I wasn't suggesting anything," Radic replied. "Just trying to understand what she does."

The two men got up to leave. Volcker gave Nolan his card and asked her to call immediately if she heard from Carol Sloan.

As they were about to exit, Radic asked one final question, "Is there someone who works here whose nickname is the Dude?" he asked.

"The Dude?" Nolan asked, scrunching her nose a bit. "The Dude? We're not very big on nicknames here, detective, but I can tell you that I don't know of any 'dude' except the one in the movies."

Chapter Six: A Mental Health Day

Rosemary's call to Allegheny General Hospital came as a surprise to her colleagues. Her first sick day ever. Rosemary's boss put it this way: "She must be sick as a dog!"

After a leisurely breakfast, in her pajamas, Rosemary got dressed and drove to Highland Park. She didn't want to be present when the police searched her apartment. And the Pittsburgh Zoo was her favorite refuge when things were not going her way.

The Pittsburgh Zoo, which occupies seventy-seven acres, just south of the Allegheny River, is one of six zoos in the U.S. to boast an aquarium as well as a zoo. The aquarium is where Rosemary began, making a beeline for the sea lion exhibit.

As a young girl, Rosemary had learned that sea lions will beg and twirl on command, even without food as a lure. Pretending to be holding a biscuit, she could coax a gullible sea lion to pirouette on its hind legs, twirling in the hope of a tasty treat. The routine never grew old!

After spending a few happy moments with the sea lions, Rosemary made her way to the small mammals exhibit. There, she found some ring-tailed lemurs, as cute as could be, grooming one another in a wonderful gesture of cooperation. Some meerkats nearby were equally attentive to their comrades' dirty coats.

The sloths were less energetic than the other small mammals, but equally fascinating. Rosemary never ceased to be amazed by the positions they adopted while sleeping—upside down, curled around a tree branch, anything but flat on the ground with tufts of grass for a pillow. Imagine the

CHAPTER SIX: A MENTAL HEALTH DAY

muscles required to grip a branch for hours while sleeping. Amazing!

Next stop: an obligatory visit to pay her respects to the zoo's Komodo dragon. Too grotesque to be endearing, the Komodo dragon still intrigued her. Its steely gaze bespoke grim determination: if a plump rodent were nearby, it didn't stand a chance. There was something compelling about such a relentless predator.

As always, Rosemary ended her visit with a triumphal tour of the African savanna. Several elephants were visiting their favorite watering hole. Giraffes munched lazily on tree leaves far beyond the reach of the other animals. In another contained area, three lions growled fiercely at spectators when not swatting flies with their magnificent tails.

Any feelings of guilt for having played hooky disappeared as Rosemary left the zoo behind her. She felt rested, refreshed, and ready to face the world again, including demanding patients and a missing roommate.

***

After discussing the case, Volcker and Radic agreed to split up. Volcker would visit Carol's parents and then inspect Carol's apartment, while Radic would return to Carol's place of work.

At Dobson and Baker, Radic met with Cynthia Nolan in her office. He declined a cup of coffee and got right down to business.

"Ms. Nolan, can you tell me the kinds of projects Carol Sloan has been working on since she joined your firm?" he asked.

"Well, detective, I'd say they fall into three basic categories," she replied.

"The first is tax preparation…and auditing, if it comes to that," she began. "Carol does tax prep work for three of our local malls. Not the shops that serve customers but the firms that actually own the malls."

"So what does that entail?" he asked.

"Well, she needs to understand each firm's business, its legal status, its history, and its relationship to bigger enterprises, assuming that it's a subsidiary," she explained.

"Sounds pretty complicated," Radic observed.

"It is, detective, but Carol is really good at her job," she replied. "One of my very best workers. In fact, she was promoted about a year ago."

Radic nodded. "And her second set of projects?" Radic asked.

"She verifies estimates for construction projects," Cynthia explained. "Homes, office buildings. It's kind of like a second opinion. If you're shelling out two million for a new home, or fifty million for a new office building, you often want a second opinion before taking the plunge."

"Okay," Radic replied. "Anything else?"

"Well, she does some intellectual property work from time to time," Cynthia responded. "For example, she's been advising a local company that wants to market some Harry Potter mugs. There are questions of copyright involved."

"That sounds more like law than accounting," Radic observed.

"Well, it's a bit of both," Nolan explained. "She works with a lawyer at a downtown law firm. But the accounting effort is not just incidental. If you're able to convince J.K. Rowling's people that a Harry Potter product is worth marketing, then the next question is: how much do you have to pay them to get the copyright waived? That's where Carol comes in. She tells the company whether they have the cash to manufacture and distribute the product AND pay the copyright fee."

"Has any of the work Carol's done for any of these clients triggered some dissatisfaction? Any complaints?" Radic asked.

Nolan sighed. "The relationship between an accountant and a client is always potentially fraught with controversy," she responded. "Sometimes a client wants you to push the boundaries. You just have to push back."

"Did that ever happen with Carol?" he asked.

"Well, to be perfectly frank, it happens with ALL of us from time to time," she answered. "In Carol's case, one of the three malls has a reputation for, shall we say, creative financing. This got them into trouble in a New York state court a couple of years ago. Luckily, we were aware of the case before the issue arose. So when someone ran a similar idea up the flagpole, Carol quickly shot it down."

"Were there any repercussions?" Radic asked.

CHAPTER SIX: A MENTAL HEALTH DAY

"Not really," she replied. "There was some bellyaching for a while, some back and forth. I had a conversation with an executive vice president who wasn't very happy about it. But the bottom line is we're still doing the accounting for this particular mall owner. And the other two as well."

* * *

Rosemary returned home from the zoo feeling almost normal again. That feeling did not last long, as she scrutinized her apartment.

Carol's room was a mess, with dresser drawers open and clothing scattered all over the floor. Fortunately, Rosemary's room seemed fine. But the kitchen, inexplicably, looked like a couple of meerkats had gone exploring for food. To make matters even worse, stale cigarette smoke permeated the air.

Hopping mad, Rosemary got on the phone at once. "Is this Officer Volcker?" she asked in a snippy voice.

"Yes," he answered.

"This is Rosemary Dunne," she said, "and I have a bone to pick with you! I gave you the key to my apartment in good faith. You and your people have totally trashed the place. It looks like a pigsty. And someone's been smoking cigarettes. Is this how the police reward citizens who are trying to help with a case?"

Volcker said nothing at first. Then he replied: "Ms. Dunne, I don't know what to say. I haven't been to your apartment since last night. I was going to come over this afternoon."

This time, Rosemary was at a loss for words. Then, finally, she responded: "What? You weren't here? Then who the hell was?"

Chapter Seven: Legal Constraints

The last thing Radic expected to see in Mulroy's squad car was a rubber chicken dangling from the rear-view mirror.

"A St. Christopher's statue would seem to be more up your alley, Mulroy," he observed.

Mulroy just rolled her eyes.

"You want me to get rid of it?" Radic asked.

"No!" Mulroy replied, with feeling. "It's better if I roll with the punches. If I remove the chicken, it will just return. If I act like it hasn't gotten under my skin, it will just blow over."

"And has it?" Radic asked. "Gotten under your skin?"

"When I was in 3rd grade, some kids at my public school would taunt me because I got ashes on my forehead on Ash Wednesday," she recalled. "When I started crying, it just encouraged them and made matters worse. In 4th grade, they taunted me again, but I didn't react. In 5th grade, the taunting stopped. Sometimes, you just have to take a punch."

"You're wise beyond your years, Mulroy," Radic said, and meant it.

* * *

Volcker asked a female police officer and a technician to join him at Rosemary Dunne's apartment. He wasn't sure what Rosemary's emotions would be.

The Rosemary Dunne who greeted him at the door was no longer angry, but she was very afraid, rattled. Well, who wouldn't be?

Volcker did his best to reassure her and to keep her occupied. "Ms. Dunne, we're going to sort all of this out," he promised. "And your apartment will be ship-shape by tomorrow. I promise! But we're going to need your help."

Rosemary nodded, at a loss for words.

At Volcker's insistence, Rosemary conducted a preliminary search of Carol's bedroom to see if anything was missing while technicians dusted for fingerprints and Volcker explored other rooms.

A half-hour later, Rosemary reported that two items were missing: Carol's laptop and an olive-green briefcase from work.

Volcker invited Rosemary to join him in the kitchen.

"Do you and Carol have any hiding places in here?" he asked. "Any cookie jars where you keep pocket money or bills?"

"We have a cookie jar, but it contains actual cookies," she said. "The bills should all be in Carol's room. She's an accountant and she's also the leaseholder. She handles all of our bills. I just write her checks for the rent and the utilities."

"How about spare keys?" he asked.

"We're not dumb enough to leave a spare key under the doormat, if that's what you mean," she said. "Each of us has a key. And we've also given a spare key to Bonnie Larson two doors down, just in case."

"So, no one else has a spare key?" Volcker probed. "I'm sure you understand this is very important. Not your parents? Not her parents? No ex-boyfriends?"

"No to all of those questions, detective, except for Carol's parents," Rosemary said. "I just can't say about them. But I'd be surprised. Carol visits them. But they don't visit us."

Anticipating a search that could last well into the evening, Volcker asked Rosemary if there was somewhere she could go for a few hours while they continued to investigate.

"I've already called my friend Martha," Rosemary said, no longer keeping her fear in check. "I just don't feel safe here right now. Martha has agreed that I can crash with her for a while."

Volcker conceded that might be for the best. He wrote down Martha's phone number and address and promised to keep Rosemary's apartment under surveillance, just in case. He also promised that the kitchen would look presentable again, though some items might not be in their usual places.

* * *

Mulroy's assignment was simple: share the sketch of Vazzy, the homeless guy, with as many of Sloan's co-workers as possible. Luckily, almost all of them were sitting at their desks and didn't object to a brief interruption. After surveying about two dozen employees, Mulroy reached a pretty firm conclusion: Vazzy might have a connection to Carol Sloan, but he was not known to her fellow workers.

Glancing at her watch, still too early to reconnect with Radic, Mulroy decided to drop by to see Lexie Davodny before she began her river patrol.

"Eager for another ride?" Davodny asked with a grin.

"Not until I invest in a wet suit and some blood pressure medicine," Mulroy responded.

"Well, the offer still stands, if you have a change of heart," Davodny said.

Mulroy produced the sketch artist's drawing. "Any chance you've seen this man?" she asked. Davodny grew serious for a moment and took a long, hard look. "There's something about him that seems familiar," she said, finally. "But I see a fair number of scruffy characters on the river. River rats, I call them. It could be I've met him. I just don't know."

* * *

The law firm Radic needed to visit was located at One PPG Place, in Market Square. Designed by the legendary architect Philip Johnson, the building was forty stories tall and featured 231 glass spires. Reflections from other buildings in Market Square enhanced its charm. It reminded Radic of Princess Elsa's ice castle in the movie Frozen, which he had seen with a young friend.

CHAPTER SEVEN: LEGAL CONSTRAINTS

Rob McPherson escorted Radic to a plush conference room with a spectacular view of the plaza below. After a brief exchange, a cup of coffee appeared, delivered by an actual person, not a robot, as at CMU.

Radic downplayed the gravity of the situation. "We're still hopeful that Carol Sloan is just on vacation," he said. But McPherson seemed smart enough to recognize that the police would not be bothering him if they didn't have cause for concern.

"I'm fond of Carol, and I can't bear the thought of any harm coming to her," he said. "I checked with my boss, and she's agreed that I can share whatever you need to know about the work Carol and I have been doing together."

"Thank you," Radic said. "So let's begin with the basics. Who are you working for?"

"It's a small business based here in Pittsburgh. They manufacture kitchenware and have been doing so for maybe twenty-five years. Dimitri's Sturdy Dishes, run by a Greek family. Pretty successful. They have a small manufacturing plant in West Mifflin, and they gross about $20 million a year. More than enough to pay the bills."

"Dimitri's Dirty Dishes?"

McPherson laughed. "That's STURDY, not DIRTY! A little Greek humor."

"When I think about kitchenware, I don't usually think that it would require the services of a lawyer. What exactly is the intellectual property element?"

"Well, normally, there wouldn't be any intellectual property issues. Most of what they produce is pretty ho-hum stuff. Serviceable, durable, good enough for your bowl of raisin bran in the morning. Not very exciting. But then, two years ago, the top dog came up with a brilliant idea. He called it Muggles."

"Muggles?"

"Yes, Muggles. More specifically, a line of mugs featuring some of the most popular characters in the Harry Potter series."

"Ah, ha! That's where the intellectual property issues kick in."

"Exactly! In order to manufacture and distribute mugs like that, you need to get permission from the copyright holder."

"And that would be?"

"Originally, J. K. Rowling, the fabulously successful author of the Harry Potter books. But now Warner Brothers, which acquired the copyright when they agreed to turn her books into movies."

"And is Warner Brothers okay with this idea, with Muggles?"

"Well, probably not, but we're still waiting to hear back. Sometimes, you luck out. For example, there's a company that decided to make some t-shirts that feature an otter wearing glasses and a Gryffindor scarf. As in: Harry Otter."

"Cute. And was Warner Brothers okay with that?"

"I don't know for sure, but they're doing it, which probably means someone said yes. The design was clever, the scope was limited, there was a tie-in to the Monterey Aquarium, which is a good cause. Warner Brothers may have decided to let sleeping otters lie."

"But not in this case?"

"Probably not. This is a much more ambitious project. The company wants to make mugs featuring Harry, Hermione, Ron Weasley, Hagrid, Professor Dumbledore, Professor McGonagall, and Dobby the House Elf. The cast of characters is larger; the resemblances are stronger."

"But if the cash is right? What if there's a side payment?"

"Well, yes. But the other issue is that producing all these mugs and calling them muggles doesn't sit well with J. K. Rowling and her reps."

"Why not?"

"Because they're NOT muggles!" McPherson laughed. "You and I, detective, we're muggles. Carol is a muggle. The mayor of Pittsburgh is a muggle. But these creatures are wizards, witches, half-wizards. If you put their images on mugs and sell them as muggles, you're violating the sacred canon. You're distorting Holy Scripture. You're committing heresy!"

"You're not joking, are you?"

"Not in the least. So I've told Carol to be cautious. And she's told her client the same thing. Don't mess with J. K. Rowling. Don't do anything you'll regret. Doing battle with her would be scarier than doing battle with

Lord Voldemort!"

"And did your client get the message? Did he back off?"

"Hard to say. He produced some prototypes or images with help from a graphic designer and sent them to England for their review. That's perfectly fine. But he wanted to actually manufacture and sell some mugs to show just how charming they could be. I warned him NOT to do that. That would be like crossing the Rubicon."

"So, did he cross the Rubicon?"

"I don't know, detective. But if he did, Carol is one of the few people on earth who would know about it."

Chapter Eight: Food for Thought

With so many new developments, Radic, Mulroy, and Volcker agreed to meet for dinner at six p.m. Volcker was still sifting through evidence at Carol Sloan's apartment, but the chosen restaurant helped convince him to take a break: Primanti Brothers in the Strip District. At five to six, Volcker let Radic know that he was on his way and asked him to order a Pitts-burger for him. Well done.

First opened in 1933, Primanti Brothers was legendary for its Pitts-burger. Many restaurants serve French fries and cole slaw on the side. Primanti Brothers serves French fries and cole slaw *inside* the sandwich, along with a delicious burger and condiments.

"I don't see any blueberries on the menu, Mulroy," Radic said.

"Don't worry about me, detective," she said. "I've wolfed down a Pitts-burger or two in my day, and I just may do so tonight."

In fact, Mulroy ordered a hoagie, while Radic ordered a Pitts-burger, plus one for Volcker. Soft drinks all around. Volcker arrived 10 minutes later.

"Have you met Snapper Volcker?" Radic asked.

"We've met," Mulroy said. "But they call you Snapper? Do you snap at people a lot?"

Volcker laughed. "I snap lots of photos."

"As a hobby?" Mulroy asked.

"Well, that too," Volcker replied. "But I take lots of photos at work."

"Snapper likes to have a visual record of people who are important to a case," Radic explained.

"You mean like suspects?"

CHAPTER EIGHT: FOOD FOR THOUGHT

"Anyone involved in the case," Radic said. "You could be next!"

"Well, not police," Volcker protested. "But anyone in the missing person's inner circle."

"What's the point?" Mulroy asked.

"Well, for example, a few years ago, I was trying to locate a missing person," he said. "I interviewed several people who knew her. Days later, one of them went missing, too. We had a devil of a time finding a photo of her, which made the search pretty complicated and which led to some bad outcomes. After that, I decided to take more pictures."

"Okay, I get that," Mulroy said. "But don't people object to your taking their photo?" she asked.

"Well, I try to be subtle about it. Like I'll take a group shot, not a headshot," he explained. "That's less threatening. If someone objects, I make the case and hope to persuade them. Otherwise, I look on the Internet. One way or the other, I usually get a photo."

The break-in at Carol Sloan's apartment was the first order of business when the sandwiches arrived. As Volcker saw it, the intruder was most likely the person responsible for Carol's disappearance. "According to her roommate," Volcker explained, "almost no one else had a spare key. Carol's parents didn't have one, which I can confirm. Rosemary's parents didn't have one. A neighbor had one, but she says she hasn't used it in two years."

"Were there any signs of forced entry?" Mulroy asked.

"None," Volcker replied. "Unless Rosemary left a window open, which she strongly denies, someone used Carol Sloan's key to get into the apartment."

"Anything missing?" Radic asked.

"We're still working on that," Volcker said. "Carol's briefcase isn't there, including various papers from work. And her laptop is missing."

"Maybe we can get access to her e-mails through work," Mulroy suggested.

"That would definitely help," Volcker said. "Meanwhile, one of our techs dusted for fingerprints. We should know in a day or two whether the intruder left any prints behind."

"So, all of this is consistent with our murder call," Radic said. "Our caller said that someone killed a woman, though he didn't say who she was. Carol

Sloan said she was in the Bahamas, but she could have been drugged, or under duress."

"Any luck in tracking down the caller?" Volcker asked.

"We think he's homeless," Radic said.

"And he might be a river rat," Mulroy added. "Someone who uses a cheap boat for transportation."

"We think he's spent time under a bridge," Radic added.

"We also think he looks like this," Mulroy said, producing the sketch. "His name or nickname could be Vazzy."

"Any sightings?" Volcker asked.

"Lexie Davodny of the River Rescue unit MIGHT have seen him in a boat," Mulroy said. "But she's just not sure."

"And the murderer?" Volcker asked. "Did anyone have a motive to kill Carol Sloan? Her roommate gives Carol rave reviews. A good person. Not much of a drinker. Doesn't have much of a love life."

"Except for the Dude," Radic interjected.

"The Dude?" Mulroy asked.

"Someone she met through work," Volcker replied.

"Maybe a guy she met at work who wants to manufacture Harry Potter mugs," Radic added. "The Dude could be the owner of a small kitchenware company in West Mifflin."

Volcker looked at his watch and stood up to leave. Radic asked a final question: "So, what's your bottom line? Is Carol Sloan our murder victim?"

Volcker sighed. "Two kinds of people go missing. Troubled people and people in trouble. Based on all reports, Carol Sloan was not a troubled person. So, that leaves option B. So far, there's no clear link between Sloan and your call from the bridge. But she disappeared a few days before your call. The timing is right. I hate to say it, but it could be her."

Volcker returned to the Sloan apartment after ordering a slice of apple pie to go.

Radic and Mulroy remained behind. Radic ordered coffee, Mulroy ordered tea. They agreed to pass on dessert after learning that there was no blueberry pie in the kitchen.

CHAPTER EIGHT: FOOD FOR THOUGHT

"So," Mulroy began. "I've never been part of a murder investigation before. Are we getting nearer to a solution? Or are we just chasing our tails?"

"Well," Radic said. "We don't have a confirmed victim. And we don't have any good evidence on who committed the murder. Our eyewitness is still the key. If he calls again, we've arranged to record the call. But he's been as quiet as a church mouse since Sunday night."

"Have you thought about why he doesn't want to be found?" Mulroy asked.

"I'm guessing that he's scared shitless," Radic replied.

"He did sound scared on the phone call," Mulroy agreed. "But he also sounded pretty cagey. Like someone who didn't want to tell us the whole story. Maybe he wants to protect the murderer and not just himself."

"That's entirely possible," Radic said. "But the only way to find out is to track him down."

"Why not smoke him out?" Mulroy asked. "Why not release the sketch?"

"I'm tempted," Radic replied. "Believe me. We could put the sketch in tomorrow's *Post-Gazette*. I think Cheesy would agree if we ask him."

"So, what's the downside?" Mulroy asked.

"Well, if our witness freaks out and disappears without a trace, that eliminates our best bet to find the murderer," Radic said. "Maybe our *only* bet to find the murderer. We don't want to scare him off. It might be better to track him down through solid detective work, like what we've been doing. Canvassing the homeless communities, checking out the marinas, trying to find someone who's seen him lately and who can point us to his lair. Or, if you believe what Professor Watanabe says, figuring out which bridge he was calling from."

Mulroy thought about this for a minute. "When I was an undergraduate, I took a political science course. If an advocacy group wants to shake things up, they 'expand the scope of conflict.' It generates a bigger audience. It reshuffles the deck. Isn't that what we need to do here?"

"Let's give it one more day," Radic said. "We still have some leads. If those leads don't pan out, then we'll ask Stilton to release the sketch to the press. It's a Hail Mary pass. Do you believe in Hail Mary passes, Mulroy?"

"Never underestimate the power of faith," she said. "But sometimes it takes publicity to move mountains."

Chapter Nine: It's All Greek to Me

With Stilton's one-week deadline looming, Radic and Mulroy agreed to split up on Friday. Mulroy would visit another homeless community on the North Side and a marina on the South Side, then additional marinas on the Ohio River if time permitted. Radic would visit the kitchenware factory in West Mifflin and speak with the owner. He would also touch base with Volcker to see if Carol Sloan's apartment yielded any useful evidence.

The homeless community on the North Side was not near a bridge but was near a soup kitchen. Sensing an opportunity, Mulroy entered the nondescript building just as breakfast ended and asked to speak with the manager. The manager was very cooperative and agreed to circulate the sketch to staff members. She hadn't seen "Vazzy," but maybe someone else had.

The homeless community was smaller than the others they had visited but also more joyful. Two elderly Black men played checkers with frequent whoops and hollers. A middle-aged white man strummed a guitar while a handful of others listened to the music and occasionally applauded. The guitarist actually sounded pretty good. Maybe a successful musician before something upended his dreams?

The guitarist turned out to be Sister Mary Grace's contact person. He didn't recognize the man in the sketch. He also said that no one in his group owned a boat, as far as he knew. "Care to hear another tune?" he asked.

Mulroy agreed to one more and was impressed when the man produced a credible version of "Mack the Knife" at her request.

Ah, yes, Mulroy thought to herself as she left a five-dollar tip. Patient police work. Lots of leads, but few that actually pan out.

Noticing clouds in the sky, Mulroy decided to drive to the South Side marina rather than hitching a ride with Lexie Davodny. If she was going to get wet, it would be the old-fashioned way, through a leaky umbrella, rather than being pelted with rain on Lexie's boat.

Radic, who had left his umbrella at home, made a mad dash to his car, a block away from police headquarters. He drove through heavy rain to West Mifflin, hoping that the shower would abate by the time he arrived. It didn't, and Radic got even wetter as he ran across the street to Dimitri's Sturdy Dishes.

Radic did a double-take on meeting the owner, Dimitrios Papadopoulos. Anticipating a brash youth with Dude-like facial hair and winning looks, he was startled to have his hand pumped by a pot-bellied old man with a bald head, a gold tooth, and plaid slacks from a bygone era. "Welcome to my world!" he said with a smile.

When Radic introduced himself, Dimitri asked for clarification. "Is that Detective Radish? Like the vegetable?"

"That's close enough."

"I don't want close. I want what's right."

"Okay. Do you ever get an itch that makes you want to scratch?"

"Yes."

"My name is like when you get an itch. Rad—itch."

"Thank you, Detective RAD-ITCH. It's nice to meet you!"

Eager to get a glimpse of the plant and its workers, Radic instantly agreed when Dimitri proposed a quick tour of the factory. He donned a pair of industrial-strength ear muffs as they entered the room where stainless steel pots and pans were made. The din was barely tolerable, even with ear muffs!

His host carried a portable white board with a red magic marker as the tour commenced. Unable to be heard over the roar, he wrote occasional words to convey what they were seeing: Steel pans...Top of the line... Reasonable prices...Want one?

Next, they entered a quieter room where ceramic bowls and mugs were

CHAPTER NINE: IT'S ALL GREEK TO ME

being mass-produced. Today's mugs featured two inscriptions: World's Greatest Mom and World's Greatest Dad. It was months from Mother's Day or Father's Day, Radic thought, but then again, it probably took months to ship these items to retail stores across the country.

As if reading his thoughts, Dimitri said, "These mugs are popular all year round. Not just Mother's Day and Father's Day. Every time a mom has a birthday, this mug is a great choice! Every time a dad has a birthday, this mug is a great choice! There's always a sales opportunity just around the corner."

The workers Radic observed—both men and women—seemed purposeful, efficient, and happy. Some of the women smiled as he walked by. One or two of the men gave him a thumbs up.

If this was the den of some nefarious conspiracy, someone had designed a truly remarkable Hollywood set.

"Are you a dad?" Dimitri asked. "I'll give you a mug to celebrate."

"No," Radic explained. "I'm not a dad."

"But you have a father," Dimitri insisted. "I'll give you a mug for your father!" Under other circumstances, Radic might have agreed, but he needed to create some distance for the delicate questions that lay ahead. "No, thanks, sir, but I appreciate the offer."

Dimitri escorted Radic to a cluttered office decorated with photos from Greece, a huge ficus tree, and a painting of a striking woman with a pearl necklace and a winsome smile. "My wife, Theodora," Dimitri observed, noticing Radic's gaze. "God rest her soul. She passed away ten years ago."

"I'm very sorry to hear that," Radic said.

Dimitri shrugged. "Have you heard of Clotho, Lachesis, and Atropos?" he asked. Radic said he had not.

"In ancient Greece, they were the three Fates," Dimitri said. "When a baby was born, they appeared in three days. They decided who lived, who died, who was rich, who was poor, who was happy, who was sad. The Fates treated me well. I was blessed to have Theodora at my side for thirty years. Theodora, maybe she was not so blessed. She died too young."

"She was a beautiful woman," Radic observed.

"Beautiful! And smart!" Dimitri added. "I ran the plant. But she ran the business. I miss her badly. Every day."

"Mr. Papadopoulos, I'm sorry to trouble you, but as I mentioned over the phone, a young woman has gone missing. Her name is Carol Sloan, and I believe you have business dealings with her."

"Carol Sloan? Yes. From the accounting firm. I met her two years ago. She has a good head for numbers."

"When was the last time you saw her?" Radic asked.

"Two years ago," he replied.

"But that's when you met her. Haven't you seen her since then?" Radic asked.

"No, only once. My son, Stephanos, he meets with her."

Radic was starting to get the picture. "Did Stephanos talk with you about his conversations with Carol Sloan?"

"Stephanos is a brilliant boy!" Dimitri beamed. "He has many good ideas. He has an M.B.A.! From Pitt."

"Did Stephanos discuss with you the possibility of producing some special mugs with a Harry Potter theme?"

"Harry Potter, yes, yes. I said maybe we can do it. But first, talk with the accountant. Carol. And with a lawyer. Stephanos handles all this. A very smart boy."

"Is Stephanos here today, Mr. Papadopoulos? I'd like to speak with him."

"No, bad timing, detective. Stephanos is on vacation. I go on vacation, in August, to Greece. He watches the plant while I'm away. Then he goes on vacation in September. I watch the plant while he's away."

"Do you know where he is?"

"Some island. But not Greece! Near Cuba."

"The Bahamas?"

"That's it! The Bahamas."

"Do you happen to have a photo of Stephanos?"

"I'll show you. In his office."

Two doors down was a much nicer office featuring a walnut desk, diplomas, a canister of macadamia nuts, and posters from two Harry Potter movies. Radic also noticed a photo of a handsome young man with a beard, not unlike the iconic Dude from *The Big Lebowski*.

"Your son?"

Dimitri nodded.

"Does he like working here?"

"Very much so. He will succeed me as head of the company when I retire next year."

"That's nice. Is everyone happy with that?"

"Everyone except Basil, my brother-in-law."

"He doesn't like Stephanos?"

"No, he loves Stephanos. They're very close. But he thought he should take over for a couple of years. Until Stephanos is a little older."

"Is Basil jealous of Stephanos?"

"He's upset with *me*. I made the decision. It was never in doubt. But he'll come around. He's still close to Stephanos. Everybody loves my boy!"

Chapter Ten: Knocking on Doors

Judging from the boats on display at the McKees Point Marina in McKeesport, just east of Pittsburgh, the marina's clients were pretty well-heeled. Many of the yachts were dazzling enough to impress even Lexie Davodny.

Mulroy didn't see any small wooden boats at the dock, but there was no harm in asking. The assistant manager, a well-muscled, tanned young man, confirmed her suspicions. "In principle, we'll find a berth for any type of boat here," he said. "But the docking fees are stiff enough that you probably wouldn't want to pay them unless your boat was more expensive than a very expensive car."

Mulroy showed him the sketch of Vazzy. "No, I can't say I've seen this guy," he said. "But I can show this to my boss when he comes in. Maybe he's seen him."

Mulroy thanked the young man, gave him a card, and headed for her car. Then, a thought occurred to her. She hurried back before the assistant manager went inside.

"I've been focusing on marinas," she explained. "But maybe I need to broaden my search. Are there any other places along the river where you could buy a cheap wooden boat?" she asked.

The young man thought for a moment. "Well, yes, now that you mention it," he replied. "There's the Sandcastle River Park, just upstream a bit. And there's Kennywood Park, further upstream."

"Do they sell wooden boats? Or store them?" she asked.

"Well, not exactly," he replied. "But they *use* a lot of wooden boats. Paddle

CHAPTER TEN: KNOCKING ON DOORS

boats. Mechanical boats. Boats that bump into other boats, often on purpose, just for fun. There's a lot of wear and tear. They probably throw most of them away. But maybe some of them are salvageable. If someone wanted to buy a cheap wooden boat that had seen better days, he might try one of those two parks."

* * *

Volcker, who had completed his sweep of Carol Sloan's apartment, called Radic with two useful pieces of information.

They found prints in Carol's bedroom, which matched those of Stephanos Papadopoulos, who was in the system for having been convicted of driving under the influence several years ago.

They also had secured Cynthia Nolan's consent to share a redacted version of e-mail correspondence between Carol Sloan and Stephanos on the Harry Potter business. They hoped to have a transcript soon.

Radic complimented Volcker on his work and meant it. It was a pleasure to be working with such a skilled investigator.

* * *

Rosemary was glad to be back at work. Caring for a teenager who would never walk again after a car accident was not a cheerful experience, but at least it put things in perspective.

After giving it some thought, Rosemary told her boss the full story of Carol's disappearance but asked her not to tell anyone else at work. "I don't want anybody's sympathy. That's what we owe our patients. I'd feel better if no one else knew what was going on."

With that out of the way, Rosemary went about her business and quickly lost herself in the demands of the day. There was nothing like the relentless pressure of a hospital to make you feel needed and to distract you from everything else.

Chapter Eleven: Silhouettes in the Moonlight

Radic made a point of visiting his parents, Bert and Sara, in Butler, north of Pittsburgh, once a month. If he had the weekend off, as he did this weekend, he would sometimes drive up on Saturday morning and return to Pittsburgh Sunday afternoon.

One of the few drawbacks of visiting his parents is that he couldn't avoid thinking about his late sister, Petra, a murder victim, while he was there. Never a good idea when he was struggling with a vexing case.

But one of the many benefits of visiting his parents is that they lived near a forest, with lots of trails. Great for jogging and for clearing your head. Radic felt alert and refreshed after an invigorating eight-mile run.

After showering, he joined his parents for a hearty dinner: goulash, with snow peas, and Plavac Mali to drink, followed by coffee and nutroll for dessert. He missed his mother's Croatian cooking and told her so repeatedly, as they talked lightly about her students at school, his father's clients at work, and the ups and downs of their erratic bowling team.

The call interrupted a quiet evening at 9:10 p.m. as he was watching a Pirates game on TV with his father. It was Stilton, and his voice was urgent.

"We got another call from your homeless guy," Stilton said. "He says there's a body in Frick Park. Meet me there, at the Nature Center, as soon as you can. Mulroy is already at the scene."

"Did we get a recording?"

"Yes, thanks to you. He called the Homicide Desk, just like before. I'll

CHAPTER ELEVEN: SILHOUETTES IN THE MOONLIGHT

send it to you right away."

"Did we get a phone number this time?"

"A burner phone, again. See you soon."

Radic packed his bags while listening to the recording:

Police: Pittsburgh Police, Homicide Desk.

Caller: I'm calling to report a dead body.

Police: What's your name, sir?

Caller: I can't tell you that.

Police: Where are you calling from, sir?

Caller: Under a bridge.

Police: Where is the dead body, sir?

Caller: In Frick Park, about 50 yards from the Nature Center.

Police: How do you know?

Caller: I know the murderer. I'm sorry I couldn't prevent this. (click)

Five minutes later, after apologies to his parents for an abbreviated visit, Radic was out the door. He arrived at Frick Park one hour later. First, he saw Stilton, pacing back and forth, looking grim, surrounded by a handful of police officers and technicians. The medical examiner, Dr. Saroja Prakash, was kneeling over what appeared to be a dead body, behind a makeshift screen to afford some privacy. Nearby was a shallow grave, perhaps six feet deep, and several shovels.

Klieg lights competed with twinkling stars in illuminating the burial ground. A thick cluster of oak, maple, and beech trees seemed incompatible with the gruesome scene that lay before him. The crime itself seemed like a sacrilege, when juxtaposed with the peace and majesty of the forest.

Next, Radic noticed Mulroy, who looked ashen, grief-stricken. She was clutching something in her right hand. Evidence? No, it looked like rosary beads. Her lips were moving. She must be saying some prayers.

Radic took a deep breath before approaching Stilton, who seemed shaken by what he was witnessing. "He told us we would find a body here, and we did," Stilton said. "Mulroy is pretty sure it's Carol Sloan. But see for yourself."

Dr. Prakash, on her knees as Radic approached, stood up to give him a better view of the rotting corpse. The scene before him took his breath away. A young woman, unmistakably Carol Sloan, was wearing a dark black robe, with a scarlet and gold scarf around her neck. She was clutching some sort of stick.

Mulroy came forward to explain: "She's dressed to look like Hermione Granger, from Harry Potter. The cape is a Gryffindor cape. That's Hermione's dorm. You can tell from the color of the scarf. She's holding a wand in her hand. It's an actual wand, from Ollivanders Wand Shop. Someone went to a lot of trouble to do this."

Radic needed help to process what he was seeing. "Do we have a time of death?" he asked Prakash, a well-respected physician who had been with the city for several years.

"Nothing precise," she responded. "But judging from a few indicators, I'd say that it was probably a few days ago."

Radic thought back to the original call. "So it could have been last Sunday night?" he asked.

Prakash nodded. "That's consistent with what I'm seeing."

"And the cause of death?" he asked.

"Too early to say," she replied. "But no visible blows to the head. And no stab wounds. The gums inside her mouth are discolored. If I were to hazard a guess, I would say a drug overdose. Or poison."

Radic grimaced and thought for a moment. "Will you be able to tell whether she dressed herself?" he asked. "Or whether someone else dressed her?"

"I don't know, detective," she said. "But I will add that to my list of questions. Is there some significance to the way she's dressed?"

Radic and Mulroy made eye contact. Then Radic responded. "She was advising a small business on some financial and legal issues involving Harry Potter. The young man she was advising is a Harry Potter buff. He's been on vacation…or missing…for about a week."

At that moment, Volcker pulled up in a squad car. Rosemary Dunne, looking somber, emerged from the passenger side. "She's agreed to identify the body," Volcker explained.

CHAPTER ELEVEN: SILHOUETTES IN THE MOONLIGHT

"Thank you for coming, Rosemary," Radic said softly. "Are you sure you're up for this?" he asked.

Rosemary nodded.

The two walked slowly to the grave site, where Carol's body was now fully covered. Radic removed enough of the sheet to reveal the victim's once-beautiful face. Rosemary winced and looked away. Then she returned her gaze to the victim.

"It's Carol," she assured them. Then, fighting back tears, "Who would do such a thing?"

Radic nodded to Volcker, who took Rosemary gently by the arm to the squad car to be returned to her friend Martha's house, where she had been staying.

Dr. Prakash approached Radic. "I'm tied up tomorrow, detective, but I'll make this a high priority," she said. "Can you make an autopsy at ten a.m. Monday?"

Radic looked at Mulroy, who nodded. "That will be fine," he said. "We'll see you then."

"What do you make of this, Radic?" Stilton asked. "Are we dealing with a lunatic? Does our murderer have some kind of obsession with Harry Potter?"

"I don't know, sir," Radic replied. "But there's obviously a connection. Do you want us to brief you now or later?"

"I'll need to tell Captain Reilly something before we issue a statement to the press identifying the victim," Stilton replied. "Make sure the parents are notified. Talk with Saroja. Then call me at home tomorrow."

"Will do, sir," Radic said.

"If there's an autopsy Monday, we'll probably have a press conference Tuesday morning," Stilton said as he stepped into his car.

Radic agreed that Volcker should inform Carol Sloan's parents and that he should do so in person.

Before leaving, Radic decided that another visit to speak with Dimitri was essential, but that they should wait until after the autopsy for that. If Dimitri's son's fingerprints were detected on Sloan's body or garments, it would be a difficult conversation. They needed to know where things stood.

Finally, there was some clarity. The call from the bridge was not a hoax. But Radic felt deflated, despondent. What kind of a world is it where a 26-year-old woman loses her life just because she befriended some sad sack at work? Well, it was *his* world. Not a very happy world, as Gloria had pointed out.

Chapter Twelve: A Grim Business

Volcker's visit to Carol Sloan's parents in Sewickley did not go well. He had barely delivered the bad news when Mrs. Sloan fainted on the spot. A sniff of ammonia and a splash of cold water revived her, but something had snapped inside. She looked like she had been hit by a Mack truck.

Volcker suggested that they call an ambulance, and Mr. Sloan agreed. By the time the ambulance arrived, though, Mrs. Sloan was standing upright and shouting that she had rights as a citizen and no one was going to force her to leave her own home against her will.

A thoughtful medic suggested a compromise: a nurse would make a house call, visit with her for a while, and perhaps give her a sedative. All things considered, that seemed the best possible solution to a dicey situation.

While waiting for the nurse to arrive, Volcker was able to speak privately with Mr. Sloan for a few minutes. He confirmed that Carol had not been in touch since her disappearance, that they knew very little about her work activities, and that she was unlikely to have a steady boyfriend.

When asked about Harry Potter, Mr. Sloan was startled, not sure what the point was. But he stated firmly that while Carol had read a couple of Harry Potter books as a teenager, she was not a Potterhead. She had never dressed up as Hermione on Halloween, had never requested a photo of Hogwarts on her birthday cake, and had never visited Harry Potter World in Orlando. As if to confirm, Mr. Sloan showed Volcker Carol's room, where the fiction was pretty highbrow and where the only poster featured singer Taylor Swift.

Leaving Sewickley, Volcker decided to visit Rosemary on his way back home. Martha answered the door and immediately summoned Rosemary, who was composed. She volunteered to visit Carol's parents, which Volcker agreed would be nice, but maybe not just yet. She also offered to pack up Carol's possessions when the time came to spare her parents the ordeal.

Volcker asked Rosemary again if there was anything she remembered about the young man known as "the Dude." For example, when Carol joined him for drinks, did she say where they went?

Regrettably, Rosemary could not remember a specific restaurant or bar. But she did remember that on one occasion, Carol returned from a rendezvous with the Dude with a half-finished container of pad thai.

"Did Carol have a favorite Thai restaurant?" Volcker asked.

"If Carol was choosing the restaurant, it might have been downtown, where she works," Rosemary reasoned, thinking out loud. "But then again, if the Dude was making the arrangements, maybe it was close to where he lived."

Volcker thanked her for this and promised to be in touch soon, once final arrangements were made for Carol's funeral.

* * *

There is no good way to prepare for an autopsy. Radic knew this all too well. He couldn't tell you how many women he had dated. He couldn't tell you how many poker games he had won. But he could tell you how many autopsies he had attended. 34. Carol Sloan would be number 35.

Mulroy was greener than green. This would be her first autopsy. She prepared by donning a surgical gown, wearing a triple mask, and slathering Vicks VapoRub inside her nostrils.

"Are you ready?" Dr. Prakash asked, with sympathy in her voice. Radic and Mulroy nodded, and the doors swung open.

"Before we begin, detective, I can answer one of your questions," the M.E. said. "She did not dress herself."

"How do you know?" Radic asked.

CHAPTER TWELVE: A GRIM BUSINESS

"Because her panties were on backwards," she replied. "Circumstantial evidence but pretty compelling."

She unveiled the body and continued: "Also, you don't need a medical degree to conclude that she was restrained. Both wrists and ankles. There's a good chance that she was kidnapped before being murdered."

Radic gazed stonily at the victim's injuries. "Was she gagged?" Radic asked.

"Maybe," the M.E. responded, "though it's hard to know for sure. The inside of her mouth is a bit of a mess. Some bruising, which suggests either a gag or force-feeding, with a struggle. Also, severe discoloration, which suggests poison or drugs. We'll know when the toxicology report comes back."

"Did you get fingerprints from Volcker in Missing Persons?" Radic asked.

The M.E. looked at a card. "Stephanos Papadopoulos?" she asked.

Radic nodded.

"Yes, I have them," she said. "I'll check to see if there are any prints on the victim's clothing or accessories either today or tomorrow."

Neither Radic nor Mulroy had eaten before the autopsy, and neither was eager to eat afterwards. But they needed to decompress and share ideas, so they settled for coffee and tea at a nearby café. Optimistically, Radic also ordered two scones.

"Are you okay?" Radic asked as they settled into a booth.

"My stomach's okay, if that's what you're asking," Mulroy replied. "It's my heart that's aching. It's such a loss. Carol Sloan was a really fine person. I would have liked her. You would have liked her."

"Agreed," Radic said. "When I was younger, a senseless death like this would send me into a tailspin. I'd waver between anger and despair. I wanted to find the son of a bitch who did it and squash him like a bug. At the same time, I couldn't bear the thought of living in a world where this was possible, even routine."

"That's not a good place to be, is it?" Mulroy observed.

"No, I eventually realized that, and I think you already get that," Radic said. "Whatever pain you're feeling now, whatever pain I'm feeling now, we need to channel it and do our best to find Carol Sloan's killer. We owe her that. We owe her parents that."

"Understood," Mulroy said.

"So, what do we want Stilton to say at tomorrow's presser?" Radic asked. "Do we reveal the name of our murder suspect? Do we publish the sketch of our informant? And do we say anything about the Harry Potter angle?"

"If we say anything about Harry Potter, it will make headlines for days," Mulroy observed. "Not just in Pittsburgh but across the country, maybe even around the world. I don't think we want that. It will be a circus. Besides, if we say nothing about how Carol was dressed, and the murderer really wants the world to know, for some twisted reason, it may piss him off and prod him to call the press or call us. He might make a mistake."

"I'm inclined to agree," Radic said. "I also think the time has come for us to go public with the sketch. If Vazzy's life is at risk, then it's better for us to find him than for the murderer to find him first. Maybe someone has seen him recently at a homeless camp, or on the water, or near the water. We need to hear his story first hand, in person, not from underneath some fucking bridge every seven days."

"I'm on board with that," Mulroy said. "But what about the Dude? Or Stephanos, assuming that he's one and the same? Do we identify him as well?"

"I'd say we need a bit more information before deciding that," Radic said. "The sort of information that only his father can provide."

"So, how do you propose to play this?" Mulroy asked.

"Dimitri Papadopoulos is a sweet old man," Radic said. "Old school. He's proud of what he's accomplished. And he should be. He's an immigrant and a successful businessman. He's beaten the odds. He also adores his son—the apple of his eye. So, if he has to choose between leveling with us and protecting his son, there's no doubt what his choice will be."

"Never-the-less," he said, drawing out the word, "we have the element of surprise in our favor. So, I hate to say it, but we have to bushwhack him. Stun him. Shock him. Hit him hard. Get him upset. And see where that leads us."

CHAPTER TWELVE: A GRIM BUSINESS

"So do we say outright that we think his son has committed murder?" Mulroy asked.

"Well," Radic said. "He's not a stupid man. If we tell him that Carol Sloan has been murdered, that she's been dating his son, and that she said she was in the Bahamas last week, he's going to put 2 and 2 together."

"Okay," Mulroy said. "So we leave it to him to connect the dots?"

Radic nodded. "And if he doesn't, we connect them for him."

Chapter Thirteen: Meet the Parents

Dimitri Papadopoulos was watching a Pirates baseball game at home in West Mifflin when he greeted Radic and Mulroy at the door, accompanied by a friendly golden retriever named Spam. Not Pam, Spam. "It's her favorite food," he explained.

He seemed surprised but unconcerned by the visit to his home. "You change your mind, detective?" he asked. "You want one of my mugs?"

"No," Radic said, refusing to engage in any banter. "We're here because we thought you might be able to help us with a murder investigation," he said. "Carol Sloan is dead, and we think that Stephanos may know something about her death."

That got Dimitri's attention. He winced at the news and turned off the TV.

"The young girl, she is dead?" he asked, not fully believing it.

"I'm afraid so," Radic said.

"And she was murdered?" he asked.

"I'm sorry, but yes," Radic said.

"Stephanos will be very sorry to hear that," he said slowly.

"We want you to help us reach him," Radic said

"But first, we have a few questions," Mulroy interjected.

"Of course," Dimitri said, sitting down again. "I'd like to help."

***

Volcker's call to Carol Sloan's father produced a surprise—Mr. and Mrs.

CHAPTER THIRTEEN: MEET THE PARENTS

Sloan would be pleased to see "Carol's roommate." The sooner, the better. Mrs. Sloan was grieving but calmer. And Mr. Sloan thought the presence of someone close to their daughter could be restorative in some way.

Rosemary, eager to help and worried that she might lose her nerve if she waited longer, put on a skirt and blouse, picked up some almond croissants at La Gourmandine in Lawrenceville, and headed north to Sewickley.

Carol's home looked so normal and inviting on a quiet Sunday afternoon, like a Norman Rockwell painting; it was almost unbearable. A poplar tree on the left and a sycamore tree on the right framed the house perfectly. An ample front porch featuring two rocking chairs and a padded bench hinted at cozy family conversations in the past, though, sadly, not in the future.

Rosemary's first reaction, once inside the house, was that Volcker had exaggerated Mrs. Sloan's recovery. She was not hysterical or angry. But she was a little too calm. Like a lost soul.

The most visible sign of a troubled mind was that Mrs. Sloan insisted on sitting next to Rosemary on the couch. She clutched Rosemary's hand like a life raft, as if somehow that connected her to Carol. A living, breathing Carol.

When Mr. Sloan returned with hot tea for all, Rosemary was able to reclaim her hand, momentarily. But Mrs. Sloan promptly put her left arm around Rosemary's waist. They would remain connected, one way or the other, for the full course of the visit.

Mr. Sloan, for his part, seemed pleased to have company, though he focused almost obsessively on safe subjects.

"Carol loved pastries. Did you know that?" he asked.

"Yes, I knew she had a sweet tooth. If I brought home a coffee cake, it didn't last long," Rosemary responded.

Mr. Sloan nodded. "Carol was a good baker, too. When she came to visit, she would sometimes bake us ginger scones. Isn't that right, dear?"

Mrs. Sloan nodded.

"She would have liked this pastry," Mr. Sloan said. "Where did you say you got it?"

Although Rosemary found Mr. Sloan's pitter patter a bit peculiar, she had witnessed something similar at the hospital on occasion. Deflection. Or attention deflection. When the elephant in the room is too painful to contemplate, people sometimes concentrate on trivia and find some comfort in that.

* * *

"Mr. Papadopoulos," Radic began, "there's definitely a connection between Carol Sloan and your son, Stephanos. We're trying to determine exactly what that connection is."

Dimitri nodded.

"We know that your son met with her from time to time and that they frequently talked about Harry Potter," he continued.

"My son, he loves Harry Potter!" Dimitri agreed.

"We know that your son has visited Carol Sloan at her apartment," Radic continued.

Dimitri shrugged. "I didn't know that. But I'm glad. She seemed like a nice girl."

"Sometime last week, Carol Sloan called her roommate and told her she was taking a sudden vacation," Radic added. "To the Bahamas."

"To the Bahamas?" Dimitri asked, puzzled. "With Stephanos?"

"We don't know," Radic said. "But that could be. If so, Stephanos may have been one of the last people to see her alive." Pausing, he then added: "Or it could be that Stephanos did her some harm. Maybe there was an accident."

"NO WAY!" Dimitri exploded. "Not Stephanos. He's a good boy!"

"Maybe that's true," Radic said. "But you can see why we need to get a hold of him. If only to clear his name."

"Does somebody say my boy hurt her?" Dimitri asked.

"Not directly," Radic conceded.

This seemed to mollify Dimitri. "Okay, then. Maybe he can help you find the killer. But my son, detective, he's no killer. I raised him well. He wouldn't harm the girl. He wouldn't harm anyone."

CHAPTER THIRTEEN: MEET THE PARENTS

Radic nodded to Mulroy, who moved the conversation forward. "Mr. Papadopoulos, would you be willing to call Stephanos right now, so that we can straighten all of this out?" she asked.

"Yes, of course," he said. "I don't usually call when he's on vacation. But this is a special case."

"We'd also appreciate it if you could put him on speaker phone," Mulroy added, "so we can talk with him too."

Dimitri consented and dialed the number.

"We're sorry, but this number is no longer in service."

Dimitri tried again.

"We're sorry, but this number is no longer in service."

Dimitri stared long and hard at the phone.

"Has this ever happened before, Mr. Papadopoulos?" Mulroy asked.

Dimitri seemed shaken: "Never," he said, trying to process what had occurred. Then, rallying, "Maybe he left his cell phone behind. And got a new phone in the Bahamas?"

"Mr. Papadopoulos, where does Stephanos live?" Radic asked.

"He has an apartment in Greenfield," he answered.

"Could you take us there?" Radic asked. "Now?"

* * *

Rosemary had dealt with grieving parents before, at Allegheny Hospital, and before that, at Presbyterian Hospital where she had trained. Her strategy boiled down to two things: let the tears flow; and find some beacon in the darkness.

The tears had already flowed, and they might flow again, before she left. But how to find a beacon in the darkness?

If only there were a sibling, then that would be reason for hope. But Carol was an only child. At least Mrs. Sloan had a sister, currently living in Denver. She would be flying to Pittsburgh soon.

Rosemary peppered Mrs. Sloan with questions about her sister and learned that they were very close. She also learned that the sister was a "birder." Had she ever visited the Aviary on Pittsburgh's North Side? Wouldn't that be a nice way to spend an afternoon?

Never bashful about promoting the Pittsburgh Zoo, Rosemary also put in a good word for the two-toed sloths, the ring-tailed lemurs, and her special friends, the meerkats. The sights, sounds, and smells of the zoo might be the elixir Mrs. Sloan needed to move forward.

Rosemary was less worried about Mr. Sloan. She discovered that he was a Steelers fan, and they swapped stories about heartbreaking playoff games and quirky running backs. Maybe someday they could take in a game together, Rosemary suggested.

Two hours later, confident that the mood had changed for the better, Rosemary announced that it was time to go. She asked to be informed about funeral plans and promised to come visit again. Mrs. Sloan released her grip, at last, permitting Rosemary to stand up and say goodbye.

* * *

Stephanos' home, in Greenfield, was an unpretentious but attractive Cape Cod—a good starter home for a young bachelor. Dimitri rang the bell at Radic's urging. No one answered, so Dimitri used his spare key to open the door.

Wary that this could be a crime scene, Radic listened and sniffed before marching across the threshold. Nothing seemed amiss.

"Stephanos?" Dimitri called. "Stephanos? Are you home, son?"

"Where's his bedroom?" Radic asked. Dimitri motioned upstairs.

The bed was made. Radic, wearing gloves, opened the closet door and saw men's jackets, men's slacks, men's sweaters. No evidence of a woman's presence. He motioned to Mulroy to inspect the bathroom while he and Dimitri entered the guest bedroom, which doubled as a study.

Mulroy, also wearing gloves, opened the medicine cabinet and saw three or four sets of pills. Positioning all of them so that their labels faced her, she took a quick photo and shut the cabinet. Only one toothbrush. Still no evidence of a female visitor.

CHAPTER THIRTEEN: MEET THE PARENTS

The guest bed did not appear to have been used recently, though you couldn't tell for sure. The study's bookcase featured a row of business books, a row of miscellaneous fiction, and a row with several Harry Potter books, plus "Fantastic Beasts and Where to Find Them." No sign of a cell phone.

Noticing a filing cabinet, Radic took a quick look. It was unlocked. He also saw a laptop. If necessary, they could return later with a search warrant.

The trio trooped downstairs to the living room. "Does everything look more or less the same as the last time you were here?" Radic asked.

"The same," Dimitri said. "But no Stephanos."

"Does Stephanos have any close friends, Mr. Papadopoulos?" Radic asked. "Anyone who might know about his trip to the Bahamas?"

"My son has lots of friends, detective," he said. "He's very popular. But I don't know all the names."

"If you think of any, even friends from college or grad school, that would be a big help," Radic said.

Dimitri nodded.

Mulroy, scrutinizing the room, noticed two photos on the mantelpiece. One featured Stephanos as a young boy with his mother and father, beaming with pride. Another featured Stephanos as a teenager, with an older man at his side. Something about the older man seemed familiar.

Mulroy brought the second photo over to Dimitri. "Who is the man with your son, Mr. Papadopoulos?" she asked.

"That's Basil," he said. "My brother-in-law. Dimitri's godfather."

Suddenly, Mulroy realized where she had seen that face before. "Mr. Papadopoulos," she asked, "what is Basil's last name?"

"Vasilikas," he said. "The same as my wife before we married."

Radic instantly understood what Mulroy was thinking. "Mr. Papadopoulos, does Basil have any nicknames?"

"Nicknames?" he asked. "Some people call him Vazzy, I guess. We just call him Basil or Uncle Basil."

"Excuse me for a moment," Radic said. "I need to call Lieutenant Stilton."

Chapter Fourteen: Going Public

The press conference commenced at nine a.m. Tuesday. Stilton had the good or bad fortune of being front and center. Radic, Volcker, and Mulroy were on hand to help. Captain Reilly sent a deputy to monitor the situation and report back to him if anything went wrong.

"Ladies and gentlemen," Stilton announced. "I am sorry to report that a young woman was murdered sometime last week. Her name: Carol Sloan. She was twenty-six years old, a Pittsburgh native from Sewickley, who worked as an accountant for Dobson and Baker."

"We are looking for two men who, we believe, have information relevant to this crime. The first is Stephanos Papadopoulos of Greenfield, who knew the deceased. The second is Basil Vasilikas, the uncle of Mr. Papadopoulos. A photo of Mr. Papadopoulos and a sketch of Mr. Vasilikas will be made available to the press corps."

"Any time a murder occurs, it is a tragedy. If anyone has knowledge of this crime, we urge them to come forward. If anyone knows the whereabouts of Mr. Papadopoulos or Mr. Vasilikas, we ask them to come forward. Thank you."

A reporter from the *Post-Gazette* asked the first question. "Lieutenant, what is the evidence that a murder occurred?" he asked.

"I'm sorry, but I cannot divulge that information at this time," Stilton said.

"Can you tell us where the murder occurred?" he asked.

"I cannot tell you that either," he responded, "but I can tell you that the grave was discovered in Frick Park."

"How did you discover the grave?" he asked.

CHAPTER FOURTEEN: GOING PUBLIC

"On a tip," Stilton responded.

"From whom?" the reporter asked.

"I'm not at liberty to say," Stilton answered.

A reporter from KDKA-TV stood up. "What can you tell us about Papadopoulos? Is he a suspect?" he asked.

"We want to talk with him because he has been working on a project with Carol Sloan," he said.

"What sort of project?" he asked.

"I'm not at liberty to say," Stilton answered.

"Can you tell us where he works?" he asked.

"At Dimitri's Sturdy Dishes in West Mifflin. He's the son of the owner."

A reporter from the Tribune-Democrat raised a hand. "What can you tell us about Vasilikas? Is he a suspect?"

"Not at this time."

"Where does he live?"

"He is homeless at the moment."

"Lieutenant, can you give us more information on the victim and her background?" another reporter asked.

"I'm going to suggest that you speak with Detective Radic and Detective Volcker for that information when the press conference is concluded."

"Lieutenant, can you tell us whether you believe that this was a random killing or whether Ms. Sloan was targeted for some reason?" someone asked.

"We do not believe that this was a random killing," Stilton said.

***

Early in the afternoon, Radic received a call from the M.E.

"Detective, this is Saroja Prakash. I thought you'd like to know that we received a preliminary report from toxicology."

"And?" Radic asked.

"Well, there were residues of two harmful substances in her stomach. Sleeping pills. A lot of them. Maybe enough to kill her. I don't know for

75

sure yet."

"And the other?"

"The other is more interesting. Have you heard of something called PFOA?"

"PFOA? I don't think so."

"Well, it's a non-stick substance. Perfluorooctanoic acid. Until recently, it was widely used in making pots and pans, to prevent food from adhering to the surface. It was an ingredient in Teflon."

"And today?"

"Well, it's been banned by the FDA since 2017 because it's carcinogenic. Today, you're supposed to use something else when making dishware, like PFBS or Gen X."

"Was the dose large enough to kill her?"

"We don't know that yet. We'll continue to investigate. It's not the sort of substance you routinely see in a murder investigation."

"So what does all this mean?"

"Well, detective, it might mean that two people tried to murder the victim in different ways. Or that she tried to kill herself and someone else also tried to kill her, maybe not realizing what she had already done. Or that someone tried to kill her with one of the substances and botched it, then used another substance to get the job done properly."

"It was a long, protracted death?"

"I'm afraid so."

"Would the sleeping pills be available over the counter?"

"Yes."

"And PFOA?"

"Most likely, you'd have to work at some kind of kitchenware manufacturing plant to have access to that."

"Any prints?"

"No, sorry. Whoever did this really didn't want to get caught."

Chapter Fifteen: Forbidden Thoughts

Radic groaned as he reached over to turn off the alarm. Despite the wear and tear of the Sloan case, he was determined to get in some daily exercise. Well, it was no longer daily. At best, perhaps twice a week. Still, he hoped to squeeze in two hours of physical activity before his workday began.

A key motivator was the Tough Mudder obstacle course in Slippery Rock, scheduled for October third. Radic had participated three years in a row and was eager to do so again, despite multiple bruises from his last outing.

The adrenaline rush. The teamwork. The sense of accomplishment. Even the bruises—black and blue badges of courage. Deeply satisfying. And, incidentally, a welcome respite from the stresses and strains of work.

Radic had some misgivings, of course. Who wouldn't? Hopefully, the event's planners would dispense with the Arctic Enema this year. Brrrr!

Radic was also anxious to avoid another sprained ankle, as in his very first Tough Mudder race. Lieutenant Stilton was none too happy about that, which limited his mobility for over two weeks.

But that was where careful planning and training came in. Plyometric routines, like frog hops, broad jumps, and tuck jumps. Tabata workouts, featuring 20 seconds of intense physical exercise punctuated by 10 seconds of rest. High planks, burpees, and squat thrusts. A great way to begin the day!

Luckily, a friend would be picking him up at five a.m. Together, they would do a range of calisthenics, followed by a five-mile run with ankle weights. Then, a final round of calisthenics. If one of them flagged, the other would buck him up. With insults or words of encouragement, whatever it took.

His partner was none other than Lucas Renfert's son. Norbert Renfert was fit, trim, and quick. Not as strong as Radic but very athletic. A marathon runner, he sped through Pittsburgh's somewhat hilly course with impressive times. In fact, he came in second two years ago.

Renfert arrived on schedule and with a boombox, featuring the latest Tabata hits: Taki Taki, Juice, Shivers, and Watermelon Sugar. His t-shirt was defiant: "Life Begins at the End of Your Comfort Zone."

"You look like shit!" he cried cheerfully.

"I feel like shit!" Radic replied.

"Well, I have just the right cure. Some Tabata workouts, a five-mile run. And a kale smoothie as your reward!"

"I'll have to pass on the kale smoothie," Radic replied. "Too much work to do. But as for the rest of it, bring it on!"

They left Radic's apartment and headed out into the still night to a nearby park in the Mexican War district. Pittsburgh seemed incredibly beautiful at this time of the morning. If you gazed at the rivers at night, from afar, you saw not water but the mirror images of the city's magnificent skyscrapers, doubling the visual impact. It was relatively quiet, except for sporadic squawks from the aviary nearby.

"My Dad says you have a particularly tough case," Renfert said

"You're violating the Tough Mudder workout rule," Radic grumbled. "Police business is off limits when we're working out."

"We're just driving," Renfert said. "We're not torturing ourselves yet."

"I'm sorry," Radic replied. "I didn't mean to snap at you. Which proves your point, I guess. This case has gotten under my skin."

"It was a young girl," Renfert said softly. "With her whole life ahead of her. You'd have to be pretty hard-hearted not to be affected. And you're not hard-hearted."

Radic said nothing.

"Besides," Renfert added, "it probably reminds you of Petra. It has to."

"Don't want to go there," Radic responded. "At least not now."

CHAPTER FIFTEEN: FORBIDDEN THOUGHTS

"Okay, okay," Renfert said. "I get it. Besides, we've arrived. Let's see what you're made of, big guy. Are you a Tough Mudder, or what?"

Radic thought of his sister Petra often but tried to think of her only in good times, not bad. Above all, he tried *not* to think of her when he was working on a homicide, especially when the case was not going well, and most especially when the victim was a young woman. Those cases were like a dagger to his heart.

Radic had been close to his sister growing up. As younger children, they were pals. They went to the pond together, in good weather to swim, in cold weather to skate. He accompanied her when she sold Girl Scout cookies door-to-door. "You're my good luck charm," she used to say and would reward him with his own box of Thin Mints after making the rounds.

Together, they lobbied their parents for a dog. It was a long, relentless campaign—a war of attrition. Eventually, their parents caved because the nagging just plain wore them out. The result—Sparky—a golden retriever who became their beloved companion and who enriched their lives in multiple ways. Even Mom and Dad became big fans.

As both of them grew older, they acquired their own friends but still enjoyed a special relationship. When Branko started playing Little League baseball, Petra would occasionally show up to cheer him on to victory or take the sting out of a defeat. When Petra took up singing, Branko would sometimes attend her concerts, in the high school auditorium at first and eventually in more visible venues like the county fair.

Petra was an excellent student, which inspired Branko to make time for homework as other activities intruded. When he struggled with Geometry, Petra lent a helping hand, especially as their mother was often busy grading homework assignments from the elementary school where she worked. Petra also helped him with his Spanish lessons.

When Petra graduated from college, at Duquesne University, she announced that she would be joining the Peace Corps. Branko and his father were supportive and enthusiastic. It seemed cool and exactly the right fit for Petra. She spoke Spanish fluently, she was smart and practical, and she had a generous spirit. She also loved to travel.

When Petra announced that she would be posted in Guatemala, only her mother raised objections. "You're so young, Petra!" she lamented. "And that's so far away! What if something goes wrong? Who's going to be there to protect you?"

Logically, Petra addressed all of her mother's concerns: One, I'll be living in a peaceful rural community; two, there will be plenty of supervisors, both Americans and Guatemalans; three, Peace Corps volunteers are well-liked because of the good work they do; four, No one targets Peace Corps volunteers; and five, if something goes wrong, the State Department will protect us.

Petra's letters and postcards from Panajachel, Guatemala, were effusive in their praise of both Guatemalans and the Peace Corps. She worked mainly on water purification projects, which involved teams of Americans and Guatemalans sharing sweat, toil, and a little bit of expertise to get new water purification systems up and running. Within months, they were making great progress. Also, Petra's Spanish was improving and she was getting to know the local citizens better.

Then one night Petra mysteriously disappeared from the Peace Corps compound. No one knew where she went or whether she had gone voluntarily. None of her colleagues had any inkling of a boyfriend. Nor had there been any known problems in or near the compound. In short, no one had a clue what had happened to Petra.

Branko's father contacted the State Department immediately after getting a distressing call from one of Petra's Peace Corps friends. After checking in with the U.S. Embassy in Guatemala City, the State Department promised to send a special envoy to Guatemala and to mobilize the local police.

When seven agonizing days had passed, and nothing resembling a clue had surfaced, Branko's father asked his employer for a leave of absence and flew to Guatemala himself. Branko continued to go to classes—his senior year in high school—but he was distracted and worried. Branko's mother was so distressed that she took a leave of absence from work and made sitting by the telephone her full-time occupation.

Kidnappings are hard to investigate in your own country, even harder to

CHAPTER FIFTEEN: FORBIDDEN THOUGHTS

investigate in a developing country where both technical resources and a sense of urgency are often lacking. That, at any rate, became Branko's firm opinion, after numerous late-night conversations with his deeply frustrated father.

Three weeks after her disappearance, Petra's body was discovered in a makeshift grave in a cow pasture 35 miles north of Panjachel. An autopsy concluded that the cause of death was a sharp blow to the head with a heavy object. Mercifully, there was no evidence of sexual violence.

Despite interviews with dozens of friends, neighbors, and local officials, the police never charged anyone with a crime. Distraught and disillusioned, the Peace Corps disbanded its team in Panajachel. Branko's father returned home and returned to work. Branko's mother also returned to work. But the sound of laughter disappeared from the Radic household for years to come.

It was around that time that Branko hatched the idea of becoming a policeman. Part of it was outrage—anger at a criminal justice system that had failed his family. Part of it was atonement—a desperate effort to protect others in lieu of the cherished sister he had failed to protect. Another part of it was sheer curiosity. How better to make sense of his family's tragedy than to understand the cat-and-mouse game that doesn't always pay off?

Snapping out of these bittersweet reflections, Radic returned to the task at hand. This case was solvable. He was convinced of that. For Carol's sake, and, yes, for Petra's sake, he would solve this crime. With Mulroy's help. With Stilton's support. One bird at a time.

Chapter Sixteen: Hoping for a Break

Anticipating a surge of calls following his press conference, Lieutenant Stilton established a hotline for calls concerning Carol Sloan's murder and the two men of interest to the police. The hotline was to be staffed twenty-four/seven. All credible calls were to be directed to Mulroy, who would decide which ones to pass along to Radic.

The Pittsburgh police's experience with hotlines was mixed but largely favorable. About fifty percent of the calls were easily dismissed. About forty-five percent were credible, on the surface, but led nowhere. The final five percent? Well, that was the reason to establish a hotline.

The most interesting call received on Monday came from someone who claimed that he saw Stephanos and Carol get into a car together near her apartment in Shadyside two days before Rosemary Dunne reported her missing. The eyewitness, a neighbor, said that both seemed to be laughing. No evidence that she was leaving against her will. And no luggage.

This seemed credible because it was already known that Stephanos had visited her apartment. It suggested that they were hanging out together…but not going to the Bahamas together. At least not that night. So, what went wrong? And when?

Radic circled back to Rosemary and learned that she had actually gone out for dinner with Martha on the night in question. She was not at home to meet Stephanos or to see Carol leave. So it all fit.

With encouragement from Mr. and Mrs. Sloan, Rosemary dutifully packed up Carol's possessions and placed them in carefully labeled boxes. Rosemary also agreed to select a pretty dress for Carol's burial. Even though

CHAPTER SIXTEEN: HOPING FOR A BREAK

the funeral service on Friday would be small and the casket would be closed, the Sloans wanted Carol to look her best.

Given the circumstances of Carol's death, Rosemary was especially attentive to the possibility of discovering something—anything—that might help the police to locate her killer and abductor. But, between the thief (who had presumably taken her laptop and her briefcase) and the police (who had removed all documents except for the lease to the apartment), there was not much to discover.

An autographed baseball from Pirates slugger Andrew McCutchen confirmed that Carol had been a Pirates fan. A book on Pennsylvania state parks and another on the Appalachian Trail, with handwritten notations on distances, indicated that Carol was a hiker. A couple of Taylor Swift CDs signaled her musical tastes.

But these were mere fragments that hinted at a life, not Carol, the three-dimensional person. Rosemary found that she missed Carol more than she thought she would. Perhaps because of the savage way that her life had ended. Or perhaps because she had forged a special connection with Carol's grieving parents.

Whatever it was, Rosemary looked forward to the week's end, when hopefully she could start to put her own life back together again. She would need to catch up on paperwork at Allegheny Hospital. She would need to find a nice present for Martha, to thank her for being such an amazing friend. She would also need to find a new roommate, or move. Yes, there was a lot to do.

* * *

Cynthia Nolan agreed to meet with Volcker when Radic explained that he had another appointment. She was willing to share selected e-mail conversations from Carol Sloan's desktop at work, but she wanted to do so in person and after a police signature, just in case legal issues arose.

Volcker joined Nolan in her office, where a computer technician was sitting by her side. Nolan produced a two-page document. Volcker asked that someone photograph the signing to make it more official (and to add a photo to his collection). The key excerpts from the transcript were riveting:

papadops@ddishes.com: I think we should produce a lot of mugs and sell them quickly, before someone else beats us to the punch.

csloan@d&b.com: I'd strongly advise against that. You don't have the cash to produce large numbers of mugs that you may not be allowed to sell. And you certainly don't have the cash to withstand a major lawsuit.

papadops@ddishes.com: But I can get the cash.

csloan@d&b.com: From whom?

papadops@ddishes.com: Don't worry about that. I can get it!

Cynthia Nolan could not shed any light on this exchange, except to say that the lawyer, Rob McPherson, might know more. She also promised that her technician would continue to scrub the computer for additional exchanges between Carol and anyone at Dimitri's Sturdy Dishes.

"Can you give us communications between Carol and the lawyer?" he asked.

"I'll need to check on that," she said, "but he's been very cooperative so far. With a little nudging, I think he'll say yes."

Volcker briefed Radic on this new development by phone and e-mailed him the transcript moments later. Radic thanked him and promised to get back in touch soon.

Despite his growing conviction that Stephanos was the murderer, Radic was convinced that Basil was the key to the case. Basil knew what was going on. He might even know why. In his gut, Radic believed that if he could track down Basil, he could crack the case.

But Basil was elusive. No home. No phone. Just a boat that was barely serviceable and seemed to have no regular berth. Under a bridge. But which one?

This brought Radic back to the bridge lady at Pitt. Though far-fetched on the surface, the bridge lady was the only person who might be able to help him narrow his search from 446 bridges to a more manageable number—maybe a dozen. With Mulroy sifting and winnowing the phone calls, he needed to sift and winnow the bridges. Radic decided that it was time to

CHAPTER SIXTEEN: HOPING FOR A BREAK

pay the bridge lady a call.

Chapter Seventeen: A Day at the Park

Hotlines seem to attract kooks. And pranksters. Mulroy was not amused when someone reported that Carol Sloan had been abducted by a UFO. Someone also reported seeing her at a Pirates game. A bit more plausible, perhaps. But the game took place on the night that Carol and Stefanos were seen together at her apartment. After establishing the timeline, Mulroy concluded that Carol and Stephanos would, at best, have arrived at the ballpark in time to catch two innings worth of baseball. So much for that tip. The way the Pirates were playing these days, two innings would definitely not have been worth the effort.

Mulroy decided to take a break from hotline call duty Tuesday morning. Volcker was kind enough to spell her for a couple of hours. With Radic's blessing, she was heading to Kennywood Park.

For Mulroy, as for many Pittsburghers, Kennywood Park brought back many fond memories. One of the park's many charms is that it includes some colorful, mildly spooky rides for younger kids, plus some exciting, state-of-the-art roller coasters for teenagers and young adults.

Mulroy recalled riding one of them, the Phantom's Revenge, as a teenager—a terrifying but exhilarating experience. Routinely cited as one of the top three roller coasters in the U.S., it reaches speeds exceeding 85 miles per hour and is beloved by roller coaster enthusiasts.

Mulroy anticipated that the park would be closed, given the time of year. Its regular season typically ran from sometime before Memorial Day to Labor Day. Still, she assumed that someone, at least, would be minding the store.

CHAPTER SEVENTEEN: A DAY AT THE PARK

When she arrived, she was encouraged. Several construction workers were transporting equipment and lumber from the parking lot to one of the rides. Clearly, some repair work was in progress.

Mulroy followed the snake line of workers to the work site, which turned out to be Noah's Ark, one of her favorites. Wistfully, she recalled the dark, narrow corridors, the shrieking animals, and the vibrating floor that hinted at doom and gloom. Sweet!

Judging from the look of things, a wooden elephant and a wooden rhinoceros were being replaced. A loud buzzing sound suggested that other work was also in progress. She hoped that Noah had a good set of ear muffs!

Mulroy asked one of the workers who was in charge of the construction work. She eventually tracked down Hector Garcia, who ordered a five-minute break so he could answer her questions.

"Who's in charge of the park today?" she asked.

Garcia shrugged. "You can try the administration building," he said, motioning to a white-framed building nearby. "But I'd be surprised if anybody's there."

"Well, who do you report to when decisions need to be made?" she asked.

"That would be Jasper Fitzpatrick," he said. "He comes to the park most afternoons for a half hour or so. Would you like his phone number?"

Mulroy nodded and called Fitzpatrick, who agreed to meet her in one hour. With time on her hands, she decided to visit the lagoon where she remembered seeing a fleet of rowboats years ago. The lagoon shimmered in the sunlight and looked very welcoming on a pretty fall day. She didn't see any boats, though. Where could they be?

Next, Mulroy moseyed over to the Old Mill, the oldest ride still operating today and another of her favorites. Here, parents and young children would climb aboard an old wooden boat to be propelled through a dark, winding tunnel. Haunting, piercing sounds would punctuate the darkness, along with sudden jerky movements. Very scary to a young girl! But no boats here either.

The hour passed quickly, and Mulroy was almost disappointed when

Fitzpatrick arrived. He shook her hand and asked how he could help.

"We're conducting a murder investigation, and we're trying to locate an informant who may be using an old wooden boat on one of the three rivers," she began. "We've been told that you sometimes sell your boats at the end of the season. Is that true?"

"A murder investigation?" Fitzpatrick asked. "The young girl who was mentioned in the newspaper?"

"Yes, that's right."

"Well, to answer your question, we DO sell some of our boats at the end of the season. If they're battered and bruised. They don't have to be in mint condition for continued use, but we don't want to give anyone splinters, and we want all of our boats to be seaworthy."

"So, who actually sells the boats?"

"Ah, well, you know, this is a seasonal park, open to the general public four months of the year. Most of our workers are seasonal employees. So the person who would sell the boats is Jake Jacoby. He works in the North Hills somewhere when we're closed."

"And he would know who has purchased the boats?"

"Well, for the last two years, at least. Not from memory. But he would know where the bills of sale are in the administration building. If he's willing to come out here sometime, I'll let him into the park. And you too."

"Where are the boats right now? The ones that are still being used?"

"We take them out of the water during the off-season to reduce wear and tear. Jacoby will be happy to show you the boats if it's important."

Chapter Eighteen: Disposing of Poisons

Radic got a chillier reception on his second visit to the kitchenware factory. The boss's son and heir apparent had been identified as a party of interest in a murder case. Not exactly good publicity. Rightly or wrongly, some employees would wind up blaming the police.

Radic found Dimitri on the factory floor, wearing bulky ear muffs. Radic waved. Dimitri nodded and soon returned to the front office. "Not a good day for my company or my family, detective," he said.

"I'm sorry about that, Mr. Papadopoulos. I truly am. But when a murder takes place, we have to follow our leads wherever they take us."

"I understand that. I really do. Just remember what I told you, though. My son is a good boy. You can count on that!"

Radic nodded without getting into a debate.

"Now, how can I help you?" Dimitri asked.

"Do you have a chief chemist at the plant? Someone who purchases and stores chemicals used in the production process?"

Dimitri looked puzzled and hurt. "Is this some witch hunt, detective? Are you trying to put me out of business?"

"No, not at all," Radic replied. "A particular chemical has surfaced during our investigation. I need to talk with someone who can tell me whether you use it here."

"What chemical?"

"PFOA."

"We used to use that until a few years ago, I think. But no more. It's not allowed."

"Can someone verify that?"

"Stephanos could, but of course he's not here. You could talk with Jim Trojanowski. He has a chemistry degree and an environmental engineering degree. He makes sure we comply with the federal rules, whatever they say. I'll introduce you. But no funny business!"

"No funny business."

"We'll be straight with you," Dimitri promised. "But you have to be straight with us. A two-way street."

Dimitri went to fetch Trojanowski and returned five minutes later. He invited Radic to use his office while he spoke with his employee.

Trojanowski was tall and thin, with a prominent nose. He looked to be in his forties, with a touch of grey in his closely-cropped hair. He had been briefed on who Radic was and why he was there.

"I'll be honest with you, detective," he said. "You're barking up the wrong tree if you think Stephanos committed a horrible crime. Or any crime. The worst thing he's ever done is drink one beer too many and get caught while driving home. And that was years ago."

"I understand," Radic said. "We're just investigating leads. We haven't made up our minds. We're just trying to learn more about your workplace."

"Fair enough. The boss said that I should talk with you and that I should be straight with you. So that's what I intend to do."

"Thank you. So, how long have you worked for Dimitri?"

"Four years. Going on five.

"Where did you work before that?"

"Koppers. Downtown."

"What did you do there?"

"I was a chemist. I worked on steel and aluminum products. My job, in a nutshell, was to make them stronger, more durable."

"And what do you do here?"

"I'm a chemist here too. But my work is more specialized. I help Dimitri and Stephanos to make pots, pans, dishes, and mugs."

"Do you have a degree in chemistry?"

"Yes, I majored in chemistry at Pitt. And I have a Master's in Environ-

CHAPTER EIGHTEEN: DISPOSING OF POISONS

mental Engineering, also from Pitt."

Radic nodded. "So, what can you tell me about PFOA?"

"Ah, yes, Dimitri mentioned that. We used to use it here, in producing our pans. It's great if you don't want food to stick to the surface. And no one does. But it was banned in 2017. So we stopped using it then. We now use something else instead."

"You can confirm that?"

"Yes, I can. It happened on my watch."

"So, what happened to the PFOA after you stopped using it?"

"A good question! Well, you can't simply put it in the trash. And you can't go dump it in the Monongahela River. That would be unthinkable! And illegal. But there aren't a lot of good options after that. If it were low-level radioactive waste, you could send it to a low-level radioactive waste depository. But it's not. So, for something like that, that's carcinogenic and banned, we would store it in the Skull and Crossbones shed."

"The Skull and Crossbones shed?"

"Yes, let me show you." They exited the main building and headed out back, where Radic saw a half dozen sheds or garages. One of them prominently displayed a skull and crossbones.

"Voila!" Trojanowski said. "The Skull and Crossbones shed."

"It's in here?" Radic asked.

Trojanowski nodded. "Here, I'll show you," he said. Using a key from his pocket, Trojanowski opened the creaky door. Inside were numerous containers. Some of them looked like paint cans. Others looked like barrels made of steel.

Trojanowski used a pocket flashlight to illuminate a corner of the shed. "In that corner over there, you have PFOA. I come in here at least twice a year to check the inventory. And I know it's there because I catalogued it about a month ago."

"Who has access to this place besides you?"

"Stephanos. But he would have no reason to come in. He's like Dimitri. Great on the business side, not so keen on the chemistry."

"But he does have a key?"

"That's correct. He has a key to this building and to all the other buildings on the premises. Everyone knows he's going to be the boss when Dimitri retires."

"Does Dimitri also have a key?"

"Yes. But he probably hasn't been out here in years."

"Anyone else?"

"Nope, that's it," Trojanowski said, exiting and locking the door.

"Would PFOA have been used by other businesses in Pittsburgh?"

"Yes. Dozens. Maybe hundreds. It was a very useful substance."

"And all of them would have handled it the same way?"

"Well, I can't answer that question, detective. If a Pittsburgh firm were a subsidiary of a bigger outfit, they might ship their toxic chemicals to another plant if they're no longer in use. I just can't say."

Radic thanked Trojanowski for his time. "One last question. Do you know anything about Stephanos' social life?" he asked.

Trojanowski paused before answering. "Stephanos is popular with the ladies. But I don't think he's ever brought one of them to work or to the annual company picnic. He keeps his private life private."

"Do you know if he's been seeing anyone in particular?"

"Maybe yes, maybe no. We don't just talk about pots and pans at work. We talk about the Pirates, the Steelers, the changing beer industry, maybe a little politics. But I don't believe he's mentioned a lady friend lately."

Chapter Nineteen: Bridge Lessons

It was easy for Radic to spot the Music Department's building on the Pitt campus. For one thing, he heard the telltale sounds of a classical piano composition wafting gently from one of the building's practice rooms. For another, the name of the structure gave it away: Music Building.

Actually, the building looked more like a rectory than a traditional academic building. Which it was, not that long ago. Before that, Radic recalled, it was the first location for Pittsburgh's public television station, WQED-TV. In these hallowed halls, Fred Rogers filmed the very first episodes of the show that eventually became Mister Rogers' Neighborhood.

Radic received a cordial greeting from Josephine Donato, Associate Professor of Music. She offered him coffee, tea, or espresso. Instead of relying on a robot, she brewed some espresso herself, which turned out to be remarkably good. Within seconds, it sent welcome electrical jolts to Radic's nerve endings. Who needs a robot, after all?

Donato got the ball rolling. "Shinichi said you have a bridge problem and that you'd like to approach it from a different angle. An auditory angle. Not what a bridge looks like but what it sounds like."

Radic nodded, briefly explaining where things stood. He played the first eyewitness call for Professor Donato.

She listened intently, then listened again as he played the second call from the same man.

They shared a long moment of silence. "Very sad, detective," Donato said. "Very sad. How can I help?"

"Both of these calls were made by a homeless man who spends some time under a bridge," Radic began. "Is there any way you can help us determine which bridge it is?"

"Well," she said, "let's begin with the basics. The sound of a bridge depends on many things. The design of the bridge. The composition of the bridge. The wear and tear on the bridge. The amount of traffic. The speed of the traffic."

Radic grimaced. "It all sounds really complicated," he said. "You'd almost need a formula to figure out how a particular bridge is likely to sound."

Donato nodded sympathetically. "I know," she said. "And you don't need a formula right now. You need an answer to your question."

"Okay," she said. "Let's zero in on one factor we haven't discussed. Did you and Shinichi talk about expansion joints?"

"He said something about that," Radic recalled. "They help a bridge to adjust to changes in the weather, from spring to summer, from fall to winter."

"That's the basic idea," Donato said. "Most bridges are primarily made of concrete. Expansion joints help to prevent the concrete from buckling by allowing the bridge to expand when the temperature is high and to contract when the temperature is low. But some bridge beams are made of steel, and steel and concrete expand and contract at different rates."

"Why is that important?" Radic asked.

"Because bridges that combine concrete and steel tend to be noisier than bridges that use concrete alone. If a bridge's substructures are made of the same material, they're quieter; if they're made of differential material, they're louder. Play the first recording again, and we'll listen to cars coming into contact with the expansion joints. That will be the loudest sound you hear."

Radic replayed the first tape while Donato listened intently.

"Okay," she said with a grin. "I'm pleased to report that your bridge's expansion joints have a very distinctive sound. All expansion joints are noisy. They tend to drive neighbors crazy, especially if they have trouble sleeping at night."

"But expansion joints experience more stress and strain on some bridges

CHAPTER NINETEEN: BRIDGE LESSONS

than others," she continued. "When they come into contact with a car's tires, they produce different sounds. Some joints sound like a subway car pulling into a station. Soft and gentle. Clickety-clack. Clickety-clack. Others sound more like a wrestler being thrown to the mat. Ka-thump, ka-thump."

"Okay," Radic said. "I'm with you so far. And this one?"

"This one sounds like a bowling alley! I hear duck pins falling as someone bowls a strike. Thwack-thwack-thwack. Your bridge has a very distinctive signature, detective. Find yourself a bridge with expansion joints that remind you of a bowling alley. That's your mystery caller's bridge!"

Chapter Twenty: Back at the Park

Jake Jacoby knew a lot about boats. He grew up in Key Biscayne, Florida, where his father took wealthy customers on fishing expeditions in private yachts. During the summer, Jacoby helped his father repair boats that got banged up. Over time, he got to know the difference between a boat that was fixable and one that was ready for the scrap heap.

At Kennywood Park, his job was to make sure the boats were safe and attractive. He and a small crew patched boats up after collisions and other mishaps and repainted them when time permitted. As they approached the Administration Building, Mulroy asked him how he had found an employer who was willing to have him work only nine months a year.

"I drive a school bus!" he explained. "It works perfectly, except in May when school's still open, and the park is open too. During May, I get about five hours of sleep a night. And I can't put in that many hours in the park. But then again, at the beginning of the season, our boats are in pretty good shape anyway. In some crazy way, it all sort of works out."

The Administration Building was deserted, but Jacoby had gotten a key from Jasper Fitzpatrick. As soon as they entered the building, Mulroy got a partial answer to one of her questions. The main reception area was teeming with boats—red boats, blue boats, green boats, red-white-and-blue boats, boats with stars, one boat with antlers, another with wings—all stacked tightly together, ready for the winter ahead.

"There's less wear and tear on the boats if we store them indoors during the bad weather," Jacoby explained. "We can't fit all of them here. But we try to shoehorn them in wherever we can."

CHAPTER TWENTY: BACK AT THE PARK

Jacoby opened a small office, fished out a key for a rusty gray filing cabinet, and extracted two thick folders with receipts.

"This is where we keep our receipts for boat sales!" he exclaimed. "I know it's horribly old-fashioned, but this is an old-fashioned park. You're the first person who's ever asked to see the receipts. Tell me what you're looking for."

Mulroy explained that she was hoping to find a boat sale to a Mr. Basil Vasilikas, sometime over the past two to three years.

"Well, that's roughly the time period covered here," Jacoby said. "Not all of the receipts are boat sales, though. We also sell pinball machines, whack-a-mole games, popcorn poppers, snowcone machines. You name it. We once sold a player piano. Why don't you take this folder, and I'll take the other one?"

Mulroy agreed. Minutes later, Jacoby crowed with satisfaction. "We have ourselves a boat!" he exclaimed.

Sure enough, there was a receipt, from about a year earlier, for a boat sold to Basil Vasilikas, for $1,650.00.

"Did he pay by credit card?" she asked.

"Sorry."

"By check?"

"No. He paid cash.

Mulroy whistled softly. "Any address?"

Jacoby shook his head.

"A phone number?"

Again, he shook his head.

Mulroy's face conveyed deep disappointment.

"Hey, wait a second!" Jacoby exclaimed. "I remember this one."

"My initials are here. J.J. And the boat we sold him was OM 156."

"You know each of your boats by number?" she asked, incredulous.

Jacoby laughed. "Not exactly. But that means the boat we sold him was from the Old Mill. OM-156."

"Why is that important?"

"Well, it means that it wasn't just an old wooden boat. It was a pretty heavy boat with a steel bar on it, for steering through the tunnel of the Old Mill. This boat would stand out in a crowd!"

Mulroy brightened at the news. She reached into her right pocket and fished out a dog-eared copy of "Vazzy's" sketch.

"Was this the guy?" she asked.

"The very same," Jacoby said. "Beefy, swarthy, serious, intelligent, and very particular."

"Particular?"

"Yes, he specifically requested a boat from the Old Mill. He said he used to work the ride years ago. It had some special significance for him."

"You don't say!" Mulroy exclaimed.

"I do say," Jacoby retorted.

"Do you happen to remember how Vasilikas removed the boat from the park?" she asked.

"Well, kind of, yes. We put it on a dolly and brought it out to the parking lot."

"Do you remember what kind of car he had?"

Jacoby thought for a moment. "I see a lot of cars, a lot of trucks. But I'm pretty sure it was a U-Haul. A rental."

"Can you get me a picture of the type of boat you sold him?"

"Better yet, I'll let you take your own picture. The Old Mill is just around the corner."

Jacoby locked up, and they walked over to the Old Mill.

"I don't see any boats," Mulroy said.

"They're all inside," he said. "Luckily, I have a key."

Jacoby opened a door that revealed a narrow waterway. At the entrance was a sturdy boat, about 12 feet in length, with a seat that could possibly fit three people. Sure enough, there was a steel bar in front. Mulroy squeezed onto a narrow platform next to the boat, took three shots from different angles, and pronounced herself satisfied.

Jacoby, noticing a half-eaten sandwich and a Coke can on the platform, removed both, shaking his head. "I hope it wasn't a park employee who left this here. That's a no-no. The park is supposed to be spotless when we

CHAPTER TWENTY: BACK AT THE PARK

close up."

"Maybe a construction worker?" Mulroy asked. "They repair rides during the off-season, don't they?"

"I like the way you think," Jacoby grinned as he locked the door. "That makes me feel a bit better."

Mulroy thanked Jacoby profusely and quickly exited the park. She was eager to tell Radic about her discovery.

She texted him but he was busy. Well, they could confer tomorrow if need be. In Sewickley. At Carol Sloan's funeral.

Chapter Twenty-One: The Lord is My Shepherd

Whoever designed modern funeral services clearly never consulted the dead. That, at any rate, was Radic's considered opinion. Is it realistic to try to reproduce the highlights of a person's life with a short eulogy, a prayer card, or a tombstone? Is it possible to convey the depth of one's sorrow through flowers, somber dress, and condolences? And isn't it perverse to compound a family tragedy by expecting a party for throngs of imbibers, noshers, and well-wishers just moments after the burial of the deceased?

Somehow, despite the challenges, the Sewickley community and its first Unitarian Church managed to capture some of the vibrancy of Carol Sloan's short life and some of the pathos of her death. A huge photo of Carol on her college graduation day, grinning ear to ear, reminded everyone of her upbeat spirit and her professional success. A tasteful floral display featuring lilies, roses, and chrysanthemums brightened up the church. A performance of Faure's Pie Jesu by a soprano from the Pittsburgh Opera Company brought tears to many eyes.

The Rev. Bartholomew Mulligan, who knew the parents and who remembered Carol from her early youth, managed to strike an artful balance between grief and hope. He conceded that many legitimate questions about Carol's death were unanswered and might remain so for a while. He cautioned against despair but welcomed expressions of grief. He told a few stories that hinted at Carol's keen intelligence, grit, warmth, and

CHAPTER TWENTY-ONE: THE LORD IS MY SHEPHERD

generosity of spirit.

Rosemary occupied a seat in the front pew, at the insistence of Mr. and Mrs. Sloan. She also agreed to do a reading from Psalm 23 as part of the service. Mrs. Sloan had progressed to a new stage, which Rosemary hoped was peace, acceptance, or transcendence. She seemed calm and not clingy. The presence of her sister, from Denver, seemed to be helping. Mr. Sloan, in contrast, was sobbing softly, finally unable to suppress his grief.

Radic, Mulroy, and Volcker hovered near the back of the church, mainly to pay their respects, but also hoping to learn something relevant to the case from a former teacher, a college friend, or someone they had already met during the course of their investigation, after the service. Later, Volcker hoped, he could take some photos. But not at the funeral itself. Even he would not cross that line.

Radic, like Volcker, looked a bit out of place, unaccustomed to wearing a jacket, a white shirt, and a tie. Mulroy looked more at home, wearing gray slacks, a green blouse, a religious pendant, and pumps. She joined in the singing while her colleagues did not.

Cynthia Nolan was there, as expected, with at least a dozen co-workers. Carol's lawyer friend, Rob McPherson, was there. Surprisingly, Dimitri Papadopoulos was also in attendance. He looked forlorn, dabbing his eyes with a handkerchief. Was he weeping for Carol? Or for his beloved son, whose whereabouts were unknown and who was under suspicion for murder?

Radic's cell phone was on "vibrate" when he received the call from Lieutenant Stilton. Funeral or no funeral, he knew to pick up.

"Radic, are you at the church?" he asked, a note of distress in his voice.

"Yes," Radic replied.

"Evacuate immediately!" he ordered. "We've just received a bomb threat!"

Radic began to blubber something but was immediately silenced. "NOW!" Stilton bellowed.

The Rev. Bartholomew Mulligan was reciting the Lord's Prayer when Radic raced to the front of the church. He nodded apologetically to the minister and turned to face the congregation.

"I'm so sorry," he said, loudly and clearly, flashing his warrant card to signify that he was with the police. "But everyone MUST leave the church right now. We've just received a bomb threat."

Volcker and Mulroy sprang into action, shepherding frightened mourners out of the church as quickly as they could. Most, including the organist, needed no cajoling and scampered to safety. But the Rev. Mulligan stood his ground. And the Sloan family refused to budge. Dimitri Papadopoulos also remained in his pew with a puzzled look on his face.

Sensing what was going on, Radic approached Rosemary Dunne and whispered in her ear, "Get them out of the church, Rosemary, NOW, so we can do our job."

Radic quickly checked his texts to see if Stilton had left additional instructions. He found a new message: Caller sez bomb in bathroom.

Radic raced to the back of the church and found the most plausible bathroom door, which was indeed a bathroom. He looked behind the toilet. No bomb. He looked at the sink. No bomb.

Then he noticed a gray metal box on an ancient radiator. The box was attached to the pipes with a padlock. And it was ticking ominously. This was no hoax.

Radic raced back to the front of the church, where Rosemary was using her powers of persuasion to coax Mrs. Sloan to exit. "I won't leave Carol!" Mrs. Sloan moaned. "I won't leave my girl!"

Mulroy had returned to the church while Volcker was keeping everyone at a safe distance across the street.

Relying purely on instinct, Radic lifted Mrs. Sloan off the ground, kicking and screaming, and carried her out of the church.

Following Radic's lead, Mulroy grasped the remaining mourners, shoving when necessary, and hustled them all outside.

Radic was confident that a bomb squad from Pittsburgh would arrive soon. But Sewickley was 20 minutes away from downtown Pittsburgh. Even if the crew left when Stilton received the call, they would be 10 minutes away. Or worse.

How much time did they have? In a James Bond movie, you would know

CHAPTER TWENTY-ONE: THE LORD IS MY SHEPHERD

the number of seconds left before an explosion. Should Radic try to defuse the bomb? Was there a way to defuse the bomb?

Not sure of his next move, Radic saw Mulroy deposit the remaining mourners across the street and run back to join him just outside the church.

"Will you come back inside with me?" he asked.

Mulroy gulped, then nodded.

Together, they sprinted to the front of the church. The casket was heavy but on rollers. Carefully but briskly, they rolled the casket down the aisle to the back of the church and then, after one nerve-wracking bump, just outside the church.

As if on cue, the pallbearers separated themselves from the rest of the mourners and rushed across the street. Volcker joined them.

With three people on one side, four on the other, they hoisted the coffin and moved it down the church steps and across the street, in a herky-jerky motion that reflected both respect and urgency. Fifty seconds later—though it seemed much longer—Carol Sloan was across the street.

Radic promptly texted Stilton:

Everyone out of church. Safe.

He received a reply:

Good work. Stay put.

Chapter Twenty-Two: A Delicate Situation

The Sewickley Fire Department arrived first, followed by an ambulance. After conferring briefly with Radic, the fire department proceeded to evacuate a handful of nearby residences, as quickly as possible. Meanwhile, paramedics offered assistance to shaken mourners, including Mrs. Sloan, who, sadly, seemed to be in a state of shock again.

The Pittsburgh bomb squad arrived ten minutes later, with sirens blaring and lights flashing. Stilton accompanied them in a separate car, and Captain Reilly arrived moments later.

Radic explained that there was a ticking time bomb in the bathroom and offered to take them there. Stilton overruled this. Only two bomb squad members would enter the building after receiving clear directions from Radic.

Somehow, Radic found time to speak with the Rev. Mulligan, who had been a good sport about all of this but who had a pressing question. Clearly, the service would not continue, at least not today. But what about the burial, scheduled for one p.m.? Radic promised an answer soon.

The hearse was sitting directly in front of the church. With Stilton's approval, Radic ordered the funeral director to drive it to a safer location, one block away, and to leave it there until further notice.

A handful of mourners politely asked if they could move their cars from the parking lot, but Radic demurred. No one was to cross the street for the

CHAPTER TWENTY-TWO: A DELICATE SITUATION

time being, until the bomb squad had done their work. And at that very moment, the bomb squad appeared.

Two men in body armor, looking like astronauts preparing for a space launch, exited the police van and conferred with Radic. They wanted to know more about the size of the bomb, the color and texture of the wires, and the nature of the container.

Their leader, dressed in civilian clothes, carried a walkie-talkie. Whatever the two men discovered, he would know instantly. And everyone within earshot as well.

After a nod from Stilton, the two bomb squad men entered the church while everyone else held their collective breath.

Officer X: It's a primitive device. But it could be dangerous.

Leader: Take an X-ray to see what's inside.

Officer X: Roger.

Leader: What do you see?

Officer X: It looks like there are some explosives inside.

Leader: Any chemical residues on the outside?

Officer X: Could be.

Leader: Take a swab and come back out. Both of you.

Within seconds, the two men hustled out of the church

The leader produced a kit, which he used to test the swab. They named a chemical Radic didn't recognize. Apparently, cause for concern.

Leader: I'm sending Hugo in. Put a camera in there. Hugo will make the cut.

Officer X: Right, boss.

With an assist from the two men, Hugo appeared—a three-foot tall robot with spindly legs and a strange pair of hands. The left hand seemed to be for gripping, while the right hand seemed to be for cutting.

The two men escorted Hugo into the church, along with a camera on a tripod. Their conversation resumed.

Leader: Is the camera in place?

Officer X: Yes, sir.

Leader: Place Hugo's cutting hand as close to the wires as you can without touching them.

Officer X: Roger.

Leader: OK. That's good. I can see it on the screen. Return to base.

The two men hustled out of the church, leaving Hugo behind.

Leader: Hugo, I want you to cut the wire. Understood?

Hugo: Yes, sir.

Leader: Lower your right hand slowly.

Hugo: Yes, sir.

Leader: Stop!

Hugo: Yes, sir.

Leader: Good, Hugo. Now, cut!

The tension was so acute that Radic could hardly bear it. He looked at Mulroy, who returned his gaze, without flinching.

BOOM!

Everyone heard the explosion. Radic waited for a second explosion. Mercifully, none came.

Radic looked at the screen in the leader's hand. There was smoke and debris. No sign of Hugo yet.

The leader said nothing for what seemed like a minute. The two costumed men said nothing as well. Finally, the leader ordered, "Assess the damage, fetch Hugo if you can, and come back immediately."

Radic watched the screen as two blurry figures eventually appeared. He caught a glimpse of Hugo, then turned his eyes to the church entrance. Hugo was being carried by one of the men underneath his arm.

"We think that did it, sir," one of the men reported. "The bathroom is a mess, but the damage is contained."

"Any fires?" he asked.

"None that we could see, but there could be a spark."

The leader nodded and spoke briefly with the fire crew chief. Within seconds, the fire crew unfurled an industrial-strength firehouse and approached the building. They sprayed the damaged area with a forceful stream of water as mourners began to express feelings of relief.

Hugo had been injured. His right hand was a mess and would need to be

CHAPTER TWENTY-TWO: A DELICATE SITUATION

replaced. He was dusty and discolored. But he would live to see another day.

Radic arranged a brief conversation with Lieutenant Stilton, Captain Reilly, and the Rev. Mulligan, together. With encouragement from Radic, they agreed that it would be okay to proceed with the funeral if the parents wished.

Again, Radic enlisted Rosemary to act as intermediary. After conferring with Mr. and Mrs. Sloan, she simply nodded. The Sloans were ready to give Carol a proper burial.

The funeral director was told to bring the hearse to the sidewalk where Carol's coffin rested. The pallbearers would then do their duty.

Meanwhile, Volcker and Mulroy escorted mourners in small groups to the parking lot, where they had two choices: they could go home after leaving a name, address, and phone number; or they could wait for the funeral procession to begin. Every single person agreed to join the funeral procession.

Radic would join the procession, too, but first, he needed to speak with Stilton. "Were you able to record the call, sir?" he asked.

Stilton nodded and pulled out his cell phone. "I think it's a different caller this time. And definitely, a different M.O. He called 911."

"Does that mean we know where he was calling from?" Radic asked.

"Roughly," Stilton replied. "We know he was calling from a Greenfield shopping center. Nothing more specific than that. He was using a burner phone, like the other guy."

Radic nodded and listened to the call.

Operator: 911. What's your emergency?

Caller: There's a bomb in the church.

Operator: Which church?

Caller: The Sewickley Unitarian Church.

Operator: Where is the bomb exactly, sir?

Caller: It's in the bathroom.

Operator: Stay on the line, please.

Caller: Hurry. You only have a few minutes.

(click)

Radic was chilled by the message and the voice—a voice he hadn't heard before.

"It's not Vasilikas, is it?" Stilton asked.

"No, sir, it's not," Radic replied.

"Stephanos?" he asked.

"There's only one way to find out," Radic said.

Within seconds, he produced Dimitri Papadopoulos. Still shaken, he looked like he could use medical attention. Or a friend.

Stilton played the call while both men looked at Dimitri.

"Do you recognize the voice?" Radic asked gently.

Dimitri moved his lips, but no words came out.

"Dimitri?" Radic asked.

"It's my son!" he said, with horror in his voice. "It's Stephanos!"

Chapter Twenty-Three: Picking Up the Pieces

If Radic and Mulroy had hoped to do patient, stealthy police work to find Vasilikas before Stephanos found him first, that hope was now dashed.

All of Pittsburgh was buzzing about the "two fugitives"—one a fugitive from justice, the other a fugitive from terror. The ambitious young entrepreneur and his homeless uncle. The prince and the pauper.

The local media knew far more about the murder and the bombing than they had learned directly from Stilton. Every organization has leaks, and the Pittsburgh Bureau of Police was not immune from them.

The *Post-Gazette* and a local TV station reported that Stephanos was linked to the bombing and that he knew Carol Sloan from work. They also reported that Basil had alerted the police to Carol's murder and had directed them to the makeshift grave site in Frick Park.

Not to be outdone, a renegade national news outlet had given them names. Stephanos was now the Church Bomber. A jilted lover, a corrupt businessman, a domestic terrorist. Take your pick. Basil, for his part, was the Witness on the Run—homeless except for a dilapidated boat who might tell all if only the police could track him down. In some accounts, he was portrayed as a cross between Popeye and a mob snitch.

It was a small mercy that no news outlet, local or national, had yet picked up on the way in which Carol Sloan had been dressed or, more broadly, on the Harry Potter connection. Nor had the Sloan family been informed, officially or unofficially. But that was just a matter of time. The clock was ticking.

On the bright side, Radic, Mulroy, and Volcker were being hailed as heroes. They would be commended for bravery and valor by Captain Reilly himself at some point in the future. Along with members of the bomb squad and, yes, Hugo.

But meanwhile there was a case to be solved. And the ground rules had changed.

First, Radic and Mulroy were to report to Stilton, twice a day. Stilton would report to Reilly once a day. Or more often, if needed.

Second, a seasoned Homicide detective, Anthony Scuglia, would be paired with Volcker, who would continue to work on the case with permission from Missing Persons. His knowledge was too valuable to ignore.

Third, all requests from Radic for technical and logistical support were to be honored immediately, with no questions about budgets or lines of authority.

Fourth, no one was to speak with the mass media except Stilton. And Stilton would confer with Reilly before releasing any important information about the case.

The overall message was clear: the PBP would leave no stone unturned to make progress on this case.

* * *

The hotline call ricocheted from Scuglia to Mulroy and from Mulroy to Radic, still composing his report at home. Stilton had given him until five p.m. to complete it.

"It's from someone at the general aviation terminal in West Mifflin," Mulroy reported excitedly. "He read about Carol Sloan's funeral in the *Post-Gazette*. He says she was scheduled to fly to the Bahamas."

Radic couldn't believe his ears. His working assumption had been that Carol Sloan's trip to the Bahamas was pure fiction. "Tell him we'll be there in less than an hour. I'll meet you at headquarters in 15 minutes."

CHAPTER TWENTY-THREE: PICKING UP THE PIECES

As he drove to pick up Mulroy, Radic tried to recall what little he knew about the Allegheny County Airport, located ten miles from downtown Pittsburgh in the southern part of West Mifflin. Most of its flights, he remembered, were corporate flights or general aviation flights, featuring licensed pilots who fly recreationally or who transport passengers or precious cargo for a hefty fee through private bookings.

Mac McCarthy greeted Radic and Mulroy, as promised, at Hangar # 9. Behind him stood a small airplane, big enough to hold three people.

After brief introductions, McCarthy got to the heart of the matter. "I recognized the name Carol Sloan from my manifest," he said. "She was scheduled to fly out of Pittsburgh a week or two ago, but the flight never took place."

"Where was she flying?" Radic asked.

"To Nassau. In the Bahamas."

"Non-stop?"

"No, they were to refuel in Ft. Lauderdale."

"Someone was flying with Carol?"

"Stephanos Papadopoulos. He's the one who booked the flight."

"And the pilot?"

"That would be me."

"When was the flight canceled? And why?"

"It was canceled at the very last minute. We were already fueled up and ready to go."

"And the reason?"

"None given. Just that they wouldn't be able to make it. I offered to rebook them, but the gentleman declined. I told him he would forfeit his five-hundred dollar security deposit. He said something like: So be it. Or I understand. So be it, I think."

"And no word from either of them since?"

"Not a peep."

"Did Papadopoulos book by phone or in person?"

"By phone."

"How did he sound to you? When he booked the flight?"

McCarthy paused to think. "Well, I guess I'd say he sounded happy. Most people who fly to the Bahamas are happy. It's a vacation paradise. But he was *really* happy. Maybe because of his lady friend."

"And how did he sound when he canceled the flight?" Radic asked.

"Not happy. Not as friendly as before. Disappointed. Serious. Almost like a different person. And no explanation. I appreciate some sort of excuse, even if it's a lame one. But I got nada from him."

"Did he tell you what his plans were for the Bahamas in his original call?" Mulroy asked.

"As a matter of fact, he did," McCarthy recalled. "He asked my advice for a hotel, and I recommended the SLS Baha Mar. He liked the sound of it and said he was going to book a room there. I don't know if he did, of course."

"What is it he liked about the Baha Mar?" Mulroy asked?

"He liked that it was pretty fancy and that it had a spa," McCarthy said. "He said his lady friend would like that."

"Is that what he called her?" Mulroy asked. "His lady friend?"

"No, now that I think about it," McCarthy said. "I think he called her his fiancée."

Chapter Twenty-Four: The Best Thai Dish in Pittsburgh

Stilton struggled to process the new information, just as Radic and Mulroy had.

"Is it possible that Papadopoulos and Sloan were actually engaged?" he asked.

"We don't know, sir," Radic replied. "All we know is that Papadopoulos claimed that they were."

"So he could have been lying?" he asked.

"Absolutely," Radic said. "Maybe he was obsessed with Sloan. Maybe it was wishful thinking."

"What do you propose?"

"We have only one brief sighting of the two of them together. But we know that they went to a Thai restaurant together, at least once. We're going to canvas every Thai restaurant we know of. In case someone saw them there together. We're also going to reach out to some of Stephanos' friends. Maybe he confided in one of them."

"Good," Stilton said. "Anything else?"

"We need to track down Vasilikas quickly. If he's still alive. And we need to learn more about him. Why is he homeless? Something happened. But what? When? At this point, he's the key to the case. But he's also a big question mark. We know what he looks like. We know what he sounds like. We know he can handle a boat. But that's about it. We need to learn more about him."

"And who can help you with that?" Stilton asked.

"Well, his brother-in-law, for starters," Radic replied. "Dimitri."

"Anyone else?"

"Dimitri might be able to point us to some other people."

* * *

Though not known for its South Asian cuisine, Pittsburgh is blessed with a number of outstanding Thai restaurants. Volcker and Scuglia were instructed to visit each and every one of them, with photos of Stephanos Papadopoulos and Carol Sloan in hand.

They started with Thai Me Up, on the South Side. The owner recognized neither face, but promised to circulate the images and get back in touch if anyone remembered them.

Next, they turned to the Silk Elephant in Squirrel Hill, halfway between Stephanos' apartment and Carol's apartment. The owner was not in when they dropped by, but a staff member agreed to show him the photos as soon as he arrived.

Nicky's Thai Kitchen is popular enough to have three separate locations in Pittsburgh—one on the North Side, one in the North Hills not far from Sewickley, and one downtown.

Volcker and Scuglia decided to start with the downtown restaurant and were glad they did. The owner, an amiable gentleman dressed in a bright green apron, instantly recognized Carol Sloan, though he knew nothing about her death.

"I don't have time for the news," he explained. "I work twenty-four/seven. But I'm VERY sorry to hear that Carol is dead. She was a good customer. And a nice person. Murdered? Who would do such a thing?"

"Did she ever come here with a young man?" Scuglia asked.

"No," the owner replied. "I would have remembered. We often talked when she came here for lunch. But she was usually alone."

"What did you talk about?" Scuglia asked.

"Well, we often discussed Thai food," he responded. "She worked as a waitress at one of our other restaurants near Sewickley when she was younger. We talked about how to get the noodles just right for pad thai. Not too brittle, not too soggy."

"Did she ever mention a boyfriend?" Volcker asked.

"She said something about a young man," he recalled. "But I never met him. Maybe someone else did."

"Did she mention his name?"

The owner shook his head. "No, all I know about him is that he knew a lot about different kinds of dishes."

"You mean like pad thai or shrimp scampi?"

"No, I mean like the dishes you serve them in. The dishes you have to wash after every meal. Carol said he was in the dish business."

* * *

Mulroy received a warm embrace from Lexie Davodny when she tracked her down at the harbor. "You're a hero, my friend!" she said. "I'm SO proud of you!"

"Whatever I did, it was pure instinct," Mulroy said.

"Well, that may be, but you have great instincts. Do your Mom and Dad know about what went down?"

"They're down in Florida," Mulroy replied. "I deliberately didn't tell them. They worry enough about me."

"Well, maybe there's a way to tell them without scaring them," Davodny suggested.

"I'll think about it," Mulroy replied. Then, reaching into her pocket, "I have another picture for you."

Davodny took a look, and her eyes widened. "I've seen this boat before!" she exclaimed.

"When and where?"

"About a year ago, on the Mon," she said.

"Are you sure it was the Mon and not one of the other rivers?" Mulroy asked.

"Absolutely!" Davodny replied.

Next, Mulroy showed her Vazzy's sketch, for the second time.

"Well, I wasn't sure the first time," Davodny said, "but yes, that was probably the guy. I remember the boat clearly because it's like an amusement park boat, not a regular boat. The guy, I don't remember so well. He was scruffy and scrappy. We had words. But I had no good reason to detain him or to ticket him."

"Did he have anything in his boat?"

"A satchel or a backpack. Maybe some food."

"How would you describe his mood? How did he come across?"

"Well, it's been a while," Davodny replied. "Guarded. Nervous. Suspicious. On edge. But not hostile. Not belligerent."

"Did he say where he was going?"

"Well, I saw him near the Fort Pitt Bridge, heading east on the Mon. He said he was almost home. So probably somewhere near there."

Mulroy checked her watch. It was time to go. Radic had scheduled a meeting with Dimitri Papadopoulos at his home, and he wanted Mulroy to be there.

Chapter Twenty-Five: Ancient History

Dimitri's buoyant self-confidence, so evident when Radic first met him, had taken a hit. His son was missing and a murder suspect. Somehow, his brother-in-law was also involved. His business was getting savaged in the press. His world had turned upside down.

"Do you have someone you can talk to about all this?" Radic asked. "A friend? A relative? Someone at work?"

Dimitri took the question as a kind gesture and nodded in appreciation. "Father Kristoff. I meet with him this afternoon."

"We're trying to find Stephanos," Radic assured him. "And whatever he's done, we'll treat him fairly."

Dimitri nodded more perfunctorily at that, probably skeptical.

"But that's not why we're here," Radic said. "We want to ask you some questions about Basil."

Dimitri acknowledged the request with a grim snort and motioned for the two officers to take a seat.

"We know next to nothing about Basil," Radic began. "He has no police record and, until recently, his name never appeared in the local newspaper. What can you tell us about him?"

Dimitri looked at the ceiling for a long time before responding. Clearly, the subject was a painful one.

"Basil is my wife's younger brother," he began. "Theo's parents moved to Pittsburgh from Athens when she was five years old. Basil was born one year later, in Pittsburgh."

"Basil was a very smart boy. Good at math. Less good with people. He got into fights with other boys. That's good, that's bad. He learned to take care of himself. But he also stood out in a crowd. Other boys teased him."

"When he turned 18, Basil should have gone to college. But that wasn't his plan. In fact, he didn't have a plan except to get high with his friends. And to shake people down for money when he needed it."

"Did he have a job?" Radic asked.

"I gave him work in the assembly line at the factory. He didn't like it. And sometimes, he'd just quit. But then he would come back again, with his tail between his legs. Lots of apologies. Lots of promises."

"Did he ever snap out of it?" Mulroy asked.

"Yes," Dimitri said, brightening. "He got better when Stephanos was born. He loved that boy from the very start. We made him Stephanos' godfather. He was very gentle with him. He was a good uncle. He was our # 1 babysitter."

"Did he ever go to college?"

"Yes, he did. He attended Allegheny County Community College and eventually got a degree. We paid for it."

"Was he still working at the factory?"

"Not for long. He got a job as an accountant with a defense contractor in Washington, D.C. He left Pittsburgh for several years."

"How long did that last?"

"Until he joined the Army."

"Wow! What brought that on?" Mulroy asked.

Dimitri laughed. "He saw a Tom Hanks movie. Saving Private Ryan. He got the idea from that."

"When did he join?" Radic asked.

"2003."

"Ouch."

"That's right. He joined the Army, went to basic training. A few months later, he was fighting in Iraq. In Fallujah."

"I've heard about that. A bloody battle. It must have been tough."

"Basil is a tough guy, detective. Fierce. He won a medal for bravery. We were very proud of him."

CHAPTER TWENTY-FIVE: ANCIENT HISTORY

"How long did he stay in the Army?"

"Three years. He left under a cloud. Something bad happened. We never understood what it was."

"What did he do next?"

"He came home to Pittsburgh."

"How did he seem when he returned?"

"Do you know the story of Odysseus, detective?" Dimitri asked.

"The Greek who fought for years in the Trojan War and was the hero of the Odyssey?" Radic responded.

Dimitri smiled. "I knew you were a smart guy, detective. You read good books. You remember how Odysseus was when he came home?"

"Yes," Radic replied. "He had changed a good deal, physically, mentally, emotionally. Some strange men had taken over his farm, but they didn't recognize him. He remained in disguise until he could figure out a way to destroy them and recover his property and his wife."

Dimitri smiled again, sadly. "When Odysseus came home, the world looked very different. When Basil came home, the world looked very different. More importantly, Basil WAS very different."

"How so?" Mulroy asked.

"He saw very bad things in Iraq. And maybe he did some bad things in Iraq. When he came back, he was a bitter man. An easy conversation was a difficult conversation with him. An easy decision was a difficult decision for him."

"PTSD?" Mulroy asked.

"Yes, I know what that is. Too much stress. Too much killing. Probably so."

"What did you do?"

"Basil's mom had died, and Basil's dad was too sick to help. So Theo said. We have to take him in. And I said, of course, we'll take him in, we'll look after him."

"So he lived with you?"

"Yes, and I gave him a better job at the factory."

"What kind of job?" Radic asked.

"Basil is good with numbers. I put him in charge of our books."

"Did he get better?"

"For a while," Dimitri recalled. "A year, two years."

"But something went wrong?"

"That's right. Something went wrong. Well, really, two things. Basil liked to drink. He met with buddies from Iraq. They would drink till they passed out."

"And the second thing that went wrong?"

Dimitri sighed. "Gambling," he said. "Basil liked to gamble at the racetrack. He would take his monthly paycheck and spend some of it on liquor, the rest on horses. He never had any money in the bank."

"Not good," Radic said.

"No, not good," Dimitri agreed.

"So what happened?"

"Theo spoke with Basil about the gambling. She insisted that he stop. She threatened to kick him out of the house if he didn't."

"Basil was very angry. But he knew she meant it. So he stopped. At least for a while."

"But it didn't last?"

"Basil tried really hard. But gambling is, what do you say, a compulsion? His head said: don't do it! But some other voice said: take a chance, it's your lucky day!"

"How did you find out he was gambling again?"

"Well, Theo was checking the books one day. In one month, our earnings went way down, by about ten thousand dollars. Theo looked at our records and we hadn't gotten a check from one of our retailers in California. She called them, and they said, oh, we mailed you that check two months ago."

"I think I know what you're trying to say," Radic said sympathetically.

"He was stealing from us!" Dimitri exclaimed. "After all we had done for him! I was furious! Theo was furious!"

"What did you do?"

"Theo kicked him out of the house, and I kicked him out of the factory."

"So he was unemployed and homeless?"

CHAPTER TWENTY-FIVE: ANCIENT HISTORY

"Not exactly," Dimitri said. "Unemployed, yes. But we wrote him a check for $5,000 to get his own apartment. And we offered to send him to a program that helps people to recover from an addiction to gambling."

"That was very generous of you," Mulroy observed.

"He was my wife's brother," Dimitri explained. "He was family. But we couldn't have him drinking and gambling and making a mess of things. Stephanos was a teenager. He looked up to his uncle. But Basil was not a good role model for Stephanos back then."

"Did things improve?"

"Well, sort of. Basil rented an apartment in Lawrenceville. I have no idea what went on there. He didn't want to see us, and frankly, we didn't want to see him. Except for Stephanos. They got together about once a month."

"Did Basil do something about the gambling problem?" Mulroy asked.

"Not at first," Dimitri replied. "But then Theo got sick, bad sick. Three months later, she was dead."

Radic was somber. "You told us that she died young," he said.

"55. She was 55 years old."

"How did Stephanos react?"

"He was shattered. He loved his mother very deeply."

"And Basil?"

"Two days after the funeral, he came to see me. He said he wanted to stop gambling. And that he wanted to stop drinking."

"Did that happen?"

"Amazingly, it did. Basil went to a clinic in Virginia. When he came back, he was a different person. Sober. Careful with money. Dependable. He turned things around."

"You paid for the program?"

"Yes, but I'm glad that I did. It put Basil on a different path. A better path."

"But you said the other day that you're no longer on speaking terms with him," Mulroy pointed out. "What's that all about?"

Dimitri sighed.

"For a few years, Basil was great!" he recalled. "He lived like a hermit in his small apartment. He helped me out at the factory with this or that."

"As an accountant?" Mulroy asked.

"Well, we hired an accounting firm to do the hard stuff. But yes, sometimes Basil would help out with the numbers."

"You trusted him?"

"I trusted Stephanos. He said, let Uncle Basil work on R&D. Research and development. New products. New marketing techniques. There was a fixed budget for that. Stephanos could spend from it. Basil could spend from it. Only those two."

"So all of your sales, which account for most of your revenue, are handled by Dobson and Baker. But new projects are handled separately?" Radic asked.

"Exactly!" Dimitri said.

"Do you know how long Basil has been homeless?" Radic asked.

"I heard this from Stephanos a year ago," Dimitri said.

"Were you surprised?" Mulroy asked.

"Yes. I thought he had turned over a new leaf, as they say. I thought he was through with the gambling and the drinking."

"But now you're not so sure?" Radic asked.

"I haven't seen him drink in five years, since Theo died. I haven't smelled alcohol on his breath. I don't think he's been gambling, either. But I don't know much about his personal finances."

"When we spoke earlier, you said that you and Basil had a serious disagreement over your retirement plans," Radic said. "When was that?"

"A few months ago, in March," Dimitri recalled. "I told my people that I would be retiring next March and that Stephanos would succeed me."

"And Basil objected to that?" Radic asked.

"He said that Stephanos is too young and inexperienced. He said I should make HIM the C.E.O. for at least two years. Until Stephanos turns thirty."

"And what did you say?"

"I told him my mind was made up. I have 100 percent confidence in my son. I still do. I know you think I'm crazy after that phone call. But I still believe in my boy."

Chapter Twenty-Six: Another Special Request

When Martha first suggested pickleball as therapy, Rosemary thought she must be joking. Rosemary was a pretty fair tennis player, but this was a different game entirely. The ball—a wiffle ball, really—was much quicker than a tennis ball, which meant less time to position yourself for a good return.

A new racket was required—sort of like a paddle ball racket, but not quite. You couldn't just use a regular tennis racket. There was something called "the kitchen"—a kind of demilitarized zone right near the net—where special rules applied. And the scoring? Well, the only way to describe it was byzantine.

Even finding a pickleball court was a challenge. You couldn't just use a tennis court. It required a special net (shorter than a tennis net) and special courts (smaller than a tennis court). Tennis courts could be altered for these purposes, but city officials were slow to adapt.

Nevertheless, pickleball was turning out to be just the distraction Rosemary needed from her topsy-turvy life. Martha had enlisted two other friends in the cause, and they had played several games after a practice session with Martha alone.

It was exhilarating! Demanding enough physically to keep you moving, bending, scooping, and swatting in rapid succession. Demanding enough mentally to require constant calculations and recalculations—who was serving, who was receiving, where you were supposed to stand when you were allowed in the kitchen.

It was like joining a secret society with elaborate rituals, secret handshakes, strange incantations, and a new set of norms. Absorbing, fascinating, and, above all, diverting.

Rosemary was suiting up for pickleball when she got the call from Volcker. He asked how she was doing, apologized for bothering her, and then cut to the chase. A lawyer had called, with news that Carol had left behind a will. Somewhat surprising for a twenty-six-year-old. But as an accountant, Carol was more attentive to money matters than most of her peers.

"So, why are you calling me?" Rosemary asked.

"Well, for one thing, you're in the will," Volcker replied. "Enough that I thought you should know about it. Ten thousand dollars."

Rosemary said nothing at first. Then, she replied: "That was very sweet of Carol. A really nice thing to do. Though I can't imagine why she did it."

"In her will, she said she hoped you would use it to go on a safari," Volcker said.

Rosemary laughed, though she was on the verge of tears. "I once told her I wanted to go to Africa but didn't have the cash to do it. I guess she's my—"

"Your what, Rosemary?"

"My guardian angel."

"Well, she obviously thought of you as a special friend. But that's not the main reason I'm calling."

Uh-oh, Rosemary thought. What's coming next?

"I don't know how to say this, but one of her bequests is likely to upset her parents. We were hoping you could come along with us when we speak to Mr. and Mrs. Sloan."

Rosemary gulped. "Do you mean she didn't leave any money for them?" she asked.

"No," Volcker replied. "Actually, she did. Fifty thousand dollars. And a lovely note."

"Then what's the problem?" Rosemary asked.

"Well, the problem is that she's left most of her estate, such as it is, to the bomber. Stephanos Papadopoulos. Apparently, they were engaged to be

CHAPTER TWENTY-SIX: ANOTHER SPECIAL REQUEST

married."

Jarred by the news, Rosemary collected her thoughts. Then she gave Volcker an answer to his question: yes, she would meet with him sometime this afternoon if necessary, but no, she would not meet immediately. She had a game of pickleball to play. She needed something to get rid of that queasy feeling in her stomach.

* * *

Rosemary, freshly showered and about to start lunch, was not terribly surprised when Volcker arrived at her apartment at 1 o'clock sharp. She was somewhat surprised to see that Radic was with him…and Mulroy, too. Also, a man she didn't recognize, looking like a duck out of water, carrying a briefcase. That must be the lawyer, she surmised. Well, here we go again!

Volcker apologized once more, and it seemed genuine. Then he introduced Markus Estill, Esq., who was handling Carol Sloan's estate.

Rosemary invited the entourage into her small living room. Mulroy thoughtfully brought in a couple of chairs from the kitchen.

"Rosemary, we're really sorry to be pestering you again," Radic began, speaking for the group. "We've all come to admire and respect you. We're in a jam, and we think you're the right person to help us out."

Rosemary sighed. "Detective, I know you have a job to do. I've been trying to put my life together as best as I can. This isn't helping. But I want you to find Carol's killer. I really do. And I've grown very fond of Mr. and Mrs. Sloan. If you have some tough news to deliver to them, and I can cushion the blow, I'm willing to do it."

"We really appreciate that, Rosemary," Radic said. "And in return, I've gotten permission from my lieutenant to tell you some things that we're not going to tell anyone else. Before I do that, though, I need you to agree that what we say here is strictly confidential. We'll decide what the Sloans need to know soon enough, but it won't be everything we're about to tell you. Understood?"

Rosemary nodded, not at all sure she wanted to hear what Radic was about to say.

"First of all, as Detective Volcker has told you, we now have reason to believe that Carol and Stephanos were engaged to be married. I know it sounds crazy, for all sorts of reasons. But it's in her will, and we've had it confirmed by another reliable source."

"I had no idea!" Rosemary exclaimed. "She talked about 'the Dude' like he was someone she could share a few laughs with, not someone she wanted to spend the rest of her life with. It's a shock!"

"Well, not just for you," Radic volunteered. "Almost everyone else will be surprised to hear it, including, of course, Mr. and Mrs. Sloan."

Rosemary nodded.

"Second, we also have confirmation that Carol and Stephanos booked a flight to go to the Bahamas," Radic continued.

Rosemary was really puzzled now. "So when Carol called and told me she was in the Bahamas, she REALLY was in the Bahamas?"

"Not exactly," Radic said. "Something happened between the time Stephanos scheduled the trip and the phone call you received from Carol. In all likelihood, she was calling from Pittsburgh."

"But why would she lie?" Rosemary asked.

"We have no good explanation for that," Radic conceded. "We're still trying to figure that out."

Rosemary didn't quite know what to say, so she said nothing.

"Now for the tricky part," Radic said. "Did Carol ever mention some intellectual property issues she was dealing with that involved getting permission from people who run the Harry Potter enterprise?"

"No, she didn't," Rosemary said.

"Did Carol ever mention that the Dude had a special interest in Harry Potter?" Radic asked.

"What sort of special interest?" she asked.

"Well, he wanted to manufacture some Harry Potter mugs. Muggles, he called them. You can't just go ahead and do this sort of thing. You need permission. Stephanos and Carol may have had a disagreement over this matter."

CHAPTER TWENTY-SIX: ANOTHER SPECIAL REQUEST

"Muggles?" Rosemary asked.

"Yes, mugs featuring some of the most popular characters from the Harry Potter books."

Rosemary grew pale at this point and looked distressed. Mulroy went into the kitchen to fetch a glass of water while Radic called for a break.

Rosemary drank the water and composed herself. Then she turned to Volcker. "Detective Volcker, do you remember how you told me I should check to see if anything was missing after the break-in?" she asked.

"Yes," Volcker said.

"Well, you didn't ask me whether I noticed something here that WASN'T here before the break-in."

"OK," Volcker said. "I guess I didn't think of that."

Rosemary stood up and went to the kitchen. Moments later, she came back with a mug. A charming, whimsical mug featuring a credible likeness of Hermione Granger.

Rosemary addressed Volcker directly again: "This mug was here after you and your officers conducted your investigation. I thought one of your officers must have left it behind."

Volcker shook his head. "I don't think so, Rosemary."

"Well, I can tell you for sure it wasn't here BEFORE the break-in and before your visit," Rosemary said.

Volcker reached over, took the mug, and turned it upside down.

"Dimitri's," he reported. "The manufacturer was Dimitri's Sturdy Dishes."

Chapter Twenty-Seven: Sheds with Secrets

Lieutenant Stilton was not brilliant, but neither was he dense. "Does this mean that Carol Sloan was a co-conspirator in manufacturing illegal coffee mugs?" he asked.

A good question, Radic had to acknowledge as he glanced around the squad room at Mulroy, Volcker, and Scuglia. He wasn't sure he could offer an equally good answer.

"At this point, we don't think so, sir," he said. "Though anything is possible. Carol might have been persuaded by Stephanos to support manufacturing the mugs prematurely. But she's on record as having opposed it. Maybe she changed her mind as her personal relationship with Stephanos grew more intimate. Or maybe she got wind of it after the fact, threatened to blow the whistle on him, and thereby sealed her death warrant."

"Do all of you agree that Carol and Stephanos were engaged to be married?" he asked.

"I'd say that's indisputable, sir," Mulroy replied.

"Any luck in tracking down Vasilikas?"

"He's been as slippery as an eel," Radic responded. "Understandably, if he's afraid for his life. But we do have some ideas."

"Well, make that a top priority," Stilton said. "And the mug? You're assuming there are more where this came from?"

"We propose to get a search warrant to check Dimitri's factory. And another search warrant for Stephanos' home," Radic said.

CHAPTER TWENTY-SEVEN: SHEDS WITH SECRETS

"Good idea," Stilton said. "Make that happen."

"Will do, sir," Radic said.

"Also, we need to keep a tight lid on the investigation. I understand you shared some of the facts of the case with Rosemary Dunne."

"That's right, sir," Radic said. "You authorized that in advance. And it was a good decision. It led to our discovery of the Hermione mug."

"Right, right," Stilton said. "Just make sure Rosemary Dunne doesn't go blabbing to the press."

"We made that crystal clear, sir," Radic said.

"OK, OK. Get the warrant. Find Vasilikas, wherever he is. And report back to me tomorrow."

Stilton left the room, and the remaining officers exhaled. "No blood drawn," Scuglia said.

"Not yet," Radic said. "But Cheesy is getting impatient. Captain Reilly, too, from what I hear. We need a breakthrough, now!"

"A Hail Mary pass?" Mulroy asked

"If you're still praying after all this, a simple prayer might be a good idea," Radic said.

* * *

It took a day and a half to get a warrant request drafted and approved. Not bad, in the scheme of things. Judge A.B. "Pinky" Floyd of the Court of Common Pleas had read all about the case in the newspaper and was eager to help. "Don't come back empty-handed!" he admonished Radic, who nodded with a half-smile.

Three squad cars arrived at Dimitri's plant at approximately 8 a.m. Radic and Mulroy were in one, Volckor and Scuglia in a second. Two technicians were in the third car, available to bag evidence and dust for fingerprints.

Radic, who genuinely had come to like Dimitri, made no excuses or apologies as he handed him the judge's warrant. "It would help if you give us a full set of keys," he said. "And it would also help to have a word with Jim Trojanowski before we begin our search."

Dimitri had grown accustomed to bad news. At this point, he didn't even raise an objection. "I don't have all the individual keys," he said, "but I have a skeleton key in my safe." He extracted the key from the safe and handed it to Radic.

There wasn't enough space in the main office for everyone to sit down. Radic invited Dimitri and Trojanowski to sit while he explained what was about to occur.

"We have reason to believe that at least one coffee mug with a protected trademark has been manufactured here without getting prior approval from the copyright holder," he began. Then, he removed the mug from a brown paper bag.

"Do you recognize this?" he asked Dimitri.

"A Harry Potter mug?" he asked.

"That's right."

"First time I see one," Dimitri said.

"And you?" Radic asked Trojanowski.

He shook his head. "I never saw this before."

Radic turned the mug upside down. Dimitri gasped while Trojanowski flinched. "That's my name, detective," Dimitri said, "but not my signature."

Dimitri reached for a coffee mug on his desk and turned it over. Sure enough, the authentic script was different, more flamboyant. "Whoever produced this mug used my name but not my signature," Dimitri said with a hint of defiance and vindication.

"OK, so we have two options here," Radic said. "We can tear this place upside down. Or you can help us with our investigation."

"We'd like to help," Dimitri said. "No need to be destructive."

Trojanowski nodded in agreement.

"OK," Radic said. "Out back, there's a Skull and Crossbones shed. I've already been there. Does it contain anything so hazardous that my technicians should wear protective equipment beyond a mask and gloves?"

"They shouldn't open up any of the drums," Trojanowski said. "And they shouldn't light a match. Other than that, it should be safe."

"Okay," Radic said. "What are the other sheds, and what do they contain?"

CHAPTER TWENTY-SEVEN: SHEDS WITH SECRETS

"The two gray sheds are for materials that are about to be shipped," Trojanowski said. "They're already packed and sealed. Do you really have to open them up? That's a lot of re-packaging for us to do."

"Sorry," Radic said. "I can make no guarantees."

"What's in the other three sheds?"

"The green shed is the R & D building that I was telling you about, detective," Dimitri volunteered. "Only Stephanos has a key to that one, now. And me, of course."

"But Basil used to, correct?"

"Yes, Basil used to have one when he worked here."

"And he left when?"

"A year ago."

"He returned all of his keys?"

"I made sure of it," Dimitri answered.

"Do you have a key to the R&D building?" Radic asked Trojanowski.

Trojanowski shook his head. "That one is off-limits to me. But Dimitri's skeleton key should do the trick."

"What's in the other two sheds?" Radic asked.

"One of them contains raw materials that are needed for the manufacturing process," Trojanowski said. "The other is kind of like our historical archives. It contains samples of dishes, pots, and pans that were once produced but are no longer in production."

"Anything dangerous in any of the buildings, besides the Skull & Crossbones shed?" he asked.

Both Dimitri and Trojanowski shook their heads.

"OK, then let's start with the R&D building," Radic said.

The group traipsed outside without saying a word. Everyone found the situation awkward, though for different reasons.

By prior agreement, the two technicians took the lead after Radic opened up the R&D building. Using box cutters, they started with six boxes near the door.

Volcker, the cameraman du jour, took photos of the search for the record. Nonchalantly, he also took snapshots of Dimitri and Trojanowski.

The first technician reached inside one of the boxes and pulled out a mug. It featured Hagrid, the friendly giant. The second technician reached inside another box and pulled out another mug. It featured Dobby the House Elf. Both mugs were very attractive, stylish. They would be easy to sell.

At Radic's request, the technicians turned the mugs upside down. Both said "Dimitri's," but neither reproduced his signature.

Radic stepped outside and placed a call to Rob McPherson, attorney at law. He left a message: "Mr. McPherson, Detective Radic here. I'd like to speak with you as soon as possible. We have hundreds, maybe thousands, of Harry Potter mugs at Dimitri's factory. I'm going to need your advice."

Radic returned to the shed.

"So, where does this leave us, detective?" Dimitri asked.

"Well, this is mainly what we've been looking for," Radic said. "We'll pack up these boxes and give you a receipt. It's evidence in a criminal investigation. I'm going to ask the technicians to look inside the other five sheds, just to be safe. But it shouldn't take that long. After that, we'll need to look at the R&D ledgers. Then we'll call it a day."

"Fair enough," Dimitri said. "But what are you thinking, detective? What does this mean?"

"We need to take a close look at the mugs. We need to take a close look at the books. We need to find Stephanos. We need to find Basil. Then we'll know where things stand."

"This is a nightmare, detective! An absolute nightmare!" Dimitri said.

"On that, Dimitri, I think we can all agree," Radic said.

Chapter Twenty-Eight: Spider Man

Thanks to Lexie Davodny and Professor Donato, Radic was now convinced that they had a fighting chance to identify the bridge where Vazzy's calls originated. It was probably a bridge that crossed the Monongahela River. And it was a bridge that sounded like a bowling alley from below.

Radic called Mulroy and asked her to record bridge traffic underneath every bridge from the Golden Triangle to McKeesport. He explained what they were looking for (a bowling alley sound). He also asked Mulroy to visit the South Side Marina. "See if anyone recognizes Vazzy's sketch or his name."

Meanwhile, Radic decided to visit the only friend whose name Dimitri could recall from Vazzy's troubled days—his name was Spider, and he worked or used to work at a tattoo parlor on the South Side.

To his surprise, Radic discovered that the South Side was a veritable mecca for tattoo buffs, hosting a total of eight separate establishments. It wasn't until the seventh one that Radic hit pay dirt. A clerk pointed to a large, muscled man with replicas of huge insects on both arms.

"I'm Spider Donatelli," the man said. "Would you like a tat?"

Radic flashed his badge. "Well, maybe not," Donatelli said. "But plenty of cops are satisfied customers. Mark Atwood. Frenchy Frobisher."

Radic flinched at the names of two of his least favorite colleagues. "I'm sure you do good work," he said, "but that's not why I'm here. I'm told that you are or were friendly with Basil Vasilikas."

Spider let out a soft sigh and motioned Radic to sit down. Then he changed his mind. "Let's take a walk around the block," he said. "We'll have more privacy there."

"Vazzy and I were tight for quite a while," Donatelli said as they started walking. "We both served in the Gulf War, and we both had scars from it."

"My scars were visible," he said, tapping his right thigh. "Vazzy's were less visible but more serious. PTSD. Most of us had it to some degree, but he had it real bad."

"What were some of the signs?" Radic asked.

"Well, drinking for sure," Spider said. "And a dark temper. If he was drinking and in a bad mood, you didn't want to mess with him."

"Was he ever violent?" Radic asked.

"Not to me," Spider said. "Of course, I was his mate."

"To anyone else?" Radic asked.

"Sometimes he would get into a fight that could easily have been avoided," he recalled. "It would start with trash talk and go downhill from there."

"Anything serious?" Radic asked.

Donatelli shrugged: "No broken bones. A few bruises."

"When was the last time you saw him?" Radic asked.

"Well, maybe two years ago," Spider recalled. "He was working for his brother-in-law, Dimitri. Do you know Dimitri?"

"Yeah, I know Dimitri," Radic said.

"What's this about, anyway?" Spider asked. "Is Vazzy in trouble?"

"We just need to speak with him," Radic said. "Any thoughts on where he might be?"

"Well, he used to talk about a boat," Spider said. "He said it was in his Greek blood. Like Jason and the Argonauts."

"Did he own a boat?" Radic asked.

"I don't know if he ever bought one," Spider said, "but he sure talked about it a lot."

The two men stood in front of Spider's tattoo shop, featuring spider's webs and all sorts of scary-looking insects.

Radic thanked him for his time and headed back to the station.

CHAPTER TWENTY-EIGHT: SPIDER MAN

* * *

Mulroy began her "bridge tour" at the Point, or near the point, where the three rivers converged. She found a spot underneath the Fort Pitt Bridge and recorded the sounds for a minute or so.

Next, she turned to the Smithfield Street Bridge and the Liberty Bridge. She decided to focus on the South Side for this iteration, rather than criss-crossing the river. One recording for each bridge would be a good place to start.

She knew what she was looking for, or listening for, but felt a little nervous about the task. What exactly is the difference between a clickety-clack and a ka-thump? And what exactly is the sound of duckpins falling? Radic assured her that she would know it when she heard it, but she wasn't so sure.

The Birmingham Bridge, not far from Fat Heads Saloon, brought back pleasant memories of her blueberry dinner a couple weeks earlier. She and Radic had become true partners since then. She was lucky. And maybe she was doing something right.

On the other hand, were they really making progress in this frustrating case? A young woman had been murdered. Dozens of people had been placed in harm's way at her funeral. Two leading suspects were missing. Rosemary Dunne was afraid to be in her own apartment. Somehow, they needed to pick up the pace.

Mulroy located a good spot to listen to the underbelly of the Birmingham Bridge. Actually, it was not far from the homeless community she and Radic had visited.

Suddenly, she heard something. Had a truck dropped a load of lumber on the bridge? Then she heard it again. And again. Regularly. Rhythmically. It was sort of like … duck pins toppling in a bowling alley!

Mulroy quickly recorded what she was hearing, for fear that the sound waves might vanish in the morning mist. For good measure, she kept the recorder on for two full minutes. "Gotcha!" she cried, exultant. "We know you were here!"

Chapter Twenty-Nine: Brainstorming at the Squirrel Cage

Mulroy had no trouble spotting Renfert as she and Radic entered the Squirrel Hill Café. He looked very…professorial. A tweed jacket, a crisp blue shirt, and a notebook. If there were patches on his elbows, she would not have been surprised.

"Kathleen, it's a pleasure to meet you!" Renfert beamed. "In all the years I've known Branko, you're the first person he's ever invited to join us in the hallowed confines of the Squirrel Cage."

"I'm honored," Mulroy replied with a smile.

"Sometimes when my brain gets stuffy, I come to Lucas for a good defogging," Radic explained.

"Defogging. De-icing. De-lousing. I provide multiple services," Renfert responded.

"Well, my brain's stuffy too, so we definitely could use your help," Mulroy chimed in.

The threesome placed their orders. Then Renfert turned to Mulroy. "Kathleen, I don't know what Branko told you, but whatever you say here today is strictly confidential. I would never divulge anything that's said here. To me, the Squirrel Cage is like a confessional."

"Well, I was wondering about that since it's an ongoing investigation," Mulroy said. "But if Radic trusts you, then I trust you too. And I appreciate the analogy to confession. As a Catholic, it's something I can understand."

"Good," Renfert said. "I wouldn't want you to be dragged into a

CHAPTER TWENTY-NINE: BRAINSTORMING AT THE SQUIRREL CAGE

conversation that makes you uncomfortable."

"Consider me comforted," she said. "I appreciate your clarifying things up front."

With that out of the way, Radic began to summarize the state of play: "One of our suspects is Stephanos Papadopoulos, the heir to Dimitri's kitchenware company in West Mifflin. On the surface, he seems like a decent guy. He did well in school. His record is clean except for one DUI. And Carol Sloan appears to have fallen in love with him."

"BUT," he continued, "he seems to have gotten tangled up in a dodgy scheme to manufacture Harry Potter mugs and sell them on the black market. It appears that he manufactured hundreds, maybe thousands of these mugs, or Muggles, to be shipped to eager customers in two or three different cities."

"What's your proof that Stephanos manufactured the mugs?" Renfert asked.

"Well," Radic replied, "we found the mugs at his father's plant, in a shed that's off-limits to everyone except Stephanos. Also, we know from the M.E. that Carol Sloan was poisoned with something called PFOA. It's a chemical that was once used to keep food from sticking to pots and pans. We've learned that PFOA is still on the premises of the Papadopoulos manufacturing plant. And Stephanos is the only person with a key to the shed where it's stored. Except for his father, who has a master key stored in a safe."

Lucas nodded. "I see why you think Stephanos might be the perp. Anything else?"

"We also have reason to suspect that he conspired to plant the bomb in the Sewickley Unitarian Church."

"What's your evidence?" Renfert asked.

"He's the one who called us and urged us to evacuate the church," Radic explained.

"Hold on," Lucas said, "that means he knew about the bomb. But does it mean that he planted it? Wasn't he doing you a favor?"

"A fair point," Radic conceded.

"Also, why would he or anybody else plant a bomb at Carol's funeral?" Lucas asked. "I gotta say that puzzles me."

"It puzzles us, too," Radic replied. "It could be that he was trying to make a statement to us or someone else. Back off. Don't mess with me. Or that he wanted to hurt someone who would be attending the funeral."

"Any individuals in mind?" Renfert asked.

"Maybe Carol's parents," Radic said. "Because it looks like he soured on Carol. Presumably, because she rejected his Muggles idea. Maybe she threatened to expose him."

"Why abort the bombing?" Lucas asked.

"That's hard to figure out," Radic admitted, "but it might be that he didn't expect his father to be at the funeral. His father's appearance was a bit of a surprise to us and perhaps to him. Maybe he didn't want his old man to be collateral damage."

"Okay, I get the picture," said Lucas. "A fuzzy picture. But I get it. And Basil?"

Radic nodded to Mulroy, who reviewed the facts. "Basil Vasilikas, who happens to be Stephanos' uncle, has more of a checkered history than Stephanos. He served in Iraq. Suffered from PTSD. He's had a drinking problem and a gambling problem. He's homeless. He's disenchanted with his brother-in-law, Dimitri, who owns the firm. He was hoping to succeed him at the firm."

"Sounds like a motive to me," Renfert said.

"Yes, I agree," Mulroy acknowledged. "But he's the one who reported the murder to us in the first place. Later, he told us where we could find the body. Why would he do that if he was the actual murderer?"

"It's certainly odd," Renfert agreed.

"Plus, Dimitri says that Basil got help to deal with his problems and that his drinking and gambling days were behind him," Mulroy added.

Renfert scratched his beard and asked the waitress for another iced tea. "Okay," he said. "So, question number one: Do you know where either of these guys is at the moment? It sounds like you need to talk with both of them."

CHAPTER TWENTY-NINE: BRAINSTORMING AT THE SQUIRREL CAGE

Radic sighed. "Stephanos is a big question mark. He was supposed to fly to the Bahamas, with Carol Sloan, but he didn't. He's supposed to return to work this week, after a two-week vacation, but we don't expect that to happen. His cell phone is no longer in service. His home is unoccupied."

"Do you have it under surveillance?"

"Twenty-four/seven."

"Okay, good. You never know. And Basil?"

"We've had a bit more luck on that front," Mulroy replied. "We know from the initial homicide desk call that he was under the Birmingham Bridge at the time he called."

Renfert smiled and turned to Radic. "So, was Professor Watanabe helpful?"

"Yes, he was," he replied. "He told me a lot about bridges. And he referred us to another professor who helped Mulroy match the first call to the Birmingham Bridge."

"Outstanding!" Renfert said, slapping the table with his hand. "Do you think Basil lives near the Birmingham Bridge?"

"He's homeless," Mulroy replied. "We have no idea where he lives."

"Sorry to hear that," he said to Mulroy. "And sorry to interrupt. You were saying?"

Mulroy continued: "We know from folks at Kennywood Park that Basil bought an old boat, with very distinctive features. We know from the River Rescue Unit and from a homeless person that he and his boat have been spotted on the Monongahela River."

"Well, you guys have done some outstanding detective work," Renfert said. "You've definitely earned your pay over the past couple of weeks."

"That may be," Radic said, "but we don't know where Basil sleeps, we don't know where he eats, and we don't know how he pays his bills."

"No sightings recently?" he asked.

"Not a one," Radic replied.

"Okay," Renfert said, "so, question number two: Whom do you trust?"

"I'm sorry," Mulroy said, "I don't think I understand the question."

Radic spoke up. "What he means is: We've gotten to know a lot of people over the past couple of weeks. Business associates, friends, old army buddies, parents. In our gut, whose judgment do we have confidence in?"

"Precisely," said Renfert.

"Let me begin," Radic said. "Of all the people we've met, the person I *like* the most is Dimitri. He's also someone I trust, but in a limited way. He's an honest man. He's been more than straight with us. But do I trust his judgment? He's the boy's father. What father doesn't love his son? Especially an old-fashioned, hard-working, good-natured Greek from the old country."

"So, to sum up, I trust Dimitri to tell us the truth about his son and his activities," Radic concluded, "but I don't trust him to judge his son objectively. I don't think he's capable of that. For that matter, how many fathers are?"

"Okay, good, that's what I want to hear," Renfert said. "Your feelings, your hunches, your gut instincts. They may or may not be right. But you have to confront them."

"And you?" he asked, turning to Mulroy.

Mulroy cleared her throat. "I don't exactly know what the ground rules are for this thought experiment," she said. "But if you ask me, 'Whom do you trust the most?' my answer would be Carol Sloan. She's the person I trust the most."

"Explain," Renfert said.

"Everyone speaks so highly of Carol," Mulroy began. "A good daughter, a great employee, a good friend. From what we've heard, she was not just a first-class accountant but a good judge of character. She was paid to spot fraudulent business practices and to advise against them. Clients relied on her good judgment. And, according to her roommate, she was cautious when it came to men."

"With one big exception,' Radic interjected.

"Well, you might say so," Mulroy said. "But her relationship with Stephanos went far beyond a one-night stand. She knew him personally and professionally. They were engaged to be married. She made out a new will and named him as her lead beneficiary. She trusted him. She believed

CHAPTER TWENTY-NINE: BRAINSTORMING AT THE SQUIRREL CAGE

in him. What she's telling us, from the grave, is: I'm nobody's fool. And I chose him. He's the real thing!"

Radic looked uncomfortable. "What's bugging you?" Renfert asked, sensing his young friend's mood.

"You haven't asked your third question yet," he said. "Even though it's the most important one."

"Yes, I know," he acknowledged.

"What's the third question?" Mulroy asked.

"Where does the evidence lead you?" Radic said.

"Okay," Mulroy said. "But so much of the evidence is circumstantial. A lot of it comes from Basil, who may be giving us false clues."

"Yes," Radic acknowledged. "But we also have SOME direct evidence. And that's the e-mail exchange between Stephanos and Carol."

"Oh," Renfert said. "You didn't tell me about that."

"Basically, Stephanos and Carol had an ex-mail exchange on the Harry Potter mugs. Stephanos was hot to trot. He wanted to manufacture the mugs. Carol said, emphatically, no."

"No follow-ups?" Renfert asked.

"Not by email," Radic said.

"When was the e-mail exchange?" Renfert asked.

Radic thought for a moment. "About two weeks before the trip to Bermuda was to take place."

"So he could have changed his mind before the trip," Mulroy argued. "Carol could have persuaded him."

"Well," Radic said. "He did change his mind. He canceled the trip to Bermuda. Probably because he and Carol couldn't agree on the Muggles."

"We don't know that for sure," Mulroy said after a pause.

"No, we don't know what he was thinking," Radic acknowledged, "but we do know that he canceled the trip."

Renfert thought for a moment and turned to Mulroy. "What I hear you saying, Kathleen, is that Stephanos was too good a guy to have committed murder. Is that right?"

"That's right," she replied.

"Was he also too good a guy to have violated intellectual property laws?" he asked.

"If Stephanos loved Carol as much as we think, he would have dropped the idea of the Muggles," she replied.

"But he didn't," Radic replied.

"Well, someone didn't."

"You mean Vazzy?"

"Vazzy. Or someone else."

"Like who?"

"Trojanowski. McPherson. People on the edge of our investigation."

"There's another possibility," Radic added. "Maybe he dropped the Muggles idea, but only *after* producing the mugs."

"A costly mistake, if that's what he did," Renfert observed.

"Not only in terms of dollars," Radic added. "It's a mistake that may have cost Carol her life."

"So where does that leave you?" Renfert asked. "What do you think happened?"

"I think Stephanos did something stupid," Radic said. "He commissioned the mugs, despite Carol's best advice. He wanted to be a contender. He wanted to make his father proud. He made a mistake. A big mistake."

"Mistakes can be corrected," Mulroy said.

"Yes, they can," Radic agreed. "But a lot was riding on this mistake. Was Stephanos big enough to admit his mistake and face the consequences? He didn't say so in an email to Carol. He didn't say so in person to his father. Instead, he canceled a trip. A trip that was to be a turning point in his relationship with Carol. It suggests that he was having second thoughts about the engagement, not that he was having second thoughts about the mugs."

"But Carol didn't say anything to Cynthia Nolan," Mulroy objected. "If they had a falling out because he went too far with the mugs, wouldn't Carol have given her boss a heads up? Or shared her concerns with the lawyer, Rob McPherson? Also, they canceled the trip at the last minute. Days before, they were happily hanging out together, according to one of

CHAPTER TWENTY-NINE: BRAINSTORMING AT THE SQUIRREL CAGE

Carol's neighbors. Doesn't that tell us something?"

"It may simply tell us that the mugs didn't arrive until just before the trip," Radic said. "At that point, Stephanos had to decide: Carol? Or the mugs? He made the wrong decision. Carol reacted badly. Maybe she threatened to blow the whistle. Harsh words were exchanged. And things got out of control."

"I don't know," Mulroy said, shaking her head. "It reminds me of my recent trips to Kennywood Park. You know the funhouse mirrors? Tall is short. Fat is skinny. They distort reality. Somehow, I think we're looking at the case through funhouse mirrors. My instincts tell me that Carol and Stephanos were in love and that their love was more important than a bunch of mugs."

"And you, my friend?" Renfert asked.

"I believe in the power of love, too," Radic said. "And I'd like to believe that Stephanos is innocent. But the evidence tells me something else. And when push comes to shove, you have to go with the evidence."

"May I make one final point?" Mulroy asked.

"Kathleen, you can make as many final points as you'd like," Renfert said.

"I think we're putting too much emphasis on one set of e-mails," she said, "and on one set of keys."

"Say more," Renfert urged.

"Well, we've been told that Stephanos was the only one with certain keys to certain sheds," she said. "Don't keys get mislaid? Don't keys get stolen? Maybe someone borrowed the keys long enough to make copies, and Stephanos was none the wiser."

"You think Basil borrowed them?" Renfert asked.

"Basil, or someone else," she replied. "I just don't see Carol Sloan making a lifelong commitment to a reckless or dishonest man."

Chapter Thirty: A Return to Sewickley

Volcker picked Rosemary up at her Shadyside apartment, at 9:30 a.m. She had decided to return to her home, even though Stephanos and Basil were still at large. A Pittsburgh police car continued to patrol her block, just in case. Hopefully, she could resume her normal activities soon.

They were to meet Mr. Estill, the attorney, at a familiar landmark in Sewickley at 10:15 a.m. so they would all arrive together at the Sloan home. No one quite knew what to expect, but the police definitely wanted Rosemary to be there.

Mr. Sloan knew in advance that Carol's attorney wanted to discuss her will and that both Detective Volcker and Rosemary would be present.

When Volcker rang the doorbell, Mr. Sloan quickly appeared. The aroma of fresh coffee and baked goods greeted them at the front door. A good sign, Volcker thought.

Mrs. Sloan appeared, gave Rosemary a big hug, and escorted the threesome into the living room. Mr. Sloan assisted with the food and drinks.

Rosemary began the conversation by chatting amiably with Mr. and Mrs. Sloan about birds, pastries, and the sad saga of the Pittsburgh Pirates. She also asked after Mrs. Sloan's sister, who had just returned to Denver.

Detective Volcker turned to business, offering firm assurances that the Pittsburgh police were investigating every lead in an effort to track down Carol's killer. "We won't rest until we've brought her killer to justice," he assured them.

CHAPTER THIRTY: A RETURN TO SEWICKLEY

"Neither will we," Mrs. Sloan said, and he believed her.

Estill came next. He offered condolences, which seemed sincere. He said that he had only met Carol once but that she had impressed him as a very responsible person and a very nice person too. "And she thought the world of both of you," he said to Mr. and Mrs. Sloan.

At that, Mrs. Sloan teared up, but held steady, waiting for what he had to say.

"So," he began, "Carol's net worth is approximately one hundred and eighty thousand dollars—a pretty tidy sum for someone as young as she was. She's leaving fifty thousand to the two of you, along with most of her possessions. She's also leaving ten thousand to Rosemary, as a token of their friendship. The remainder of her estate, she's leaving to Stephanos Papadopoulos."

"What?" Mr. Sloan asked, incredulous. Then, turning to Volcker, "Isn't that the man the newspapers say is one of your suspects?"

"We don't like to use that term," Volcker said. "He's someone we want to talk to."

"But why would Carol leave so much money to that young man?" Mr. Sloan persisted. "Someone we've never met? And someone who might have done her harm?"

Volcker turned to Estill for help. "Well, Mr. Sloan," he said, "I don't know for sure, but the simplest explanation is that Carol and Mr. Papadopoulos were engaged to be married."

At that, Mrs. Sloan dropped her coffee cup, which shattered, spilling coffee all over the table and the floor. She stood up abruptly and left the room. Rosemary followed her into the kitchen.

"What?" Mr. Sloan asked. "How can that possibly be true?"

"Well," Estill replied. "She told me herself. She met the young man about two years ago, through work. They were planning on getting married sometime in the spring."

"But she didn't tell us!" Mr. Sloan exclaimed. "Why didn't she tell us?"

"I can't answer that question," Estill replied. "I'm sure she was going to tell you sometime soon."

Meanwhile, in the kitchen, Mrs. Sloan was quivering while Rosemary did her best to comfort her. "Did you know, Rosemary? Did you know about this?" she asked.

"I just learned, Mrs. Sloan," she said. "You have my word. Carol never told me either. It was a secret."

"But why didn't she tell us?" she asked. "Did you ever meet this young man?"

"I never met him," Rosemary said. "But she did talk about him now and then."

"What did she say about him?" Mrs. Sloan asked.

Rosemary paused, choosing her words carefully. "She said that he made her happy and that he was fun to be with."

"But the newspapers make him sound like a monster," she said. "I just don't understand."

"The newspapers sometimes get the wrong end of the stick," Rosemary said. "If Carol thought he was a good guy, then he must have been a good guy. Whatever the newspapers say. Carol wouldn't have gotten engaged to a bad person."

When Rosemary and Mrs. Sloan returned to the living room, it was evident that Mr. Sloan wanted time alone with his wife. "Thank you for coming, gentlemen," he said. And then to Rosemary: "Rosemary, you know you're always welcome here."

After mumbled goodbyes, and a couple apologies, Volcker, Estill, and Rosemary left, leaving the Sloans alone in their grief. And with many new questions to be answered.

As soon as he returned to Pittsburgh, Volcker called Radic to give him a report. Radic was not surprised. He thanked Volcker for handling a delicate situation as best he could. He also made a mental note to check with the attorney who had worked with Stephanos. If Carol Sloan had a will, maybe Stephanos had one too.

On Monday morning, Radic called the intellectual property attorney, Rob McPherson, who instantly grasped what was up. "I don't handle wills myself," he explained, "but I do recall advising Stephanos that he should have

CHAPTER THIRTY: A RETURN TO SEWICKLEY

one. Especially as he was going to become the CEO of a small business."

"And what did he say?" Radic asked.

"Well, he said he'd do it," the attorney said.

"Any idea who he would turn to for a will?" he asked.

"I suggested a woman I know," he said. "Very reputable."

"Do you have her number?" he asked.

"Sure," he said, giving Radic the phone number. "Her name is Cindy McSwigan. If she didn't do the will, you might ask Dimitri. Maybe the same person who prepared a will for Dimitri did one for Stephanos as well."

Radic lucked out. McSwigan was indeed Stephanos' estate lawyer, and she had been following the case in the news media. But she cautioned Radic that there were limits to how much she could tell him.

"If Stephanos were dead, I could give you all the information you require," she explained. "But he's not dead, just missing. That means he still has lots of legal rights."

"I understand," Radic said, "but let me put it to you this way: his reputation is clearly at stake, if you've been following the news, and his life may be at stake as well."

"Tell me more," McSwigan said.

"I can't get into the details of the case," he said, "but we have two fugitives. They may be working together. But it's also possible that one of them kidnapped the other. Or that they're having serious disagreements."

"You think Stephanos may have been kidnapped?" she asked.

"I can't go that far," Radic said. "All I can say is it's a possibility."

McSwigan thought for a moment. "What exactly are you trying to find out?"

"Two things, really," Radic replied. "Did he change his will recently? And, if he did, is one of his beneficiaries Carol Sloan?"

"The young woman who was murdered?" McSwigan asked.

"That's right," Radic replied.

"Why would he leave money to her?" she asked.

"Because we believe they were engaged to be married."

McSwigan responded with a soft whistle. She asked for time to review the file and the case law and confer with a junior colleague. She promised to get back in touch a.s.a.p.

A few hours later, McSwigan called back. "Detective, I've been in touch with one of my associates, who had a recent conversation with the gentleman we discussed."

"Okay," Radic said.

"Under Pennsylvania law, I have some freedom to divulge information on the will of a missing person, which would apply to Mr. Papadopoulos. But the law specifies that you'll need the consent of the person who has power of attorney for my client."

"And that would be?" Radic asked.

"His father. Dimitri Papadopoulos. If he consents, I can answer your two questions. And maybe a little bit more. But only if he consents."

"Does Dimitri know that he has power of attorney?" he asked.

"Well, we definitely advise our clients to inform that individual and get his or her consent. But it's up to the client. The father may or may not know."

Radic thanked McSwigan and promised to call back after speaking to Dimitri.

Chapter Thirty-One: A Request for Mugs

Radic was actually thinking about Dimitri when he got the call. He looked at the clock. 10:50 p.m.

"Detective Rad-itch?"

"Yes," Radic replied. "Mr. Papadopoulos, is that you?"

"Yes, it's me," he responded.

"I decided to call you because I trust you," Dimitri said.

"Of course, Mr. Papadopoulos. What's on your mind?"

"We got a call at the factory today. I think you should hear it. I didn't erase it."

"Is it urgent? Do you want me to come over right now?"

"Not urgent," Dimitri said. "Maybe tomorrow morning?"

"How about 8 o'clock? At your office?"

"That's good," Dimitri said. "I'll be there."

Mulroy was waiting outside police headquarters when Radic arrived at 7:30 a.m. She slid into the passenger seat, and they headed to West Mifflin.

"Any idea what the message is about?" she asked.

"No clue."

"How did Dimitri sound?" she asked.

"Worried. But not alarmed."

"Given the circumstances, that's the best we can hope for these days, I suppose," she said.

Radic grunted. They arrived a bit early, but Dimitri's car was already parked in front. They parked behind it and rang the bell. Dimitri answered it himself.

"Come in, detective, officer," he said.

He seemed subdued. Radic remembered that this was the day Stephanos was to return home from the Bahamas. Maybe that was weighing on his mind.

"Have a seat," Dimitri said, motioning to two chairs. "I got this call, and I was going to erase it. But I'm an honest man. If I learn something, I tell you. It doesn't sound good, but that's for you to decide."

Radic nodded while Dimitri played the call:

Hello. This is Mr. Smith from Chicago. I'm trying to reach Stephanos, but his phone isn't working. He sent me 100 mugs on a trial basis. We like them! We'd like 5,000 more. Please call me back. (312) 555-2901.

Radic asked Dimitri to replay the call, which he did.

"Can you excuse us for a few minutes, Mr. Papadopoulos?" he asked. Dimitri nodded, and Radic and Mulroy stepped outside.

"It sounds bad for Stephanos," Mulroy said.

"Yes, it does," Radic replied. "But, like it or not, this is a great lead. If we reach out to the caller and play our cards right, we can learn more about who's involved and the terms of sale."

"I agree," Mulroy said.

"So, here's my thought. One of us needs to pose as a salesman who works for Stephanos. Volcker might fit the bill. He'll ask the right questions and won't give the game away. We'll have him use the company phone if Dimitri agrees. We may need to get the fraud unit involved. Stilton will have to sign off on that. But we should get the ball rolling quickly. We don't want to scare 'Mr. Smith' off by ignoring him."

"Mr. Smith?" Mulroy asked skeptically.

"Right. A phony name! Do these people have no imagination?"

Radic explained his plan to Dimitri, though he omitted any reference to the fraud unit. Dimitri had only one question: "Do you think this will help you to find my boy?"

Radic paused. "I don't know for sure," Radic said. "But anything we learn about how Stephanos spent the last week or two could help us to track him down. You did the right thing, Mr. Papadopoulos."

CHAPTER THIRTY-ONE: A REQUEST FOR MUGS

"I hope you're right, detective," Dimitri said sadly. "Because right now, it feels like I'm snitching on my own son."

***

Stilton's reaction to the Muggles sting proposal was decidedly positive. When you can't solve a murder, it doesn't hurt to solve another crime while you wait. The PBP's Financial Crimes Task Force agreed to have Volcker be the front man, because he already knew the case. They did insist, however, on having a member of their unit present when the call was made and a continuing role after that.

One of the Financial Crimes Task Force members also registered a concern that no one wanted to hear: "If we hit pay dirt, we're going to need to call in the feds," he said. "Much as we'd like to do it ourselves."

"Let's cross that bridge when we come to it," Stilton said. "We have enough to worry about at the moment without having the FBI second-guess us every step of the way."

Radic sketched his plan for the group: "We want to catch 'Mr. Smith' of course, but our main goal is to find out more about Stephanos Papadopoulos, who may be guilty of Carol Sloan's murder and a bombing that threatened dozens of people. That means, for example, learning the bank account where Mr. Smith's money winds up…or an address…or a third party. Anything that leads us back to Stephanos or to someone who's working with Stephanos."

"Stephanos' absence is a plus for us, because we can use that as an excuse to ask Mr. Smith how he paid for the one hundred mugs he already has. We don't want to focus on that at first, of course. Instead, Volcker will talk about the mugs in loving detail. He will rave about them like a real salesman would. He will tell Mr. Smith there are plenty more if he wants them. He will offer the bait and then reel him in."

"Do we think that Smith knows he's involved in a shady business?" Stilton wanted to know.

"The fact that he uses an alias like Mr. Smith suggests that he knows this is not a legal transaction."

"Are we worried that he might not be willing to talk with someone other than Stephanos?" Mulroy asked.

"That's a possibility," Radic admitted. "But Volcker can work around that. He can give Smith the option of waiting two weeks for Stephanos or sealing the deal with himself right away. No cash deposit, no guarantee of the mugs he wants."

"Will we actually be shipping something to Chicago?" someone from the Financial Crimes Task Force wanted to know. "Do you want us to get in touch with people in Chicago?"

"We're open to doing that," Radic said. "If we get a good address, we can share it with the Chicago PD. You can work with them to apprehend the suspect."

The group disbanded after agreeing that Volcker should place the call at 6:15 p.m. the following day, the same time that Mr. Smith had called Dimitri's Sturdy Dishes. The chase was on. The hare was running, and the fox was in pursuit.

Chapter Thirty-Two: The Sting

Dimitri's office was beginning to look like a sound studio. State-of-the-art equipment was installed to ensure a high-quality recording, with a backup system if the main recording failed. A desk was removed to squeeze in two more chairs. Dimitri's portable whiteboard would be used for quick handwritten messages, if necessary.

Volcker was completing a crash course in Harry Potter characters and kitchenware, led by Radic, with Mulroy asking surprise questions to throw him off balance. "If the toughest questions you face come from us rather than Smith, you'll do just fine," Radic assured him.

A set of contingencies was determined in advance, concerning pricing, billing, and shipping. As for the rest, well, Volcker would have to improvise.

Dimitri himself was banished from his office, just in case he had second thoughts. But, in a gesture of solidarity, Dimitri offered Volcker a "Dimitri's Sturdy Dishes" cap. Volcker wore it with pleasure. It calmed him down and helped him feel the part better.

At 6:30 p.m., Volcker placed the call, as four other officers listened in. No one answered. Not unexpected. So Volcker left a message: This is Johnnie Eliopolos calling on behalf of Stephanos Papadopoulos. He's out of town right now but he asked me to return your call. I'm working on inventory for a while. Call me tonight or sometime tomorrow afternoon. The number is (412) 555-3421. If someone else answers the phone, be sure to ask for me personally.

Preparing for what could be a long night, Radic ordered sandwiches, coffee, and sodas from a local deli. Plus two pies, to be shared.

The chatter in Dimitri's office was strained and awkward. Everyone was a bit on edge.

At 8:26 p.m., the phone rang. Volcker waited for three rings, then picked it up.

Hello?

This is Mr. Smith from Chicago.

Mr. Smith, this is Johnnie Eliopolos.

I'd like to speak with Stephanos.

Well, I'm sorry, but Stephanos is on vacation. He's out of the country. Totally off the grid. But he's authorized me to fill your order if you like.

(pause) I'd prefer to deal with Stephanos.

Sure, that's fine. He'll be back in a couple of weeks. But I should tell you, the merchandise you're requesting is moving *very* quickly. I can't promise we'll have any left two weeks from now.

(pause) Do you have five thousand mugs in stock?

That's a big order but yes, we do. Depending on what you want. What did you get last time?

Well, I got fifty Harrys, twenty-five Hermiones, and twenty-five Professor McGonagalls.

Some of our bestsellers. And this time?

Well, I like the looks of the Hagrid mug. You guys did a great job with his beard.

Thank you.

Does that come in a bigger size? He is a giant, you know.

(Radic shakes head)

No. They're all the same size.

Even Dobby the House Elf?

Even Dobby. The big creatures, the small creatures, all the same-sized mug.

So Hagrid's not bigger, and Dobby's not smaller?

That's correct. The figures on the mug may be bigger or smaller, fatter or thinner, but the mugs themselves are the same size.

Do they all transport equally well?

CHAPTER THIRTY-TWO: THE STING

Well, we were a bit nervous about Professor McGonagall, with her witch's cap and all.

Right.

But you got some of those. How did they turn out?

Beautiful! Just beautiful. No chipping. You packed them really well.

We've been in business for twenty-five years. We take pride in our shipping.

Well, it shows. Okay, here's what I'd like: two thousand Harrys. One thousand Hermiones. One thousand Professor McGonagalls. Five hundred Hagrids. And five hundred Dobbys.

Got it.

Do you have all of those in stock?

Let me check on the Hagrids. Those were harder to make because of the beard. (pause) Yep, we have just enough.

Excellent!

Okay. So, where would you like those shipped?

Same as before.

Right. But I don't have that paperwork. It's in Stephanos' office, under lock and key. You understand why we don't have that lying about, right?

Yes, of course. I appreciate that. Okay. It's 6234 Marshfield St., Chicago, Ill. 60613.

And the payment? How did Stephanos handle your first order?

Half up front, half on delivery.

Okay, fine. Let's do it the same way. Did Stephanos have you do a direct deposit?

No. He gave me an address. Don't you have that?

Well, sure, I have our regular address. But it's better for you to send it to the same address as before. Just to play it safe.

Got it. Let me check. Okay. It says: PO Box 322, Homestead, Pa. 15120.

That sounds perfect. It's close to our shop. And how would you like the mugs shipped?

Fed Ex.

Can do. Okay. Did Stephanos give you an invoice before? Or did he just give you a number?

Just a number.

That's what I thought. Give me a minute.

Radic, who had been using a calculator, wrote down three numbers on the blackboard: one for the mugs, one for the shipping and tax, and one for the grand total.

Volcker repeated each of them out loud and then divided the grand total in two.

You should send us a check to the PO Box in Homestead in the amount of $52,106.35. Then, if everything is satisfactory at your end, you'll send us a second check for the same amount. Make both payable to Dimitri's Sturdy Dishes. Do you know how to spell that?

Yes, it's a pun. I get it. Should I put Muggles at the bottom of the check?

(Radic shook his head no)

I would advise against that.

That's what Stephanos said.

Okay, then, we're all set.

And if I want more?

Stephanos should be back in a couple weeks. And his private phone number should be working again. You can deal directly with him. Ask for me if you can't reach him.

Will do. I appreciate your help.

Don't mention it. Enjoy your mugs!

Volcker hung up the phone and let out a huge sigh of relief.

The rest of the group applauded.

"That's an A +, my man! An A+!" Radic said.

"You think I have the makings of a good salesman?" Volcker asked.

"If Dimitri had seen you in action, he would hire you himself," Radic said.

"Well, that's good to know, just in case the police thing doesn't work out," Volcker replied.

Chapter Thirty-Three: A Chance Encounter

Lexie Davodny was driving home after work at 4:15 p.m. when she saw a familiar face. Branko Radic. She nearly honked but thought better of it. Radic was about to ring a door bell. To make an arrest? But there was no sign of a squad car. Or a partner.

Instead of honking, Davodny decided to pull over and watch. Was Radic armed? Could he use backup?

A Black woman answered the door. She recognized Radic and seemed happy to see him. A total false alarm. Sometimes, your imagination runs wild.

Moments later, a boy appeared—skinny, wiry, also Black, perhaps eight years old. His face lit up like a Christmas tree when he saw Radic. Clearly, they had some history.

After a brief conversation, the boy kissed the woman and stepped outside. Radic wrapped his right arm around the boy and together they strolled to the street, where a car awaited.

Reluctant to intrude, Davodny remained silent. She would wait until Radic left and then go home.

But as Radic's car pulled away, she impulsively decided to follow him and the boy. She wasn't sure why. Curiosity, perhaps. Or lust.

Whatever the reason, she was eager to know more about the relationship between Radic and this young boy from one of Pittsburgh's tougher neighborhoods.

TOO MANY BRIDGES

The trip was short. A mile away, Radic stopped at a public park. He and the boy emerged, each clutching a Frisbee.

Isn't that one Frisbee too many? Davodny thought to herself.

But the explanation quickly became apparent. After a brief walk, Radic encouraged his protégé to toss the Frisbee in the direction of what appeared to be a trash can. The boy missed, but not badly. He fetched the Frisbee and tried again from the spot where the Frisbee landed. This time, he succeeded. Radic applauded. The boy grinned. Then Radic tossed his own Frisbee right into the trash can, or whatever it was. *Show-off!* Davodny thought to herself. But the boy didn't seem to mind. In fact, he scampered away in quest of another trash can as Radic trotted behind him.

Davodny was about to head home when it dawned on her that perhaps this might be an opportunity. Throwing caution to the wind, she locked her car and headed after the duo.

How to play this? she asked herself. *Out for a walk. I come here all the time. I don't live that far from here. I needed to unwind from work. I wanted to ask you out on a date.*

Oops! She needed to stick to a script, or else she might say something foolish.

As Radic and the boy came into view, Davodny decided that jogging might be a good excuse. She wasn't wearing sweatpants, but at least she was wearing pants. She wasn't wearing tennis shoes, but at least she was wearing casual shoes. Mustering some courage, she broke into a trot.

Radic noticed her from fifty yards away. She waved, deviated from the path, and approached him and the boy.

"Hi!" she said, eloquent as ever.

"Hi!" Radic replied. He seemed surprised but cordial.

"I didn't expect to see YOU here!" she said.

"Likewise," he replied.

"I hear you've been super busy lately," she said.

"Too busy," he replied.

"Who's your friend?" Davodny asked, nodding at the boy.

"This is Damon," Radic replied. "Damon, say hello to Officer Lexie

CHAPTER THIRTY-THREE: A CHANCE ENCOUNTER

Davodny. She also works for the Pittsburgh Police."

"Hello, Damon," Davodny beamed. "Nice to meet you!"

"Nice to meet you too," Damon replied, extending his right hand.

"Are you guys playing some sort of game?" she asked, struggling to continue the conversation.

"It's disc golf," Damon replied. "I'm pretty good, but he's beating me."

Davodny laughed. "Well, you're playing against an old man, Damon. Trust me, he's going to run out of gas soon. Don't give up yet!"

Damon seemed to appreciate her teasing at Radic's expense. But Davodny couldn't quite figure out what to say next. Unfortunately, *she* was running out of gas.

"Well, I should probably let you guys finish your game," she said. "Nice to meet you, Damon!" Then, nodding to Radic, "I hope to see you around!"

Davodny resumed her jog, heading in the same direction as before to create the illusion of an actual destination.

To her surprise, Radic yelled after her: "Lexie!"

She spun around and jogged back.

"Hey," he asked, "do you still work for the River Rescue Unit?"

"Yep," she replied.

"Do you think sometime you could give Damon and me a spin?" he asked. Then, to Damon: "Would you enjoy going out on a police boat sometime?"

Damon grinned. "Yeah, definitely!" he replied.

Davodny couldn't believe her good luck. "Sure," she said. "I'd be happy to do that. Just give me a call sometime." Then, to Damon: "But be sure to wear a poncho, young man. You're going to get the ride of your life!"

Chapter Thirty-Four: Two Stakeouts

It took no more than twenty minutes to reach an agreement with the Pittsburgh Post Office on how to conduct surveillance at their Homestead branch. It helped that Lieutenant Stilton and the head of the Pittsburgh Post Office were both members of the local Rotary club.

A quick conversation with Homestead Postmaster John Byrnes revealed that PO Box 322 did indeed belong to Stephanos, who had rented it only four months ago. It was not a particularly big box. Big enough for letters and small packages. Big enough to receive checks for illegal merchandise. All Homestead postal workers were given photos of Stephanos, with instructions to alert their boss if he appeared.

In addition, all mail destined for PO Box 322 was "red-flagged" by the Homestead Post Office, so that they would know about it before it was actually placed in the box. Stilton asked the head of the Pittsburgh Post Office whether it might be possible to open the mail in advance of delivery, but that option was flatly rejected as inconsistent with federal law.

Arranging surveillance of the Muggles' destination in Chicago proved to be far trickier. Intergovernmental cooperation between federal and local law enforcement was notoriously difficult and this certainly turned out to be true.

Almost from the point of initial contact, two different FBI units squabbled over who would be in charge. Then, the Chicago Police Department raised objections to playing any role in the operation, citing high crime, rising costs, and personnel shortages.

After a good deal of skirmishing, the parties agreed that the Chicago P.D.

CHAPTER THIRTY-FOUR: TWO STAKEOUTS

would not need to get involved at all. The FBI's Intellectual Property Rights Unit would handle the operation, in consultation with the FBI's Financial Crimes Unit, and with an assist from the Pittsburgh Police, who would track the packages and let the FBI know when they arrived in Chicago.

At that point, the FBI would dispatch an officer to Marshfield Street to take photos of the goods being delivered and accepted. They knew that the owner of the property was a Mr. Vladimir Fedorov (a far cry from Mr. Smith!) but they couldn't be sure who was on the premises or who would actually take possession of the packages.

Both Radic and Stilton expressed misgivings about the Chicago end of the deal, but it was out of their hands, and they were less concerned about intellectual property crimes than the homicide they were trying to solve. They felt reasonably confident that the Pittsburgh part of the operation had a good chance of success.

* * *

Since the Sloan case had begun, Radic had missed one of his weekly meetings with Damon. Worried that this might happen again if he wasn't proactive, he called Lexie Davodny to book an excursion on the River Rescue Unit's Jupiter boat.

Davodny asked lots of questions about Damon. How did they meet? What were his likes and dislikes? Radic explained that he had met Damon through the Big Brothers, Big Sisters program. Damon was a good kid, whose father had gone to prison for drug dealing three years ago and who was not scheduled to be released any time soon.

He did his best to summarize Damon's food preferences (popsicles), book preferences (high adventure), and favorite subjects in school (maybe geography, definitely not math). They agreed to meet at four on Thursday afternoon for a boat ride.

Squeezing in exercise while working on a difficult case was also problematic, but Norbert Renfert was a good friend...and relentless.

"Whaddaya mean, you're too busy?" he asked. "Was Muhammad Ali too busy for the Thrilla in Manila? Was Spider-Man too busy to fight Dr. Octopus? Was Napoleon too busy for the Battle of Waterloo?"

"Actually, I think Napoleon lost the Battle of Waterloo," Radic replied. "So that might not be your best example."

"Well, that's beside the point. At least he showed up. I'll meet you at the Allegheny Commons Park at 5 o'clock sharp. Be there or be square!"

"What happens if I'm not there?"

"You don't want to know!"

Chapter Thirty-Five: An Act of Piracy

Radic came close to canceling the nautical adventure. He needed time to think about Stephanos and Carol, Stephanos and Basil, and possible accomplices for the murder and the intellectual property theft. He needed time to confer with Mulroy, Volcker, and Scuglia. He needed to meet with Stilton. And, according to Norbert Renfert, he needed more exercise. In short, he had to be in too many places at the same damn time.

Damon was a mature kid. He rolled with the punches. If Radic postponed the boat trip, he would understand. On the other hand, he seemed genuinely excited by the prospect of taking a spin in a speed boat. Also, what would Davodny think if he canceled?

Radic's feelings for Davodny ultimately tipped the scales to a yes. There seemed to be some mutual interest, if his radar was correct. They worked for totally different units, so there were no ethical issues to fret over. She was fun to be with. And she was very, very sexy.

Radic picked Damon up at 3:45 p.m. His young friend was brimming with enthusiasm. As they drove to the dock, he peppered Radic with questions. How big is the boat? How fast does it go? How deep is the water? Do people swim in it?

Radic's first glimpse of Davodny at the wharf took his breath away. She was wearing a green bicorn hat, a black eyepatch, a green leotard, some sort of puffy shirt, and a bright red vest with brass buttons. Tall black boots rounded out her ensemble. She looked terrific!

"Ahoy, mateys!" she said. "Come aboard!"

The sleek Jupiter boat was festooned with confetti and flowers in honor of the occasion. Radic didn't know what to say. "Aren't you going to get in trouble for this?" he asked.

"Only if someone sees us!" she replied, with a smile and a wink of her one visible eye.

Davodny was holding a black satchel. She reached inside and withdrew two eyepatches. "One for each of you!" she beamed.

Damon eagerly donned his eyepatch and seemed very pleased. "Arghhhh!" he growled, in his best pirate voice. Radic, determined not to be a party pooper, put one on as well, after confirming that no one else was around. "Arrh," he croaked, not fully in character.

"Are you ready for the ride of a lifetime?" Davodny asked Damon.

"Aye, aye, sir!" he replied. "I mean, ma'am."

Davodny laughed. "Aye, aye, Captain, will do."

"Aye, aye, captain," he responded.

"That's the spirit!" she said, giving him a hearty pat on the back.

"I see you've brought your poncho," she said to Damon. "No pirate should be caught without one. But what about your friend?"

"I can handle a little bit of water," Radic said.

"Suit yourself, matey," she replied. "But we have a rule: any pirate without a poncho has to walk the gangplank at the end of the trip."

"Hmm," Radic said. "Maybe I'll wear a poncho after all."

"A wise choice," Davodny said, reaching into her satchel for a man-sized poncho.

"Finally," she said. "Every pirate's best friend. A life jacket."

She quickly produced three life jackets and explained to Damon how to put one on. She then showed Damon how to hold on to the railing with two hands instead of one. "Just in case it gets a bit bumpy," she explained.

With a toot of the boat's horn, Captain Davodny eased onto the Allegheny River and headed east. Suddenly, she accelerated. "Hold onto your hats, mateys!" she cried.

The Jupiter quickly overtook two smaller boats, as startled boaters tried to figure out whether three pirates had commandeered a police vessel. The

CHAPTER THIRTY-FIVE: AN ACT OF PIRACY

speed and the spray left Damon and Radic sputtering, but laughing. A good sign. Occasionally, Davodny's passengers bounced up and down, emitting gasps and groans that conveyed surprise but not distress. After ten minutes, Davodny slipped into a more comfortable speed, to give Damon and Radic a chance to enjoy the scenery.

"Where are we going, Captain?" Damon yelled, to be heard.

"Why, to the pirates' cave, of course!" she yelled back. "Meanwhile, check out the refrigerator if you'd like a snack." She motioned to a small freezer inside the cabin.

Damon stood up, unsteady at first. But he regained his footing and made his way into the cabin. He found a banana popsicle and squealed with delight. "Would you like one, Branko?" he asked.

"Maybe later," Radic replied.

"How about you, Captain?" he asked.

"I need two hands to steer this vessel," Davodny responded. Then, removing one hand from the steering wheel, she pretended that the ship was spinning out of control. "Maybe later," she laughed, as she "regained" control of the boat.

While Damon sucked happily on his popsicle, and with the boat idling for a bit, Davodny approached Radic. "How's your case coming along?" she asked.

"Two steps forward, one step backwards. I guess that's progress," he replied.

"It's a really tough case," she said with empathy, removing her eyepatch for a moment. "But you have a gift for solving difficult cases. Like the O'Herlihy case."

As she bent closer, Ravic noticed what a dazzling shade of green her eyes were. And how beautiful she was. She didn't smell like a pirate either. Her perfume was intoxicating. Why had he never reached out to her before?

Snapping back to the conversation, he acknowledged the compliment. "I got lucky," he said. "And the perp got careless."

"That's not what I heard," Davodny said. "The perp got careless because you gave him enough slack to make a mistake. Then, when he made a mistake, you reeled him in. Like a mackerel on the high seas."

"Spoken like a true captain," Radic laughed. Then, more seriously, "Mulroy says that you met Vazzy on the high seas. What did you make of him?"

"Well, I definitely met his boat, a Kennywood special," she said. "I'm pretty sure I met him too, though I'm not 100 percent positive."

"Did he seem scared to you?" he asked.

Davodny thought for a moment. "Either scared or scary. I couldn't quite make up my mind. He was definitely on the alert. Looking for someone. Whether he was the predator or the prey, I just couldn't say."

Noticing that Damon had finished his popsicle, Davodny returned to the cockpit and accelerated, though at a gentle pace. She motioned to Damon to join her, which he did. Then she pointed to the console, which featured a GPS map. "Have you seen one of these before?" she asked.

Damon shook his head.

"It's a map, like the ones you see in your geography class," she said. "Notice the blue, which is the Allegheny River. And the compass, which says we're heading..."

"East!" Damon cried.

"Exactly!" Davodny said. "I see you're good at reading maps. Now, if you look at the right river bank, what seems to be coming up?"

"It says... Woodstock Glen."

"That's right. Not many people know this, but Woodstock Glen was named after "Stinky Pete" Woodstock, one of the orneriest pirates who ever lived."

"Really?"

"Really! He was a nasty piece of work. And he never brushed his teeth. That's why they called him Stinky Pete."

"Eww! That's disgusting."

"Well, he was disgusting. But he was also a very clever pirate. And the legend says that before he died, he buried a special treasure right here in Woodstock Glen."

"Wow!"

Radic, eavesdropping, was amazed at how quickly Davodny had estab-

CHAPTER THIRTY-FIVE: AN ACT OF PIRACY

lished a rapport with Damon. He and Damon had an excellent relationship, but it had taken several weeks to build up that level of trust. For Davodny, it had taken all of 30 minutes.

Noticing the time, Radic signaled that it was time to head back. Davodny executed a Figure 8 maneuver and turned to Damon.

"What shall it be, matey?" she asked in her best pirate voice. "Fast? Or super-fast?"

Damon didn't hesitate. "Super-fast!" he exclaimed.

"Super-fast it is!" she declared. And off they went, at about 40 miles per hour, giggling and groaning as they headed back to the wharf.

Damon and Radic were permitted to keep their eye patches as mementos of their trip. "Keep the eye patch under your pillow at night, and it will bring you good luck!" Davodny yelled as they left the boat.

Damon did exactly that when he went to bed that night. And Radic did, too.

Chapter Thirty-Six: Picking Up the Mail

Letter carrier Eva Nguyen was just beginning her shift at the Homestead Post Office at 7 a.m. She was looking forward to a quiet day. The weather was nice. Mild and sunny, with light winds. It was mid-week, so there was no backlog of weekend mail. Best of all, that vicious pit bull on Montana Street had recently passed away. Someone had lost a friend, perhaps. But, honestly, among letter carriers, he would not be missed.

As she walked through the back entrance, Nguyen noticed a lone customer retrieving mail at a PO box. Not unusual. People collected their mail at all hours of day and night. But this gentleman was in the vicinity of the PO box they were supposed to watch.

She slowed down and took a good look. The postal patron looked up as she glanced his way. She breathed a sigh of relief when she noticed that he didn't look at all like the sketch her boss had shared with letter carriers and clerks the other day. He was clean-shaven, kind of homely with an asymmetrical face and a pointy nose, in his late forties, not a handsome youth with a beard. A different guy.

That's a relief, she thought to herself, as her muscles relaxed. Still, maybe she should investigate. She changed her route and walked in his direction. "Nice day we're having!" she said cheerily. The customer grunted, fumbled awkwardly for his mail, and quickly closed his box. Box 322.

He seemed furtive. Was it her imagination? Perhaps. But it was the right box, so she plunged ahead, improvising. "Did you know that we have larger boxes available? In case you get packages in addition to letters?" she asked.

CHAPTER THIRTY-SIX: PICKING UP THE MAIL

"That's okay," he replied. "Not for me." He walked quickly to the door. "Have a nice day!" she called as he exited the building.

She watched as the mystery man headed towards a blue-green Toyota Camry. Then she noticed that in his haste to leave, he had dropped a letter. She picked it up and rushed towards his car, waving the letter. But the patron was spooked. He quickly sped away as she continued to wave the letter.

Still suspicious, she noted the plate—Pennsylvania, KDY—9745 — and wrote it down on an index card. Then she looked at the letter. It was addressed to Stephanos Papadopoulos, PO Box 322, Homestead, Pa. Wasn't that the name her boss had mentioned?

Something was fishy, though she couldn't put her finger on it. She called her boss, John Byrnes. He would know what to do.

Within minutes, several police officers arrived at the scene, including Radic, Mulroy, and Volcker. Radic spoke with Nguyen briefly, quickly established that she was an eyewitness, and thanked her profusely when she produced a license plate number. His eyes widened at the piece of mail she was carrying. He couldn't open it just yet, but maybe down the road.

Postmaster Byrnes arranged for a floater to handle Nguyen's mail for the day, while Nguyen herself accompanied Radic and Mulroy to the police headquarters on the North Side. Volcker took the same route in a separate car.

A license plate check at the station quickly revealed that the owner of the car was Stephanos Papadopoulos. Radic produced a photo of Stephanos and gauged Nguyen's reaction. "Definitely not!" she said. "The customer was clean-shaven, no beard. Nerdy looking. The guy in the photo is a hunk. A bearded hunk. I'm certain it wasn't him."

Undeterred, Radic reached into his folder. Thanks to Volcker and his penchant for impromptu photos, they had pictures of Dimitri and Trojanowski, plus Rob McPherson, from a publicity photo. Also sketches of Vazzy and Gatti (Volcker had convinced Mulroy to describe Gatti to a sketch artist).

"Recognize any of these men?" Radic asked.

"Bingo!" Nguyen cried when she saw Trojanowski. "That's the guy. PO Box 322."

Radic turned to Mulroy. "Call Dimitri immediately and ask if Trojanowski is at work. Don't alert him to what's going on. Make up some excuse."

Mulroy nodded and disappeared. Moments later, she returned. "He called in sick."

Cursing in disgust, Radic asked Mulroy to get Trojanowski's home address from Dimitri.

Within minutes, they were on their way to Trojanowski's home in Highland Park while Volcker detained Nguyen for further questioning by Stilton and the FBI. Rush hour traffic was dense, so Radic took a detour through Polish Hill to avoid the worst of it. As they approached Trojanowski's residence, Radic advised Mulroy to prepare for what might be a difficult arrest.

"If he has a weapon, we need to disarm him, and quickly," he said.

"With a gun?" she asked.

"A taser would be better."

"I've done it at the academy, never in real life."

"Use it only if there's active resistance. But use it if you're at risk."

"Where should I aim if I have to use it?"

"Aim at his chest. It's a wide target. Or his back if he makes a run for it."

"No gun?"

"If it's necessary, I'll handle the gun. You handle the taser."

Two blocks from their destination, a car whizzed by in the opposite direction. Mulroy interrupted Radic, who was discussing firearms and shouted, "A Green Toyota Camry, with a plate beginning KDY. Isn't that Stephanos' car?"

Radic slammed on the brakes and reversed course. Whoever was driving the Toyota was definitely in a hurry. When Radic accelerated, he accelerated, too.

"Hold on to your hat!" Radic said, activating his siren and flashing lights.

As they raced through a quiet residential neighborhood, Radic tried to anticipate where the driver was heading.

CHAPTER THIRTY-SIX: PICKING UP THE MAIL

"What do you think?" he asked. "Where's he going?"

"I'd say the Parkway," Mulroy replied.

"See if you can get a roadblock there pronto," he said. "I'd like to avoid a showdown on the Parkway. People could get hurt."

"Will do," Mulroy said as she placed a call.

The driver was ignoring stop signs and traffic lights. Radic kept up with him, hoping desperately that no pedestrians would get in the way. Honks greeted them at every intersection.

Five minutes later, they saw the Parkway entrance. Gratefully, they also saw two police cars with flashing lights and a column of about a dozen stalled cars. The driver noticed the trap, but it was too late. Lacking a good alternative, he tried driving on the sidewalk to escape. But a mix of tricycles, recycling containers, and telephone poles made that extremely difficult. Within seconds, the car came to a screeching halt.

"It's showtime, Mulroy," Radic said. "Turn on your body-cam, now."

The driver got out of the car and raised his hands. "Don't shoot!" he said. "Don't shoot!"

Radic and Mulroy exited their car. "On the ground!" Radic barked, his gun drawn. And the man complied.

"Arms outstretched!" Again, the man complied.

The suspect on the ground was indeed Jim Trojanowski, though in disguise. He was wearing a bushy black mustache that didn't quite match his medium brown hair color. He was also wearing a Pirates cap and sunglasses.

Radic motioned to Mulroy to get closer. Mulroy proceeded with caution, a taser in her right hand.

"There's no need to use that thing!" Trojanowski cried.

"Only if you resist!" she replied.

"I won't," he said.

But he did. As Mulroy bent over to cuff him, Trojanowski executed a deft backflip, knocking Mulroy to the ground with a thud. He reached for her taser and tried to wrench it from her, but she resisted. He punched her hard in the mouth, incapacitating her, and was about to grab the taser when Radic kicked him hard in the small of the back.

Trojanowski's back buckled, and he grew limp. Moving quickly, Radic cuffed him and turned his attention to Mulroy.

Her mouth was bleeding badly from the punch, and she seemed a bit woozy. "Stay down," Radic told her. "Give yourself a minute."

With one eye on Trojanowski, Radic produced a bandana from his pocket to stanch the bleeding from Mulroy's mouth. "We'd better get you to a hospital," he said.

"Officer needs medical assistance," he reported on his walkie-talkie, describing their location. "No, not life-threatening, but make it snappy."

Meanwhile, an officer abandoned the blockade and assisted Radic in processing Trojanowski. Radic handled the final honors: "James Trojanowski, you are being arrested for reckless driving, assaulting a police officer, conspiracy to commit fraud, and other crimes. You have the right to remain silent. Anything you say can and will be held against you …"

Five minutes later, an ambulance arrived. An EMT checked Mulroy's vitals, then pressed an ice pack on top of her throbbing mouth. "I wanna talk wid 'im," Mulroy said as the ambulance beckoned.

"I'll do my best to make that happen," Radic promised her.

Mulroy nodded with relief.

"You did good work today, Mulroy," Radic said.

"I shoulda been able to cuff 'im," she said with regret.

"It happens to all of us once or twice," Radic said. "Next time, you'll have a plan. You learn from experiences like this."

"I needa learn more quickly," she said and disappeared with the ambulance.

Chapter Thirty-Seven: Time to Get Ready

Radic had no trouble convincing Stilton to delay the questioning of their star witness, so Mulroy could participate. Stilton was already a Mulroy fan, and he got very protective when one of his officers was injured in the line of duty.

Also, Trojanowski was relevant to two ongoing investigations—one local, the other federal, which meant that the PBP and the FBI needed time to agree on ground rules for interrogation.

Before any of this could be accomplished, the police had to respond to a petition from Trojanowski's lawyer claiming excessive use of force in subduing his client.

According to Trojanowski's lawyer, Melvin Hirsch, the sequence of events was: his client lay on the ground, as instructed; Detective Radic kicked him viciously in the back, causing significant bodily injury; he responded by lashing out at Officer Mulroy, who happened to be nearby.

Luckily, Mulroy's body-cam recorded the scene faithfully from the moment Radic and Mulroy stepped out of their car. The video evidence was crystal clear—Trojanowski lashed out at the police rather than vice versa.

Radic smiled grimly. This lie could come back to haunt Trojanowski because it established him as an untruthful witness. The police could use this mistake to good advantage whenever his credibility was an issue.

While Mulroy was being treated at Shadyside Hospital, Radic conferred with Stilton and set the wheels in motion. He would get a warrant to search the contents of the car Trojanowki was driving and his home as well. He arranged a meeting of the PBP and the FBI for the following morning. Finally, he set up a one-on-one with an assistant DA to discuss a range of charges.

Initial conversations with FBI agents Fromm and Fogarty did not go well. The FBI wanted a piece of Trojanowski. Although Stephanos was the target of the FBI's investigation, Trojanowski clearly knew Stephanos and was presumably doing his bidding when picking up mail at PO Box 322. Furthermore, he may have played a role in manufacturing and selling the mugs. At the very least, he had valuable inside information that could lead the FBI to their suspect.

Radic and Stilton, however, argued that Trojanowski was critical to *their* investigation. Trojanowski knew Basil and Stephanos and appeared to be in cahoots with one or both of them. He might also know something about Carol Sloan's murder. Therefore, they wanted first crack at him. Their final point: he was sitting in one of *their* jails after being arrested by *their* officers. They were not going to yield without a fight.

Eventually, after many arguments, raised voices, and threats to escalate the conflict, the parties reached a rough consensus: the PBP would go first, focusing on any information that could help them locate the whereabouts of Stephanos and Basil. The FBI would be present and could interrupt for a private word if the interrogation strayed too far afield into intellectual property issues or if they wanted to probe a particular point.

Because both parties saw Trojanowski as an accomplice, not a kingpin, either party might be tempted to use Trojanowski as a bargaining chip to get to someone else. On the other hand, the two parties had different agendas. For this reason, it was agreed that neither party would approach a prosecutor with a plea offer without the other's consent. Radic's conversations with an assistant DA would have to be tentative, preliminary.

Getting a search warrant from Judge Floyd of the Court of Common Pleas was not as easy the second time around. "There are some jurisdictional issues here, detective," Floyd said when Radic submitted the paperwork. "I

CHAPTER THIRTY-SEVEN: TIME TO GET READY

may have been a little hasty in approving your last warrant request."

"How so?"

"There are some fine points of law that I overlooked when I approved your request as worded," he said.

"Such as?"

"In retrospect," he explained, "I wish I had drawn a sharper distinction between two of your sheds: one that contained a poison that may well have been used to kill Carol Sloan and one that contained some mugs that may have violated someone's property rights. The first is clearly my jurisdiction; the second is a matter for a federal court."

"But we couldn't know in advance what would be in which shed," Radic objected.

Judge Floyd raised his hand. "I know. I know. And that will help us if this matter is ever appealed. But now that we know there are some intellectual property issues, I have to tread more carefully."

"What do you suggest, your honor?"

"Just give me a day or two to read the case law and to confer with one or two colleagues," he replied. "I think there's a path forward. I just need a little more time."

Back at the office, Radic explained the legal situation to Stilton and Volcker as best he could. No one was happy with the delay, but there seemed reason to hope. "Let's move on to other issues," Stilton suggested.

Volcker was the first person to ask two key questions: "Where is Trojanowski's car? And why was he using Stephanos' car?"

"We need to find that out," Stilton agreed. "Make that a high priority!"

"It stands to reason that someone else is using Trojanowski's car," Radic argued. "It could be Stephanos. Or it could be Basil."

"Get the make and serial number and put out an APB," Stilton ordered.

Radic reached Mulroy at home that evening.

"How are you doing, partner?" he asked.

She chuckled, which he took as a good sign. "I've been better," she said.

"You sound okay," he said.

"Well, they patched me up pretty well. And the swelling is down a bit."

"Any serious damage?" he asked.

"I lost a tooth," she replied. "And another one is chipped. It will have to be capped."

"So you'll be visiting a dentist?"

"Once the swelling goes down and my gums recover."

"Maybe they can fix your overbite!" Radic suggested.

Mulroy laughed. "I thought you said I didn't have an overbite."

"You didn't then," Radic said. "And you don't now. But if you'd like to get some dental surgery, now would be the time to do it. I'll keep you in the loop on the case. Hang in there!"

Chapter Thirty-Eight: A Reluctant Witness

The interview room was crowded. Trojanowski and his lawyer. Radic, Mulroy, and Volcker. And the two FBI agents, Fromm and Fogarty, whom the police referred to privately as Frick and Frack. In most interrogations, the focus of attention is on the suspect. But in this case, the initial focus was on Mulroy, whose lips were puffy and who had abrasions on both cheeks. She was also drooling a bit and occasionally wiped her mouth with a Kleenex.

Melvin Hirsch was taken aback. "I didn't realize that Officer Mulroy would be here," he said.

"She's part of this investigation, and she's recovered sufficiently from her injuries to participate," Radic replied.

Hirsch asked for a moment to confer with his client. Then he said, "Officer Mulroy, my client wishes to say that he regrets any harm that may have come to you as part of his effort to protect himself from another police officer."

Radic responded before Mulroy could: "Neither one of us is going to respond to that remark, because it pertains to one of many charges against your client. I suggest that we proceed."

Hirsch looked at his client, who nodded. Hirsch nodded as well.

Radic began by turning on a tape-recorder and by announcing the time, place, and names of all those present.

"Mr. Trojanowski," Radic began, "I'd like to begin with a simple question.

Two days ago, you were seen picking up mail at the Homestead Post Office, from Box # 322. Who authorized you to pick up that mail?"

Trojanowski looked at his attorney, who nodded.

"Basil Vasilikas asked me to do that, after conferring with Stephanos Papadopoulos, who was away on vacation."

"You did not receive that request from Mr. Papadopoulos directly?" Radic asked.

"No, I did not."

"When was the last time you spoke with Mr. Papadopoulos?" Radic asked.

"The day before he left on vacation."

"What did you discuss?" he asked.

"You'll have to be more specific, detective," Hirsch warned.

"Okay, did Stephanos Papadopoulos authorize you to use his car while he was away on vacation?" he asked.

"Well, Stephanos asked me to use his car while he was away, but he didn't ask me directly."

"So, how did you conclude that you were to use his car?"

"Basil told me."

"Did he tell you in person or by phone?"

"By phone."

"And did he explain why you should use Mr. Papadopoulos' car rather than your own?"

"Well, Stephanos' car is relatively small. I have an SUV. A Honda Pilot. Stephanos and Basil decided that Basil should use my SUV for a couple of weeks to haul some merchandise."

"What kind of merchandise?" Radic asked.

"I'm sorry, detective," Hirsch interjected. "But my client is not going to answer that question until you have a conversation with the District Attorney's office."

"I'll withdraw that question for the time being," he said. Then he turned to Mulroy. "I believe that Officer Mulroy has some questions."

All eyes turned to Mulroy, who dabbed at her mouth with a Kleenex before beginning. "Mr. Trojanowski," she said, slowly getting her sea legs,

CHAPTER THIRTY-EIGHT: A RELUCTANT WITNESS

"Where were you heading when you left your home suddenly two days ago?"

Trojanowski turned to Hirsch, who nodded.

"I was heading to the Pittsburgh airport," he said.

"And why were you doing that?" she asked.

"I needed time to think things over," he replied.

"You can't think things over in Pittsburgh?" she asked.

"I needed to clear my head," he replied. "I needed a short vacation."

"And why is that?" she asked.

"I've been asked to do some things at work that make me uncomfortable," he said. "I like my job. And I like my employer. But I was told to do some things that seemed reasonable at the time, but that seem less reasonable today."

"Like what?" Mulroy asked.

Hirsch intervened. "I'm afraid that my client is not prepared to answer that question at the present time," he said.

"Okay," Mulroy replied. "I understand. What was your destination?"

"Miami," he said.

"Miami?" she asked.

"Yes, I have a good friend who lives there," he replied. "I was going to stay with him for a few days. To sort some things out."

"Did Stephanos and Basil know that you were leaving town?" she asked.

Trojanowski looked at Hirsch, who nodded. "No, they did not," he said.

Radic glanced at the two FBI agents, whose body language conveyed no useful information. "We're going to take a fifteen-minute recess," he said. "We'll resume questioning after that."

* * *

The extended team of officers, plus Stilton, huddled in an anteroom nearby. Barney Fromm, from the FBI, was the first to speak up. "Well, that didn't get us anywhere," he complained. "It sounds like the lawyer won't give us squat until we have a plea bargain deal."

"Anyone else?" Radic asked.

"What's the status of our warrant request?" Stilton asked.

"We're still waiting to hear from Judge Floyd," Radic said. "He wants to confer with his counterpart from the federal courts."

"Do we have a time frame?" Stilton asked.

"Probably sometime later today," Radic said, hoping it would prove correct.

"What did we get from his personal belongings after the arrest?" Volcker asked. "Any airplane tickets?"

"Yep, he was telling the truth," Radic replied. "He was scheduled to fly to Miami. The reservation was booked the previous day."

"A return flight?" Volcker asked.

"Yep, after a long weekend," Radic said. "Of course, he might have changed his plans after thinking things over."

"I say we need to scare the shit out of him," Fromm argued. "Intellectual property crimes carry long sentences. Let's put the fear of God in him. The sooner he cops a plea, the better."

"Well, that's certainly one way to play it," Radic said. "But the way I look at it, we haven't exhausted all the possibilities yet. To you, it may seem like we've learned nothing so far. To me, we've learned an awful lot, with the promise of more to come."

"Explain," Stilton said.

"Before this morning, we didn't know whether Trojanowski was getting orders from Stephanos or from Basil. Now, it's pretty clear that he's been interacting with Basil exclusively. For the past couple of weeks, at least. That's really important."

"Admittedly, Basil might be Stephanos' mouthpiece. But I'm not sure I buy it. And I'm not sure that Trojanowski and his lawyer buy it either. Not anymore. Basil may have deceived him, claiming to have the authority to speak for Stephanos. But who says he speaks for Stephanos? Only Basil himself."

"What are you suggesting?" Stilton asked.

"He's suggesting that Hirsch actually wants Trojanowski to answer questions about Basil," Mulroy said. "He's looking for a fall guy."

CHAPTER THIRTY-EIGHT: A RELUCTANT WITNESS

"Precisely," Radic said.

"So, let's say you're right, what do you propose?" Stilton asked.

"I say we reconvene and redirect our inquiry," Radic said. "Direct the questions away from Trojanowski and towards Basil. I think Trojanowski has something to say and that Hirsch wants him to say it."

"Can't hurt," Stilton said. Then, turning to the FBI officials, "Do we agree?"

"One more round of questioning," the agent said. "Then we light a fire under his ass!"

"Are you okay with that?" Stilton asked Radic.

"I'm okay with that," he said.

"Then let's give it a try: round two!" Stilton said.

Volcker entered the interrogation room ahead of the rest to see if Trojanowski or Hirsch would like some coffee. Both said yes.

The interrogation resumed twenty-two minutes after its suspension.

"Mr. Trojanowski, when did you first meet Basil Vasilikas?" Radic asked.

"He was one of Dimitri's top people when I joined the company a few years ago."

"What was your role at that time?"

"Chief chemist."

"Did you report to him? Was he in your chain of command?"

"Not really. I reported to Dimitri."

"What was Basil's role at the company at that time?"

"He was in a small department, set apart from the rest of the shop. The R&D department."

"Who headed that department?"

"Well, it was kind of hard to tell. It was Stephanos and Basil. Just the two of them. They made decisions together."

"Any signs of friction between Stephanos and Basil?"

"No, I wouldn't say so. Two peas in a pod."

"Two peas in a pod," Radic repeated. "What does that mean exactly?"

"Well, they had very different personalities. Different styles. But on business matters, they always seemed to be on the same page."

"Always on the same page," Radic repeated. Then, after a brief pause:

"What did you think about Basil during your first days at Dimitri's?"

"Competent. Intense. Serious. Ambitious."

"In what way was he ambitious?"

"He wanted Dimitri's to be bigger, better, grander. Less of a local firm, more of a national firm."

"And Stephanos? What were your impressions of him?"

"Charming. Friendly. Considerate. Intelligent."

"Ambitious?"

"Yes, he was ambitious too. But a bit more cautious."

"A bit more cautious," Radic repeated. "So maybe not exactly two peas in a pod." Then, after a brief pause: "Getting back to Basil…were you aware of his past?"

Trojanowski looked to Hirsch. "You're going to have to be more specific here, detective," he said.

"Okay, were you aware that Basil had served in the Gulf War?"

"Yes, of course."

"Did you ever see any evidence that he was suffering from PTSD?"

Hirsch objected. "My client is not a psychiatrist," he said. "He can't possibly answer that question."

"Let me rephrase it then: did you ever see Basil lose his temper?"

Hirsch nodded. And Trojanowski responded: "Yes, I did. Many times."

"Can you give me an example?"

Again, Hirsch objected. "I'm afraid my client is not prepared to get into specifics at this time."

"Has Basil Vasilikas ever threatened you with bodily harm if you did not do something he asked you to do?"

Trojanowski looked at Hirsch. "My client is not prepared to answer that question at the moment."

Mulroy nudged Radic, who deferred to his younger colleague.

"Mr. Trojanowski, do you know where Basil Vasilikas is living at the moment?"

"No, I do not."

"Do you know if Basil has been homeless for the past year or so?"

CHAPTER THIRTY-EIGHT: A RELUCTANT WITNESS

"That may be true."

"Does he own a boat?"

"Yes, he does."

"Can you confirm that he got that boat from Kennywood Park?"

After a nod from Hirsch: "That's news to me."

"Do you know where he stores that boat?"

"No, I do not."

"How do you get in touch with Basil when you need to?"

Trojanowski turned to Hirsch, who raised his hand. "My client is not going to answer that question, Officer."

"OK, one final question. Do you believe that Basil Vasilikas is capable of committing murder?"

Trojanowski blanched and turned to Hirsch with a pained expression on his face.

"I believe that's all we have to say at the moment, Officer. Detective, I'd like the opportunity to confer with my client."

Chapter Thirty-Nine: Extra Cheese?

The best part about a stakeout in Chicago was the pizza. Where else could you find stuffed pizza that tasted so heavenly?

FBI Agent Harold (Hal) Gomar had participated in stakeouts in LA, Sacramento, Portland, Oregon, Richmond, Virginia, and Annandale, Virginia. The pizza in those locales didn't even come close.

A key factor: he was partial to stuffed pizza, a Chicago specialty. But there was something else about Chicago pizza. A June say choir. Zhu-na-say-kwah. Whatever.

At 6' 4", 255 pounds, Agent Gomar knew a lot about pizza. Food, generally, for that matter. And why not? One of life's little pleasures.

His weight was occasionally an issue in annual evaluations. "Have you thought about dieting?" "Yep, thinking about it just makes me hungry." "How often do you work out?" "I work out when my job allows it. But my job should come first, don't you think?"

These exchanges didn't bother him much. Nothing ever came of them.

Gomar was looking forward to his Giordano's pizza. As usual, he had ordered the "Meat and More Meat" stuffed deep dish pizza. Pepperoni, salami, sausage, and bacon. YUM! His thought was: maybe half for lunch, then the rest for dinner.

He was well-prepared. Back in Sacramento, he had invested in a rechargeable hot plate. There was no way he was going to eat cold pizza, stakeout, or no stakeout. Yep, his hot plate was fully charged and ready to go.

All that was missing was a couple of cold brewskis to wash down the

CHAPTER THIRTY-NINE: EXTRA CHEESE?

delicious pizza. But Gomar was scrupulous about such things. He was a professional, after all. No drinking on the job. There would be plenty of time for a couple of Old Styles back in his apartment later on.

So Gomar settled down for what could be a long wait. According to Federal Express, the shipments from Pittsburgh had arrived at O'Hare Airport at 9:34 p.m. the night before. The scheduled delivery: sometime that afternoon. 6234 Marshfield Street, in Wrigleyville. It was now 11:50 a.m. Luckily for him, Giordano's had opened at 11 a.m. He had picked up his pizza just in the nick of time.

Although he was eager to try a slice, first things first. Gomar removed his camera from its case, checked the shutter, and focused on the front door under surveillance. He had deliberately chosen a spot across the street, but not directly across the street. If the recipient had to sign for the packages, he didn't want his puss to be blocked by the delivery guy. So, he positioned his car at a favorable angle. After taking a couple of practice shots, which turned out well, he relaxed a bit. But just a bit.

In Gomar's experience, the key to a successful stakeout, in addition to some nice, warm pizza, was to stay busy. If you don't stay busy, you get bored. If you got bored, you got sleepy. Gomar shuddered at the thought of where that might lead.

One of his colleagues back in Sacramento had gotten tired on a stakeout once and fallen asleep. Probably only for a few minutes. But those few minutes ended his career.

It was a drug shipment from Mexico. He was waiting outside a deserted warehouse in Petaluma, California. Not much to do out there. Not much to look at.

By the time he woke up, the dropoff had been made, and all the criminals had disappeared. To make matters worse, they had spotted him and left a note attached to his windshield wipers: PLEASANT DREAMS! They had even taken a photo of him and mailed it to the FBI. What kind of a sick fuck would do something like that?

Three months later, after an investigation, his friend was history. The last he heard, he was managing a Walmart in West Sacramento.

Well, that was not going to happen to Harold P. Gomar. That was for damn sure! So he had done all the right things: He brought along a couple of crossword puzzles and two nicely sharpened pencils. He had loaded some Kenny Rogers classics onto his Spotify playlist. And he had checked out a book from the public library.

Although he didn't know all the details, he knew that the shipment in question featured some mugs from the Harry Potter books and movies. He had heard about Harry Potter from one of his nieces, but he never really understood what the fuss was all about. Well, now was the time to find out. Harry Potter and the Sorcerer's Stone. Not likely to put him to sleep.

Chapter Forty: Second Thoughts

"We have photos!" Volcker cried as he caught Radic at his desk, doing paperwork.

"More photos?" Radic asked. "You've been taking MORE photos? Of whom?"

"Photos from Chicago!" Volcker said.

"Oh, why didn't you say so?" he asked. Radic stopped what he was doing and looked over Volcker's shoulder as he placed hard copies of several photos on a nearby ledge.

He saw clear, crisp shots of a thin man with a beak-shaped nose and very little hair—perhaps in his late 50s. The man signed for some Fed Ex packages which, the next photo showed, piled up on the front sidewalk so that the front porch was barely visible.

Judging from the remaining photos, the man used a dolly to haul the packages to the side of his house, possibly destined for the basement.

"Do we have a name?" Radic asked.

"Vladimir Federov, the owner of the house," Volcker replied.

"Not Mr. Smith?" Radic asked.

"That's what his signature says," Volcker explained, "but the feds have identified the man in the photos as Federov."

"He has a history?" Radic asked.

"Very much so," Volcker replied, "He's a Russian oligarch of some sort. Knee-deep in shady activities. The feds are VERY excited. In fact, Frick and Frack have flown the coop. They're on a plane to Chicago."

"But they were to interview Trojanowski tomorrow morning," Radic said, perplexed.

Volcker shrugged. "I guess they have other fish to fry."

"Well," Radic said, "that simplifies things on our end. We can set aside the intellectual property stuff for a couple of days and concentrate on the murder."

Volcker nodded. "Anything new?"

"I'm to meet with Pinky Floyd on the warrant in a half hour," Radic replied. "Do you want to come along?"

"Sure thing," Volcker said. "Let me copy the photos for Stilton and then I'm free."

"How is Mulroy doing?" Volcker asked after hopping into the car with Radic.

"Okay, I think," Radic said. "She's seeing a special kind of dentist this afternoon. An orthodontist. Or maybe an oral surgeon. I think there's some question about the kind of dentist she ultimately needs to see."

"She took quite a punch," Volcker said.

"I know," Radic replied.

"She's not having second thoughts about all this, is she?" Volcker asked. "I mean, our business? Being a police officer?"

"No," Radic said. "She's a tough cookie."

"That's my impression, too," Volcker agreed. "But you'd have to be a fool not to think twice about it."

"Have you?" Radic asked. "Thought twice about it?"

"Well, I'm not in homicide," he replied. "So I don't usually see the really rough stuff."

"OK, but missing persons?" Radic probed. "Not exactly a cakewalk."

"Well, there's a lot of anxiety. A lot of worrying," Volcker agreed. "When someone goes missing, their family puts their life on hold until they reappear. And sometimes they don't. It's not easy. You have to get them through it."

"You're good at that," Radic said.

"Most of the time," Volcker said. "But sometimes it's still not enough. Like with Carol Sloan."

CHAPTER FORTY: SECOND THOUGHTS

Radic nodded. "Did you ever think of doing something else?"

"Well, photography. I've sometimes thought about being a photographer."

"And?"

"With more and more smartphones, everybody's a photographer these days," Volcker lamented. "Photos are easy to take and easy to distribute. Why pay somebody else to do it? There's not much of a marketplace left. It's a fun hobby, but it doesn't pay the bills. Besides, I like what I do. I like what WE do. It's important work."

Radic nodded appreciatively. He could not have put it better.

* * *

Mulroy's head was throbbing, but for the first time in a while, it was her temple, not her lower jaw, that was aching. She recognized it as a stress headache and tried to work through it with the help of a couple of Advils and the prospect of some Percocet at night.

She was at her desk at work. She had not been placed on administrative leave. That was a victory. Getting to interrogate Trojanowski was a big deal, and she greatly appreciated it. Both Radic and Stilton had stood up for her. Big time.

She fully understood why Stilton and Radic wanted her working in the office, at least for a few hours a day. She still had doctors' visits, including a mandatory counseling visit, that were hard to reconcile with the fast-paced developments in the case. Radic couldn't work around her schedule.

As for her teeth and her jaw, the oral surgeon was optimistic. There was a hairline fracture to her jaw, but it would heal in time. One tooth, a bicuspid, had already come out, of its own accord. Another would have to be removed shortly, followed by a tooth implant.

It was a long and somewhat unpleasant procedure—lasting many months—but pretty straightforward. Her teeth would look fine, and the new tooth would function fine, the oral surgeon assured her. And, yes, if she wanted to do something about that overbite, he would be happy to oblige.

But none of this was causing her headache. In truth, Mulroy had been unnerved by Trojanowski's knockout punch, by her inability to anticipate it, by her inability to protect herself, and by the feelings of anger she continued to feel afterwards.

She had experienced physical pain and fear at the Police Academy lots of times. She had injured an ankle and dislocated a shoulder during training exercises. She had also come close to being shot, accidentally, by another trainee, who, thankfully, had dropped out of the Academy before he could do any serious damage to himself or others.

Still, she was having troubling thoughts about her vocation. Her mother's words, from years ago, kept intruding: Kathleen, you're intelligent, you're a good person. You're good-looking, and you have lots of friends. Why would you want to become a police officer? You're not big enough. You're not mean enough. You have a gentle spirit. It's just not YOU!

Mulroy brushed these thoughts aside for the time being. They were not very productive. Normally, she would drink a cup of coffee to reboot. But a hot, acidic beverage was not the best remedy for her sensitive gums. She settled instead for a glass of water and turned back to her work.

As the new point guard for all things vehicular related to the Sloan case, Mulroy sifted through daily reports on vehicles—stolen vehicles, damaged vehicles, abandoned vehicles. She scrolled onto the relevant website, looking for matches with Trojanowski's car, now officially missing. No luck.

Next, she looked at the list of names of traffic violators. Nothing jumped out, except the name of a colleague's wife, who had been found guilty of a DUI. Oops! That could be awkward. But none of her business.

Stolen vehicles came next. Nothing obvious here. Unless…Donatelli. Where had she heard that name before? Then she remembered. "Spider" Donatelli. An old friend of Basil's. A Vincent Donatelli had reported a stolen car last night. 10:23 p.m. A 2012 Ford Bronco. The owner lived on the South Side, on Mt. Oliver Street, near St. Michael's Cemetery. Could this be Spider? Well, one easy way to find out.

"Mr. Donatelli, I'm Officer Kathleen Mulroy of the Pittsburgh Police. I'm

CHAPTER FORTY: SECOND THOUGHTS

calling about your stolen car."

"Have you found it?"

"Well, not yet. We're working on it."

"I need that car to get to work. It's very inconvenient not to have it."

"Mr. Donatelli, do you, by any chance, have a nickname?"

"Spider. I got it from one of my tattoos. I run a tattoo parlor."

"Ah, ha. So you know my colleague, Detective Radic."

"Yes, I do. I was thinking of calling him. But he's in homicide, right?"

"Why were you thinking of calling him?"

"Well, because I know him."

"Any other reason?"

"Well, maybe. But I should probably talk with him directly."

"Does it have to do with Basil Vasilikas?"

"Well, I don't know what to say. How do you know about that?"

"We're working together on the Carol Sloan case."

"Oh."

"Mr. Donatelli, if you have any fresh information on Basil Vasilikas, I know that Detective Radic would really like to talk with you about it. And, you know, it might even help us to find your car."

"I don't know."

"Mr. Donatelli, if I were to send someone out to give you a lift, would you be able to give us a fuller report on any dealings you've had with Basil Vasilikas?"

"I don't know. It's complicated."

"It won't take long. And then we can give you a lift to your place of work."

"Well, that would be good. Will Detective Radic be there?"

"I'll make sure he's here."

"Okay."

"I'll send someone to pick you up. It will just be a few minutes."

Mulroy called Volcker, hoping he would be free. He didn't respond. She looked at her watch. She was tethered to the desk. But surely, this was a high priority.

Eager to make progress, she closed her laptop and sent a brief text to

Radic and Volcker explaining the situation. She would pick up Donatelli herself. Hopefully, no one would see her sneaking out the door.

Chapter Forty-One: Legal Niceties

Volcker got the text message from Mulroy before Radic did but couldn't alert his colleague just yet. They were just finishing up with Judge Floyd. "So, what you're saying, your honor, is that we really need two warrants," Radic said.

"I'm sorry to rain on your parade, detective, but yes, that's pretty clear to me," Judge Floyd said. "If you think that a search of Mr. Trojanowski's home will help you to locate either Mr. Vasilikas or Mr. Papadopoulos, who are parties of interest in a murder investigation and a bombing incident, then I can authorize such a search. The same applies to the contents of the car that Mr. Trojanowski was driving."

"On the other hand," he continued, "as an Allegheny County judge, I don't have the authority to help you unravel an intellectual property fraud scheme that crosses state lines. That's the federal government's jurisdiction."

"So do we have to wait for a second search warrant from a federal judge?" Radic asked.

"No, I didn't say that," Judge Floyd said. "You can proceed with your search, but you're going to have to change the language in your warrant and your overall game plan. Look for clues to the whereabouts of your missing persons. Look for evidence that Carol Sloan was there. Look for blood. But if you encounter any mugs or correspondence with the Harry Potter people or correspondence with potential buyers of the illegal merchandise, you can't confiscate those items."

"But we can note what they are and where they are?" Radic asked.

"Yes, you can do that," Judge Floyd said. "But there are limits. If you see a document that's related to Harry Potter mugs, then read enough to be sure that's what it is … but no further."

"And the mail we recovered from Trojanowski?"

"As I understand it, most or all of that is likely to be related to your sting operation, which is the federal part of this case. So the F.B.I. can and should include that in their warrant, but that's not for you. Even if it's addressed to one of the men you're trying to locate. Do we have an understanding?"

"Yes, we do, your honor," Radic replied. "We greatly appreciate it."

"You'll need to rewrite the warrant along the lines we discussed, but I'll approve it quickly," he said.

"Got it," Radic replied. "Will do."

"I'm sympathetic, detective," Floyd said. "I hope you find your man. Or men. But don't pollute the waters for the parallel investigation. The FBI has jurisdiction over the intellectual property stuff. Give them a chance to do their job properly."

"Got it!" Radic said. "Thank you, your honor."

* * *

Spider Donatelli was waiting on his front porch when Mulroy pulled up in a police car. She got out of the vehicle, introduced herself, and invited Donatelli to sit in the front seat.

"What happened to you?" he asked, noticing the puffy lips and the bruises on her jaw.

"A work-related injury," she said.

"You were making an arrest?" he asked.

"Yep," she said.

"Some dudes, when they get high, you never know what they're going to do," he observed.

"Well, this dude wasn't high," she said.

"Oh," he said. "Well, I'm sorry it happened. You seem like a nice lady."

Mulroy smiled. Well, a half smile. Her mouth still wasn't working right. "Thank you," she said.

CHAPTER FORTY-ONE: LEGAL NICETIES

"Will Detective Radic be there?" Donatelli asked.

"He's on his way," she said.

"Good," he said. "He seems like a cool dude."

Mulroy smiled again. "He is," she said.

Mulroy checked her cell phone when they arrived at the station. There was a text from Volcker, five minutes ago: On our way.

She escorted Donatelli into an interview room and asked if he would like a cup of coffee. She got a cup for him, some water for herself, and returned.

"What's it like, giving tattoos to people?" she asked.

"It's great!" he said. "Really. It's like being an artist. Only your canvas is the human body."

"What kinds of tattoos are people asking for these days?" she asked.

"Well, it runs from A to Z," he answered. "Words—love, peace. Animals—a bird, a snake. Weapons—a sword, a gun. More ladies are getting them. Do you have any interest?"

"My Mom would kill me if I got one," she said.

"Well," he smiled, "Only if she knew."

"Besides," she said, "there are other ways to make a statement."

"It's not for everyone," he agreed.

Radic and Volcker arrived moments later. "Spider, it's good to see you again," Radic said, "but I'm sorry to hear about your car."

Donatelli shrugged. "I just hope you're able to find it, man. A businessman without wheels is like…I don't know, a spider without a web."

Radic laughed. "Well, we have a better chance of finding your car than finding your web." Then, more seriously, "Did Officer Mulroy explain why we're eager to speak with you?"

Donatelli nodded. "Because of Vazzy."

"Exactly," Radic said. "Have you seen him since we spoke the other day?"

Donatelli paused before answering. "I haven't seen him, but I did speak with him."

Radic's eyes widened. "Tell us more."

"Two days ago, I heard from Vazzy," he said. "He called me at work. Said he had gotten into some trouble. He asked me to meet him last night."

"Did he say what kind of trouble?" Mulroy asked.

"He said he had gotten into some difficulties because of Stephanos," he answered.

"Did he elaborate?" Mulroy asked.

"No, I thought he'd explain when we met," Donatelli said.

"But you didn't meet?" Radic asked.

"No, I showed up where he asked me to be, last night, at nine o'clock. But he never showed."

"And your car?" Radic asked.

"I waited about fifteen minutes. Then I returned to my car. It wasn't there."

"It just disappeared?" Radic asked.

"It just disappeared."

"Did you leave your keys in your car?" he asked.

"Only a fool would do that," he said. "The car was locked. Someone must have broken into it and hot-wired the ignition."

"Do you think it was Basil?" Mulroy asked.

Donatelli squirmed in his seat. "I don't know, detective. I just don't know. Vazzy is a friend of mine."

"But he might have set you up," Radic said. "Is that what you're thinking?"

"I don't know what to think," Donatelli said. "I just want my car back."

Volcker intervened. "When Basil called you two days ago, did he call your landline or your cell phone?"

"My cell phone," Donatelli said.

Volcker's eyes widened. "Did you try to call him back?"

"No answer," Donatelli said.

"But you have the phone number?" Volcker asked.

"Right here," he said. (412) 555-9214.

Chapter Forty-Two: Loose Ends Day

They were seated at a table in a conference room at police headquarters. Everyone had coffee except for Mulroy, who was sipping water. "I'm officially declaring today Loose Ends Day," Radic announced.

"Say what?" Volcker asked.

"Loose Ends Day," he repeated. "Our friends from the FBI won't be back until tomorrow. We promised that they could interview Trojanowski next, so we have to cool our heels. But that could be a good thing. We have a lot of leads to investigate. I suggest that we pause and make a list, divide up the work, and do as many things as possible before the FBI's shitstorm begins."

"As I see it, we need to put Stephanos and Basil, our main suspects, under a microscope," Radic said. "That means we need to know more about their past, their history, their associates, their mistakes. It means we need to know more about their money, their financial circumstances, and their bank accounts. We need to know more about what makes them tick. So where do we start?"

"Let's start with the money," Volcker suggested. "Can we get access to Stephanos' bank account? Would Judge Floyd approve that?"

"He's nervous about anything that might connect to the FBI's intellectual property investigation," Radic said. "But maybe a federal judge would be receptive to a request, not from us but from the FBI."

"So, get them to include the bank account in their warrant?" Volcker asked.

"I think we have a better shot that way," Radic said.

"And they would share what they find?" Volcker asked.

Radic grimaced. "I can't be certain," he said. "But Stilton would fight hard to get them to share. And they need information from us. It might be a two-way street."

"Okay," Volcker said. "So how about Stephanos' will? Do we know whether Carol is in his will, like he was in hers?"

"That's my bad," Radic said. "It's been on my to-do list for a couple of days. I just haven't gotten around to it."

"I think that qualifies as a loose end," Volcker said. "And an important one."

"I agree," Radic said.

"Have we looked to see whether Basil has an active bank account?" Volcker asked.

"He had one until about a year ago," Radic reported. "But he cleaned it out. One hundred percent. A tidy sum. About 200 grand."

"I don't get it," Volcker said, shaking his head. "He's homeless. But he had $200,000 in the bank?"

"How did we get that information?" Mulroy asked.

Radic looked around the room. "Just between us chickens, it's unofficial. I got that information, confidentially, from a friend at PNC."

No one said a word. "Anything more we can do on that front?" Mulroy asked. "Legally, that is?"

"Well, we can ask all the local banks if Basil has established an account there in recent months. I'm not holding my breath. But you never know."

"He might have used an alias," Mulroy said.

"That's exactly my concern," Radic said.

"But maybe it's part of a pattern," Mulroy said.

"How so?" Radic asked.

"Well," Mulroy said. "We know that Basil borrowed Stephanos' car for a couple of weeks, before he swapped it for Trojanowski's."

"Okay," Radic said.

"What if he also borrowed Stephanos' identity for a while?" she asked.

"Say more," Radic said.

CHAPTER FORTY-TWO: LOOSE ENDS DAY

"I mean, maybe it wasn't Stephanos who talked with Mr. Smith in Chicago. Maybe it was Basil PRETENDING to be Stephanos."

Everyone was silent, considering the possibility. "It makes sense to me," Volcker said, "If I could pretend to be Eliopoulos, Basil could pretend to be Stephanos."

Radic looked pensive, at a loss for words. "What are you thinking?" Mulroy asked.

"I'm thinking that maybe Basil has done this in other situations as well," Radic said slowly. "Remember what the airplane pilot told us the other day? Someone calling himself Stephanos made a reservation for a flight to the Bahamas. He was happy. Someone calling himself Stephanos canceled the reservation. He was like a different person. His exact words. What if he WAS a different person? What if Stephanos made the reservation and Basil, pretending to be Stephanos, canceled it?"

"By God, that might be it!" Volcker said, slamming his fist on the table. "That would explain a lot. We could ask the pilot to listen to the phone calls. He might be able to tell us who called him."

"It's worth a shot," Radic said excitedly. "It's like what Mulroy said the other day about funhouse mirrors. Maybe short is tall. Fat is skinny. And maybe Stephanos is Basil."

"What do we really know about Basil, anyway?" Scuglia asked. "He was in the military. Do we know anything about his record? He received treatment at an addiction clinic, and he's received psychiatric counseling. Can we learn something about that?"

"In my experience, the bar for getting access to medical records and psychiatric records is a pretty high one," Radic said. "But a soldier's military record is different. It's not in our database, but if we link it to a murder investigation, the Pentagon might release it to us. That's a great suggestion, Tony. I wish I had thought of it myself. See what you can find out."

Volcker and Scuglia left to pursue their assignments. Volcker would check in with the local banks. Scuglia would confer with the military.

Chapter Forty-Three: What's in a Blintz?

Harold Gomar was getting a hostile vibe from Fromm & Fogarty. Well, maybe not hostile. An arrogant vibe. Like, who was he to tell them what's what? Like he was some sort of rube from the Midwest, who didn't know his ass from a hole in the ground.

Well, he was the guy who photographed Federov accepting illegal merchandise and who had the presence of mind to put a surveillance camera near his garage in case he made a run for it through the back alley. Which he did.

Gomar was thus able to follow Federov to a warehouse where he deposited the merchandise for safekeeping. Who knows what other ill-gotten gains are stored there? Well, they'll know soon enough, thanks to his heads-up thinking.

Now, they want to fly Federov to Pittsburgh to be interrogated by some police detectives there. Fine. But couldn't they get a U.S. marshall to accompany the guy on the flight to Pittsburgh? Why did it have to be him? And why did it have to be an 8 a.m. flight? Oh well, it's part of the job.

Gomar picked up Federov at an FBI detention center in the Loop at 6 a.m., signed off on some paperwork, handcuffed him, escorted him to his car, and headed to O'Hare. "I'm your chaperone for today!" he said as Federov glowered in his direction.

Federov was sullen at first but started to thaw as Gomar made it clear that he had nothing against Russian immigrants, or Russian businessmen, or Russian food.

An hour later, they were chatting comfortably. "I like strawberry blintzes

CHAPTER FORTY-THREE: WHAT'S IN A BLINTZ?

the best," Federov was saying as they settled into their seats. "If they're in season."

"Of course," Gomar said. "You gotta make sure they're fresh and tasty. What kind of sour cream do you use?"

"I make my own," Federov replied.

"From scratch?" Gomar asked.

"It's very simple," he answered. "I'll tell you."

The plane touched down at 11:15 a.m. By the time Gomar arranged for a rental car, it was nearly lunchtime. Fromm and Fogarty wouldn't be back for another couple of hours. "You know of any good Russian restaurants in Pittsburgh?" Gomar asked.

"Can I use my cell phone to call a friend?" he asked.

"Be my guest," Gomar said, handing him the phone. "So long as you speak English. No Russian. You understand?"

Federov nodded. Forty-five minutes later, they were seated at Kavsar, a Russian restaurant on the South Side. Federov urged Gomar to try some beef stroganoff. Plus some strawberry blintzes. With caviar.

"I don't know about the caviar," Gomar said.

"Try it! You'll love it!" Federov assured him. And he did.

After ordering coffee, Federov thanked Gomar for a truly delicious meal. Then he asked a question: "Am I in serious trouble?"

Gomar nodded.

"Because of the Harry Potter mugs?"

Gomar nodded again. "And because it ties in with a murder investigation."

"Murder!" Federov squealed. "I'm just a businessman. I never committed murder!"

"Well, no one's saying you did," Gomar assured him. "But the stakes are higher than you might have thought."

Federov sat glumly, no longer savoring the sumptuous Russian meal. "Agent Gomar," he asked, "what do you suggest? What should I do?"

Gomar thought about the situation a bit. Normally, he didn't advise suspects. But in this case…

"Vladimir," he said, "If I were in your shoes, I'd try to be as helpful as possible. You're not blameless. But you're not the guy they're after. If you can help identify the guy behind the Harry Potter mugs, and if he turns out to be the murderer, it's bound to help you when it comes to charges. Odds are they'll be grateful."

Federov nodded slowly. "They're beautiful mugs!" he said. "Have you seen them? Do you know the story of Harry Potter?"

"Tell me more, Vladimir," he said. "I started reading one of those books and couldn't put it down. Harry seems like a righteous dude. But his foster parents? They're the worst!"

Chapter Forty-Four: Following the Trail

Scuglia was the first to hit pay dirt. A contact at the Pentagon checked with his superior and got permission to release the record of Basil Vasilikas. It made for interesting reading.

He had enlisted in the U.S. Army at age thirty-three, in 2003. After training for ten weeks at Fort Benning, Georgia, he deployed to the Persian Gulf. While there, he saw combat on several occasions. His commanding officer, a Major Whitby, described him as "intrepid and utterly fearless."

He re-upped for a second tour of duty in 2006. A few months later, he was reprimanded for an altercation with a fellow enlisted man. A scuffle had broken out in the barracks. Afterwards, PFC Raoul Ramirez had to be treated for severe bruises to the shoulders, neck, and face. Vasilikas, the assailant, was placed on administrative leave. Then a few days later Vasilikas was accused of being the ringleader of a black market scheme that included unauthorized transactions with radical Muslims.

Vasilikas received a dishonorable discharge in late 2006. He was found guilty of reckless endangerment, intent to commit mayhem, and financial misconduct. His commanding officer summed up the evidence: "Private Vasilikas has a violent streak, which makes him a fierce soldier in the field but which, sadly, puts other service men and women at risk. He also has shown a reckless disregard for limits on commercial transactions on a military base. He is no longer fit for military service."

A contemporaneous report from a psychiatrist was appended, with terminology that Scuglia did not understand, plus fingerprints, as requested.

Scuglia shook his head as he put away the report. "What a loser!" he muttered to himself.

* * *

Based on Radic's tip, Volcker decided to begin with PNC's bank manager. Volcker explained that they were conducting a murder investigation and that they were checking with local banks to see if Stephanos had an account with them. He did not reveal that he already knew the answer to his own question.

The bank manager acknowledged immediately that Stephanos had an account with them, but he indicated that he could only reveal more if there was a writ from a judge.

Volcker explained that Judge Floyd had already authorized a search of Stephanos' apartment and his place of employment. This carried some weight with the bank manager, who suggested that the police amend the warrant to include his bank account. If approved by Judge Floyd, he would divulge the information.

Radic reached out to Stephanos' lawyer, Cindy McSwigan, who had gotten permission from Dimitri to share the contents of Stephanos' will. According to McSwigan, Stephanos had indeed changed his will, designating Carol Sloan as the lead beneficiary for one of two bank accounts in case of his death. Radic passed that information on to the rest of the team.

He then enlisted Mulroy to join him on a trip to the general aviation airport in West Mifflin. When they arrived, "Mac" McCarthy, in Hangar # 9, was standing beside a Piper Mirage single-engine prop plane with its hood open and was engaged in an animated conversation with another man. "I'm in the middle of an inspection, Detective," he explained. "Could we talk in maybe 30 minutes?"

Radic agreed, eager to have McCarthy's undivided attention. He and Mulroy took refuge in a nearby diner, then returned in 45 minutes. McCarthy was much more relaxed.

"Sorry about that, Detective, Officer," he said. "I need to get my plane inspected after every 100 hours of air time. Otherwise, the FAA won't allow

CHAPTER FORTY-FOUR: FOLLOWING THE TRAIL

me to fly."

"How did it go?" Mulroy asked.

"Just fine," he said. "I'm good to go. So, how can I help you?"

Radic explained that they needed help to confirm the identity of whoever called to reserve the flight to the Bahamas and later canceled it. "I'm going to share some highly sensitive phone calls with you," he said. "You are not to disclose what they contain to anyone under any circumstances."

McCarthy's expression became more serious. "Understood," he replied.

Radic decided to start with Stephanos, playing the call that revealed the bomb in the Sewickley Unitarian Church. "Do you recognize the voice?" he asked.

"Yes, I do," he said. "That's the guy who called."

"Okay, next, I have a call from someone else." This time, he played the first call from Basil.

"Do you recognize that voice?" he asked.

Now McCarthy was confused. And he said so.

"Let me play both of them again," Radic suggested. And he did.

"What do you think?" he asked.

"Okay," McCarthy said. "The man who made the reservation was your first caller. A younger man. He sounded much happier then. We had a good conversation. But he's the guy."

"And the second man?" Radic asked.

"Well, he's older, more serious," he replied. "Now that I think about it, he might have been the one who called to cancel the reservation. He wasn't on the phone that long, so I can't be absolutely sure. But the second guy might have conned me into thinking he was someone else. It's definitely possible."

"Thank you very much, Mr. McCarthy," Radic said. "We appreciate it."

"What happened to the first guy?" he asked. "The one who was going to the Bahamas with his girlfriend?"

"That's what we're trying to find out," Radic said.

"And the second guy?"

"We're trying to figure that out, too," he said.

TOO MANY BRIDGES

* * *

After checking in with Radic, Scuglia reached the M.E. "Saroja, have you finished your report on the Papadopoulos home?" he asked.

"Just about," Prakash said. "I hope to write something up this afternoon."

"Well, before you do, we have a new set of prints we'd like you to consider," he said.

"From whom?" she asked.

"Basil Vasilikas," he said.

"You've caught him?" she asked.

"No, we should be so lucky," he said. "But we have his prints."

"I thought Radic said he wasn't in the system," she said.

"Well, he's not in our system," Scuglia explained. "But he is in the military's."

"Ah, ha," she said. "Got it. Okay. Bring them in, and I'll check them against what I have. Then I'll write up the report."

* * *

That evening, Radic was dog-tired and out of sorts. He hadn't exercised in a few days. His refrigerator was nearly empty. He had no social life. But he needed to amend the search warrant for Judge Floyd. He needed to read a new e-mail from the M.E. He needed to touch base with the FBI to set the stage for tomorrow's interrogation. As usual, there was too much on his plate.

Radic had nearly completed the warrant when he got a call from Gloria.

"Branko, how are you doing?" she asked, sounding a bit tipsy.

"Gloria, I'm surprised to hear from you," he said. "Are you okay?"

"Branko, I think I made a big mistake," she said. "I miss you. I want to see you."

Radic straightened up in his chair, searching for the right words. "Gloria, you didn't make a mistake. You were right. My job is twenty-four/seven. In fact, I'm working on stuff right now. We should go our separate ways."

CHAPTER FORTY-FOUR: FOLLOWING THE TRAIL

"But I miss you!" she exclaimed, bursting into tears.

"Now, Gloria, don't do that," he said. "It's for the best. You know that. And I know it, too. It just took me a while to realize it."

"Are you seeing someone else?" she asked.

"That's not the point," he said. "The point is that you deserve someone who can give you his undivided attention. And that's not me."

"I guess I shouldn't have called," she said. "You've hardened your heart. Don't worry, you won't hear from me again." Then she hung up.

Radic stood up and paced around his apartment, angry but not sure whether he was angry with Gloria or with himself. Gloria had a way of getting under his skin, of making him feel callous and shallow. Well, he wasn't. He had to remember that. Besides, Gloria didn't know her own mind. Tomorrow, in the light of day, she could easily have a different opinion.

He needed to get back to work. But he also needed to get his personal life in order. This was no way to live. On an impulse, he picked up the phone.

"Lexie, it's Branko Radic. How are you doing?"

"Hi Branko, nice to hear from you. How's Damon doing?"

"He's fine," he said. "He really enjoyed the boat trip. It was very nice of you to do that."

"He's a very sweet boy. I'd be happy to do it again."

"Well, I'm sure he'd love that."

"Hey, I heard that Mulroy got banged up pretty bad the other day. Is she okay?"

"Well, she's still sore, and she's going to need some dental surgery."

"Ouch!"

"But she's going to be fine. And she's back at work."

"Good. Maybe I'll give her a call."

"I'm sure she'd appreciate that. Hey, I was wondering if you might like to go out to dinner some night?"

There was only a brief pause. "Sure, Branko, I'd enjoy that."

"The next couple of days are going to be pretty crazy," he said. "How about Friday night?"

"Perfect," she said. "Are you thinking pirate food? Fish and chips?"

Radic laughed. "Well, I think we can do a bit better than that. Do you like Thai food?"

"I LOVE Thai food!" she said.

"I know a place. You'll like it, I think. Shall we say 6:30?"

"Perfect," she said.

"If you give me your address, I can pick you up then."

Radic returned to his work in a far better frame of mind. He finished up at 11:15 p.m., went to bed, and quickly fell asleep.

Chapter Forty-Five: Taking the Fifth

Radic was looking forward to the next session with Trojanowski with mixed emotions. He was eager to hear directly from Trojanowski what he knew about Basil and Stephanos. After all, he had worked closely with both of them. Recently too.

On the other hand, Radic knew that this round belonged to the FBI. He did not look forward to being a potted plant, though he knew that was exactly what was expected of him. Well, he could play that role if he had to.

Fromm and Fogarty were in their usual quarrelsome mood when he greeted them at headquarters. They had flown in from Chicago the night before after a two-hour delay at O'Hare. Not happy campers.

Apparently, another FBI agent from Chicago was babysitting Vladimir Federov (aka Mr. Smith) in a holding cell nearby. With luck, they would get around to him later in the day.

As before, Trojanowski and his lawyer were escorted into an interview room. Volcker set up the equipment and fetched coffee. Then Fromm, Fogarty, Radic, and Mulroy entered the room. Stilton and Volcker remained outside.

Radic motioned to Fromm to do the honors. Fromm announced the cast of characters for the tape and began his interrogation.

Immediately, Hirsch, the attorney, interrupted the proceedings. "Mr. Fromm, I think I should tell you that my client will be pleading the Fifth unless and until we receive assurances from the U.S. Attorney and the district attorney that they will exercise appropriate prosecutorial discretion if my client cooperates."

Fromm looked like he was ready to burst a blood vessel. "Do you realize how serious the federal charges against your client are, Mr. Hirsch?" he asked. "Your client is facing multiple charges and what could easily be a long prison sentence."

"My client is fully aware of the situation, I can assure you," Hirsch said. "In fact, that's precisely why my client is exercising his constitutional rights."

"You don't know who you're messing with, pal," Fromm said, looking very irritated.

Sensing that things might be heading south, Radic intervened. "Agent Fromm, might I suggest that you and I hear Mr. Hirsch out privately before we resume the interrogation?"

Fromm looked at Fogarty, not sure of his next step. Fogarty thought for a moment and then nodded.

Shaking his head in exasperation, Fromm spoke into the mic: "We are suspending the interview of Mr. Trojanowski, on the advice of his counsel, at 9:03 a.m." Fromm, Radic and Hirsch departed. Stilton escorted them to an unoccupied room down the hall and left them to it.

"This had better be good," Fromm grumbled.

"It WILL be good, I assure you," Hirsch said with a smile: "Agent Fromm, Detective Radic, my client, is prepared to give you valuable information in return for favorable consideration. Let me cover the essential points: First, my client will give you the checking account number and password of Stephanos Papadopoulos. He will also give you a summary of all deposits into that account over the past two weeks. Second, my client will tell you in specific terms who was involved in sending 5,000 mugs to Mr. Smith in Chicago and under what circumstances. Third, my client will give you a complete list of additional clients who have expressed an interest in obtaining mugs. Fourth, my client will give you a comprehensive list of all mail he picked up at PO Box 322 over the past two weeks."

"And in return?" Fromm asked.

"In return, we ask that all local charges against my client be dropped, because he was acting at the behest of his employer. We will cooperate with the federal investigation. At the conclusion of that investigation, we

CHAPTER FORTY-FIVE: TAKING THE FIFTH

propose a sentence of six months in a work-release facility."

Fromm snorted. "That's it?" he asked.

"Those are our conditions," Hirsch replied.

Fromm turned to Radic, who suggested that they confer in private, which they did.

"What are you thinking?" Radic asked.

"I just hate to see this bastard walk, which is roughly what Hirsch is proposing," Fromm said.

"I agree," Radic said. "Also, he's giving us some stuff we don't really need and not giving us stuff we desperately need."

"Say more," Fromm said.

"Well, we already know who's been sending letters to PO Box 322 over the past two weeks."

"Right."

"Plus, we're about to get court approval to look at Stephanos' bank accounts—not just the checking account, but the savings account as well. I just dropped off a revised warrant at Judge Floyd's chambers early this morning."

"I didn't know about the banking accounts," Fromm said. "That's good news."

"I have a more basic problem with Hirsch's offer, though," Radic said. "It doesn't really help us to find either of our principal suspects. And it doesn't help us to determine who killed Carol Sloan."

Fromm got the point. "What do you suggest?"

"We need three things," Radic said. "First, we need to know how to find Basil. Maybe Trojanowski doesn't know exactly where he is. But he knows a hell of a lot more about Basil's habits than we do. He might be able to help us. Second, we need a fuller explanation of who had access to the PFOA, which was used to kill Carol Sloan. I strongly suspect that Trojanowski knows more than he's saying about that. Third, we need to question him about the Hermione Granger costume."

"The what?" Fromm asked.

"It wasn't released to the press, and Trojanowski may not know about

211

it, but before Carol Sloan was buried, she was dressed up as one of the leading characters in the Harry Potter books. Hermione Granger, wizard extraordinaire. We don't know if Basil or Stephanos did that. Trojanowski might have seen something relevant that points us to the killer."

Fromm responded less defensively than before. "What do you want to do?"

"Give me a chance to up the ante with Hirsch. If he's willing to give us more information, I'm okay with the reduced sentence for the federal crime. And I can live with dropping some of the local charges. But not ALL of the charges. He assaulted a police officer. He hurt her badly. There's no way we're going to drop that charge, and that's got to involve some additional jail time. But I'm willing to drop the other local charges. If my boss agrees, of course."

"I'll need to get approval, too," Fromm acknowledged.

"Okay," Radic said. "Let me make the case to Hirsch. If he agrees to give us more, then you and I can take the next steps. With luck, you can speak to the U.S. attorney, and I can speak to the D.A. today or tomorrow."

Fromm nodded. "Let's do it," he said. "Let's get these bastards!"

"Agreed," Radic said.

Hirsch was noncommittal after hearing Radic out. He asked to confer with his client alone. Then, he reported that his client would need additional time to think things over. Radic and Fromm agreed to sound out the two prosecutors in case Trojanowski said yes. They all agreed to meet again the following morning.

"Shall we bring in Mr. Smith?" Fromm suggested.

"Why not?" Radic said. Then, with a touch of irony in his voice: "It could be the perfect ending to the perfect day."

* * *

Gomar got the word that the FBI and the PBP were ready to interview Vladimir Federov. "Can I sit in?" he asked.

"We already have too many people inside," Fromm said. "But you can

CHAPTER FORTY-FIVE: TAKING THE FIFTH

watch."

The ground rules changed once the interview began. "I'm not willing to say anything unless Agent Gomar is present," Federov said.

Fromm looked at Fogarty. Fogarty looked at Radic, who shrugged. "Agent Gomar?" Fromm yelled in the direction of the camera. "Your presence is requested in the interrogation room."

Gomar did his best to suppress a grin. He wasn't sure that a vote of confidence from a suspected felon was a feather in his cap. But if it got him inside, why not?

After the preliminaries, Fromm got down to brass tacks: "Mr. Federov," he said. "Did you purchase five thousand Harry Potter mugs from a Mr. Eliopoulos earlier this month?"

"Yes, I did," he said.

"Did you realize at the time that this transaction was illegal?"

"No, I did not," he said.

"How can that be, Mr. Federov?" he asked. "If you thought this was a legal purchase, then why did you masquerade as Mr. Smith?"

"It was clear from the outset that Mr. Papadopoulos viewed this sale as a private sale, for special customers only," he said. "It was also clear that he wanted the transaction to be hush-hush. I simply responded in kind."

"What led you to believe that the transaction was to be hush-hush, as you put it?" Fromm asked.

"In our initial conversation, Mr. Papadopoulos said that he wanted to corner the market before other suppliers learned about the sale of the mugs. He also indicated that there were some disagreements within the firm as to when the mugs should be sold."

"The firm being?"

"Dimitri's Sturdy Dishes."

"Did he elaborate on what the disagreements within the firm were about?"

"No, he did not."

"Have you used an alias, before, Mr. Federov?"

"Not normally," he said. "But under unusual circumstances, if I'm really interested in a certain product, I do what needs to be done."

"Even if it's against the law?" Fromm asked.

"As I say, Agent Fromm, I had no reason to believe that these transactions were illegal. All I knew was that there were certain steps I needed to take in order to obtain the merchandise. I'm a simple businessman, Agent Fromm. If a vendor tells me to pay by check, I pay by check. If a vendor tells me to send my check to a certain address, I send it to that address. If a vendor tells me to call him on his private line, I call him on his private line. The vendor determines the terms of the sale. Not me."

"Do you seriously expect us to believe that you had no suspicions that these transactions were illegal?" Fromm asked.

"Suspicions? I sometimes have suspicions. When I make a purchase at a pawn shop, I may wonder about where the merchandise came from. When I make a purchase from a brand new firm, I may wonder whether they have fully complied with OSHA requirements, EPA requirements, FTC requirements. But Dimitri's is a good business with a good reputation. Whatever suspicions I might have with other firms, I didn't have them in this case."

"You're a smooth talker, Mr. Federov, I'll give you that," Fromm said. "Have you reported these purchases to the IRS?"

"As I'm sure you're aware, Agent Fromm, I only need to report my purchases and my sales at the end of the calendar year," he said. "Have you reported YOUR recent purchases to the IRS?"

"That will be enough of that," Fromm said, increasingly frustrated.

Mulroy raised her hand. "Agent Fromm, is it okay with you if I pursue a related line of questioning?" she asked.

Fromm was about to object. Then he looked at Mulroy's swollen jaw, her crooked smile, and the Kleenex she was using to dab her mouth. "Yes, Officer Mulroy, you may do that," he said.

"Thank you, Agent Fromm," she said.

"Mr. Federov," she said, "how many times have you spoken with Stephanos Papadopoulos by phone?"

"Twice," he replied. "First, when he called me to let me know about these wonderful mugs. And second, when I called him to place my order."

CHAPTER FORTY-FIVE: TAKING THE FIFTH

"Very good," she said. "And how would you describe his voice?"

"I'm sorry," he said. "I'm not sure I understand the question."

"Would you say that he was young or old? Well-educated or not well-educated? Friendly or serious? Chatty or to the point?"

Federov looked at Gomar, who simply nodded.

"Okay, well, I'd say that he sounded middle-aged. He didn't use fancy words, but he seemed intelligent. He was on the serious side. He had a good product to sell. He didn't need to go through any sort of song and dance. What's the expression? He had me at hello."

"Mr. Federov, if I were to play a tape for you, would you be able to tell us whether it's the voice of the person you recognize as Stephanos Papadopoulos?"

He looked at Gomar, who nodded.

"Okay, I can do that," he said.

Mulroy played the tape alerting the PBP to the presence of a bomb at the Sewickley Unitarian Church.

Federov was visibly shaken. "I don't know anything about a bomb," he said. "That's terrible. Just terrible. No one should ever do such a thing."

"Thank you for that sentiment, Mr. Federov, but please answer my question," Mulroy said. "Is that the voice of Stephanos Papadopoulos?"

"No, it is not," he said.

"You're sure?"

"Yes, I'm sure."

"One more tape for you, Mr. Federov, if that's okay?"

Federov looked at Gomar, who nodded again. Then she played the tape telling the police that a murder had occurred.

"Do you recognize that voice, Mr. Federov?" she asked.

Federov swallowed. "A murder. How horrible! I have nothing to do with that. I would never get involved in such a thing."

"We appreciate that," Mulroy said. "But what can you tell us about the caller's identity?"

"That's Stephanos Papadopoulos," he said. "I'm sure of it. That's the man who sold me the Harry Potter mugs."

215

Chapter Forty-Six: Say Ah!

Mulroy was feeling good about the case. Basil, the eyewitness, was morphing into Basil, the master criminal. Someone who assumed his nephew's identity, usurped his authority and expropriated his car. Ostensibly, with Stephanos' permission, to sell mugs while he was away. But, more likely, without Stephanos' approval, since it was doubtful that Stephanos had gone anywhere. Clearly, the case was moving in a different direction, with Basil as the prime suspect. Things were looking up.

But Mulroy's jaw was throbbing. It hurt to eat. It hurt to brush her teeth. She would need to take a Percocet to sleep, even if it made her drowsy tomorrow.

She checked her email. Radic had gotten a report from Prakash, identifying fingerprints from four people in Stephanos' home: Stephanos, Dimitri, Carol Sloan, and Basil Vasilikas. The last set of prints, according to Prakash, was found in multiple rooms and were fresh. It almost looked like Basil had been crashing in Stephanos' apartment. How could we not have noticed?

Scuglia also had an interesting finding to report. He called the number Donatelli had given them…and got a recorded message from none other than Jim Trojanowski. Her nemesis! Which could mean that Basil had borrowed the guy's car AND his phone. Or that he and Basil were connected to this case like Siamese twins. Mulroy was starting to feel drowsy, thanks to the Percocet. She shut her laptop and soon fell asleep.

When Mulroy awakened, at 6:30 a.m., she did not feel good at all. She

CHAPTER FORTY-SIX: SAY AH!

was still sleepy, and her jaw still hurt. As much as she hated to do it, she was going to have to call in sick. At 8:01 a.m. she called her oral surgeon and made an appointment for later in the day. She alerted Radic and Stilton. She ate some applesauce and, with difficulty, a piece of toast. Then she took a couple of Advil and went back to bed.

* * *

Radic tracked down a senior assistant DA and summarized the case in person, with as many nuances as possible. It helped that Judge Floyd had already highlighted some of the trickier legal issues, which he wove into his narrative. The assistant DA, Jonathan Grimaldi, was sympathetic and thought his boss would be too. He promised to talk with the DA later in the day and call back.

Meanwhile, Fromm had reached out to an assistant U.S. attorney, who was intrigued. A self-described Potterhead, he was eager to prosecute someone who was violating J.K. Rowling's intellectual property rights. "We just need to figure out who we're prosecuting first," he said. "The best way to do that is to get a plea bargain from Trojanowski," Fromm argued. "Okay," the deputy U.S. attorney said, "let me make the case to my boss."

Mulroy reawakened at 11:30 a.m., just in time for another painful meal. Dutifully, she retrieved her trusty jar of applesauce. She couldn't face another piece of toast, so she made herself some oatmeal, let it cool off a bit, and then ate it slowly. She also tried a piece of cheddar cheese, which didn't do her any harm. Mission accomplished, she said to herself.

Noticing the time, Mulroy decided she'd better head to the dentist's office. She put her laptop in a satchel and headed out the door.

At the dentist's, she was treated with great courtesy by the staff, who seemed to know her back story. A technician took X-rays, trying hard not to hurt her. She also gave her something medicinal to gargle with. Then she told her to wait. Dr. Kim would be with her shortly.

Mulroy opened up her laptop and visited her new favorite website, with everything you always wanted to know about Pittsburgh vehicles. She was starting to nod off when she noticed a familiar name—Vincent Donatelli. "Whoa!"

She straightened up in her chair and took a closer look. Donatelli's car had been spotted by an airport security officer. It was illegally parked in a tow-away zone, not far from the United Airlines ticket counter. The officer had the presence of mind to remove it to a safe location at the Greater Pitt airport and to leave his name and phone number.

"How are you doing, Officer Mulroy?" Dr. Kim asked. Mulroy was startled. She had almost forgotten where she was.

"Excuse me, doctor," she said, "but could I send a quick e-mail before we begin? It's kind of important."

"Of course," he said with a smile. "I need to look at your X-rays anyway. Go right ahead."

Mulroy texted Radic: "Spider's car found at Greater Pitt. Call (412) 555-6428. Ask for Paul Tabor."

"Okay, doc," she said when the doctor returned. "I'm all yours!"

After looking at the X-rays and checking Mulroy's mouth, Dr. Kim gave her a report: "Well," he said, "I have good news and bad news. The good news is your jaw fracture is no worse. In fact, it's healing nicely. The bad news is that your gums are pretty inflamed. That probably means that you have an infection. Not unusual in cases like this. So, I'm going to put you on antibiotics immediately. Hopefully, it will work its magic in a few days. Then we can take another look."

Mulroy grunted. "I know, I know. It's a setback," Dr. Kim said. "It's no fun. But I'm pretty sure the antibiotics will clear this up."

"It hurts to eat," Mulroy said. "Any suggestions?"

"Do you like Lebanese food?" he asked. "Hummos and pita bread. Maybe some stuffed grape leaves as well. All at room temperature. And, of course, some applesauce."

Mulroy laughed. "I'm already well acquainted with applesauce," she said. "But Lebanese sounds great. I'll get some on my way home."

* * *

CHAPTER FORTY-SIX: SAY AH!

Spider Donatelli's Ford Bronco got more attention in one afternoon than it had received over its previous ten years. With Donatelli's consent, police technicians proceeded to collect prints from every visible surface and lots of invisible surfaces, too.

They checked out the trunk and found nothing except some old copies of Tattoo Society magazine, a handful of tattoo needles, a Pueblo blanket, and a cooler with nothing in it but grime and mold. They checked out the glove compartment and found assorted papers, a pack of Life Savers, and a V.F.W. card.

After an initial scan, prints were rushed to Saroja Prakash, who agreed to make them a high priority. Donatelli, naturally, wanted to know when he would be getting his car back. "Sometime soon," Radic assured him and hoped it was true.

Radic and Fromm both got encouraging reports from their respective prosecutors. The D.A.'s office was reassuring—if Trojanowski offered credible evidence on who the killer was and how to find him, they would drop most charges against him, except assaulting a police officer. The U.S. Attorney's office included more caveats in its response. If Trojanowski clearly identified the mastermind behind the Muggles scheme and helped them to reel in several customers who knowingly purchased illegal goods, they could live with a year in federal prison. Fromm thought that Hirsch would bite.

Vladimir Federov's fate depended on how many other customers were caught up in the net and his willingness to identify Basil Vasilikas as the vendor in a federal trial. Since he was not yet represented by counsel, they were less concerned about him at the moment.

**

Saroja Prakash was true to her word. Within hours, she called Radic to report two matches from her fingerprint analysis.

"One set belongs to the owner," she said. "Vincent Donatelli. His prints are all over the car."

"And the other?" Radic asked.

"The other is Basil Vasilikas," she said. "His prints are on the steering wheel, the gear shift, and the ignition. Also, the door handle to the driver's side of the car."

"Not the trunk?" Radic asked.

"Not the trunk," she replied.

"Well, we don't think he had a key," Radic said. "So all of that makes sense."

"What's your conclusion?" Prakash asked.

"It's not good," Radic said. "It looks like Vasilikas stole the car, abandoned it at Greater Pitt, and headed off into the wild blue yonder."

"Disappointing," Prakash said. "You were so close."

"We're checking with the airlines to confirm," Radic said. "So far, no hits."

"A fake ID?" she asked.

"Always possible," he said. "Even with today's security."

"Well, let me know if I can help with anything else," she said.

"I will," Radic said. "But you've already been a big help."

Radic needed a few minutes to collect his thoughts. With lots of help from Mulroy, Volcker, Scuglia, and, yes, even the FBI, he had broken the case wide open. They had evidence pointing to a new suspect and, if Trojanowski agreed to squeal, additional evidence to put him behind bars.

But now, it seemed, their prime suspect had left town. Destination unknown. Probably with a fair amount of cash. And Stephanos? Dimitri's only son and the apple of his eye? They had no idea where he was or whether he was in league with Basil. Were they looking for a hardened criminal, a reluctant co-conspirator, or another victim?

At times like this, Radic couldn't help but think about Petra, whose killer had never been brought to justice. It filled him with rage.

He thought of his own parents, who would never hear their daughter's laughter again. He thought of Carol Sloan's parents, who seemed so kind and so devoted to their little girl.

He wondered what he could possibly do next. What could he tell his team to give them hope? The FBI's intellectual property case was moving right along. But his murder investigation had stalled. Somehow, he had to think

CHAPTER FORTY-SIX: SAY AH!

of a new angle. Somehow, he had to reboot.

Chapter Forty-Seven: Lost but Not Found

It was hard to distinguish between night and day without a watch and without windows. Hunger was a clue. If he got really hungry, it meant, probably, that several hours had passed.

Perhaps it was his imagination, but he also detected a faint hint of sunlight for hours at a time. For the time being, he was defining that as day and everything else as night.

Occasionally, but rarely, he thought he detected voices. In his head? In real life? They were always muffled, never nearby. But at least they offered some hope. Assuming they were real.

It had taken him quite a while to get even a rough sense of his surroundings. At first, he was too drowsy to think straight or to think at all. Drugs, no doubt. Gradually, he became more aware of his environment and his predicament.

One thing for sure: he was near a body of water. But what type? A river? A stream? A lake? A sewer? Maybe he was in a culvert near the Monongahela River. That would make sense.

It was cold much of the time. He had blankets; thank God for that. And he had food and water. Nothing fancy but enough to get by. Bread. Peanut butter. Dry cereal. Occasional sandwiches. Sometimes carrots or beans.

What he didn't have was mobility. His right foot was manacled and connected to an iron bolt attached to the floor. Only a blacksmith could have pried it loose.

CHAPTER FORTY-SEVEN: LOST BUT NOT FOUND

A thick rope approximately ten feet long permitted him to reach a makeshift commode. The stench of his own waste was overpowering at times. Fearful though he was of another visit from his captor, he hoped that he would return. At least the commode would be emptied out.

Stephanos thought back to how suddenly the situation had spiraled out of control. The Harry Potter mugs had seemed like a splendid idea. Like his uncle Basil, Stephanos believed in taking chances, in thinking boldly. He authorized the production of prototypes, which turned out surprisingly well.

But he drew a line in the sand after that. Carol was adamant that he would be putting his father's company at risk if he manufactured and sold large numbers of "muggles" without prior authorization from the Harry Potter folks. He sided with her and not with Basil.

That seemed to settle things at first. But Basil had already set the wheels in motion to do much more than that, using his own nest egg or private funding from investors whose identity was never revealed. He had manufactured thousands of mugs without approval from Stephanos or his father. And he wanted to sell them on the black market.

"I can't put the genie back in the bottle," Basil had said. "What's done is done. We have no choice but to move forward."

Stephanos was firm. "I can't do that, Basil. It wouldn't be legal. It wouldn't be fair to my father. It wouldn't be right for the firm."

"It's that bitch," Basil said, his voice thick with contempt. "She has you wrapped around her little finger."

"I make up my own mind," Stephanos said.

"Then choose," Basil said. "It's me…or her!"

Stephanos said, frankly, that the choice was easy. Even if there were no legal or moral concerns, Carol was more than his accountant and more than just a friend. She was now his fiancée.

Basil was livid. "You're marrying that whore?" he fumed.

"We fly to the Bahamas tomorrow," he said. "We'll announce our wedding plans when we return."

Stephanos had seen Basil angry before, but never this angry. His rage was volcanic. His eyes bulged, his face turned beet red, and he started sputtering.

"How could you?" he said. "You've ruined me! How could you?"

"No, Basil," he said. "You've ruined yourself. My father and I have both tried to help you, to work with you. Again and again. But you've repaid our kindness with resentment and reckless behavior. My father was right about you. You're a ticking time bomb. Well, I'm not willing to let you destroy my life or my father's company. You're on your own!"

In retrospect, that speech was the match that lit the fire. Basil tackled him, punched him repeatedly in the face, and probably hit him with some sort of blunt instrument, at which point he must have lost consciousness. His scalp was still sore from that blow.

The precise sequence of events after that was blurry. He had a dim recollection of being back in his own bed, but groggy and unable to move. After that—a day, a few days, a week?—he was moved to his current location, though he couldn't remember how.

Incredibly, things got even worse. Apparently, Basil had kidnapped Carol. Poor, innocent Carol. So sweet, so gentle, so loving. Who knows what he did to her? And then, according to Basil, she was dead. Just like that. Basil claimed it was suicide. An overdose of sleeping pills. But Stephanos was not that gullible. If Carol was dead, it was certain that Basil had killed her.

For a while, Stephanos held out hope that Basil's story was just a ruse—a lie aimed at convincing him to sign off on the production and sale of thousands of muggles. But a *Post-Gazette* article, furnished by Basil, made two things crystal clear: Carol had, in fact, been murdered…and Stephanos, inexplicably, was suspected of having committed the crime.

Showing no mercy, Basil then planted a bomb in the Sewickley church where Carol's funeral was being held. Exactly why was unclear. At this point, he was acting like a lunatic. Totally unhinged, obsessed with the mugs, ranting and raving, hell-bent on making a profit and vindicating himself. Minutes from detonation, Basil demanded that Stephanos call the police and let them know about the bomb. Stephanos refused, suspecting that Basil would use the call to shift blame for the bomb. But Basil taunted him with the knowledge that Carol's family was in danger and informed

CHAPTER FORTY-SEVEN: LOST BUT NOT FOUND

him that Dimitri was there as well. To protect his father and Carol's parents, Stephanos would have to comply. Reluctantly, he made the call.

It was beginning to dawn on Stephanos that he had to make a move and make it quickly. Somehow, he had to escape from this prison, wherever it was. But how?

Basil was a formidable foe. He was tough and strong. Even without being manacled, Stephanos would be at a disadvantage. Basil had a reputation for getting into fights and winning them. In a fight, he would be mean, vicious. Stephanos would suffer a severe beating unless he handled it just right.

Was there a chance that Stephanos could appeal to Basil's better nature? Any possibility of rekindling an uncle's love for his nephew? Any chance to appeal to his decency, his humanity? Once upon a time, yes. But now? At best, it was a long shot. In all probability, that ship had sailed.

Well, maybe he could bargain with him. Basil wanted cash, and Stephanos had plenty of it. Under duress, he had given Basil the password to his checking account. Thus far, he had not given him access to his savings account. Would that be a tempting offer? His life for $300,000 or $400,000 in cash? But how could he guarantee that Basil would keep his end of the bargain?

The more he thought about the possibilities, the more he returned to his original idea. A fight. But not a fight to the finish, which he would surely lose. A ruse, a trick. To gain what? Time? Keys?

And then a thought occurred to him. Did Basil carry a cell phone with him? If he could stun him and disable him for just a minute, he could use his phone to call 911 and get the operator to trace the call. Basil would be extremely upset when he recovered. He might even try to kill him. But maybe, just maybe, he would flee if he thought the police were on their way.

This line of thinking led Stephanos to search for something resembling a weapon. Something to catch Basil by surprise. To even the odds. Something sharp or hard.

Chapter Forty-Eight: Into Thin Air

Flight attendants are harder to track down than airline ticketing clerks. But flight attendants get better, longer looks at passengers than clerks do, who simply watch customers for three seconds as they place their tickets onto a scanner. Volcker focused on them after assuring himself that no one named Basil Vasilikas had boarded a recent flight.

His goal was to talk with key flight attendants in person, so he could share Vazzy's sketch and gauge their reactions. He began by reaching out to flight attendants from any airline with a Miami-bound flight on the day Donatelli's car was discovered at Greater Pitt. Miami seemed an obvious choice, since that was Trojanowski's destination. The relationship between Trojanowski and Vasilikas remained murky, but there was a good chance they were connected at the hip.

Over the course of two days, Volcker was able to speak with four of five flight attendants. All of them said categorically that Vasilikas had not been on the Miami flight. "How can you be sure?" Volcker asked. "Because he's kind of scary-looking," one of them answered. "He's the kind of guy you notice."

Volcker broadened his search to all United flights on the day in question. Trojanowski had booked a flight through United. Why not Vasilikas?

For such a large number of flights, he needed a different strategy. Working through United's Pittsburgh manager, he sent emails to all the relevant flight attendants stating that the PBP needed information on the gentleman in question (sketch attached). Of 16 emails, he got two hits: one said he might

CHAPTER FORTY-EIGHT: INTO THIN AIR

have been on a flight to Dallas, another said he might have been on a flight to Chicago.

Volcker zeroed in on the two maybes and took a close look at all the middle-aged males on the two flights. One of them was wanted for a crime but was clearly a long-time Chicago resident. Volcker passed the information along to the Chicago PD with his compliments. Another passenger did indeed look like Vazzy, based on a photo ID, but he turned out to be a fine, upstanding citizen, a Lions Club Man of the Year from Fort Worth.

All in all, it was a slow, tedious process. Stilton was growing impatient. Even Radic, normally so understanding, was bugging him twice a day for updates.

After four days, Volcker reached a sad conclusion: Basil Vasilikas had left Pittsburgh, but his destination was unknown. The trail was cold.

* * *

While the search for Basil was underway, Radic was following up on other leads. Thanks to Dimitri, he had the name of one of Stephanos' closest friends. Doug Howley had been in China on a business trip for several days. Now, back in Pittsburgh, he was ready to talk with the police.

Radic and Howley met for coffee near Market Square at 10:30 a.m. Howley knew from an early newspaper article that Stephanos was missing and possibly in trouble, but he did not know about the church bombing and was very surprised to hear that Stephanos was somehow involved.

Radic asked him to start from the beginning: how did he first meet Stephanos, and when?

"We met in third grade," he recalled. "My family had been living in Zelionople. My dad got a job in Pittsburgh, and I found myself attending a strange grade school in a strange community. I had left lots of friends behind, so it was a difficult time for me. I was miserable."

"And Stephanos?" Radic asked.

"He went out of his way to make me feel welcome," he said. "He invited me to his home for dinner, and we became good friends. He was very kind to me. And he was fun to be with."

Radic nodded. "And you've kept up with him since then?" he asked.

"Absolutely!" Howley said. "We played football together in high school. I was a wide receiver. Stephanos was an offensive tackle. He looked out for me on and off the field."

"Did you keep in touch in college?" Radic asked.

"Pretty much. We both went to Pitt. And we both majored in business. Stephanos was already being groomed for his dad's pots and pans business. I was more interested in international finance. We took different courses. But we went to ball games and movies now and then. We double-dated once or twice. We hung out together when we could."

"Did you ever meet Stephanos' Uncle Basil?" he asked.

Howley sighed. "I saw he was mentioned in the newspaper. Yeah, I met Basil a few times, and I heard about him a lot from Stephanos."

"What were your impressions?" Radic asked.

"He was a Dr. Jekyll-Mr. Hyde sort of a guy. One minute, he might be warm and friendly. The next minute, he might be on your case about something. Then he could be snide and sarcastic."

"How would you describe Stephanos' relationship with Basil?" Radic asked.

"Well, it was complicated. It changed over time."

"How so?" Radic asked.

"When I first met Stephanos, it was Uncle Basil this and Uncle Basil that. They were VERY close. Then Basil went off to Iraq. And when he returned … well, I don't know. I was just a kid, but I sensed that something was different. Something bad had happened, though I never heard what."

"What did Stephanos say about the situation?"

"He said Uncle Basil is having a hard time; we're trying to help him. Basil was no longer reliable. Sometimes, he was supposed to pick Stephanos up from school, but he wouldn't show up. Stephanos struggled to make sense of it all. But it was pretty clear that Basil had been knocked off his pedestal."

"Did things improve?" Radic asked.

CHAPTER FORTY-EIGHT: INTO THIN AIR

"Well, not immediately. I think Basil became a family project. I don't know what Stephanos actually felt. Sometimes love. Sometimes embarrassment. And then Stephanos' Mom died. That was a terrible blow."

"Did you know his Mom?" Radic asked.

"I loved his Mom! She was always super nice to me. And I love his Dad! I even worked for him for a couple of years to help pay my college bills. He's one of the nicest guys I know."

"To get back to Basil, did things improve?"

"Yes, they did, but in a sad way. When Stephanos' Mom died, that's what it took to get Basil back on track. He went into rehab and disappeared for a while. Then he came back, better and stronger."

"And he returned to work?" Radic asked.

"Yes, I think Stephanos deserves most of the credit for that. His Dad was really fed up with Basil, and I can understand why. He just didn't trust him. But Stephanos kept saying: We need to give Uncle Basil a chance. He has lots of good ideas. He has good business instincts."

"Do you think that's true?" Radic asked.

"Well, what matters is not what I thought. I had my doubts. But Stephanos was bound and determined to rehabilitate Uncle Basil. He'd carved out an R&D unit at Dimitri's. He and Basil worked together there. They pushed the envelope a bit together. They had a couple successes, like skillets that were easier for old people to handle. I thought it was working."

"But you don't know for sure?" Radic asked.

"No, I don't. With Basil, nothing is easy. But I thought things were pretty good."

"Carol Sloan," Radic said. "Did you meet her?"

"I did, and I really liked her!"

"And Stephanos? What did he think of her?"

"Well, I'd say his thinking evolved. At first, Carol was this fussbudget who was telling him to cool his jets whenever he and Basil would come up with a brilliant idea: 'Better safe than sorry, Stephanos. Better safe than sorry.' But later he came to think of her as a smart, caring person who was looking out for him and his Dad and the firm."

"Did you know that they were engaged to be married?" Radic asked.

"Yes, I did. Stephanos told me before my trip to China and before his trip to the Bahamas."

"What did you think?"

"I thought they were made for one another. I've never seen him happier. And Carol loosened up as she got to know Stephanos better. He became more like her; she became more like him."

"Did Stephanos ever talk with you about Muggles?"

"Oh, you know about those, do you?"

"Yes, what did he say about them?"

"Well, he was very excited. And Basil was excited too."

"Did you ever see one?"

"Well, I saw drawings. They looked pretty cool."

"Did you ever hear Carol and Stephanos talk about the mugs together?"

"No, I knew that she wanted them to go slow and that Basil was all gung ho. I think Stephanos was in the middle somewhere."

"Have you ever seen Stephanos harm anyone?" Radic asked.

Howley said nothing for a moment. "On the football field? Or off?" he asked.

"Both," Radic said.

"On the football field, he was a fierce competitor. He was a hard hitter. I benefited from that. I caught passes, thanks to his blocking."

"And off the field?" Radic asked.

"Off the field, he's a VERY sweet guy," he said, tearing up. "Gentle and kind. I pray to God that nothing has happened to him. But if it has, I'd be willing to bet that good old Uncle Basil is somehow behind it."

Chapter Forty-Nine: Butterflies

Radic had butterflies in his stomach as he rang Lexie's doorbell. He had once arrested a close personal friend for cocaine possession. He had delivered bad news to grieving parents. He had watched a sure-fire conviction unravel in court. Somehow, this was tougher.

But then he saw Lexie in the flesh. She greeted him with a dazzling smile. She was wearing a black pencil skirt and a Kelly Green cashmere sweater. She looked amazing!

"Where's your eyepatch, matey?" she asked.

Radic laughed and relaxed. "Sorry, I left it at home."

It felt so good to be in the company of an attractive woman and not to be burdened by the challenges of a difficult case. If only for a few hours.

"I hope you like Thai food," Radic said, vaguely remembering that they had covered this ground before.

"So long as the fish doesn't come from the Monongahela," she said.

"Isn't the Mon supposed to be pretty clean these days?" he asked.

"That's what they say," she admitted," but when you see it up close and personal like I do every day, I'm not so sure."

As they entered the restaurant a few minutes later, Radic observed that several men noticed his arrival. Perhaps they recognized him from the newspapers. Then he realized that they were not looking at him at all. Lexie clearly had admirers here, which was fine with him.

Lexie ordered a martini, while Radic asked for a Thai beer. They decided to try some Tom Yum soup.

"Yum Yum," Lexie said approvingly.

"Tom Yum," Radic corrected her with a smile.

"Ha, ha," she said.

Over soup, Radic learned that Lexie had been a Navy brat, moving from base to base as her father was reassigned: Norfolk, Greece, Spain, New Orleans, Guam. It was hard at times, but it forced her to learn to make friends quickly. "Is that how you got interested in boats?" he asked.

"Well, I was keen on planes first," she said. "My Dad encouraged me to get a pilot's license, which I did. I sometimes go on short flights just for fun."

"Aren't you afraid of engine failure? There's not much of a backup plan in those one-prop planes, is there?"

"Well, sure. There's a parachute. That's your protection. I've gone parachuting a few times, just in case. And for the adrenaline rush. It's exhilarating!"

"You don't go race car driving, do you, by any chance?"

"How did you know?"

"You're amazing! Is there anything you CAN'T do?"

Lexie paused. "Well, I can't whistle," she confessed.

"You're kidding! Not at all?"

"Not at all," she said.

"Let me hear," he said.

"No. I don't want to make a public spectacle of myself."

"Go on. There aren't that many people here."

Lexie wrinkled her eyebrows, pursed her lips, and burst out laughing.

"Try again," Radic said. "But first, lick your lips, and try closing your eyes. No distractions. No pressure. Think positive thoughts."

Lexie closed her eyes, scrunched her face, licked her lips, and puckered up. "Pffft! Pffft!"

This time, Radic burst out laughing. "Really? Pffft? That's the best you can do?"

"Don't make fun of me," she warned. "I'm a sensitive person!"

"Sorry. Sorry. Okay. Try making an O with your mouth and place your tongue firmly beneath your lower teeth."

Lexie complied as best she could. "Thuhhh! Thuhhh!"

CHAPTER FORTY-NINE: BUTTERFLIES

Radic snorted involuntarily, then apologized. "Here, watch me whistle. Then imitate what I do."

Lexie watched and listened as Radic whistled a fragment of a popular song. "You didn't make an O," she chided.

"I didn't?"

"No, you didn't. You've been giving me bad advice! It's not my fault."

Their main courses arrived: Pad Thai Beef for Radic, Grilled Trout with Banana Leaf for Lexie.

"You may think you're off the hook because your dinner arrived, but this whistling lesson is not over, my friend," Radic said. "Not by any means."

Lexie protested. "I can only handle so much public humiliation in one evening."

The food was delicious, and the conversation flowed easily. After coffee, Radic asked Lexie if she might be up for some music.

"Sure," she said. "What did you have in mind?"

"There's a jazz club downtown," he said. "Con Alma, in the Cultural District. Do you know it?"

"I know it to see it, but I've never been inside."

"I checked, and Benny Benack III is going to be there tonight," he said.

"Benny Benack III?" she asked. "Who was the first? And who was the second?"

"Well, Benny I was a trumpeter. According to my Dad, he used to play Beat 'em Bucs at Pirate games. Benny II is a saxophonist, a good one."

"And Benny III?"

"He's a trumpeter. He sings, too."

"Perfect!" she said. "Let's go."

They found seats easily at Con Alma and settled in for the first set. Radic ordered a Smithwick's. Lexie decided to try one, too.

Benny was charming and entertaining. He played some up-tempo songs and bantered with the audience. He closed the set with a ballad, "The Nearness of You."

As they huddled together and listened to the music, Lexie reached over and held Radic's hand. Then she rested her head on his shoulder.

Radic drove Lexie home. She asked if he'd like to come in, and he did. It was a cozy two-bedroom apartment with a bowl of fruit on the dining room table.

She kissed him firmly on the lips.

"So you can pucker well," Lexie observed. "That's a start."

"It's the next step that's harder," Radic replied.

"Not necessarily," Lexie said.

And she was right. It wasn't hard at all.

Chapter Fifty: Push-Ups

Despite the dire circumstances, despite his fear, despite his pain, Stephanos felt better than he had in days. At least he had a plan. Thanks to a can of peas.

Basil had opened the peas with a can opener and hadn't removed them from the can. More importantly, he hadn't disposed of the lid, which Stephanos had found near a damp wall. The can was sharp but the lid was sharper still. It could be a formidable weapon.

He knew, though, that a weapon would not be enough. He needed to get stronger quickly. Unlike his uncle, Stephanos had never experienced boot camp. But he had seen enough movies to get the basic idea.

He began with twenty push-ups. Then rest. Twenty sit-ups. Then rest. Twenty clam shells on the left side. Then rest. Twenty clam shells on the right side. Then rest.

After that, he tried running in place. The manacle on his left ankle made this difficult, but he eventually acquired a kind of rhythm that felt comfortable and productive.

After a half hour of these and other exercises, he felt exhausted. But he also felt energized. He would try it again in a few hours.

In some ways, the greatest challenge he faced was boredom. No human company. No cell phone. No Spotify. No television.

The first mind game he tried was simple: He began a sentence with the letter A and ended the sentence with a word beginning in B. Then he began a sentence with the letter B and ended it with a word beginning in C. It kept him alert.

From there, he segued to Spanish grammar: Yo tengo, tienes, el tiene, nosotros tenemos, vosotros teneis, ellos tienen. Tuve, tu tenias, el tuvo, nosotros tuvimos, vosotros tuvisteis, ellos tuvieron.

Singing was more satisfying, especially the music of Mac Miller, the Pittsburgh rapper whose death at age 26 had affected him deeply:

And the Nikes on my feet keep my cipher complete
Nike, Nike, Nike, Nike, Nike, Nike, Nike, Nike, Nikes
And the Nikes on my feet keep my cipher complete
Nike, Nike, Nike, Nike, Nike, Nike, Nike, Nike, Nikes

Twice a day, he crafted a plan of attack. But only twice a day. So much was riding on this that he grew agitated and fearful every time he thought about different scenarios. It wasn't good to dwell on this. But he had to think it through.

Two ideas occurred to him. The first was to play dead. If he didn't move at all, surely Basil would approach him to see if he was fast asleep or stone cold. Then he could pounce. The second idea was to pretend to be sick. To claim he had a fever. Would Basil put a palm on his forehead, as in the good old days? Or would he tell him to ride it out?

Neither idea was foolproof, so he toyed with other possibilities. He could offer to sign a document granting Basil full access to his bank account. But did banks really work that way? Wouldn't he need to do this in person? And why offer to do something that might reduce his value to Basil as a living, breathing human being?

One problem with all of these ideas: Stephanos was not a very good liar. Never had been. And Basil was as cunning as they come. Somehow, his body language and his tone of voice needed to be convincing.

He rehearsed his lines and tried to anticipate Basil's response.

Stephanos: Basil, I'm really not feeling well. I think I have a fever.

Basil: Does this look like a hospital? Do I look like a nurse? Toughen up.

OK, back to square one. What if he were to throw up in the corner? He'd have to live with the stench for a couple of days. But it would be tangible evidence that he was sick. It would not require an Oscar-winning performance.

CHAPTER FIFTY: PUSH-UPS

Stephanos: Basil, I'm really not feeling well. I can't keep my food down.

Basil: Does this look like a hospital? Do I look like a nurse? Toughen up.

This was getting frustrating. Maybe he should try reasoning with Basil instead. But no, that was naïve. Basil was too far gone. His beloved uncle had turned into a monster. He had to think like a soldier. He had to think like a killer. He had to think like Basil.

And then Mother Nature intervened. The more he thought about throwing up, the more nauseous he became. He found a spot near the toilet and heaved. Again and again. Well, that settles that, he thought.

As he drifted into sleep, he saw two people. His sweet, thoughtful mother, so caring, so warm, so full of life. And his hard-working, decent, exuberant, dependable father, who had taught him the difference between right and wrong, in business and in life.

He didn't think about Carol. He couldn't. It was too painful. It was as if that part of his brain had been lobotomized. He needed to think, hard. But he also needed NOT to think about her.

Chapter Fifty-One: A Brief Respite

Pittsburgh's citizens were remarkably peaceful for nearly two days, and Radic and Lexie took full advantage of the lull. After attending to chores at his own apartment for a couple hours, Radic returned to Lexie's apartment with a gym bag and a bouquet of fresh flowers.

They agreed to go jogging together mid-afternoon, followed by a home-cooked meal. Lexie was very impressed by Radic's exercise regimen before the jog. She was less impressed by his Spotify list.

"Where did you come up with this stuff?" she asked. "Do your friends know that you listen to this crap?"

"Actually, my playlist comes from a friend," he replied.

"Well, that's an excuse, I suppose," she said. "But we're going to have to work on that."

Following a vigorous jog, Radic and Lexie showered together. Lexie had picked up a couple of steaks and some odds and ends at the grocery store. After firing up the grill, Lexie handled the steaks while Radic tossed a salad, boiled corn on the cob, and checked his e-mail. Nothing urgent. "Thank God!" he thought.

When Lexie came back inside, they enjoyed a nice bottle of pinot noir with the meal and basked in the warmth of a new relationship.

"Are you ready to resume where we left off?" Lexie asked.

"Do you mean with your whistling lessons?"

"Not exactly what I had in mind," she answered. Within minutes, the lights were out. After making love, Lexie reached over to stroke Radic's scratchy cheek. Then she grasped his earring playfully.

CHAPTER FIFTY-ONE: A BRIEF RESPITE

"It takes a self-confident man to wear an earring like this."

Radic laughed.

"Is there a story behind it? A long-lost love?"

Radic said nothing.

"Oops!" Lexie said. "Did I touch a nerve? You don't have to answer if you don't want to."

"No, that's okay," Radic said. "It was Petra's earring."

"Petra?"

"My sister."

"I didn't know you had a sister."

"Well," Radic said. "I don't anymore. She's dead. But it reminds me of her. I think about her just about every day."

"How did she die?"

Radic said nothing for a moment. Then: "She was murdered."

"Oh, my God! I'm so sorry."

"I still have moments when I have trouble processing Petra's death. Especially because her murderer was never caught. But most of the time, Petra's death helps to motivate me. To do good police work."

"You must have been very close," Lexie said softly.

"We were. She was fun to be with. And she always had my back."

"How old were you when she died?"

"I was a junior in high school."

"Was she killed here in Pittsburgh?"

"No, in Guatemala. She was in the Peace Corps."

"How very sad! To die so young. And while serving her country."

Radic nodded.

"That's tough to take."

"It is," Radic acknowledged. "But wearing her earring keeps me connected to her. And it helps me to stay safe. At least, that's the way I look at it. When I'm out on assignment, I think of her as my guardian angel."

Lexie said nothing. She embraced Radic and held him tight. Soon, they both fell asleep.

***

The following morning, after breakfast, Radic and Lexie talked about their relationship and how to handle it. They agreed to be discreet at the office and to tell none of their colleagues.

"Not even Mulroy?" Radic asked.

"Not for the moment," Lexie answered. "Let's give ourselves some time."

They went out to lunch. Lexie had Pilates that afternoon. Radic left her and headed home, after telling her twice how amazing she was.

The Sloan case continued to weigh on his mind. They needed to find Basil and Stephanos and had no clue where either was. But somehow, that burden was lighter with Lexie in the picture.

Chapter Fifty-Two: A Day at Wrigley Field

It was the top of the ninth inning at Wrigley Field, and the Cubs were in trouble. They had blown a five-to-one lead with a foolish fastball down the middle to the Braves' clean-up hitter with bases loaded. Now the Braves were rallying again, with a man on second base. Harold Gomar ordered another Old Style to calm his nerves. Visiting Wrigley Field was not for the faint of heart. The tension was interrupted by a phone call. A 412 area code. Pittsburgh. Should he take it or not? It was probably one of those assholes from headquarters. Fromm or Fogarty. The batter popped up to retire the side. Cradling his beer between his legs, Gomar took the call.

"Is this Agent Gomar?"

"Yes," Gomar replied. "Vladimir, is that you?"

"Yes, it's me."

"Are you still in Pittsburgh?"

"Yes, that's what I wanted to talk about."

"Vladimir, I want to help, I really do. But there are limits to what I can say to you."

"I understand. But I need your advice. I value your advice."

Gomar paused. "Okay, shoot."

"I need a lawyer."

"I agree."

"I have a lawyer. In Chicago. A good one."

"Is he Russian?"

"Well, yes. I know him. I trust him."

Gomar paused. "It's good to have a lawyer that you trust. But will the Pittsburgh Police trust him? Will my colleagues at the FBI trust him?"

"What are you saying?"

"Do you have something you can give the Pittsburgh Police and the FBI that might reduce your sentence?"

"As a matter of fact, I do."

"Then my advice would be: Hire a lawyer, but not a Russian lawyer. And definitely not someone with a connection to the Russian mafia."

A long pause. "But those are the people I know."

"I know. But that's not the path to freedom."

"What is?"

"Well, there's no guaranteed path to freedom. But if I were in your shoes, I'd do two things. Hire a good lawyer with a spotless reputation. Better yet, hire a good Pittsburgh lawyer with a spotless reputation. Maybe your guy can suggest one."

"And the second thing?"

"Leak like a sieve."

"Thank you, Agent Gomar, I really appreciate it. That's what I'll do."

"Don't mention it."

"Oh, and Agent Gomar, I hate to bother you. But there's one more thing."

"What is it?"

"Do you like cats?"

"Do I like cats?"

"It's been two days now, and no one has looked in on Miss Natasha. I'm beside myself with worry."

"Vladimir, that's not something I can do for you. "

"What do you suggest?"

"Maybe that's a job for your Russian lawyer."

* * *

CHAPTER FIFTY-TWO: A DAY AT WRIGLEY FIELD

Several hours later, Lieutenant Stilton got a call from a well-regarded Pittsburgh attorney, Jeffrey Diamond. He said that his client was Vladimir Federov and that he had something to tell the PBP and the FBI in return for immunity.

"What can he possibly tell us that would get him immunity?"

"My client is prepared to testify that the same individual who sold him the Harry Potter mugs sold him something else a year earlier."

"You mean like pots and pans?"

"Not exactly."

"Well, what exactly?"

"Well, it was skillets."

"What's so special about skillets?"

"Well, these particular skillets didn't have a patent."

There was a long pause. "Mr. Diamond, give me your number. I'll have Detective Radic call you later today."

Radic was intrigued but also irritated by Stilton's text message asking him to call Federov's new lawyer. Despite Judge Floyd's warning, Stilton seemed to be pushing Radic towards the FBI's share of the case. Fromm and Fogarty would not be happy if he had a private conversation with an attorney who was knee-deep in intellectual property issues.

After a moment's thought, Radic decided to call the FBI before contacting Federov's lawyer. He didn't mind being on the FBI's shit list, but Judge Floyd was quite another story. He would need his help again in the future and didn't want to jeopardize his goodwill if he could avoid it.

Agent Fromm was definitely intrigued by Federov's offer. A two-front war, in this instance, could help them make a stronger case against Dimitri's Sturdy Dishes or whoever was behind the sketchy sales. It could also give them more bargaining power with Trojanowski and his lawyer. He proposed a joint meeting with Federov's lawyer, which Radic promptly arranged.

At this point, Radic was getting a splitting headache. Too much carousing with Lexie? Too many competing interests to manage? He leaned strongly towards the second explanation. Popping a couple of Advils, he started prepping for another round of legal skirmishes.

Chapter Fifty-Three: A Man's Best Friend

On learning that Spider Donatelli's car could, at long last, be returned to its rightful owner, Mulroy jumped at the chance to do so. She had grown fond of the quirky tattoo artist, and she hoped she might be able to extract more information from him about the ever-elusive Basil Vasilikas. After determining that he was at home, she offered to bring his car to his doorstep.

Spider's Ford Bronco was not the most beautiful car on the planet. It had a dented right rear fender, rust-colored splotches under the chassis, an ugly key scratch on the driver's side, and a hood that didn't quite close. But when Spider was reunited with his car after nearly two weeks apart, the rapture in his eyes was marvelous to behold.

"There she is!" he beamed. "Looking so sweet! I've missed you, honey. I'm sorry I took you for granted. Baby, you're the best!"

Mulroy had seldom heard a grown man gush so effusively about a daughter or girlfriend, much less a Ford Bronco. She wondered what he would say if he owned a Porsche.

"Detective Radic said to tell you he's sorry it took so long," she said. "We had to search it from top to bottom. But the good news is we've given it a good cleaning, free of charge. And all your possessions are in the trunk."

"Thank you, thank you," he said. "I really appreciate it."

Then, narrowing his gaze and speaking confidentially, "Do you know who took it?"

"Well," Mulroy said, lowering her voice, "I'm probably not supposed to tell you this, but based on the fingerprints, it was your pal. Basil Vasilikas."

"He's no pal of mine if he stole my car," he said, shaking his head. "You think you know someone."

"From what you said the other day, it sounds like you got to be pretty close to Basil when you were in Iraq," she said.

"Yes, we were close back then," he said. "A small group of us. Like brothers."

"Do you, by any chance, have any photos of you and Basil from the war days?" she asked.

"Yes, I do," he said. "Not that many. But I keep them in a special place. Would you like to see them?"

"Yes, I would," she said.

They went inside. Amidst the chaos of Spider's dimly-lit living room, Mulroy spotted tattoo magazines, empty Coca-Cola cans, peanut shells, Chinese food containers, and dust bunnies that probably went back a long way. Did he even own a vacuum cleaner?

Spider excused himself and returned shortly with a leather bag. He reached inside and pulled out a bunch of photos, some crumpled and bent, others in good shape.

"This pouch is all that's left of my service to our country," he said ruefully. "A bunch of photos, my discharge papers, and a medal of valor."

"What was the medal for?"

"Well, I got it for rescuing a wounded officer in the middle of a firefight," he said.

"Can I see it?"

He lifted the medal out of a red velvet case and opened it slowly. It was a Bronze Star.

"You should be very proud," Mulroy said, with feeling. "It was a very brave, courageous thing that you did."

"Thank you, Officer, thank you. It's nice of you to say that. I wish I could say that I felt brave at the time, but honestly, I just felt scared. Whatever I did was pure instinct."

He invited Mulroy to have a seat on the couch, after clearing it up a bit, and fetched a couple of Coca Colas.

CHAPTER FIFTY-THREE: A MAN'S BEST FRIEND

"Your jaw seems less swollen than the last time I saw you," he observed. "How are you feeling?"

"A bit better," she said. "Thanks for asking. I still need to get some dental work, which I'm not looking forward to. But after that, it should be okay."

"Maybe YOU deserve a Bronze Star," Spider suggested.

"Sometimes I think so," Mulroy said.

While sipping his Coke, Spider identified the men and women in the photos, with a lively running commentary on each. After a few photos, Mulroy realized that she had yet to see Basil.

"Is Basil in here somewhere?" she asked.

"Yes, yes, sorry." He rifled through the rest of the photos. "Here he is. Here's Keys in all his glory," he said.

Mulroy stared at a somewhat rakish-looking young man with a rifle at his side and a sneer on his face. He looked like one tough hombre.

"What did you just call Basil?" she asked.

"Keys," Spider said. "That was his nickname."

"I thought his nickname was Vazzy," Mulroy said.

"Well, over here, yes," he said. "But over there, he was Keys."

"Why's that?" she asked.

"He had more keys in his pockets than anyone in our platoon. He had a key to the mess hall, which was very valuable after hours if you wanted a midnight snack. He had a key to the supply room, which was pretty cool if you wanted a mattress that wasn't lumpy."

"Am I correct in assuming that he wasn't supposed to have these keys?"

"Yes, that's correct. God only knows how he got them. But that made him a really good guy to know."

"And did one of those keys get him into trouble?" she asked.

Spider looked up at her quizzically.

"We have his military record," she explained.

"Ah," he said. "I should have guessed. Well, that's right. If it had just been a little petty thievery, no one would have bothered. But Keys always had his sights set on something bigger, bolder. He was a dreamer, and his dreams got the better of him. That's what got him into trouble."

"The black market," Mulroy said.

"Yep, a little horse-trading here and there, so what? But he was trading a lot of stuff with some pretty shady characters."

"Did you know about it at the time?"

"Well, I knew about the little stuff. Late-night hamburgers. An extra pillow for your bed at night. But no, I had no idea about the other stuff. If I had, I'd have wanted nothing to do with it. Way too risky."

"So, what are YOUR dreams, Spider?" Mulroy asked.

Spider smiled. "You're gonna laugh at me, but I'm already living the dream. I have my own tattoo shop. I'm a successful businessman. And I'm an artist. Customers recommend me to other people. Customers come back for more. My tattoos help people to express themselves, and they help me to express myself. Isn't that cool? Who could ask for more?"

Mulroy noticed the time and called an Uber to get back home. She thanked Spider for sharing his mementos with her, especially his Bronze Star. "It was an honor to see it," she said.

On the way home, she thought about Spider, his tattoo parlor, and his medal. She also thought about "Keys" Vasilikas. An idea was starting to form in the back of her head. She was eager to share it with Radic and Volcker. Hopefully, they would be able to meet sometime soon.

Chapter Fifty-Four: A Roll of the Dice

A door opened or closed. A definite clanging sound. Not an ordinary door. Metallic perhaps. Then, more noises. But no words. One person. One man. It could only be Basil.

Stephanos tensed up, his entire nervous system on red alert. He listened attentively and tried to get his bearings. No hint of light. It must be nighttime.

More clanging. Then, a swishing sound. Water. The sound was rhythmic, steady. Like someone rowing a boat.

Stephanos reached underneath his water bowl to make sure the tin can lid was there. He grabbed it with his right hand and made a fist so it could not be seen. Then he curled up in a fetal position. It was time to execute his plan. It was time to play possum.

The clanging and the rowing persisted. Then it stopped. Basil hopped out of the boat or whatever he was in. He shined a flashlight in his direction. Luckily, Stephanos was facing the other way, so he wasn't tempted to squint.

"Stephanos!" he said. "Stephanos! I've come with food."

No response.

Stephanos heard a few footsteps, then felt Basil's hand on his shoulder. He remained limp. He wanted Basil to turn him over a full embrace so that he would be as close to him as a mother with a newborn child.

"Stephanos!" he said. "Are you sick?"

As Basil enveloped his upper torso, Stephanos grabbed Basil's shirt for leverage. He lashed out furiously, aiming for Basil's neck, hoping to sever his jugular vein. He heard a terrible cry and chose a second target, carving a gash into his uncle's thigh. At this point, he opened his eyes.

Basil was bleeding from his neck. But he was also kicking violently. A kick landed in Stephanos' lower back and sent him skidding backwards on his butt. He lost his precious lid.

Basil had produced a handkerchief from his left pocket and was trying to stanch the bleeding. Stephanos tackled him and knocked him over, sending the flashlight skittering into the corner. He reached for Basil's right pocket with his empty left hand. He felt keys, but no cell phone.

This time, Basil kneed him in the groin. It was terribly painful, but Stephanos kept his eyes on the prize—Basil's left pocket. He kicked him hard in the head with his manacled foot. This diverted Basil long enough for Stephanos to reach inside Basil's pocket for the cell phone. He extracted it just as Basil landed another vicious blow, this time with an elbow to the chin.

Stephanos was stunned but somehow managed to hold onto the cell phone. Distancing himself as best he could from Basil, he found the green phone icon. To his surprise, he noticed that he was holding his own phone. Not thinking straight, he dialed his father, instead of 911, as originally planned. Sadly, he found himself in voice mail.

"Dad." Heavy breathing. "It's Stephanos." Panting.

"I'm a prisoner. I don't know where. Uncle Basil…"

Basil wrestled the phone from his nephew and ended the call. He picked up his keys, limped to the boat, and disappeared into the darkness without saying a word.

Stephanos surveyed the scene. He had received some precious food and water. And he had acquired a flashlight, which he promptly shut off to save the battery. His hands were scraped, his groin hurt, and his back was throbbing. But he had survived.

On the other hand, he had botched the call. He should have called 911 so the police could locate and rescue him. *Damn!* At least his father now knew the truth. But would that be enough?

Stephanos heard a clanging sound. Like the closing of a prison gate. Then silence. Dead silence. He was alone again. Free from Basil, perhaps. But

CHAPTER FIFTY-FOUR: A ROLL OF THE DICE

isolated, unreachable. With very mixed feelings, he fell asleep.

Chapter Fifty-Five: A Familiar Voice

Radic was sound asleep when he received the call. He looked at the clock. 6:03 a.m. "Hello?" he croaked.

"Detective Rad-itch, this is Dimitri. I'm sorry to trouble you so early in the morning."

"That's okay, Dimitri."

"I got a call from Stephanos in the middle of the night. It was interrupted. I'm very worried about my boy."

"What did he say?"

"Basil is holding him prisoner somewhere."

"Play back the voice mail. I need to hear it."

Radic groaned after listening. "I wish he had called 911," he complained. "We'd be able to trace the call."

Dimitri said nothing.

Radic quickly pivoted. "He's alive, Dimitri," he said. "That's the most important point."

"But where is he, detective?"

"That's what we're going to find out. Don't give up hope. Never give up hope! I'll call you back later in the day."

Radic thought about going back to sleep, but he was too excited. Instead, he brought his case notes into the kitchen, brewed a cup of coffee, and sat down with a sheet of paper and a pen.

Q1: Is Stephanos still in Pittsburgh? Yes. Or probably yes.

Q2: Being held prisoner? Yes. Or probably yes.

Q3: By Basil? Yes. Or probably yes.

CHAPTER FIFTY-FIVE: A FAMILIAR VOICE

So, was Basil's dramatic theft of Spider's Ford Bronco a ruse? Apparently so. By stealing the car and leaving it at Greater Pitt, he gave the police two false impressions: that he was no longer in Pittsburgh and that he no longer had access to a car. But quite possibly, he still had access to Trojanowski's car. Basil had reasoned, correctly, that the police would not make finding that car a high priority if he was presumed to be elsewhere. Very clever! Clearly, they had underestimated their mystery caller and eyewitness.

But where could Stephanos be? And where could Basil be? In the same place? And where was that?

Apparently, Basil still had unfinished business in Pittsburgh. He had a chance to leave town and he didn't take it. Why?

What was the nature of his unfinished business? It must have to do with Stephanos. Presumably, the mugs. But maybe something more than the mugs.

So where would Basil go if he thought no one was looking out for him any longer? Stephanos' home? That was under surveillance. But maybe he could slip through the net. He was a slippery enough character.

Somewhere else? Trojanowski's home? Perhaps. Surely, Basil knew that Trojanowski was in police custody. They should send two officers there as soon as possible. They might luck out.

Any other possibilities? Spider's home? Spider seemed like a victim of a car theft, not a co-conspirator in an intellectual property crime. But who knows? Maybe the close bonds from Iraq remain strong. Maybe Spider was the perfect accomplice—willing to have his own car "stolen" to keep his buddy from being caught by the police.

Chapter Fifty-Six: A Disturbing Dream

Rosemary had been sleeping well, but tonight was an exception. She saw Carol in her dreams, a wraith-like figure, beckoning her to the graveyard because she had something to tell her. She tried to follow Carol, but her legs wouldn't move.

In her dream, she detected a sinister presence, though she couldn't specify what it was. Someone who wished her harm. She looked behind her in the misty graveyard, but saw no one. She heard a noise, but it was just the rustling of leaves in the wind.

She smelled the foul odor of cigarettes, one of her least favorite smells. "No smoking!" she shouted to no one in particular. Then she realized that it was just a dream. She woke up with a start.

But her mind kept spinning illusions. She still smelled the cigarettes, and she felt unsafe. She decided to get up and get a glass of water. She reached for her nightgown.

"Don't get up, Rosemary!" someone said in a deep male voice. Rosemary screamed—a piercing scream of pure terror.

"And don't scream again, or I'm going to have to hit you," he warned.

Rosemary saw a shadowy figure in the darkness and did what he told her.

"Who...who...are you?" she sputtered.

"I'm someone who needs your help," the man said. "You're a nurse. I've been wounded. I want you to patch me up. Then I'll be out of your way."

Rosemary remained silent.

"I have your cell phone, and I've locked all the doors. I have a gun. So don't even think about making a run for it."

CHAPTER FIFTY-SIX: A DISTURBING DREAM

"Why should I believe you?" she asked at last. "Why should I believe that you'll let me go if I do as you ask?"

"I have no quarrel with you," he said. "You help me, and I'll let you live. That's the deal. Take it or leave it."

Rosemary paused only briefly. "I'll take it," she said firmly.

"Smart girl," he said. "Now, here's what I want you to do…"

The man standing before Rosemary looked strong, menacing, but unsteady on his feet. She noticed a blood-soaked tourniquet wrapped around his neck and evidence of a nasty wound on his right thigh, judging from the congealed blood on his pants.

At his instructions, Rosemary walked slowly to the hallway closet, wearing nothing but panties and a loose-fitting top. She extracted a towel, two facecloths, gauze, ointment, and a plastic tub.

"I'll need hot water," she said. "And scissors."

"Small scissors only," he said, "and I'll be watching you very closely when you use them."

Rosemary nodded.

"You can fill the tub with hot water," he said.

"I'd like to put on my clothes," she said.

"Don't press your luck," he said.

Rosemary instructed the man to sit on the edge of her bed. He closed the bedroom door, then did as she suggested while holding a revolver in his right hand.

Rosemary told him to remove his shirt, but he acknowledged that he couldn't do so. With his permission, she removed his shirt and slowly removed the bloody tourniquet.

She gasped when she saw the damage. "This is really serious," she said. "You need to get to an E.R."

"Not going to happen," he said. "Do what you can."

Rosemary bathed the wound with hot water as best she could. Her patient winced whenever she got close to the point of entry.

"You're going to need stitches," she said.

"Do it," he ordered.

255

"I'm not authorized to do that," she objected. "I can take stitches out. I can't put them in."

"Have you observed doctors do it?" he asked.

She nodded.

"Then do it," he barked.

"It's really painful without an anesthetic," she warned.

"Do it anyway," he insisted.

"I'll need thread," she said. "And a needle."

"Where?" he asked.

"In the hall. The same closet."

"We'll go together," he said.

After getting the needle and thread, Rosemary put some disinfectant on the wound, which was about two inches wide. Then, she began to sew.

Her patient cried out in pain at the first stitch. But he insisted that she continue. At one point, Rosemary thought he was going to pass out. But his tolerance for pain was remarkable. Five minutes later, Rosemary indicated that the job was done.

"Bind it," her patient said, "and move on to the next one."

Rosemary bound the wound with gauze, feeling a mix of emotions. Her lifelong commitment to patient care kicked in, plus her survival instincts. She had no intention of taking risks with this scary man. But she desperately wanted to escape and had not given up hope of doing so, gun or no gun.

She removed her patient's shoes and then his trousers. His second wound was not as wide or as deep as the first, but it was not a pretty sight.

She bathed the second wound with hot water, then applied some disinfectant to it.

"Stitches?" her patient asked.

"I don't think they're absolutely necessary here," she said.

"Honestly?" he asked.

"Honestly."

After a few seconds, he responded. "Bind the wound." And that's what she did.

The patient stood up, in his underwear. "Do you have any men's clothing

CHAPTER FIFTY-SIX: A DISTURBING DREAM

here?" he asked.

Rosemary shook her head.

"You're sure?"

She nodded.

"Sweat pants, then. And a pullover."

Rosemary pointed to a dresser drawer. "Okay?"

Her patient nodded. Rosemary fetched the clothes.

"Put the pants on first," he said. And Rosemary did exactly that, doing her best to avoid the wounds.

"Now, the pullover. And no funny business," he warned, brandishing the gun.

Rosemary complied.

"Now, find me some duct tape," he said.

"Duct tape?" she asked.

"Duct tape," he responded. "That is, if you want to live."

Rosemary and her patient walked slowly into the kitchen, to get the duct tape. She actively considered making a run for it, but her patient seemed stronger, more confident. And he still had the gun.

She handed him the duct tape.

"Sit down," he said, motioning towards a kitchen chair. "Place your hands behind the chair," he said. Rosemary did as he said. She grunted as he fastened the duct tape to the back of the chair, and she started to tear up, feeling less confident than before.

"Now, your feet," he said. He bound her feet to the front chair legs. Then he disappeared for a moment, returning with a facecloth.

He inserted the facecloth into her mouth, despite her protests. Then he duct-taped her mouth shut.

Rosemary tried to say, "My phone?" But it sounded like gobbledygook. Her patient seemed to anticipate her question.

"Your phone?" he asked. "I'm taking it for safekeeping."

"Don't leave me this way," she pleaded, though it sounded unintelligible.

Her patient disappeared one last time. She heard the sound of a toilet flushing. Then he reappeared, holding his gun in one hand, her phone, and some painkillers in the other.

Without a word, he disappeared into the night, or what now had become daybreak. She heard a car start nearby. And then there was silence.

Chapter Fifty-Seven: The Ties that Bind

Rosemary felt a lump in her throat and started to sob, but quickly thought better of it. Get a hold of yourself, she thought. You're alive. And there's got to be a way out of this mess.

As she looked around the kitchen, such a cheerful place normally, so terrifying at the moment, Rosemary considered her options.

The duct tape felt tight around her wrists and feet. She tried to move her right leg, then her left. A little more give on the right, but it would be hard to get the duct tape off either foot.

Besides, she really needed to free her hands. Any chance of doing that?

Rosemary looked for something sharp that might help to secure her release. Her kitchen knives stood at the ready on the counter but were not reachable. There were a couple of sharp corners on the kitchen table that might do some damage to the duct tape if she rubbed vigorously enough. But how to get there?

Whatever she did, she didn't want to wind up on the floor, fully bound, like Gulliver, only inaudible. That would be even worse than the status quo. At least now she could see if someone came to the front door.

With that in mind, she thought about the morning mail. She knew the mail lady by name—Gabby—they were on friendly terms. If she could somehow get rid of the duct tape on her mouth, before the mail delivery at 10:30 or so, she just might be able to get Gabby's attention.

In his haste to leave, her patient had taped her mouth shut but had not wrapped the duct tape behind her head. If she could dislodge the duct tape from one side of her mouth, she had a fighting chance of getting rid of the facial duct tape altogether. Then hopefully, the face cloth.

As she thought about her predicament, Rosemary noticed her dustbuster and the cord that connected it to electrical power. It wasn't that far away.

If she could detach the plug from the electrical outlet, it would give her something reasonably sharp to cut at the duct tape. But then she realized that it would be loose. If her hands were free, that would do. But her hands weren't free. She needed something sharp and stationary, not something sharp and mobile that she couldn't manipulate with her hands.

Frustrated, Rosemary decided to start from scratch. Surely, there was something that could work. If only she thought it through.

Relaxing just a bit, Rosemary stopped scanning the kitchen for sharp objects and stared long and hard at her not so portable prison—the chair to which she was attached. Although her mobility was limited, she just might be able to stretch her upper torso so that her taped face touched the seat of the chair.

The trick would be to make this maneuver without toppling the chair. Slowly, Rosemary stretched her right side as far as she could, aiming for the chair seat. She found herself using muscles that she had long forgotten, even with the addition of pickleball to her life.

Her first pass was encouraging. She almost made it. She tried again. This time, she made contact. Her shoulder hurt from the stretching, but she didn't lose her balance. She straightened up again. *Okay,* she thought to herself. *This one is for all the marbles.*

Chapter Fifty-Eight: Free at Last

Radic was driving to police headquarters when he got a call from the central dispatcher on his walkie-talkie. "Detective Radic?"

"Yes?"

"We have a call for you from a mail lady. From the Post Office? She's been trying to reach you on your cell phone. She says it's urgent. Something about Rosemary Dunne."

"I'll take it right away," Radic said as he pulled over to the side of the road.

He saw three calls in a row from an unfamiliar phone number and called back.

"Detective Radic?" a female asked.

"Yes."

"I'm Gabby Sanders from the Post Office, and I'm at Rosemary Dunne's apartment," she said.

"Yes?"

"She's bound with rope or tape and can't move. She needs help!"

"Is she okay?"

"I think so."

"Is anyone with her?"

"I don't think so."

"Can you wait there until I arrive? It'll only be ten minutes."

"Of course."

Radic called Volcker. "Meet me at Rosemary Dunne's apartment."

"Rosemary?"

"She's tied up. Literally."

"I'm on my way."

Volcker was the first to arrive. "Rosemary, it's Max Volcker. Are you okay?"

"Yes, but I can't move!"

"No key under the doormat?"

"No."

Volcker looked at the door, then at a nearby window. He opted for the window, using a rock to break the glass. A minute later, he was inside.

Rosemary was seated in a kitchen chair, wearing nothing but her underclothes. Her hands and feet were bound. A gag lay on the floor near the chair. Her lip was bleeding, but there were no other signs of injury. She looked frightened but not hysterical.

Volcker spotted the knives on the kitchen counter and used one to remove the duct tape, releasing Rosemary's hands and feet.

Rosemary bolted to the bathroom. "I'll be right back," she said.

Volcker heard water running, a toilet flushing. Rosemary reappeared, wearing a nightgown.

"Rosemary, are you okay? We should probably get you to a hospital."

"I think I'm okay," she said.

There was a knock at the front door. "Max?"

"Coming!" Volcker said as he opened the door for Radic.

"Rosemary, are you okay?" Radic asked.

"I'm fine," she said, "but I'm getting a little tired of uninvited guests."

"You don't mean us, do you, Rosemary?" Volcker asked with a smile.

"No, detective," she said. "I invited you."

"Who was it who did this to you?" Radic asked.

"I think I know, but he never actually told me his name," she said. "He was badly injured in a fight, and he wanted me to patch him up. He knew I was a nurse."

Volcker pulled out his cell phone and scrolled down to the sketch of Basil. "Is this the guy?"

"He's the one," she said.

"Basil Vasilikas," Volcker said.

CHAPTER FIFTY-EIGHT: FREE AT LAST

"That's what I thought," Rosemary said. "Stephanos' uncle."

"He was injured?" Radic asked.

"Pretty badly," she said.

"Where exactly?"

"In the neck. A two-inch cut. Deep. Also one in the thigh. Not so bad."

"Did he hurt you?" Volcker asked.

"No."

"What did he have you do?" Volcker asked.

"I bathed the wounds and applied some disinfectant," she said. "He insisted that I stitch up the neck wound. That's a first for me."

"Do you know how he got in?" Radic asked.

Rosemary shrugged.

"He probably has a key," Volcker said. "Carol's key."

Rosemary's composure flagged at this point. She started sobbing.

Then she rallied. "I need to get dressed and go to work," she said. "I'm already late."

"Rosemary," Volcker said gently. "That's probably not a good idea. Let me call your boss and explain the situation. I'm sure they'll understand."

Rosemary hesitated, gazing at Volcker. Then she nodded her head and gave him her boss' name and number.

"When will this ever end?" she asked Radic.

"Soon, Rosemary," he said. "Soon."

Chapter Fifty-Nine: The Keeper of the Keys

Reflecting on her conversation with Spider Donatelli over a breakfast of lukewarm oatmeal and applesauce, Mulroy remembered that Basil was not the first "keyster" to surface in this case. She had another memory of someone with so many keys on his key chain that he couldn't fit all of them in his pocket—Jake Jacoby.

The other time she had thought about keys was in Dimitri's office. Dimitri had a skeleton key, which he kept locked in the office safe. Now, why would he do that? Not because he was careless or forgetful. But because he had reason to worry that the key might be stolen. Or copied.

By whom? Stephanos? Certainly not. Dimitri trusted him implicitly. Trojanowski? Perhaps. Her blood boiled at the very thought of the man. She would love to see him charged with yet another crime or infraction. Basil? Certainly. Maybe it had happened before.

Basil might very well have a key to all the sheds on Dimitri's compound. He might have a key to Stephanos' apartment. He might even have a key to Trojanowski's home. Come to think of it, he probably had a key to Carol Sloan's apartment. She shuddered at the thought.

Which brought her back to Jacoby. If Basil was obsessed with keys, might he have obtained keys to Kennywood Park when he was an employee there? And might he have copied or kept those keys? Might this be his hideaway, at least during the off-season? Spider Donatelli's neat division of the world between Iraq and the U.S. made sense in the abstract but not in reality.

CHAPTER FIFTY-NINE: THE KEEPER OF THE KEYS

Once a thief, always a thief. Once a key fanatic, always a key fanatic.

She gave Jacoby a call. Jacoby was pleased to hear from her and asked about the case. She told him enough to impress upon him the urgency of her request. Jacoby had just delivered a busload of schoolchildren to their elementary school. He was not due back until 2:20 p.m. If Jasper Fitzpatrick agreed, he would get the keys and meet her at the park entrance at 10:30 a.m.

Mulroy tried to reach Radic, but he didn't pick up, so she sent him a text. Moments later, she was on the road to Kennywood Park.

Jacoby's smile faded when he saw Mulroy's black-and-blue face. "What the hell happened to you?" he asked.

Mulroy explained as they entered the park and strode towards the Old Mill. "I hope they give that bastard a long sentence for what he did to you!" he said with feeling.

"I was brought up not to wish anyone ill," she said. "Even if someone hurts you. But part of me wishes exactly the same thing."

When they reached the entrance to the Old Mill, Mulroy noticed that the door was ajar and that there was blood on the pavement. Jacoby was about to enter when she held up her hand to stop him. "I'd better call for backup," she explained, using her walkie-talkie to make the request. She also texted Radic.

"Is there nothing we can do until they arrive?" Jacoby asked.

Mulroy thought about it. She didn't have a gun, but she did have her taser. And she now felt that she could use it if necessary.

"Open the door, slowly!" she said.

A row of ornate boats greeted her. On the seat of the lead boat, she saw more blood. "This is the police!" she shouted and listened in awe at the echoes...the police...the police.

"Is anybody there...ere...ere?"

Then she heard a faint response: "Help...elp...elp! I'm in here...ere...ere!"

Mulroy motioned to Jacoby, who flicked on a light and then an electronic switch that activated the fleet of boats. With a sudden shudder, the boats began to move. Mulroy and Jacoby hopped into the second one, to avoid the bloody seat, and turned on their cell phone flashlights for better illumination.

"It's the police...ice...ice!" she cried. "We're here to help...elp...elp!"

Then she heard a response: "Thank God...od...od!"

Stephanos Papadopoulos was standing up when Mulroy and Jacoby arrived. He looked thin, gaunt, weary, and distressed. His beard was scraggly, his clothes were torn. A far cry from the legendary Dude she had imagined.

The stench was overpowering. A combination of poop, urine, vomit, and blood. She gagged at the smell.

Then she noticed the manacle attached to his left foot. *How horrible!* she thought to herself. *How evil would someone have to be to do this to a fellow human being?*

"Are you Stephanos?" she asked.

He nodded.

"Is anyone else here?" she asked.

"No," he responded. "He went away. I was able to wound him. With a tin can lid."

"Who?" she asked. "Who did this to you?"

"My uncle," he replied. "Basil."

Jacoby attended to Stephanos as Mulroy called in the news on her walkie-talkie.

"Are you okay, man?" Jacoby asked.

"Lots of bruises," Stephanos said. "Can you get rid of this?" he asked, nodding towards the manacle.

Jacoby bent down and examined it closely. "I don't have a key for it," he said. "It's not Kennywood property. But maybe I can find something."

"Kennywood?" Stephanos exclaimed. "Kennywood? The Old Mill?"

"The very same," Jacoby said.

Stephanos stifled a half-laugh. "I should have guessed," he said. "I should have guessed."

"Paramedics are on the way," Mulroy said. "Do you need anything right away?"

CHAPTER FIFTY-NINE: THE KEEPER OF THE KEYS

Stephanos started to cry. "I need...I need..."

"What do you need?" she asked softly, putting an arm around his shoulder.

"I need Carol. I need Carol."

Stephanos crumpled to the ground, sobbing uncontrollably. His body heaved with sorrow. Mulroy crouched and did her best to comfort the poor man who had lost so much. "Officer Mulroy...roy...roy? Are you there...ere...ere?"

"Stay there...ere...ere!" she shouted. "One of us is coming out...out...out!"

Turning to Jacoby, "Can you go fetch them?" she asked.

"Of course," he said. Then, motioning to Stephanos, "Maybe I can find a bolt-cutter."

"Good idea," she replied.

Jacoby left quickly, activating the boats and making the loop back to the entrance. Minutes later, a flotilla of boats arrived, with several police officers and two paramedics. Jacoby was not among them. Presumably, he had gone to fetch tools.

The EMTs sprang into action, checking Stephanos' blood pressure and asking him basic questions about his injuries.

One of the EMTs drew Mulroy aside. "Do we know how long he's been here?" she asked.

"It could be as long as three weeks," she said.

"Unbelievable," the EMT said. "He seems to be doing remarkably well under the circumstances, but we need to get him to a hospital. And we need to get this chain off."

"Do you have anything in your kit that could do it?" Mulroy asked.

"Not really," the EMT replied, "but the guy you were with said he knew where to find something."

Jacoby returned a few minutes later with a toolbox and a passenger Detective Radic.

"I decided to hitchhike," Radic said with a grin. "How's he doing?"

"We should get him to a hospital a.s.a.p," Mulroy said as Jacoby bent over the manacle, yanking and twisting with what appeared to be a pair of bolt-cutters.

"Has he said anything about Basil?" Radic asked.

"Only that he's responsible for this," she said.

"Stephanos," Radic said, bending down to touch the prostrate man on the shoulder, "I'm Detective Radic. We're going to get you to a hospital."

Stephanos nodded but said nothing, apparently overwhelmed, perhaps in a state of shock.

Radic stepped back to make a quick phone call. Then he returned and crouched down. "Stephanos, there's someone who would like to speak with you."

He held the phone next to Stephanos' ear. The booming voice was familiar. "Stephanos!" he exclaimed. "Stephanos, are you okay?"

Stephanos gasped with joy at the sound of his father's voice. "Dad? Dad? I'm okay. It's going to be okay."

A snipping sound and a nod from Jacoby confirmed that Stephanos was finally free. Radic turned to the EMT. "Which hospital?" he asked.

"Mercy," she said.

Radic retrieved his phone. "Dimitri, we'll meet you at Mercy Hospital." Then, to the EMTs, "Let's roll."

Gingerly, an EMT escorted Stephanos to one of the boats. She wrapped him in two blankets and gave him water to drink. Mulroy and Radic followed in another boat while several police officers remained behind. Jacoby agreed to explain boat protocols to someone after calling Jasper Fitzpatrick to brief him on the morning's extraordinary events.

Chapter Sixty: Reunited

The ride from Kennywood Park to Mercy Hospital was short but surreal. Glancing back at the amusement park, Radic saw magnificent roller coasters and other alluring rides fronted by an assortment of police vehicles with flashing lights. The Old Mill was now a crime scene.

He followed the ambulance as it zipped forward, its siren blaring. It sped quickly through city streets, followed by a small convoy of police and civilian cars.

Unintentionally, his mind produced a barrage of images from the last few weeks: Carol Sloan's ransacked apartment, her costumed corpse in the woods, the frantic exit from the Sewickley Unitarian Church, the terrifying bomb explosion, the heart-stopping car chase, Trojanowski's difficult arrest.

Most of all, he saw Dimitri's multiple faces: buoyant and self-confident as he escorted Radic through the factory he had built from scratch, anguished when he learned that Stephanos was missing, deflated and confused when he heard Stephanos calling in the bomb threat.

He also thought of Mulroy and their conversation at the Squirrel Cage just a week ago. He had trusted the evidence, which pointed to Stephanos; she had trusted her instincts, which pointed to Basil. She had been proven right.

The ambulance stopped suddenly at the Mercy Hospital entrance. A handful of medical personnel appeared from out of nowhere, grabbed the stretcher from the ambulance, and quickly disappeared into the hospital.

Radic parked nearby and waited for Mulroy, who had just pulled in behind him. "You did the impossible, Kathleen," he said to her. "You saw through the funhouse mirrors!"

Mulroy laughed. "It helps when the perp has a key fetish," she said.

"It was a great catch," he said. "Stephanos probably owes his life to you."

"But we're no closer to catching Basil," she lamented.

"Don't be so sure," Radic said. "Stephanos may be able to help us. He knows Basil better than anyone."

"I sure hope so," Mulroy said.

Radic and Mulroy made their way through the well-scrubbed corridors of Mercy Hospital until they reached the E.R. Stilton was waiting for them there. Next to him was Dimitri, looking concerned but hopeful.

"Detective," he said, grasping Radic's right hand with both of his, "I can't thank you enough for returning my boy to me. I knew I could count on you."

"Officer Mulroy deserves a lot of the credit," Radic said. "She's the one who thought we should give Kennywood Park a closer look."

"Thank you, officer," Dimitri said to Mulroy. "I cannot tell you how grateful I am. Can I give you a hug?" he asked.

Mulroy teared up and looked at her boss. Stilton nodded his head, and Dimitri gave Mulroy a warm embrace.

"I'm glad we were able to find him," Mulroy said. "He's been through a lot. But I think he's going to be okay."

"My boy, he's strong," Dimitri said. "How do you say it? When the going gets tough?"

"The tough get going?" Mulroy asked.

"That's my boy!" he said.

At Stilton's suggestion, Mulroy returned to the office to write up what she had witnessed at Kennywood Park. Stilton also returned to work.

Radic remained behind with Dimitri, waiting for a report from the emergency room physician. It was a long wait, and Dimitri nodded off while Radic grabbed coffee, two sandwiches, and the morning paper.

At three p.m., Dr. Daniel Fazio appeared. "Mr. Papadopoulos?" he asked. "Yes," Dimitri replied, trying to focus on the stranger before him.

CHAPTER SIXTY: REUNITED

Radic introduced himself. "Do you know the back story?" he asked.

"My attending physician spoke with Lieutenant Stilton before Stephanos arrived," he said. "He briefed me."

"How's my son, doc?" Dimitri asked.

"Well, your son took a nasty blow to the face," he replied. "A punch. Or maybe a kick. His face is swollen, but his jaw is intact. He also has a bruised groin. And some abrasions on his hands and arms. But we've given him some pain medication. And I don't see any lasting damage from those external injuries."

"I'm relieved to hear it," Dimitri said.

"But that's not what worries me. He's badly dehydrated. That can cause organ failure if it goes on too long. And from what I understand, he may have been held prisoner for two to three weeks."

Radic nodded. "That's what we suspect," he said.

"There are psychological scars to worry about, too. He could have nightmares. He could become distrustful. But first things first. We're going to get some blood samples, urine samples. We'll do some tox screens. We'll have a better sense of where things stand by tomorrow."

"Any idea when I can speak with him?" Radic asked. "We're eager to find the man who did this to him. The trail grows colder the longer we delay."

"I understand, I truly do," Dr. Fazio said. "But at this point, the patient is sound asleep."

"And when he awakens?" Radic asked. "I really need to talk with him then."

Dr. Fazio sighed. "Mr. Papadopoulos, are you okay with some questions?"

Dimitri nodded. "I want to help. The man who did this is my brother-in-law. He's dangerous. Crazy. The police need to find him before he hurts somebody else."

"Okay, then," Dr. Fazio said. "Ten minutes when he awakens later today. Maybe more tomorrow if there are signs of progress."

"Thank you, doctor," Radic said.

Dimitri and Radic kept vigil over Stephanos in a private room after Radic gave Stilton a progress report. A nurse checked in from time to time, but they were otherwise alone. Dimitri wanted to know more about Trojanowski, whom he had trusted and liked.

"Is he a bad person?" he asked.

"We don't know yet. Maybe bad. Maybe just weak. We'll know more soon."

"Did he hurt Stephanos? Did he hurt the girl? Carol?"

"We don't know, Dimitri. His lawyer won't let him talk until we work out some sort of arrangement."

Dimitri shook his head.

"With some people, the more you do to help them, the more they take advantage of you."

"I know how you feel."

At around eight p.m. Stephanos stirred. Dimitri noticed and stood up immediately. He clasped his son's hand. "Stephanos? Stephanos? It's me! Your Dad!"

Radic saw an eye flutter. Then, the left eye opened. And the right.

"Dad?" he asked. "Where am I?"

"Mercy Hospital, son. The docs are looking after you."

"What happened to me?"

Dimitri looked at Radic.

"Stephanos, I'm Detective Radic. Do you remember me from Kennywood Park?"

Stephanos nodded slowly. "I think so. And the lady cop."

"That's right. That was Officer Mulroy. We have some questions for you. Is that okay?"

Again, Stephanos nodded.

"Who brought you to Kennywood Park?"

"Basil," he said. "My uncle."

"Do you remember how he got you there?"

He shook his head. "He must have drugged me. It's all a big blur."

"I understand," Radic said. "Don't worry about it. Some of it may come back. Why didn't you go to the Bahamas?"

Stephanos winced at the memory. "Basil came to my home. I was packing.

CHAPTER SIXTY: REUNITED

He said he had kidnapped Carol. He agreed to take me to see her. He wanted me to talk with her about something. But then. I don't know. I can't remember what happened next."

"Did he say why he kidnapped Carol?"

"He and I had an argument. Over some mugs. Harry Potter mugs."

"We know about the Muggles," Radic said.

"Basil blamed Carol when I decided that we couldn't go ahead with the Muggles. Basil got VERY upset," he said. "But it wasn't Carol's fault. I made the decision. We didn't have the legal authority."

"Do you know if he hurt Carol?"

Stephanos struggled for words. "He said it was suicide, a drug overdose. But I don't believe him."

"Did you hurt Basil at Kennywood?"

"Yes, I did."

"How did you manage to do that?"

"A can of peas," he said.

"A can of peas?"

"Basil left me a can of peas and forgot to take away the lid. It was sharp. I used it to attack him and get his cell phone. It was the only thing I could do."

"No one's blaming you for that, son," Dimitri interjected. "Are they, detective?"

"No, Dimitri, of course not. How badly did you hurt him?"

"I went for his jugular vein. He was bleeding badly. And I got him in the thigh. He fought back, but then he left. A day ago? Two days ago? I lose track."

Stephanos' eyes started to flutter. A nurse came in. "Detective, the patient needs to get some rest."

"I understand," Radic said. "Just one more question. Stephanos, do you have any idea where your uncle would go if he's badly hurt? A friend's house? One of the homeless communities?"

Stephanos was running out of energy. "What makes you think that Basil is homeless?" he asked.

273

And with that, Stephanos was fast asleep.

Chapter Sixty-One: A New Game Plan

Radic was not much of an expert on stocks per se, but it was clear to him that Trojanowski's stock had plummeted in value now that the police had access to Stephanos. In all likelihood, no one knew Basil—his habits, his quirks, and hopefully his whereabouts—better than Stephanos.

So, Radic began the staff meeting with a question: "Do we want to strike a deal with Trojanowski?"

Volcker was the first to weigh in: "If we want to prosecute Basil, then we need Trojanowski to confirm that Basil was the mastermind behind the Harry Potter scam. He can tell us what Basil's instructions were in loving detail. A lot of what Basil did was probably without Stephanos' knowledge or consent. If we're able to locate Basil and bring him in alive, Trojanowski is likely to be the lead witness for the prosecution. Trojanowski probably didn't witness the murder, but he did witness the intellectual property fraud. So, we need him, no matter how much we dislike him."

Scuglia disagreed: "I'm all in favor of prosecuting people for the Harry Potter caper. That includes Basil and Trojanowski. But we need to keep our eyes on the prize, and that's our murder case. I don't think Trojanowski knows anything about the murder. He just doesn't help us on that front. Stephanos is a better source for anything incriminating that has to do with Carol Sloan. I say, keep Trojanowski on ice until we extract as much information as we can from Stephanos."

Radic looked at Mulroy. Her jaw was no longer black and blue. She was still not drinking hot coffee, but she had graduated from water to Coca-Cola.

She was still not eating potato chips, but her diet had broadened beyond hummus and applesauce. At the moment, she looked uncomfortable, like she wanted to be somewhere else.

Stilton intervened. "Mulroy," he said. "What do you think? We'd like to hear your opinion."

Mulroy sighed. "This is tough for me. I'm trying to be objective, but it's hard for me to be objective about Trojanowski."

"Just tell us what you think," Stilton said gently.

"Well, I don't want to make any more concessions to Trojanowski than we have to," she began. "But Basil is a slippery character, and he's no dummy. He's on our radar screen right now. If he wants to get back at Stephanos, why not lie low for a while, then strike when our guard is down? We can't keep Stephanos under surveillance forever, can we?"

"No, we can't," Stilton agreed.

"How's Basil going to lie low if he's homeless?" Volcker asked.

"Well, that's an interesting question," Radic observed. "We've been assuming that he's homeless. But what if that's not true?"

Stilton looked surprised. "I thought we all agreed that he was homeless," he said.

"Well, almost all of us agree," Radic said.

"Who disagrees?" Stilton asked.

"Stephanos," he replied.

"You're kidding!" Stilton said.

"He raised questions about it, at any rate," Radic said. "Just before falling asleep. I'm going to follow up with him later today."

"But why would Basil pretend to be homeless?" Stilton asked. "Who in his right mind would do that?"

"Well, he's a master of misdirection," Radic replied. "It's like what Mulroy once said—this case is like the funhouse mirrors at Kennywood. Basil has distorted his image in lots of different ways. That's enabled him to keep one step ahead of us."

"So what does that imply for us?" Stilton asked.

"It means we have to find out where he is," Radic said. "And maybe that

CHAPTER SIXTY-ONE: A NEW GAME PLAN

means on dry land. He may be living in an actual home."

"As I see it, we have two excellent witnesses now," Mulroy observed. "Trojanowski knows a lot about the Harry Potter scheme. Stephanos knows a lot about everything else. Let's get as much information as we can from both of them and blow this case wide open!"

"Radic?" Stilton asked.

"That's my opinion, too, sir," Radic said. "I think the time is ripe to get information from Stephanos, from Trojanowski, and from Federov, too."

"What will our friends from the FBI say?" Stilton asked.

"Basil is still the kingpin," Radic replied. "We have to convince them that it pays to make some concessions to Trojanowski and to Federov. Trojanowski can lead us to Basil. Federov can lead us to other buyers. There will still be enough prosecutions to keep the feds happy."

"Okay," Stilton said. "I'm on board. I want you to learn everything you possibly can about Basil Vasilikas. I want to know his blood type. I want to know where he cuts his hair. I want to know where he shops. I want to know his favorite foods. I want to know whether he's drinking again. I want to know what part of Pittsburgh he considers home. I want you to find that son of a bitch and bring him to justice!"

"Yes, sir," Radic said. "That's what we'll do."

Chapter Sixty-Two: A Whiff of Soap

Radic's visit to Mercy Hospital yielded two surprises. First, Stephanos was wide awake. The color in his cheeks was redder. His eyes were more animated. And his scraggly beard was gone. He smiled as Radic entered the room. "Nice to see you, detective," he said.

The second surprise was the presence of his friend, Doug Howley. "Good to see you again, detective," Howley said. "And thank you for rescuing Stephanos."

Something else was different, too, though Radic couldn't put a finger on it. Maybe it was Dimitri, who didn't leap forward to shake his hand. Everyone was polite, but somehow the mood had changed.

"You're looking much better," Radic said. "How are you feeling?"

"The docs fixed me up pretty good," Stephanos said. "I'm safe, thanks to you and Officer Mulroy. And I had my first warm meal in three weeks. Chicken, roasted potatoes, and asparagus. I'm feeling pretty good."

"Glad to hear it!" Radic said. "So, are you up for a few questions?"

There was an uncomfortable silence, eventually broken by Dimitri. "We're very grateful to you, Detective Rad-itch, for everything that you've done. And Stephanos will be happy to answer your questions. But we've decided that he should have a lawyer present when he does."

These words, which Radic had heard many times before, felt particularly painful when spoken by Dimitri, whom he had come to think of as an ally, even a friend.

"It was my idea," Doug Howley said. "Stephanos has nothing to hide. But some people have done some very bad things in the name of the firm and

CHAPTER SIXTY-TWO: A WHIFF OF SOAP

in his name. And Stephanos has been forced to do some things that he didn't want to do. Under the circumstances, we think it makes sense to be cautious. I can give you the name of Stephanos' lawyer. He will be more than happy to set something up."

Radic said nothing for a few moments. Then he turned to the patient. "Stephanos, you have every right to an attorney. And I understand why you might want one, even if you have nothing to hide. But we're trying as hard as we can to bring a killer to justice. Your uncle. He's badly injured at the moment. You know this yourself. What you don't know is that he was able to have his wounds treated and patched up. He may be recovering even as we speak. If he does, he could strike again. And you're his number one target. Or he could leave Pittsburgh and never return, in which case he would never pay for the murder we believe he committed. A murder that cost the life of the woman you loved."

No one said a word for a long time. Then Dimitri spoke: "What do you suggest, detective?"

"I suggest that we draw a line in the sand between two types of questions: On one side of the line are questions relating to your company and the Harry Potter mugs. On the other side of the line are questions relating to the whereabouts of your brother-in-law. We need Stephanos' help to track down Basil, and we need his help right now."

Dimitri thought for a moment. "Can you give us a few moments?" he asked.

"Of course," Radic said. "I'll just step outside."

As he waited in the corridor, Radic thought back to his senior thesis defense at Carnegie Mellon years earlier. He had presented his findings and answered questions from a panel of distinguished professors, including Lucas Renfert. For ten agonizing minutes, he paced back and forth, awaiting the committee's verdict.

It had ended happily, with hearty congratulations and a celebratory lunch. He had received a "distinction" for his thesis.

But how would this group decide? Distrust of the police these days was high. He thought that he had earned the trust of the Papadopoulos family.

But who knew for sure?

Dimitri opened the door after ten anxious minutes. "Detective, we've reached a decision. Come inside, and we'll explain."

Radic reentered the room, grateful that it was a single.

"Detective, I've gotten to know you over the past three weeks. You've treated me fairly. I think you'll treat Stephanos fairly. So we agree to your line in the sand. Anything Stephanos can say that leads you to Basil; he wants to help. But Stephanos is not fully recovered from his injuries, and he's on medication. If you ask a question that we think crosses the line in the sand, we will say so. And Stephanos will not answer that question. Do we agree?"

"I appreciate that, Dimitri," Radic said. "And I'm fine with that arrangement."

"Okay, then," Dimitri said. "Pull up a chair. And ask away."

"Thank you, Dimitri," Radic said. Then to Stephanos: "Before you drifted into sleep yesterday, you said something that surprised me. You said, I think, that you weren't convinced that Basil is actually homeless. What makes you think that?"

Stephanos looked at his father, who nodded his head.

"Well, Basil has been homeless on and off over the past two years. At those times, he's probably been based at the homeless camp near the Birmingham Bridge. And he's used that crazy boat of his to get around."

"What's with the boat?" Radic asked.

"Well, it probably goes back to Jason and the Argonauts. Uncle Basil sometimes sees himself as a Greek hero. A tragic Greek hero. Whatever it is, he's always adored boats. And he eventually bought one from Kennywood Park."

"You've seen the boat?" Radic asked.

"Yep, it's from the Old Mill. I should have put two and two together. He worked there years ago."

"Do you know where he stores the boat?" Radic asked.

"Somewhere near the Monongahela River."

"But you don't know exactly where?"

CHAPTER SIXTY-TWO: A WHIFF OF SOAP

"No, sorry. I'd say Basil has gone out of his way to keep that a secret. Like so many other things."

"So, what you're saying is he HAS been homeless, right?" Radic asked.

"Yes, that's right. But I've often had the sense that Basil has a base of operations other than the homeless camp. Maybe he crashes with a friend. Maybe he has a hideaway apartment somewhere."

"What makes you think that?" Radic asked.

"Well, two things, really," Stephanos said. "First, he's usually clean-shaven. Which means that he has access to an electrical outlet."

"Interesting," Radic said. "But couldn't he use a straight razor?"

"That's a possibility," Stephanos acknowledged. "But Basil has a bit of a tremor from his Iraq war days."

"That's true," Dimitri chimed in.

"So he might be a little nervous about using a straight razor."

Radic nodded. "How about a food bank? They have electrical outlets where you could plug in a shaver."

"Basil is a very proud man, Detective. I'm not saying he'd never go to one under any circumstances. But he sure wouldn't like it. I just don't think he'd go there on a regular basis."

Radic nodded again. "You said there was a second clue that leads you to believe he's not truly homeless."

"Yes, there is. Body odor."

"Say what?"

"Well, the absence of body odor. Basil doesn't smell like a homeless man. On the contrary, he usually smells like soap. Even over the past few weeks, when he was holding me prisoner, I'd be willing to swear he's had access to a shower."

"Interesting," Radic said. "Aren't there showers that homeless people can use?"

"That's not something I can answer, Detective," Stephanos said. "I'm just telling you what I've observed. Despite lots of ups and downs, Uncle Basil smells pretty good, and he shaves maybe every other day. Does that sound like a homeless person to you?"

Chapter Sixty-Three: A Difficult Conversation

The FBI did not make concessions gladly. But now that Basil Vasilikas was within their sights, Fromm and Fogarty were willing to reduce Trojanowski's sentence in return for valuable intelligence. The U.S. attorney signed off on this arrangement.

In a nutshell, all parties agreed that Trojanowski would serve no more than two years in a minimum-security federal prison in return for satisfactory answers to several key questions. The FBI insisted on taking the lead in the interrogation, which would focus primarily on the intellectual property side of the case. Stilton was fine with that, so long as Radic got to ask some questions and so long as Trojanowski's assault on Mulroy would be adjudicated through local courts.

The FBI and the U.S. attorney agreed to an even sweeter deal for Federov, who, after all, was just a buyer. In return for his testimony and documents that could help to convict Basil Vasilikas, Federov would serve no more than one year in a minimum-security federal prison. As with Trojanowski, the FBI would ask questions first, followed by Radic.

At Trojanowski's insistence, and despite objections from Radic, Mulroy was excluded from the interrogation. Mulroy's facial wounds had healed considerably but not completely. Trojanowski and his lawyer found her presence disconcerting. Stilton agreed to this arrangement, arguing that there would be ample opportunity to adjudicate Trojanowski's assault later on.

CHAPTER SIXTY-THREE: A DIFFICULT CONVERSATION

Agent Fromm wore crisp beige slacks, a light blue shirt, a gray sports coat, and well-polished black shoes for the occasion. Agent Fogarty wore gray pants, a white shirt with cuff links, and a tie.

After establishing Trojanowski's employment history at Dimitri's Sturdy Dishes, Fromm zeroed in on the Muggles.

FROMM: Mr. Trojanowski, who first told you about the idea to design and manufacture some Harry Potter mugs, known as Muggles?

TROJANOWSKI: That would be my employer's son, Stephanos Papadopoulos.

FROMM: What exactly did he say about the mugs?

TROJANOWSKI: He said that he and his uncle Basil were excited by this possibility and that they were thinking of taking some first steps.

FROMM: And his uncle Basil would be?

TROJANOWSKI: Sorry. Basil Vasilikas.

FROMM: Did Stephanos Papadopoulos indicate to you that there might be some legal barriers to producing and selling these Muggles?

TROJANOWSKI: Yes, he did.

FROMM: What exactly did he say?

TROJANOWSKI: He said that they were conferring with a lawyer in order to determine how to proceed.

FROMM: Did he say who that lawyer was?

TROJANOWSKI: Not at the time. But I later learned that the lawyer was Rob McPherson.

FROMM: Who told you that?

TROJANOWSKI: I believe that was Stephanos.

FROMM: At what point did you see drawings for these mugs, known as Muggles?

TROJANOWSKI: Well, I can't be precise about that. But I'd say maybe six weeks later.

FROMM: Who actually produced the drawings?

TROJANOWSKI: Initially, it would have been Stephanos and Basil. Later, they hired a graphic designer to do it properly. Those are the drawings I saw.

FROMM: And when did you actually see some Harry Potter mugs?

TROJANOWSKI: Well, that took more time. I'd say maybe six months later.

FROMM: Do you know who authorized the production of those mugs?

TROJANOWSKI: I assume that it was Stephanos.

FROMM: Why do you assume that?

TROJANOWSKI: Because a decision like that would have to come from the top.

FROMM: But the top, as you put it, was Dimitri Papadopoulos, the owner, not Stephanos Papadopoulos, the owner's son.

TROJANOWSKI: Well, that's true. But it was commonly understood that Stephanos would succeed Dimitri someday. So, if Stephanos approved something, I assumed that he had Dimitri's blessing.

FROMM: Can you tell us how many mugs were produced initially?

TROJANOWSKI: It was my understanding that there were six.

FROMM: Six?

TROJANOWSKI: Yes, enough to see what different Harry Potter characters would look like. Not enough to spook the lawyers.

FROMM: We come back to the lawyers again. Did you ever see any written communications from Dimitri's lawyer or from the Harry Potter lawyers?

TROJANOWSKI: No, that would be above my pay grade.

FROMM: So you don't know if the Muggles idea was ever officially approved?

TROJANOWSKI: Well, the first step was to produce some prototypes, which we did. The next step was to mass-produce the mugs. Once we cleared the legal hurdles.

FROMM: Once you cleared the legal hurdles. But from what you said, you don't actually know if those legal hurdles were cleared. Isn't that correct?

TROJANOWSKI: (squirming) Well, yes and no.

FROMM: How can that be? Isn't it either yes or no?

TROJANOWSKI: Well, a few months ago, I was told that we were good to go and that we were going to produce the mugs.

CHAPTER SIXTY-THREE: A DIFFICULT CONVERSATION

FROMM: And who told you that exactly?

TROJANOWSKI: That was Basil.

FROMM: Not Stephanos?

TROJANOWSKI: That's correct.

FROMM: Did you ever get confirmation that Stephanos was on board with this decision?

TROJANOWSKI: Yes.

FROMM: From Stephanos?

TROJANOWSKI: Indirectly.

FROMM: You mean from Basil?

TROJANOWSKI: Well, yes, Basil said that Stephanos was on board.

FROMM: Were those his exact words?

TROJANOWSKI: Well, something like that.

FROMM: Did it ever occur to you to ask Stephanos directly? Or to ask Dimitri directly?

TROJANOWSKI: (squirming) Well, that's not how a company works. You don't go to the top for confirmation of every decision that's made.

FROMM: But this wasn't just any decision, was it? You knew up front that there was considerable doubt about the legality of producing these mugs, didn't you?

TROJANOWSKI: Considerable doubt? Some doubt, for sure. But it's up to other people to make these decisions. Not me.

FROMM: What exactly did Basil Vasilikas say when he told you the mugs were going to be mass-produced?

TROJANOWSKI: He said that time was of the essence and that we were going to make this a high priority.

FROMM: Meaning what?

TROJANOWSKI: Meaning that we were going to work on this after hours. In the evening and on Sundays so that it didn't interfere with our other work.

FROMM: And who told you this?

TROJANOWSKI: Basil.

FROMM: Not Stephanos?

TROJANOWSKI: Not Stephanos.

FROMM: Didn't that make you suspicious?

TROJANOWSKI: Well, in retrospect, maybe it should have. At the time, I didn't pay much attention to the situation.

FROMM: In truth, didn't you have reason to believe that Basil was doing this behind Stephanos' back? Didn't you have reason to believe that you were engaging in an illegal activity?

At this point, attorney Hirsch intervened: "Agent Fromm, I object to the tone you're taking with my client. The purpose of this conversation is not to determine my client's guilt or innocence. That's off the table because of the plea bargain."

"I'm sorry if this line of questioning offends you or your client," Fromm replied icily, "but this gets to the very heart of the case, which is that a decision was made to manufacture and sell large numbers of Harry Potter coffee mugs without the legal authority to do so."

"That may be true," Hirsch said, "but my client had no way of knowing that."

"Well, in fact, he did have a way of knowing that," Fromm replied. "He could simply have asked Stephanos. Or he could have asked Dimitri."

"My client has already explained that a certain level of trust is necessary in any business enterprise," Hirsch countered. "He was not obligated to go beyond his immediate superior."

"But it's not at all clear that Basil was his immediate superior," Fromm countered. "In fact, he had previously been sacked from the firm. He had no actual authority outside of the R&D shop. His role was to develop ideas, not to approve them. Your client was surely aware of this."

Trojanowski grew visibly agitated as the conversation ensued. Recognizing the signs, Hirsch asked for a recess, which Fromm reluctantly granted.

Radic had seen Fromm in action before and sensed that nothing he could say would divert him from his chosen path. Still, he couldn't resist the urge to say something. "What are you trying to accomplish?" he asked.

"I want to find out what he knew and when he knew it," he responded. "And knock that smug look off his face."

CHAPTER SIXTY-THREE: A DIFFICULT CONVERSATION

"Well, we get smug looks all the time," Radic said. "In my view, life's too short to worry about them."

"Okay, Mr. Smarty Pants, what would you do if it were up to you?" he asked.

"Well, if it were up to me, I'd cut to the chase. And then do some backfilling."

"And how would you do that?"

"I'd ask him a simple question: Do you have any reason to believe that Basil ordered the mugs without Stephanos' consent?"

"You think he'll answer that question right off the bat?"

"Yes."

"Well, go ahead and ask it yourself. Then, if he doesn't answer it, we'll go back to my way: building a record, methodically, with one factual question after another."

The meeting reconvened. Fromm explained that Detective Radic would like to ask a question.

"Mr. Trojanowski, do you have any reason to believe that Basil ordered the mugs without Stephanos' consent?" Radic asked.

Trojanowski looked to his attorney, who nodded.

"Yes, I do."

"Please explain."

"I heard them arguing about it one night after work. Basil said he went ahead and mass-produced the mugs even though the lawyers hadn't approved it. Stephanos said that was the wrong decision, and he was not okay with it."

"How was the dispute resolved?"

"Stephanos said he was going to tell his father."

"And then what?"

"And then I left."

"If you knew that Stephanos was opposed to selling the mugs, why did you continue to aid and abet Basil?"

Trojanowski raised his hands above his head in a gesture of exasperation.

"I tried to back out, but Basil wouldn't let me."

"What do you mean, 'He wouldn't let you?'"

"He told me that if I didn't do exactly what he said, he would beat me to a bloody pulp. And then he would go after my family."

"Did you believe him?"

"I don't always believe what Basil says. But when he said that, with the devil's own look in his eyes, yeah, you're damn right I believed him. I was scared to death!"

The room was silent for at least 30 seconds.

Then Radic spoke: "I have one final question before Agent Fromm resumes his questioning. Do you have any idea where Basil stores his valuables? Cash, private papers, that sort of thing?"

"I don't know for sure," Trojanowski said. "But I have a hunch."

"What's your hunch?" Radic asked.

"About a week ago, Basil asked me to give him a lift. He had me pick him up in West Mifflin, where Homestead Duquesne Road meets Thompson Run Road. Right in front of Al Cheapo's storage place. He had a lot of paperwork with him that night. I'm guessing that he stores some of it at Al's."

"Thank you, Mr. Trojanowski," Radic said, standing up. "And thank you, Agent Fromm. I'll leave you to finish up the questioning. I have an errand to run."

Chapter Sixty-Four: New Evidence

Mulroy was reviewing vehicle reports and stewing over her snub. She knew that Stilton was trying to reconcile competing goals when he excluded her from Trojanowski's interrogation. She also knew that the assault charges had not been dropped.

Still, it stung. Anything connected to Trojanowski was now deeply personal to her. Every time she felt the absence of a tooth with her tongue, she thought of Trojanowski. Every time she looked at her purple face in the mirror, she thought of Trojanowski. Every time she booked a dental appointment, she thought of Trojanowski.

Her phone rang. She was tempted to ignore it until she noticed that the caller was Radic.

"Mulroy, are you free?"

"Aren't you supposed to be quizzing Mr. T.?"

"I left early. We have a lead."

"Where shall I meet you?"

"Out front. Five minutes."

Mulroy grew excited when Radic explained the tip.

"Do you think he stores his boat there?"

"Unlikely, I'd say. It's not terribly close to the river. But papers. Clues to his movements. Clues to his plots. Clues to his whereabouts. Something's gotta be there. I can just feel it!"

Radic pulled into the lot for Al Cheapo's Self Storage, spotted a clerk, and identified himself as a police officer.

"We're looking for Al," he said.

"Al who?" the clerk asked.

"Al Cheapo."

The clerk laughed. "There is no Al Cheapo. That's just a gimmick to attract attention. But we do have an owner. Would you like to speak with him?"

A mousy man with calloused hands, faded blue jeans, and a raggedy plaid shirt emerged from a small office in the back.

"Mike Rich," he said, extending a hand. "How can I help you?"

Radic was tempted to ask how a Mr. Rich became a Mr. Cheapo but decided to pass. He produced a sketch of Basil from his shirt pocket.

"We're looking for this man. We have reason to believe that he might rent a storage unit here."

The owner studied the sketch and raised his eyebrows. "That looks like Basil," he said. "Hey, Bart, come 'ere a sec!"

"Does that look like Basil to you?"

The clerk nodded. "Yes, it does."

"Is he in trouble?" Rich asked.

"Would it surprise you if I said he was?"

Rich shrugged. "I know him, and I like him. But, no, it wouldn't surprise me. He's a tough guy. And he has a temper."

"We'd like to see his locker," Radic said.

Rich looked worried. "Detective, I'd like to help, but I have obligations to my clients. It's just that…"

Radic interrupted him. "Mr. Rich, I know what you're going to say. So you listen to what I'm going to say. This man is wanted for murder and two counts of kidnapping. If you insist on a warrant, I'll get one. I'll also launch an investigation into your finances, your code compliance history, your employees' records, and anything else that occurs to me while I'm waiting to get my warrant."

Rich held up his hands apologetically. "Detective, detective, there's no need to play hardball. You made your point. I'll show you his locker. We like to help the police."

Basil's locker was big enough to fit a gym bag and some papers, but no

CHAPTER SIXTY-FOUR: NEW EVIDENCE

boat.

"Just this? Nothing bigger?"

Rich nodded. "We have bigger units, but Basil doesn't rent one."

"How long has he rented this?"

"I can check. Two years, maybe."

Rich opened the locker, and Radic reached inside after donning gloves.

"Do you have a shopping bag?" he asked. "Maybe two?"

Rich nodded and fetched two cloth bags. Mulroy transferred papers into one bag, everything else into another.

"How often does Basil drop by?" Radic asked.

Rich thought for a moment. "Maybe once a week."

"What does he talk about?"

"Well, boats. The Iraq War. He's a vet, you know."

"I know. What else?"

"Well, let's see, mugs. Coffee mugs."

"How so?"

"He asked to see my coffee mug, which is pretty ordinary. He asked if I might be interested in upgrading to a Harry Potter mug."

"A Harry Potter mug?"

"Yeah, he said his company was going to be producing a whole bunch of them. He wanted me to buy some."

"What did you say?"

"I said, 'Who the hell is Harry Potter'?"

Chapter Sixty-Five: Sifting and Winnowing

Volcker, Scuglia, and Mulroy gathered at Radic's apartment that evening to sift through the treasure trove of material they had acquired from Al Cheapo's.

"Mulroy, can you handle pizza yet?" Radic asked.

"If it's cold!" she replied.

"That's no fun," he lamented.

"At this point, even cold pizza makes my mouth water. I can't eat hummus and applesauce anymore. Bring it on."

"Okay," Radic replied. He ordered three large pizzas and two salads.

"We're going to need two sifters and a scribe," Radic announced.

"I can sift," Volcker announced.

"Me too," Scuglia said.

"I guess I'm the scribe," Mulroy said.

Radic fetched beers and sodas from the refrigerator, and the crew got down to work.

The first item to attract the group's attention was a bright orange life preserver, presumably for Basil's boat. "Write down the brand name and model number. Maybe we can figure out where he bought it," Radic instructed.

The second item was a thick, heavy legal tome entitled "Fundamentals of U.S. Intellectual Property Law" by Amanda Reid. It was well-used—dog-eared, with certain passages underlined with a magic marker. "Wow!"

CHAPTER SIXTY-FIVE: SIFTING AND WINNOWING

Volcker marveled. "He was serious about the legal stuff."

"Maybe he was hoping to convince Stephanos to take the plunge," Scuglia said.

The third item of interest was a bottle of Woodford Reserve, unopened. "At least he has good taste," Volcker observed.

"Can you tell where he bought the bourbon?" Radic asked.

"I put a bunch of receipts together in the green bag," Mulroy reported. "Maybe it's in there."

"Let's switch to the receipts for a while," Radic suggested. "That will tell us where he shops."

Mulroy emptied a bunch of receipts and other odds and ends on the kitchen table.

"Okay, what do we have?" Radic asked.

A half hour and three pizzas later, the group had a much better sense of Basil's geographic center of gravity. Receipts from Dick's Sporting Goods, Fine Wine and Good Spirits, Giant Eagle, Target, and Lowe's Home Improvement. Many of the receipts were from stores on East Waterfront St., in Homestead. "Are the receipts from different weeks or the same week?" Radic asked.

Mulroy checked. "They're from different weeks."

"Good!" Radic exclaimed. "That means he shops there regularly."

"What did he buy from Lowe's?"

Mulroy checked. "Duct tape!" Mulroy shouted. "He bought duct tape!"

"Check the date," Radic said. "Is it before or after Carol's body was discovered?"

"Before," Mulroy said. "September 13."

"What else did he buy from Lowe's?"

"A lamp, a flashlight, some wood, some nails."

"Why would he buy a lamp if he's homeless?" Volcker asked.

"Good question," Radic said. "Dunno."

"How about Giant Eagle?" Radic asked.

"There's a lot of stuff here," Mulroy replied. "What are you looking for?"

"Well, for starters, a can of peas," Radic replied.

Mulroy sifted through over a dozen receipts, covering three to four weeks. "I see minestrone soup. Beets. Wax beans. Carrots. I see peas! I see peas!"

"And the date for the peas?"

"It's recent," Mulroy replied. "About a week ago."

"It all fits," Radic said.

"Yes, but what does it tell us?" Scuglia asked. "Where is he?"

"This is his shopping center, on the waterfront in Homestead," Radic replied. "If we wait for him there, sooner or later, he's going to show up."

"Unless he's one step ahead of us," Volcker said ruefully.

"But we have one thing in our favor," Radic said.

"What's that?" Volcker asked.

"There's a good chance he's going to need fresh bandages, medicine, painkillers," Radic said.

"He's a motivated shopper," Mulroy chimed in.

"We need to alert Stilton," Radic said. "And we need to position people at the key stores: a pharmacy, a grocery store."

"CVS?" Mulroy asked.

"For sure," Radic said.

"Giant Eagle?"

"Absolutely!"

"Target?"

"Maybe."

"Where are we going to find the personnel for this?" Mulroy asked.

"We're so close, we can't allow him to slip through our fingers again. I think Stilton will support us."

Radic was about to adjourn when he thought of something.

"Mulroy, when you look at the receipts, at Giant Eagle and at CVS, do you ever see a *Post-Gazette*?"

Mulroy was surprised by the question. "No, I don't think so. Let's check."

Scuglia, Volcker, and Mulroy sifted through the receipts again and looked up at Radic.

"Not a single newspaper," Mulroy reported.

"Okay," Radic said slowly. "What do you make of that?"

CHAPTER SIXTY-FIVE: SIFTING AND WINNOWING

"It seems very odd," Volcker said. "If I were suspected of murder and kidnapping, I'd want to know what the police are saying. I'd want to know every detail."

"Exactly," Radic said. "So what does that tell us?"

"He doesn't care what other people think about him?" Scuglia volunteered.

"I don't think so," Radic said.

"He reads the paper at a local library?" Volcker suggested.

"Not a bad guess," Radic said. "But a public library is a bit too public. Maybe something else."

"He already has a subscription!" Mulroy exclaimed. "So he doesn't need to buy newspapers every day."

"Bingo!" Radic said.

"You think he has a subscription? And a home where it's delivered?" Volcker asked.

"That's what I think. Because that's what Stephanos thinks. We could be wrong. But why else would he buy a lamp? I suggest that one of us check out the Post Gazette's subscription list. Look for Basil Vasilikas. But also look for Basil Whatever. Look for Whatever Vasilikas. Look for Whatever Papadopoulos. Change his name around. Maybe something will turn up."

"I'll do it first thing tomorrow morning!" Volcker promised.

"Great! Let's meet with Stilton at 9 o'clock. I'll set things up."

Chapter Sixty-Six: A Bridge to Somewhere

"There's more Basils who read the *Post-Gazette* than you might think," Volcker said.

"How many exactly?" Radic asked.

"Ten."

"Any that live in Homestead or West Mifflin?"

"There's one that lives on the South Side," Volcker reported. "And one that lives in Braddock."

"Check them out," Stilton ordered. "Begin with public records. If one looks promising, we'll pay him a visit."

"How many Stephanoses did you get?"

"Only one," Volcker reported. "And he lives in McKees Rocks."

"Check him out, too," Stilton said.

"Anyone else?" Radic asked.

"We have a Papadopoulos in Ambridge."

"That's pretty far north," Radic said.

"Nevertheless, check him out," Stilton said.

"Store surveillance, sir?" Radic asked.

"48 hours," Stilton replied. "Choose your top two or three stores, and we'll put some people there around the clock."

"Armed?" Radic asked.

"Armed."

"And if nothing happens?"

CHAPTER SIXTY-SIX: A BRIDGE TO SOMEWHERE

Stilton looked grim. "We'll cross that bridge when we come to it."

* * *

Mulroy was relaxing at home as best she could. She was scheduled to stake out the Homestead Giant Eagle from ten a.m. to six p.m. the following day. It was exciting to be close to catching a murderer. But it was also frustrating. They had traced Basil to a shopping center that occupied about two hundred and sixty-five acres of land. But could he be trapped? She wasn't so sure.

Mulroy turned on the TV and flipped the channels. She laughed when she saw one of her options: "Harry Potter and the Chamber of Secrets."

Why not? she said to herself.

Harry and Ron Weasley were flying to Hogwarts, without permission, in Ron's father's car. Ron, a terrible driver, crashed into a Whomping Willow and broke his wand. They would have hell to pay when Angus Dumbledore discovered what they did. It would be even worse when Ron's parents found out.

Mulroy was about to turn off the TV and go to bed when she thought of something. She made a mental note to follow up on it.

The following morning, after a semi-normal breakfast with lukewarm oatmeal and blueberry jam on untoasted bread, Mulroy called the *Post-Gazette* and asked for the subscription department.

She identified herself and tracked down the staffer who had spoken with Volcker the day before. She gave the staffer a list of names and asked her to call back if she got a hit. A half-hour later, the staffer called.

"We have a match," she reported.

"What's the name?" Mulroy asked.

"Draco Malfoy," the staffer said.

"I should have guessed!" Mulroy exclaimed. She requested an address and got it. "Thank you, thank you, thank you. We really appreciate your help!"

Mulroy immediately called Radic. No response. Then she called Stilton.

No response. Next, she called Volcker. No response.

"Where the hell are they?" she said aloud.

Determined to pursue the lead, Mulroy left a text for Radic: "A Draco Malfoy subscribes to PG. Address is 205 Blackmore St. in Duck Hollow. I'm going to check it out."

With that, Mulroy grabbed a taser, locked her apartment door, got in her car, and drove to Duck Hollow.

Mulroy remembered hearing about the community from her parents, who grew up in nearby Swissvale. It was a community of only a few dozen residents, with one rickety bridge connecting it to the outside world. The bridge was reportedly so fragile that when residents needed a new appliance, delivery vans would deposit it on the near side of the bridge. Later, residents would wheel the appliance to its destination on a dolly.

Mulroy had never actually visited Duck Hollow, though she knew how to get there. It was not far from the Homestead Grays Bridge, named after a famous all-Black professional baseball team.

When she arrived, she laughed at the sign: Duck Hollow—Population: Just Enough! If someone wanted to live quietly without being noticed, this was surely the place to be.

Remembering the story of the rickety bridge, Mulroy decided to park her car outside the village limits. Besides, she didn't want to draw attention to herself as she snooped around. She got out of her car and locked it.

The wooden bridge creaked and groaned as Mulroy approached the tiny community. Her first impression was that Duck Hollow could be a Hollywood set for a sitcom filmed in the 1950s. She almost wondered if the homes were three-dimensional. She took a peek behind one of them. It seemed to be a full-fledged home. But there was a rusty Schwinn bike in the driveway. Laundry hanging on a clothesline. A statue of the BVM in the front lawn. She felt like she was in some kind of time warp.

Warily, Mulroy approached 205 Blackmore, gripping her taser. She saw no car, but there was a garage. She noticed that there was no *Post-Gazette* in the driveway, but there was a *Post-Gazette* in another driveway. The resident was probably home.

CHAPTER SIXTY-SIX: A BRIDGE TO SOMEWHERE

Mulroy started to feel tense. Her teeth began to chatter. Her skirmish with Trojanowski must have spooked her, plus everything she had heard about Basil Vasilikas.

At the same time, Mulroy noticed the garage door open up. Quickly, she sprinted to the side of the house, hiding behind an arbor vitae as best she could. From that vantage point, she watched as a car moved down the street towards the bridge. It was a Honda Pilot that fit the description of Trojanowski's long-lost car.

As the car disappeared around the bend, Mulroy realized that she had been holding her breath. She exhaled deeply and tried to calm herself. She checked her phone. No response from Radic or anyone else. "Damn them!"

She sent Radic a text: "At 205 Blackmore. Someone left in T's car. Could be B."

Sensing an opportunity, Mulroy stood up and walked to the back of the house. She peeked into the living room, which seemed quite ordinary. No feminine touches, like a vase with flowers. A photo of some sort sat on the mantel.

Mulroy eased slowly to the other side of the house, where she saw a bedroom with an unmade bed. Squinting, she tried to see what was on the dresser top. It looked like … a gauze bandage, with medicine nearby. Now, her heart was pounding. She was peering into the lion's den.

Mulroy turned the corner, to the front of the home. Her legs were getting a bit wobbly. She paused to check her cell phone. Still no replies. She sent a text to Stilton: Send someone to 205 Blackmore. Duck Hollow. Now!

As she turned the corner, Mulroy couldn't believe her good luck. The resident—presumably, Basil—had left the garage door wide open! It was like an invitation to step inside.

Without thinking about legal issues or her personal safety, Mulroy walked into the empty garage, where she noticed some boating gear but no boat. She tried the door to the inside of the home, and, magically, it opened up.

Mulroy checked her phone one last time. Nothing. She licked her lips, breathed deeply, pulled the taser out of her pocket, and stepped inside.

The photo she had seen from the back was now visible. It featured a younger Basil and a very young Stephanos flashing a smile. It was touching but horrifying if you thought about the back story. This man had killed his nephew's fiancée, kidnapped and imprisoned his nephew, and basically wreaked havoc on his sister's family, who had opened their hearts to him. He was a fiend, a monster, a cruel and evil man. Then she heard the garage door shut behind her.

"You must be Officer Mulroy," a man with a deep voice said.

"Don't come any closer," she said. "I have a taser."

"I noticed that," the man said, "but I have a gun."

As he entered the living room, Mulroy saw that he was telling the truth. The man who stood before her was even scarier than the man whose sketch she had been carrying around for three weeks. She hadn't expected him to be so bulky, so intimidating. The vacant stare in his eyes reminded her of soulless snakes she had seen on TV, who gazed intently at their prey before they struck. She didn't know what to do.

"Now, slowly, I want you to drop that taser and kick it towards me," Basil said.

Mulroy did nothing.

"Now!" he shouted. Mulroy complied.

"Good girl!"

"Now I want you to drop your cell phone and kick that towards me, too," he said.

Mulroy complied.

"Now, I want you to sit down on the living room couch and enjoy my hospitality. Meanwhile, let me see what you've been saying to our friends in the police department."

Mulroy sat down, looking for a safe exit. The back door? The bathroom? It wasn't obvious. She also tried to gauge her captor's strength. Was he healthy? Did he have a fever? Was he quick on his feet?

"Naughty girl!" he said, shaking his head after reviewing her phone texts. "You've made it very difficult for me to remain in this beautiful community where everyone minds their own business. I'm going to have to punish you for that."

CHAPTER SIXTY-SIX: A BRIDGE TO SOMEWHERE

Mulroy gulped but said nothing.

"But first, I have to ask you for your car keys," he said. "Yes, when I saw a car just outside Duck Hollow, I sensed that something wasn't right. When you've served your country overseas, you learn to recognize when you're in danger."

Mulroy tossed her keys in his direction. She realized that she was running out of options.

"How are you feeling?" she asked. "Do you need to visit a hospital?"

"Ah, the fake sympathy move," he said sarcastically. "Well, thank you so much for asking. I had a fever, but it's down. Turns out Carol's roommate is a very good nurse."

"Don't you want to know how Stephanos is doing?"

It was the wrong question. "That son of a bitch tried to kill me!" Basil screamed, his eyes bulging. "Did he tell you that?"

"You kidnapped him and imprisoned him," Mulroy retorted. "How could you do such a thing to your own nephew?"

"He betrayed me!" Basil yelled. "I had a vision of a bigger, greater company. I went out on a limb for Stephanos and Dimitri. Stephanos sawed that limb off."

"What you did was illegal," Mulroy said. "Surely, you understand that. From Professor Reid's book."

Basil was surprised. "How do you know about that book?" he asked. Then it dawned on him. "Oh, so you've been to Al Cheapo's. I should give that son of a bitch something to remember me by, but I'm afraid I'm running out of time. And so are you!"

"You don't have to kill me!" Mulroy pleaded. "Why not just tie me up?"

"All out of duct tape, I'm afraid," Basil responded.

Mulroy thought for a moment. She needed to keep him talking. "Don't you want to know how I found you?"

"No one was supposed to find me here. The most isolated community in Pittsburgh. How DID you find me?"

"The *Post-Gazette*."

"A story?" Then it dawned on him.

"My subscription!"

"We looked for Harry Potter characters."

"Very clever, my dear. You're clever enough to belong to Slytherin."

"That would not be my choice."

"No, I guess not."

Mulroy heard a rustling sound near the garage door. Had the cavalry arrived?

"Basil, are you okay?" The scratchy voice was that of an old woman. She walked through the garage into the living room and stopped.

"Basil, what's going on?" she asked. "And why are you pointing a gun at that young woman?"

"I'm a police officer, ma'am," Mulroy said. "We're having a bit of a disagreement."

"Margaret, I wish you hadn't done this," Basil whined.

"Done what, Basil? I just wanted to see if you're okay. But something's not right."

"Margaret, I'm afraid I'm going to have to ask you to stand over there with Miss Mulroy," he said.

"I'll do no such thing," she said defiantly. "I'm going to call the police."

As Margaret tried to exit through the garage, Basil grabbed her by the arm and shoved her to the ground with a thud. Mulroy, seeing an opportunity, tackled him and squeezed his neck with her hands as hard as she could. Basil screamed like a wounded lion, but he was a powerful man. He tossed Mulroy into the air like a sack of potatoes and looked frantically for his gun, which had been lost in the scuffle.

The gun landed next to Margaret. Though shaken by her fall, she managed to grab it and point it at Basil. "Don't even think about it, honey," she warned. "I'm a crack shot."

Basil shimmied backward on his legs, creating some distance from Margaret and getting close to the garage door.

"Give me the gun, Margaret," Mulroy said.

Basil decided to run for it. But Margaret aimed and fired.

She winged him—in the arm, it appeared. Then he ran in the direction of

CHAPTER SIXTY-SIX: A BRIDGE TO SOMEWHERE

the Duck Hollow bridge. Mulroy grabbed the gun with no objection from Margaret. "Call 911!" she ordered as she chased after Basil.

With a head start and little ground to cover, Basil was almost at the little bridge when Mulroy spotted him. "Stop, or I'll shoot!" she yelled. But Basil kept on running.

Mulroy sprinted in his direction. Her shoulder throbbed painfully from Basil's body toss, but she ignored it and focused on her man.

As Basil reached her car and unlocked it, Mulroy heard a police siren in the distance, but getting closer. Basil started up her car and headed away from the siren. Mulroy aimed at her right rear tire and took two shots. No luck. She aimed at her left rear tire. "Pfft!" She watched as the car waddled forward like a wounded duck.

Mulroy approached the car warily, her gun drawn. It suddenly dawned on her that there was a service revolver in the glove compartment. Would Basil think to look?

Just in case, Mulroy took cover behind the nearest tree. At the same time, two police cars pulled up. Radic emerged from one of the police cars, his gun drawn.

"He might have a gun!" Mulroy yelled.

It was a timely warning. Basil emerged from the car, a gun in hand, and aimed at Radic, who had just retreated behind his car. A bullet caromed off the car; another skipped off a nearby rock.

"You're surrounded, Basil," Radic yelled. "Put the gun down."

With a war whoop, Basil fled into the nearby woods, zigging and zagging in an apparent effort to avoid being shot.

Chapter Sixty-Seven: A Daring Escape

For someone who was recovering from two stab wounds and who had just been shot in the arm, Basil was remarkably agile as he raced into the woods. Within seconds, he was no longer visible.

"I'm going in after him," Radic yelled to Mulroy. "Secure his home in case he circles back!"

"Will do," Mulroy shouted. "Be careful!" With a nod, Radic disappeared into the dense underbrush.

Once in the woods, Radic paused, hoping to hear Basil's footsteps ahead. But a chorus of birds and crickets made it difficult to identify any human sounds. Traffic from the Homestead Grays Bridge didn't help either. Maybe he had become a little too sensitive to bridge noises.

Would Basil head to the river or to civilization? Logically, he should flee to Pittsburgh's city streets, where he could blend in, bide his time, and try to escape after dark.

But was Basil logical? Or was he obsessed with the river, as Stephanos and Dimitri believed? Would Jason and the Argonauts try to escape from danger by land or by sea?

After vacillating for a few moments, Radic made his choice: Basil was Poseidon, not Ares. He would head to the river.

Radic pivoted to the river trail, then reconsidered. Basil had a gun, and he would not hesitate to use it. On reflection, it was safer to stay in the woods, getting close to the trail but avoiding the trail itself.

As he moved towards the river, Radic thought he heard a door open or close. Could Basil have access to a second car? Then he heard the sound of

CHAPTER SIXTY-SEVEN: A DARING ESCAPE

laughter and a conversation. As he edged closer, he noticed a young man and his son heading to the river to fish.

"Damn it," Radic cursed softly. Having no choice, he hailed the startled man, flashed his badge, and gestured for him to join him in the woods.

Surprised and confused, the man complied. Radic quickly explained the situation, instructing the startled father to return to his car immediately and come back to fish another day.

The man got the picture, took his son by the hand, and jogged back to his car. Moments later, the car sped away. Radic breathed a sigh of relief. But he had lost precious time.

Then, out of the corner of his eye, he noticed a shed in the woods. Approaching cautiously, he saw that the door was open. "Come on out with your hands up!" he cried. No response. Slowly, using trees for cover, he circled behind the shed, reluctant to place himself in the line of fire.

From behind, he saw a small, dirty window in the back of the shed. Crouching and walking like a monkey, he made his way to the back of the shed and peeked through the window. It was empty. Quickly, he scampered to the front and entered the dilapidated wooden structure.

It was certainly big enough for a boat. He saw lumber, paint, spare parts, tools, and remnants from a meal or two. This must be the hideaway for the Argo or whatever Basil called his Kennywood boat. But the boat itself was gone.

Cursing himself, Radic sprinted to the river. As he grew closer, he heard the rhythmic sound of waves lapping softly against the shore. Then, in the distance, he saw a man in a boat. It must be Basil paddling out to sea.

Radic pulled out his cell phone and called Stilton, who answered immediately.

"Sir, are you in Duck Hollow?"

"Yes, I'm with Mulroy. Did you find him?"

"He's in his boat, heading west."

"Damn!" Stilton replied. "Track him until he disappears. Give us visual reports. I'll contact the River Rescue Unit."

"Sir?" Radic asked.

"Yes?"

"A helicopter?"

"I'll contact the state police and try to get one."

Radic looked again at Basil's boat. Unlike before, when it seemed to be moving at a steady pace, it now appeared to be drifting. He squinted, trying to get a better view of Basil himself. There seemed to be a person inside the boat—but not moving at all. Was he tired? Dead?

Or was he even there? Suddenly, Radic began to question his first premise—was Basil even in the boat? Or had he simply pushed the boat out to sea with something bulky inside to hint at a human form?

This was the decoy of all decoys. The man who had tricked them through sleight of hand was tricking them yet again.

Fearful once more, Radic looked around him, realizing that Basil could still be in the woods with a gun—a gun that he would not hesitate to use. He sought cover behind a nearby elm tree, trying to keep his wits about him.

Then, another thought occurred to him. Gazing at the bridge, he looked carefully at each segment until he reached a point midway to the top. Was it his imagination, or did he see a flash of orange there? The same blood-orange color as a life jacket?

In awe at the man's audacity, Radic continued to observe as the splotch of orange got higher and higher in his line of sight.

He called Stilton again.

"Lieutenant?"

"Radic?"

"I want you to send two squad cars to the Homestead Grays Bridge. Position one at the north end. And one at the south end."

"To look down at the boat?"

"No, to look down at the bridge. He's climbing the bridge!"

"He's what?"

"He's just traded his bishop to save his queen."

"What the hell are you talking about, Radic?"

"He's just given up his boat to save his life. There's no man in the boat.

CHAPTER SIXTY-SEVEN: A DARING ESCAPE

It's yet another illusion."

"The copter?"

"It will just spook him. He thinks he's fooled us. Let him think that."

"Cancel the copter?"

"Definitely. We want to surprise him."

"And you?"

"I'm leaving now. I want to be on top of the bridge when he gets there."

"Mulroy?"

"Tell her to meet me with a car at the entrance to Duck Hollow."

Chapter Sixty-Eight: The View from the Bridge

P*ost-Gazette* reporter Evan Kobosky got the tip from his sister-in-law, Brenda, who worked down the hall in the Circulation Department.

"Evan, are you still covering the story about that poor girl who was murdered, and they found her body in Frick Park?"

"Yeah, the police have shifted 180 degrees. They're looking for the uncle now, not the nephew. Didn't you see my article?"

"Sorry, Gracie and Auggie have both been home sick. I haven't had time to go grocery shopping, much less read the paper."

"I hear something's going around," he said.

"Well, they'll recover. But the guy they're looking for is Basil Vasilikas, isn't it?"

"Yeah," Evan said with curiosity.

"Well, I got a call from one of the police officers. Max Volcker?"

"Yeah, he's one of the key players."

"He gave me several names to check on our subscription list, and Vasilikas was on the list."

"Okay," Evan said. "Is he a subscriber?"

"Well, here's where it gets interesting. He's NOT a subscriber, at least not officially. But another cop—Kathleen Mulroy—called me back and gave me another list of names. And we got a hit."

"What's the name?"

"Draco Malfoy."

CHAPTER SIXTY-EIGHT: THE VIEW FROM THE BRIDGE

"Draco Malfoy? From Harry Potter?"

"That's the one."

Evan took a moment to process the information. "How did she react?"

"She got very excited."

"She did? Do you have an address?"

"Yep, but you can't let on how you found out. I don't want to get fired."

"My lips are sealed. Thanks, Brenda. I may just pay Mr. Malfoy a visit."

Kobosky looked up the address. Duck Hollow. Population. What? You gotta be kidding! You could really go off the grid there.

His heart pounding, he grabbed a notepad and headed out the door.

As he approached Duck Hollow, Kobosky saw three police cars and another car that looked like it had been in an accident. No sign of Officer Mulroy. He did see Lieutenant Stilton, looking agitated, engaged in a tense conversation on his Walkie-Talkie.

Then two of the police cars left hurriedly, as if in hot pursuit. Kobosky decided to follow them. No sirens, but they were traveling very fast. The first vehicle stopped just before the Homestead Grays Bridge while the other vehicle continued. Kobosky found a parking spot nearby and waited to see if he recognized any of the officers. One of them was Max Volcker, also an investigator in the Sloan case. Yep, something was definitely up.

Volcker and the other officer, whom he didn't recognize, were behaving oddly. They kept looking at the bridge, but furtively. Then Volcker ordered the other officer to remain behind while he sauntered casually over to the bridge and peered downward. He then returned to the squad car, where an animated conversation took place.

Kobosky called a friend who sometimes listened in on PBP dispatch calls. Maybe he could figure out what was going on.

Intrigued, his friend agreed to tune in and call back.

Meanwhile, Kobosky reached into his glove compartment for a pair of binoculars, from a recent birding expedition. They might come in handy.

Volcker strolled nonchalantly back to the bridge again, this time peering over the other side of the bridge.

Kobosky got a call.

"They're looking for a guy in a boat," his friend reported.
"Do you have a name?"
"Basil, no last name."
"That's all I need."
"It's confusing, though."
"What's confusing?"
"Some people think the guy is in a boat. Others seem to think he's climbing the Homestead Bridge."
"You're the best! Gotta go!"

As Kobosky was trying to decide his next move, another police car arrived. Detective Radic, the lead investigator, got out of the car, followed by Officer Mulroy. After a brief conversation with Volcker, Radic walked to the bridge and peered over. Meanwhile, Volcker and Mulroy started talking with pedestrians. Within seconds, a handful of pedestrians scampered across the bridge while others headed back in the opposite direction after some mild protests.

Kobosky got another call. "River Rescue says they've spotted the guy climbing the bridge."

"Which end?"

"North."

"That's my end. How far up?"

"Two-thirds of the way, they're saying."

"You're one in a million."

Putting two and two together, Kobosky was starting to get the picture. The police were trying to eliminate all pedestrian traffic. But they didn't want to draw attention to themselves. They were setting a trap for the climber. Draco. Or Basil. Probably one and the same.

The case was coming to a head. And he was there. With the police preoccupied, Kobosky made a beeline for a rough trail on the northeast side of the bridge that led down to the riverbank. He positioned himself there, behind a holly tree, and took out his binoculars.

It took a while to adjust the lenses, but he finally got a sharp image. Scanning slowly, he zig-zagged horizontally, then vertically. Bingo!

CHAPTER SIXTY-EIGHT: THE VIEW FROM THE BRIDGE

A man in an orange flak jacket was climbing the damn bridge. He must have nerves of steel. Or he must be truly desperate. One false move, and he was history.

As he zoomed in, Kobosky judged that the man was maybe 30 feet from the top. He took out his i-phone and took a few shots. Then he turned to his binoculars again.

"Mr. Kobosky, I'm afraid I'm going to have to ask you to leave immediately." It was Detective Radic.

"But…but…"

"And we could really use your binoculars, if you don't mind."

"But…but…"

"You'll get your story, pal, but it will be much easier to write if you're alive to write it."

"But…but…"

"He's armed and dangerous, Evan, and I don't think he's a great believer in freedom of the press."

Radic escorted Kobosky to his car, confiscated the binoculars, and gave them to Mulroy, who essentially positioned herself where Kobosky had been.

Cars and trucks continued to whiz by in both directions, oblivious to the drama that was unfolding. If you were climbing the bridge, you probably wouldn't know that anything was amiss.

Kobosky called his friend. "I've been grounded. What are they saying?"

"They want him on top of the bridge. Then they'll make their move."

"It makes sense," Kobosky conceded before hanging up.

At this point, the police were no longer peering over the edge of the bridge. Presumably, they were getting all the information they needed from Mulroy.

Pedestrian traffic across the bridge had ceased, though about three dozen onlookers were clustered together about fifty yards north of the bridge, gawking with undisguised curiosity.

A clue that something was finally happening came when Mulroy gave Radic a hand signal, eliciting a nod.

Moments later, Kobosky saw a man's face at the railing and then an upper torso. He took out his cell phone and pressed the VIDEO button. The man hoisted himself up and vaulted onto the sidewalk. A startled motorist honked, then another. But no one stopped.

The man, clearly Basil Vasilikas, looked exhausted. He glanced in both directions and walked slowly north, clutching something in his right pocket.

Suddenly, Radic, Volcker, and another officer appeared, out of nowhere, with pistols. "You're surrounded, Basil!" Radic hollered. "Arms up!"

Vasilikas hesitated, then complied, tossing his gun to the ground.

The police rushed forward, but as they did so, Vasilikas hoisted himself onto the railing of the bridge.

"Don't do it, Basil!" Radic pleaded.

Vasilikas looked uncertain for a moment. Then he spoke: "I have one request," he said.

"What's that, Basil?" Radic asked, inching closer.

"Tell Spider I'm sorry about his car."

With that, Vasilikas jumped off the bridge, splashing into the water below seconds later.

Chapter Sixty-Nine: A Front-Page Obituary

Radic retrieved the *Post-Gazette* from his front stoop, poured himself a cup of coffee, black, no sugar, and eagerly read the article that appeared on the front page:

DEATH OF A SALESMAN by Evan Kobosky

A strong but troubled man climbed the Homestead Grays Bridge Wednesday, despite multiple wounds from a fight with his nephew and a battle with police. Within seconds after his astonishing ascent, he took his own life by plunging 108 feet into the Monongahela River.

The man, Basil Vasilikas, 54, has been the subject of a manhunt for several weeks. His ascent up the Homestead Bridge took approximately 34 minutes; his descent took approximately four seconds. His rise and fall at the bridge are an apt metaphor for a life marked by many ups and downs.

As an enlisted man in the U.S. Army, Vasilikas received a commendation for valor in Iraq. Months later, he received a dishonorable discharge.

He helped to transform his brother-in-law's dishware company in West Mifflin, Dimitri's Sturdy Dishes, into a successful small business. Later, he would be fired for stealing $10,000 from his family.

He struggled with alcoholism and an addiction to gambling as a young adult. Later, he would conquer both, only to succumb to ambition and greed so all-consuming that it dulled his sense of right and wrong.

Pittsburgh police believe that Vasilikas killed Carol Sloan, a 26-year-old accountant whose unwelcome but legally sound advice on a complicated intellectual property matter angered him so much that he decided to kidnap and kill her.

According to police, Vasilikas also kidnapped and imprisoned his nephew, Stephanos Papadopoulos, who sided with Sloan and opposed Vasilikas, triggering a battle royale between the two and an orgy of violence that included a bombing at Sewickley's Unitarian Church, where Sloan's funeral was taking place.

Unlike Sloan, Papadopoulos survived a brutal beating and imprisonment at the Old Mill in Kennywood Park, where he was held captive in chains. As reported by the *Post-Gazette*, Papadopoulos was able to surprise his uncle and wound him with a vegetable can lid when his uncle checked up on him several days ago.

Another victim, Rosemary Dunne, a nurse and Sloan's roommate, was bound and gagged after Vasilikas demanded that she treat him for wounds sustained at the Old Mill. According to Dunne, Vasilikas agreed not to kill her if she treated his wounds.

Had he lived, Vasilikas, known to some friends as "Vazzy," would have been tried for murder, kidnapping, domestic terrorism, and a variety of other serious offenses. Although these things are difficult to predict, prosecutors say it is likely that he would have been convicted.

At the heart of the dispute between Vasilikas and other members of his family was a disagreement over a proposed scheme to manufacture thousands of Harry Potter mugs without the approval of Warner Brothers, which owns the copyright to all things having

CHAPTER SIXTY-NINE: A FRONT-PAGE OBITUARY

to do with Harry Potter.

Although the legal issues are arcane, lawyers say that a proposal for a new product can be substantiated through drawings or a handful of mock products but that the sale of these products is illegal without explicit authorization from the party who owns the copyright.

Rob McPherson, a lawyer who worked with Sloan and with Papadopoulos, puts it this way: "If you have a bright idea that requires copyright approval, you can sketch it out on paper, you might even be able to produce a few samples. But you can't sell the things without the copyright holder's consent."

According to the PBP and the FBI, which is handling the intellectual property issues, Vasilikas and a confederate, James Trojanowski, manufactured and sold thousands of Harry Potter mugs on the black market without prior approval, thus violating federal intellectual property law.

The mugs, known as Muggles, featured a variety of popular Harry Potter characters, including Hermione Granger, Angus Dumbledore, Professor McGonagall, and Dobby the House Elf. Vasilikas sold thousands of these items, despite a veto by Papadopoulos, as recommended by Sloan.

Originally considered homeless by the police, Vasilikas spent several months in and out of a homeless community near the Birmingham Bridge on the South Side. However, he earned enough money on the black market to purchase a home in Duck Hollow, where PBP officer Kathleen Mulroy confronted him on Wednesday, triggering the dramatic events that culminated at the Homestead Grays Bridge.

The family drama, which produced three kidnappings, one bombing, one murder, and one suicide, has generated national attention, including coverage in *The New York Times*, the *Wall Street Journal*, and *Forbes* magazine.

In an interview with the *Post-Gazette*, PBP Lieutenant Charles

Stilton praised Detective Branko Radic, Officer Kathleen Mulroy, and Detective Max Volcker for their work on the Sloan case.

"These are some of the finest police officers I have been privileged to serve with," Stilton said. "They demonstrated exceptional intelligence, skill, and courage in solving an unusually complicated and difficult case."

Radic, the lead investigator, played a key role in exposing Vasilikas' complicity in several crimes and in apprehending Vasilikas on top of the Homestead Bridge, though his capture proved short-lived.

Mulroy was instrumental in rescuing Papadopoulos at Kennywood Park and in linking Vasilikas to a home in Duck Hollow. Mulroy was recently injured in a fracas with Trojanowski, chief chemist at Dimitri's Sturdy Dishes, currently in custody at the county jail.

Volcker is said to have played a critical role in locating persons involved in the intellectual property crime, which is expected to lead to additional indictments as the investigation continues.

The future of Dimitri's Sturdy Dishes, the West Mifflin kitchenware company, is still unclear. Police believe that the owner, Dimitri Papadopoulos, Stephanos' father, was completely unaware of the criminal activities that have clouded his company's reputation.

A confidential police source said this: "Dimitri is completely blameless in all of this. He is a good egg whose brother-in-law committed some horrible crimes and who came close to killing his son. He is cooperating fully with the police."

Nevertheless, Dimitri's Sturdy Dishes could face some legal liability if it can be shown that the firm was negligent in allowing a rogue employee—Vasilikas—to manufacture and sell merchandise without legal approval or the owner's consent. Dimitri's is being represented by McSwigan & O'Rourke.

The *Post-Gazette* has learned that Stephanos Papadopoulos is currently debating whether to succeed his father as the C.E.O. of

CHAPTER SIXTY-NINE: A FRONT-PAGE OBITUARY

the firm. The younger Papadopoulos reportedly was engaged to be married to Carol Sloan and is said to be deeply distraught by the recent turn of events.

According to a PBP spokesman, Basil Vasilikas will be buried later this week at an undisclosed location. The Papadopoulos family will be handling expenses.

* * *

Radic fetched a second cup of coffee and read the article more slowly. He had three immediate reactions:

First, he recognized himself as the confidential police source. He hoped his unambiguously positive comments about Dimitri would help him and his firm bounce back from a public relations disaster and a legal quagmire. Dimitri deserved a break. And Stephanos, too.

Second, he made a note to call Kobosky and thank him for saying nothing about the Hermione Granger costume that Carol Sloan was wearing when her body was discovered in Frick Park. Kobosky knew the facts, but Radic had argued strongly against publishing them. If disclosed, that macabre twist would be unsettling and embarrassing to the Sloan family and the Papadopoulos family. It did not need to be revealed to the public.

Third, he thought that the article did an excellent job of capturing the many contradictions that marked Basil Vasilikas' life. What was missing from the article was a sense of his keen intelligence. He had been a formidable adversary. In truth, he had outsmarted the police on multiple occasions. His ultimate capture was a credit to the police force, as Stilton suggested, but it was also a matter of good luck. He had come very close to slipping through their fingers.

Chapter Seventy: When the Going Gets Tough

It was a cool, crisp autumn day with bright sunshine, blue skies, and a soft breeze. Judging from the festive atmosphere and the large crowd, the gathering could be a county fair or a church picnic. But Lexie knew better. It was the Tough Mudder competition, being held this year in Butler, Radic's home town.

Lexie was pleasantly surprised as she joined the spectators in the staging area, sitting on portable bleachers. She hadn't expected to know anyone except Radic, who was counting on her for moral support, plus band-aids and a stretcher, if necessary.

But she spotted Mulroy, laughing heartily at a joke from a handsome young man at her side. *Mulroy, you sly devil!* she thought to herself.

"Nice to see you, pal!" she said.

"You too, Lexie."

"Who's this gorgeous man who's chaperoning you today?"

"Lexie Davodny, I'd like you to meet Jake Jacoby."

"Nice to meet you, Jake. Your name rings a bell, though I can't remember why."

"Jake has been in the *Post-Gazette* a bit," Mulroy explained. "He helped us out at Kennywood Park."

"Of course!" Lexie exclaimed. "You're the guy who knows all about Kennywood's boats. I'm a bit of a boat person myself."

"Lexie is with the River Rescue Unit at PBP," Mulroy explained.

CHAPTER SEVENTY: WHEN THE GOING GETS TOUGH

"Cool!" Jacoby said. "I've seen you guys out there."

"What do you do when you're not repairing boats and rescuing kidnap victims?" Lexie asked.

"Well, I drive a bus. A school bus."

"You ever thought of being a police officer? You seem to have a cool head in a crisis."

"I don't think so," Jacoby said, shaking his head. "I prefer a job where the worst thing that can happen is that someone throws up in the back of the bus."

"Does that happen often?"

"Not on my watch. I take curves very slowly to make sure it doesn't."

Mulroy waved at someone and motioned for him to join them in the stands.

A tall, Black, distinguished-looking man with a tweed jacket and corduroy pants approached them. "Kathleen, so nice to see you here!" he said, greeting Mulroy with a hug.

"You too! Let me introduce you to two friends."

"Professor Renfert, this is my friend Jake Jacoby, whom I met at Kennywood Park."

"Nice to meet you, Professor."

"Please. Call me Lucas. Otherwise, I'll have to get out a red pen and start grading papers."

"Okay, Lucas. Got it."

"And this is my friend Lexie Davodny, who works with the River Rescue Unit."

"It's a pleasure, Lucas," Lexie said. "I've heard a lot about you from Radic."

Renfert raised his eyebrows.

"Lexie and Radic are friends," Mulroy explained.

"Got it," he said, drawing his own conclusions.

"Are you here to cheer Radic on to the finish line?" Lexie asked.

Renfert settled in beside them. "I have two dogs in this fight. There's Radic, of course. But there's also my son Norbert." He motioned towards the competitors. "He's the one over there trying to persuade Radic not to withdraw from the race."

"No way!" Lexie laughed. "Radic will finish this competition if they have to drag him out on a stretcher."

"Well, let's hope it doesn't come to that," Renfert said. "I hope both young men leave the battlefield with their limbs and their dignity intact."

Mulroy snorted. "There's too much mud here for anyone to have a shred of dignity by the time this is all over."

Lexie made a face, looking down at her stylish clothes. "Am I going to be expected to give Radic a hug at the end of the race?"

"That's entirely up to you," Mulroy said.

"I don't think I dressed right for this occasion. I should have worn sweatpants, a pullover, and some wellies."

Suddenly, the background music switched from loud to very loud, from guitars and violins to trumpets and cymbals, from easy listening to militaristic.

A puff of yellow smoke and the stench of sulfur permeated the air. A boorish man got hold of the loudspeaker and announced that the Tough Mudder competition was about to begin.

Lexie felt a thrill of excitement for Radic, who had prepared so diligently for this big moment, also a frisson of apprehension, in anticipation of some of the ordeals to come.

The competition began with a taunt: "Sissies, step aside! This is what separates the men from the boys, the women from the girls, the moose from the mice. It's the moment of truth: Are you Tough Mudders, or what?"

"WE'RE TOUGH MUDDERS!" the competitors chanted in unison.

"I can't hear you!"

"WE'RE TOUGH MUDDERS!" they chanted again, even more loudly.

"I still can't hear you!"

"WE'RE TOUGH MUDDERS, YOU SON OF A BITCH!"

"That's more like it. Let the games begin!"

As Lexie watched the events unfold, walking or trotting to keep up with the competitors, she found herself snickering, cheering, cursing, and gasping in horror as the contestants demonstrated courage that could easily

CHAPTER SEVENTY: WHEN THE GOING GETS TOUGH

be described as foolishness.

A middle-aged man seemed determined to bulldoze his way through the obstacle course. If he couldn't climb an embankment, he clawed, kicked, and chewed to get to the other side. The taste of dirt seemed to motivate him. With every disgusting chew, he found new energy and seemed to be progressing better than most.

Moments later, a young woman put the competition's PG rating to the test. After losing her bra in a muddy swamp filled with bobbing logs, she scampered forward braless, hoping that no one would notice, with so much mud. A judge intervened, whistling her to a stop but offering her a new bra instead of disqualifying her. She continued on with a grunt in lieu of thanks.

As for Radic and Renfert, they kept moving forward, undaunted by setbacks, unembarrassed by humiliating spills. Each looked after the other. If Renfert faltered while climbing a moving wall, Radic, already on top, extended a helping hand. If Radic struggled with icy water cold enough to paralyze you, Renfert reached out to yank him to dry land. Clearly, they were a team.

Her companions kept up a good pace on the sidelines, offering cries of encouragement for the most part. "Make me proud, son!" Renfert yelled. "You can do it!" "Mind your knee!" Mulroy yelled. "Don't break your goddamn knee!"

At times, the crowd was a problem. As people stopped to gawk, the spectator path got congested and sometimes slippery, with mud from the course leaking onto the sidelines. Lexie had to maneuver a bit to get to the fourth course, and that's where she stumbled. Eager to avoid the couple in front of her, she stepped on a wobbly rock. With a scream, she fell sideways, twisting her left ankle in the process. "Ouch!" she squealed.

Luckily, Mulroy was right behind her. "Lexie, are you okay?" she asked. "Ugh!" she responded.

"You look a little pale," Mulroy said. As spectators tried to avoid Lexie, with limited success, Mulroy decided to get her out of harm's way. "Jake?"

Together, Mulroy and Jacoby hoisted Lexie to her feet, and she limped to a bench with their support.

"Try to put some weight on it," Mulroy suggested.

"I can't!" she said.

"Let me get someone from First Aid," Jacoby suggested, retracing his steps despite the surging throng. At this point, Lucas Renfert was far gone, oblivious to what had happened.

The First Aid medic reached a quick, though indecisive, verdict: "You have a sprained ankle at best, a broken ankle at worst. I'm gonna tape you up. Come back to the main tent when you can, and we'll take an X-ray for you."

"This is embarrassing," Lexie said. "I feel like such a klutz."

"Officer Mulroy!"

A thin, gray-haired woman emerged from the crowd and headed in their direction. "I thought I recognized you," she said. "From TV."

Mulroy didn't quite know what to say.

"I'm Branko's mother, sweetheart, he always speaks so highly of you!"

"Mrs. Radic, how very nice to meet you!" Mulroy said, breaking into a grin. "Shouldn't you be following your son to the finish line?"

"Pfft!" she said dismissively. "It's like a stampede out there. I was lucky to get out alive."

"Your husband?"

"He's in the mix. That's fine with me. What happened to you, honey?" she asked, turning to Lexie.

"I got caught in the stampede," she said ruefully. "I'm Lexie Davodny, also with the PBP. I'm a friend of Branko's."

"Well, it's nice to meet you, dear," she said. "I hope it's just a sprain."

"I hope so, too," Lexie said. "We're going to get an X-ray in the main tent."

Mulroy introduced Jake Jacoby to Mrs. Radic. "Do you two want to go back to the race?" Mrs. Radic asked. "I can stay here with your friend."

Mulroy looked at Lexie. "Go ahead," Lexie said. "I'll be fine. Look for us here. Or back at the main tent."

With Mrs. R's blessing, Mulroy and Jacoby darted off in search of their favorite warriors, hoping to catch the last few events.

CHAPTER SEVENTY: WHEN THE GOING GETS TOUGH

"What do you do for the police department, honey?" Mrs. Radic asked.

"I work for the River Rescue Unit. It's pretty cool. I get to ride a boat every day."

"Well, that *is* pretty cool. And, hopefully, not as dangerous as Branko's line of work. I worry about him so much."

"Well, he did an amazing job of solving the Carol Sloan case."

"I know. I know. We're very proud of him. And when he solves a case like that one, well, it's a kind of therapy for some of the bad things that happen in life."

"Do you mean Petra?" Lexie asked softly.

Mrs. Radic eyed Lexie intently. "I'm getting the impression that you're more than just a friend. You know about Petra?"

Lexie nodded.

"Well, we don't like to talk about her that much. But the truth is that Branko became a policeman because of her."

"I know," Lexie said.

"And it pains him deeply when a young person is killed. Like Carol Sloan. It brings back memories."

Lexie nodded.

"But then, when he brings a killer to justice…I don't know…it's kind of like a cloud disappears, at least for a while. It's like he's evening the score somehow. Do you know what I mean?"

Lexie nodded again.

"Don't tell him I said all of this. It's just psychobabble."

"No," Lexie said. "I'd say you're very wise, Mrs. R. You got it exactly right."

"Well, it's very kind of you to say that, dear. So, what do you say? Shall we walk slowly back to that main tent? Maybe we can beat the rush."

"But…I…"

"I know. I know. I look pretty weak. But I can support you. I go to yoga once a week. And it's not that far away. Let's limp over there together. Slowly."

Acknowledgements

I've been reading murder mysteries for so many years that it almost feels like breathing. There is something deeply satisfying about being given a puzzle on a matter of grave importance, the chance to solve it, and an authoritative answer on whether you've solved it correctly.

It wasn't until COVID that I actually thought about writing a mystery myself. Out of tragedy, an opportunity emerged. How better to spend time isolated from friends and colleagues than to enter an imaginary world through a secret portal and create a fable with a puzzle for others to solve?

As it turns out, I wasn't isolated at all. In fact, I have received so much amazing support and advice while working on this project from family, friends, and generous members of the mystery writing community that this was half the fun. As in Murder on the Orient Express, where it took multiple murderers to commit a single crime, it took multiple readers and critics to produce this book.

I will begin by thanking those who helped me at the very beginning, by looking at early drafts of first chapters: Nancy Pfenning, Frank Pfenning, Helaine Mario, and Lori Rader-Day. When you're just starting out, with wobbly legs, thoughtful suggestions are worth their weight in gold.

I would also like to thank those who read the entire manuscript and critiqued it mercilessly but kindly: Robin Stacey, Laura Kalman, Carl and Christy Van Horn, Deb Walther, Susie Hogan, and John DeDakis. Their encouragement was reassuring, but their recommendations for change were even more welcome.

Accustomed to empirical research as a public policy professor at Georgetown University, I was surprised by how much empirical research was needed to write a credible mystery. For their sage advice on bridges, small airplanes, intellectual property rights, search warrants, 911 calls, and police procedures, I am deeply grateful to Larry Cole, Greg de Lissovoy, Rebecca Tushnet, Ken Gormley, Matt Brown, and Bruce Coffin.

For excellent advice on the wild and wacky world of fiction publishing, I benefited greatly from conversations with Jeffrey Higgins, Lori Duffy-Foster, and K.L. Murphy. Patti Fors was kind enough to encourage Level Best to take a look at my manuscript, and Shawn Reilly Simmons did a great job of critiquing the penultimate version and getting the book to press.

As always, I am indebted to my wife Rosie Zagarri and our daughter Angela Gormley for their unflagging support for my "second career."

About the Author

Bill Gormley is Distinguished University Professor Emeritus at Georgetown University. This is his first murder mystery.

AUTHOR WEBSITE:
  https://billgormley.com
  Podcast: Profs on Cops, available through Apple and Spotify.

SOCIAL MEDIA HANDLES:
  Bill Gormley (Facebook)
  @billgormley25 (twitter or X)

Also by Bill Gormley

Books on public policy and bureaucratic politics published by Brookings Institution Press, Harvard University Press, Harvard Education Press, Princeton University Press, and others.

For example:

Everybody's Children: Child Care as a Public Problem

Organizational Report Cards

The Critical Advantage: Developing Critical Thinking Skills in School

Taming the Bureaucracy: Muscles, Prayers, and Other Strategies